Praise for CHRIS

'A ripping detective yarn with the ... ... to follow in the golden bootprints of Rebus ... The plotting is watertight, the setting cracklingly criminal and the language a cut above your usual potboiler'
                                                                                                    Scotsman

'Banville may have swapped the literary novel for crime, but he hasn't abandoned writing with elegance and beauty, to which he has added an absorbing plot, beguiling characters and evocative settings. He may well be the first author to add to his Man Booker a Gold Dagger, the prize for crime fiction ... Black has quickly learnt the essentials of crime writing: his pacing is impeccable, and the story is replete with shocks and surprises'
                                                                    Marcel Berlins, *The Times*

'OK, he's a superb stylist, but can he plot? The answer is yes ... The numerous characters are each distinct and credible, atmosphere fairly reeks from every page. Banville's control and pacing cannot be faulted, and the final outcome is bleak, creepy and almost unbearably moving. As for the writing ... you're in for a treat. Freshly minted images of startling originality and precision have always characterised Banville's prose, but such insights are leavened here by a measure of the quotidian and the humdrum that rarely features in his mainstream novels. It would be absurd to say that Banville writing as Black is better than Banville writing as Banville, but in a different and yet fascinatingly similar way he is every bit as good and deserves to win a new, broader readership with this fine book ... If there's any justice, Banville should be able to add the CWA Gold Dagger to his heap of trophies' Michael Dibdin, *Guardian*

CHRISTINE FALLS

BENJAMIN BLACK is the pen name of acclaimed author
John Banville, who was born in Wexford, Ireland, in 1945.
His novels have won numerous awards, including the Man
Booker Prize in 2005 for *The Sea*. He lives in Dublin.
Christine Falls is the first book in Benjamin Black's
celebrated Quirke series, which is now a major
BBC TV series starring Gabriel Byrne.

BENJAMIN BLACK

CHRISTINE FALLS

A Quirke Mystery

PICADOR

First published 2006 by Picador

First published in paperback 2006 by Picador

This edition published 2013 by Picador
an imprint of Pan Macmillan, a division of Macmillan Publishers Limited
Pan Macmillan, 20 New Wharf Road, London N1 9RR
Basingstoke and Oxford
Associated companies throughout the world
www.panmacmillan.com

ISBN 978-1-4472-3731-0

1 3 5 7 9 8 6 4 2

A CIP catalogue record for this book is available from the British Library.

Typeset by SetSystems Ltd, Saffron Walden, Essex
Printed and bound by CPI Group (UK) Ltd, Croydon, CR0 4YY

Visit **www.picador.com** to read more about all our books
and to buy them. You will also find features, author interviews and
news of any author events, and you can sign up for e-newsletters
so that you're always first to hear about our new releases.

To Ed Victor

SHE WAS GLAD it was the evening mailboat she was taking, for she did not think she could have faced a morning departure. At the party the night before one of the medical students had found a flask of raw alcohol and mixed it with orange crush and she had drunk two glasses of it, and the inside of her mouth was still raw and there was something like a drum beating behind her forehead. She had stayed in bed all morning, still tipsy, unable to sleep and crying half the time, a hankie crushed to her mouth to stifle the sobs. She was frightened at the thought of what she had to do today, of what she had to undertake. Yes, she was frightened.

At Dun Laoghaire she paced back and forth on the pier, too agitated inside herself to stand still. She had put her luggage in the cabin and had come back down to the dock to wait, as they had told her to. She did not know why she had agreed to what had been asked of her. She already had the offer of the job in Boston, and now there had been the prospect of the money as well, but she suspected it was more that she had been afraid of Matron, afraid to refuse when she had asked if she would bring the child with her. Matron had a way of sounding the most intimidating when she spoke the softest. *Now, Brenda,* she had said, looking at her with those goggle eyes of hers, *I want you to consider carefully, because it's a big responsibility.* Everything had felt strange, the sick sensation in her stomach and the burning in her mouth from the alcohol, and the fact that she was not wearing her nurse's uniform but the pink wool costume she had bought specially to go away in—her going-away suit, as if she was getting married, when instead of a honeymoon she would have a week of taking care of this baby, and not a hint of a husband. *You're a good girl, Brenda,* Matron had said, putting on a smile that was worse than one of her glares, *may God go with you.* She would need His company, all right, she thought mournfully now: there was tonight on the boat, then the train journey tomorrow to Southampton, and then five more days at sea, and then what? She had never been out of the country before, except once, when she was little and her father took the family on a day trip to the Isle of Man.

A sleek black motor car was edging its way through the crowds of passengers going towards the boat. It stopped when it was still a good ten yards away from her, and a woman got out at the passenger side with a canvas bag in her hand and a bundle in a blanket in the crook of her other arm. She was not young, sixty if she was a day, but was dressed as if she was half that, in a grey suit with a narrow, calf-length skirt belted tightly at the waist, her little pot belly sticking out under the belt, and a pillbox hat with a bit of blue veil that came down below her nose. She walked forward over the flagstones, unsteady in stiletto heels, her painted-on mouth pursed in a smile. Her eyes were small and black and sharp.

'Miss Ruttledge?' she said. 'My name is Moran.' Her fancy accent was as fake as everything else about her. She handed over the bag. 'The baby's things are in there, with her papers—give them to the Purser when you get on board at Southampton, he'll know who you are.' She examined Brenda closely, making slits of her little black eyes. 'Are you all right? You look pale.'

Brenda said she was fine, that she had been up late, that was all. Miss Moran, or Mrs, or whatever she was, smiled thinly.

'The parting glass, eh?' She held out the bundle in the blanket. 'Here you are—don't drop it.' She laughed shortly, then frowned at herself and said, 'Sorry.'

What struck Brenda first about the bundle was the heat: it might have been a lump of burning coal that was wrapped in the blanket, except that it was soft, and that it moved. When she held it against her breast something in her insides flipped like a fish. 'Oh,' she said, a weak gasp of surprise and happy dismay. The woman was speaking to her again but she was not listening. From deep down in the folds of the blanket a tiny, filmy eye was regarding her with what seemed an expression of dispassionate interest. Her throat thickened and she was afraid the morning's waterworks might start up again.

'Thank you,' she said. It was all she could think to say, although she was not sure who it was she was thanking, or for what.

The Moran woman shrugged, pulling her mouth up at one side in a sketch of a smile.

'Good luck,' she said.

She walked back rapidly to the car, her high heels

clicking, and got in and pulled the door shut. 'Well, that's done,' she said, and through the windscreen she watched Brenda Ruttledge, still standing where she had left her on the dock, gazing into the opening in the blanket, the canvas bag forgotten at her feet. 'Look at her,' she said sourly. 'Thinks she's the Blessed Virgin.' The driver made no comment, only started up the car.

I

1

IT WAS NOT the dead that seemed to Quirke uncanny but the living. When he walked into the morgue long after midnight and saw Malachy Griffin there he felt a shiver along his spine that was to prove prophetic, a tremor of troubles to come. Mal was in Quirke's office, sitting at the desk. Quirke stopped in the unlit body room, among the shrouded forms on their trolleys, and watched him through the open doorway. He was seated with his back to the door, leaning forward intently in his steel-framed spectacles, the desk lamp lighting the left side of his face and making an angry pink glow through the shell of his ear. He had a file open on the desk before him and was writing in it with peculiar awkwardness. This would have struck Quirke as stranger than it did if he had not been drunk. The scene sparked a memory in him from their schooldays together, startlingly clear, of Mal, intent like this, sitting at a desk among fifty other earnest students in a big hushed hall, as he laboriously composed an examination essay, with a beam of sunlight falling slantways on him from a window somewhere high above. A quarter of a century later he still had that smooth seal's head of oiled black hair, scrupulously combed and parted.

Sensing a presence behind him Mal turned his face and peered into the shadowy dark of the body room. Quirke waited a moment and then stepped forward, with some unsteadiness, into the light in the doorway.

'Quirke,' Mal said, recognising him with relief and giving an exasperated sigh. 'For God's sake.'

Mal was in evening clothes but uncharacteristically unbuttoned, his bow-tie undone and the collar of his white dress shirt open. Quirke, groping in his pockets for his cigarettes, contemplated him, noting the way he put his forearm quickly over the file to hide it, and was reminded again of school.

'Working late?' Quirke said, and grinned crookedly, the alcohol allowing him to think it a telling piece of wit.

'What are you doing here?' Mal said, too loudly, ignoring the question. He pushed the spectacles up the damp bridge of his nose with a tap of a fingertip. He was nervous.

Quirke pointed to the ceiling. 'Party,' he said. 'Upstairs.'

Mal assumed his consultant's face, frowning imperiously. 'Party? What party?'

'Brenda Ruttledge,' Quirke said. 'One of the nurses. Her going-away.'

Mal's frown deepened. 'Ruttledge?'

Quirke was suddenly bored. He asked if Mal had a cigarette, for he seemed to have none of his own, but Mal ignored this question too. He stood up, deftly sweeping the file with him, still trying to hide it under his arm. Quirke, though he had to squint, saw the name scrawled in large handwritten letters on the cover of it: *Christine Falls*. Mal's fountain pen was on the desk, a Parker, fat and black and shiny, with a gold nib, no doubt, twenty-two carat, and more if it was possible; Mal had a taste for rich things, it was one of his few weaknesses.

'How is Sarah?' Quirke asked. He let himself droop sideways heavily until his shoulder found the support of the doorjamb. He felt dizzy, and everything was keeping up a flickering, leftward lurch. He was at the rueful stage of having drunk too much and knowing that there was nothing to be done but wait until the effects wore off. Mal had his back to him, putting the file into a drawer of the tall grey filing cabinet.

'She's well,' Mal said. 'We were at a Knights dinner. I sent her home in a taxi.'

'Knights?' Quirke said, widening his eyes blearily.

Mal turned to him a blank, expressionless look, the lenses of his glasses flashing. 'Of St Patrick. As if you didn't know.'

'Oh,' Quirke said. 'Right.' He looked as if he were trying not to laugh. 'Anyway,' he said, 'never mind about me, what are you doing, down here among the deadmen?'

Mal had a way of bulging out his eyes and drawing upwards sinuously his already long, thin form, as if to the music of a snake-charmer's flute. Quirke had to marvel, not for the first time, at the polished lustre of that hair, the smoothness of the brow beneath, the untarnished steely-blue of his eyes behind the pebble-glass of his specs.

'I had a thing to do,' Mal said. 'A thing to check.'

'What thing?'

Mal did not answer. He studied Quirke and saw how drunk he was, and a cold glint of relief came into his eye. 'You should go home,' he said.

Quirke thought to dispute this—the morgue was his

territory—but again suddenly he lost all interest. He shrugged, and with Mal still watching him he turned and weaved away among the body-bearing trolleys. Half-way across the room he stumbled and reached out quickly to the edge of a trolley to steady himself but managed only to grab the sheet, which came away in his hand in a hissing white flash. He was struck by the clammy coldness of the nylon; it had a human feel, like a loose, chill cowl of bloodless skin. The corpse was that of a young woman, slim and yellow-haired; she had been pretty, but death had robbed her of her features and now she might be a carving in soapstone, primitive and bland. Something, his pathologist's instinct perhaps, told him what the name would be before he looked at the label tied to her toe. 'Christine Falls,' he murmured. 'You were well named.' Looking more closely he noticed the dark roots of her hair at forehead and temples: dead, and not even a real blonde.

He woke hours later, curled on his side with a vague but pressing sense of imminent disaster. He had no memory of lying down here, among the corpses. He was chilled to the bone, and his tie was askew and choking him. He sat up, clearing his throat; how much had he drunk, first in McGonagle's and then at the party upstairs? The door to his office stood open—surely it was a dream that Mal had been there? He swung his legs to the floor and gingerly stood upright. He was light-headed, as if the top of his skull had been lifted clear off. Raising an arm, he gravely saluted the trolleys, Roman-style, and walked stiffly at a tilt out of the room.

The walls of the corridor were matt green and the woodwork and the radiators were thick with many coats of a bilious yellow stuff, glossy and glutinous, less like paint than crusted gruel. He paused at the foot of the incongruously grand, sweeping staircase—the building had been originally a club for Regency rakes—and was surprised to hear faint sounds of revelry still filtering down from the fifth floor. He put a foot on the stair, a hand on the banister rail, but paused again. Junior doctors, medical students, nurses beef to the heel: no, thanks, enough of that, and besides, the younger men had not wanted him there in the first place. He moved on along the corridor. He had a premonition of the hangover that was waiting for him, mallet and tongs at the ready. In the night-porter's room beside the tall double-doors of the main entrance a wireless set was quietly playing to itself. The Inkspots. Quirke hummed the tune to himself. 'It's a Sin to Tell a Lie'. Well, that was certainly true.

When he came out on to the steps the porter was there in his brown dustcoat, smoking a cigarette and contemplating a surly dawn breaking behind the dome of the Four Courts. The porter was a dapper little fellow with glasses and dusty hair and a pointed nose that twitched at the tip. In the still-dark street a motor car oozed past.

'Morning, Porter,' Quirke said.

The porter laughed. 'You know the name's not Porter, Mr Quirke,' he said. The way that tuft of dry brown hair was brushed back fiercely from his forehead gave him a look of permanent, vexed surmise. A querulous mouse of a man.

'That's right,' Quirke said, 'you're the porter, but you're

not Porter.' Behind the Four Courts now a dark-blue cloud with an aspect of grim intent had begun edging its way up the sky, eclipsing the light of an as yet unseen sun. Quirke turned up the collar of his jacket, wondering vaguely what had become of the raincoat he seemed to remember wearing when he had started drinking, many hours ago. And what had become of his cigarette case? 'Have you a cigarette itself to lend me?' he said.

The porter produced a packet. 'They're only Wood-bines, Mr Quirke.'

Quirke took the cigarette and bent over the cupped flame of his lighter, savouring the brief, flabby reek of burning petrol. He lifted his face to the sky and breathed deep the acrid smoke. How delicious it was, the day's first searing lungful. The lid of the lighter chinked as he flipped it shut. Then he had to cough, making a tearing sound in his throat.

'Christ, Porter,' he said, his voice wobbling, 'how can you smoke these things? Any day now I'll have you on the slab in there. When I open you up your lights will look like kippers.'

The porter laughed again, a forced, breathy titter. Quirke brusquely walked away from him. As he descended the steps he felt in the nerves of his back the fellow's suddenly laughless eye following him with ill-intent. What he did not feel was another, melancholy gaze angled down upon him from a lighted window five storeys above, where vague, festive forms were weaving and dipping still.

*

Drifts of soundless summer rain were greying the trees in Merrion Square. Quirke hurried along, keeping close to the railings as if they might shelter him, the lapels of his jacket clutched tight to his throat. It was too early yet for the office workers, and the broad street was deserted, with not a car in sight, and if not for the rain he would have been able to see unhindered all the way to the Pepper-canister Church, which always looked to him, viewed from a distance like this down the broad, shabby sweep of Upper Mount Street, to be set at a slightly skewed angle. Among the clustered chimneys a few were dribbling smoke; the summer was almost over, a new chill was in the air. But who had lit those fires, so early? Could there still be scullery-maids to haul the coal bucket up from the basement before first light? He eyed the tall windows, thinking of all those shadowed rooms with people in them, waking, yawning, getting up to make their breakfasts, or turning over to enjoy another half-hour in the damp, warm stew of their beds. Once, on another summer dawn, going along here like this, he had heard faintly from one of those windows a woman's cries of ecstasy fluttering down into the street. What a piercing stab of pity he had felt for himself then, walking all alone here, before everyone else's day had begun; piercing, and pained, but pleasurable, too, for in secret Quirke prized his loneliness as a mark of some distinction.

In the hallway of the house there was the usual smell he could never identify, brownish, exhausted, a breath out of childhood, if childhood was the word for that first decade of misery he had suffered through. He plodded up the stairs with the tread of a man mounting the gallows, his sodden shoes squelching. He had reached the first-floor return when he heard a door down in the hall opening; he stopped, sighed.

'Terrible racket again last night,' Mr Poole called up accusingly. 'Not a wink.'

Quirke turned. Poole stood sideways in the barely open doorway of his flat, neither in nor out, his accustomed stance, with an expression at once truculent and timid. He was an early riser, if indeed he ever slept. He wore a sleeveless pullover and a dicky-bow, twill trousers sharply creased, grey carpet slippers. He looked, Quirke always thought, like the father of a fighter pilot in one of those Battle of Britain films, or, better still, the father of the fighter pilot's girlfriend.

'Good morning, Mr Poole,' Quirke said, politely distant; the fellow was often a source of light relief, but Quirke's mood this early morning was not light.

Poole's pale, gull's eye glittered vengefully. He had a way of grinding his lower jaw from side to side.

'All night, no let-up,' he said, aggrieved. The other flats in the house were vacant, save for Quirke's on the third floor, yet Poole regularly complained of noises in the night. 'Frightful carry-on, bang bang bang.'

Quirke nodded. 'Terrible. I was out, myself.'

Poole glanced back into the room behind him, looked up at Quirke again. 'It's the missus that minds,' he said, lowering his voice to a whisper, 'not me.' This was a new twist. Mrs Poole, rarely glimpsed, was a diminutive person with a furtive, frightened stare; she was, Quirke knew for a fact, profoundly deaf. 'I've lodged a strong complaint. *I shall expect action*, I told them.'

'Good for you.'

Poole narrowed his eyes, suspecting irony. 'We'll see,' he said menacingly. 'We'll see.'

Quirke walked on up the stairs. He was at his own door before he heard Poole closing his.

Chill air stood unwelcoming in the living room, where the rain murmured against the two high windows, relics of a richer age, which no matter how dull the day were always somehow filled with a muted radiance Quirke found mysteriously dispiriting. He opened the lid of a silver cigarette box on the mantelpiece, but it was empty. He knelt on one knee and with difficulty lit the gas fire from the small flame of his cigarette lighter. With disgust he noted his dry raincoat, thrown over the back of an armchair, where it had been all the time. He rose to his feet too quickly and for a moment saw stars. When his vision cleared he was facing a photograph in a tortoise-shell frame on the mantelpiece: Mal Griffin, Sarah, himself at the age of twenty, and his future wife Delia laughingly pointing her racquet at the camera, all of them in tennis whites, walking forward arm in arm into a glare of sunlight. He realised with a faint shock that he could not remember where the picture had been taken; Boston, he supposed, it must have been Boston—but had they played tennis in Boston?

He took off his damp suit, put on a dressing-gown and sat down barefoot before the gas fire. He looked about the big, high-ceilinged room and grinned joylessly: his books, his prints, his Turkey carpet: his life. In the foothills of his forties, he was a decade younger than the century. The nineteen fifties had promised a new age of prosperity and happiness for all; they were not living up to their promise. His eye settled on an artist's articulated wooden model, a foot high, standing on the low telephone table beside the window, its jointed limbs arranged in a prancing pose. He looked away, frowning, but then with a sigh of annoyance rose and went and twisted the figure into a stance of desolate abasement that would better suit his morning gloom and burgeoning hangover. He returned to the chair and sat down again. The rain ceased and there was silence but for the sibilant hiss of the gas-flame. His eyes scalded, they felt as if they had been boiled; he closed them, and shivered as the lids touched, imparting to each other along their inflamed edges a tiny, horrible kiss. Clearly in his mind he saw again that moment in the photograph: the grass, the sunlight, the great hot trees, and the four of them striding forward, young and svelte and smiling. Where was it? Where? And who had been behind the camera?

2

IT WAS AFTER LUNCH by the time he could get up the
energy to drag himself into work. As he entered the
pathology department, Wilkins and Sinclair, his assistants,
exchanged an expressionless glance. 'Morning, men,'
Quirke said. 'Afternoon, I mean.' He turned away to hang
up his raincoat and his hat, and Sinclair grinned at Wilkins
and lifted an invisible glass to his mouth and mimed
drinking off a deep draught. Sinclair, a puckish fellow with
a sickle of a nose and glossy black curls tumbling on his
forehead, was the comedian of the department. Quirke
filled a beaker of water at one of the steel sinks ranged in
a row along the wall behind the dissecting table and carried
it cautiously in a not quite steady hand into his office. He
was searching for the aspirin bottle in the cluttered drawer
of his desk, wondering as always how so much stuff had
accumulated in it, when he spotted Mal's fountain pen
lying on the blotter; it was uncapped, with flecks of dried
ink on the nib. Not like Mal to leave his precious pen
behind, and with the cap off, too. Quirke stood frowning,
groping his way through an alcohol haze back to the
moment in the early hours when he had surprised Mal
here. The presence of the pen proved it had not been a

dream, yet there was something wrong with the scene as he recalled it, more wrong even than the fact of Mal sitting here, at this desk, where he had no right to be, in the watches of the night.

Quirke turned and walked into the body room and went to Christine Falls's trolley and pulled back the sheet. He hoped the two assistants did not see the start he gave when he found himself confronted with the corpse of a half-bald and moustached old woman, the eyelids not quite closed and the thin, bloodless lips drawn back in a rictus that revealed the tips of a row of incongruously white, gleaming dentures.

He returned to the office and took Christine Falls's file from the cabinet and sat down with it at his desk. His headache was very bad now, a steady, dull hammering low down at the back of his skull. He opened the file. He did not recognise the handwriting; it was certainly not his, nor that of Sinclair or Wilkins, and the signature was done in an illegible, childish scrawl. The girl was from down the country, Wexford or Waterford, he could not make out which, the writing was so bad. She had died of a pulmonary embolism; very young, he thought vaguely, for an embolism. Wilkins entered the room behind him, his crêpe soles squeaking. Wilkins was a big-eared, long-headed Protestant, thirty years old but gawky as a schoolboy; he was unfailingly, excessively, infuriatingly polite.

'This was left for you, Mr Quirke,' he said, and laid Quirke's cigarette case before him on the desk. He coughed softly. 'One of the nurses had it.'

'Oh,' Quirke said. 'Right.' They both gazed blankly at

the slim silver box as if expecting it to move. Quirke cleared his throat. 'Which nurse was it?'

'Ruttledge.'

'I see.' The silence seemed a demand for explanation. 'There was a party, upstairs, last night. I must have left it up there.' He took a cigarette from the case and lit it. 'This girl,' he said, in a brisk voice, lifting the file, 'this woman, Christine Falls—where's she gone?'

'What was the name, Mr Quirke?'

'Falls. Christine. She must have come in some time last evening, now she's gone. Where to?'

'I don't know, Mr Quirke.'

Quirke sighed into the open file; he wished Wilkins would not insist on addressing him by his name in that crawlingly obsequious way every time he was called on to speak. 'The release form,' he said, 'where's that?'

Wilkins went out to the body room. Quirke searched in the desk drawer again and this time found the aspirin bottle; there was one tablet left.

'Here you are, Mr Quirke.'

Wilkins laid the flimsy pink sheet of paper on the desk. The unreadable signature on it, Quirke saw, was the same, more or less, as the one in the file. At that moment he realised suddenly what had been odd about Mal's pose here at the desk last night: although Mal was right-handed, he had been writing with his left.

Mr Malachy Griffin was conducting his afternoon rounds of the obstetrics wing. In three-piece pinstriped suit and red bow-tie he swept from ward to ward, stiff-backed, erect, his narrow head held aloft, a gaggle of students shuffling dutifully in his wake. On the threshold of each room he would pause theatrically for a second and call out, 'Good afternoon, ladies, and how are we today?' and glance about with a broad, bright, faintly desperate smile. The big-bellied women, torpid on their beds, would stir themselves in shy expectancy, straightening the collars of their bed-jackets and patting their hairstyles, thrusting hastily under pillows the powder compacts and the hand-mirrors that had been brought out in anticipation of his visit. He was the most sought-after baby-doctor in the city. There was about him a certain tentativeness, despite his great reputation, that appealed to all these mothers-soon-to-be. Husbands at visiting time sighed when their wives began to speak of Mr Griffin, and many a boy-child born here at the Holy Family Hospital was obliged to venture out upon the obstacle course of life bearing what Quirke was sure would be the not inconsiderable handicap of being called Malachy.

'Well now, ladies, you're grand, grand—all grand!'

Quirke hung back at the end of the corridor, watching with sour amusement Mal making his stately progress through his domain. Quirke sniffed the air. Strange, to be up here, where it smelled of the living, and of the newborn living, at that. Mal, coming out of the last ward, saw him and frowned.

'Have a word?' Quirke said.

'As you see, I'm on my rounds.'

'Just a word.'

Mal sighed and waved his students on. They walked a little way off and stopped, hands in the pockets of their white coats, more than one of them suppressing a smirk: the love that was not lost between Quirke and Mr Griffin was well known.

Quirke handed Mal the fountain pen. 'You left this behind you.'

'Oh, did I?' Mal said neutrally. 'Thanks.'

He stowed the pen in the inside breast pocket of his suit; how judiciously, Quirke thought, Mal performed the smallest actions, with what weighty deliberation did he address life's trivia.

'This girl, Christine Falls,' Quirke said.

Mal blinked and glanced in the direction of the waiting students, then turned back to Quirke, pushing his spectacles up the bridge of his nose.

'Yes?' he said.

'I read the file, the one you had out last night. Was there a problem?'

Mal pinched his lower lip between a finger and thumb; it was another thing he did, had always done, since childhood, along with the fingering of the spectacles, the twitching of the nostrils, the loud cracking of the knuckles. He was, Quirke reflected, a living caricature of himself.

'I was checking some details of the case,' he said, trying to sound offhand.

Quirke lifted his eyebrows exaggeratedly. 'The case?' he said.

Mal shrugged impatiently. 'What's your interest?'

'Well, she's gone, for a start. Her corpse was—'

'I don't know anything about that. Look, Quirke, I have a busy afternoon—do you mind?'

He made to turn away but Quirke put a hand on his

arm. 'The Department is my responsibility, Mal. Stay out of it, all right?'

He released Mal's arm and Mal turned, expressionless, and strode away. Quirke watched him quickening his step, drawing the students into his wake like goslings. Then Quirke turned too and walked down the absurdly grand staircase to the basement and went to his office, where he was aware of Sinclair's speculative eye upon him, and sat at his desk and opened Christine Falls's file again. As he did so the telephone, squatting toadlike by his elbow, rang, startling him with its imperious belling, as it never failed to do. When he heard the voice that was on the line his expression softened. He listened for a moment, then said, 'Half five?' and put down the receiver.

The greenish air of evening was softly warm. He stood on the broad pavement under the trees, smoking the last of a cigarette and looking across the road at the girl on the steps of the Shelbourne Hotel. She wore a white summer dress with red polka dots and a jaunty little white hat with a feather. Her face was turned to the right as she gazed off towards the corner of Kildare Street. A stray breeze swayed the hem of her dress. He liked the way she stood, alert and self-possessed, head and shoulders back, her feet in their slim shoes set neatly side by side, her hands at her waist holding her handbag and her gloves. She reminded him so much of Delia. An olive-green dray went past, drawn by a chocolate-coloured Clydesdale. Quirke lifted his head and breathed in the late-summer smells: dust, horse, foliage, diesel fumes, perhaps even, fancifully, a hint of the girl's perfume.

He crossed the street, dodging a green double-decker bus that parped its horn at him. The girl turned her head and watched him without expression as he approached, stepping over the street's dappled sunlight and shade, his raincoat on his arm and a hand thrust stiffly into a pocket of his double-breasted jacket and his brown hat at a perilous tilt. She noted his frown of concentration, the way he seemed to have difficulty walking on those improbably tiny feet of his. She came down the steps to meet him.

'Do you make a habit of spying on girls like that?' she said.

Quirke stopped before her, one foot on the edge of the pavement. 'Like what?' he asked.

'Like a gangster casing a bank.'

'Depends on the girl. Have you anything worth robbing?'

'Depends what you're after.'

They were silent a moment, watching each other, then the girl smiled. 'Hello, Nuncle,' she said.

'Hello, Phoebe. What's wrong?'

She gave a grimacing shrug. 'What's right?'

They sat in the hotel lounge in little gilt chairs and had tea and plates of tiny sandwiches and tiny cakes on a tiered cake-stand. The high, ornate room was busy. The Friday evening horsy crowd was up from the country, all tweeds and sensible shoes and braying, overbearing voices; they made Quirke feel on edge, and when he squirmed the curved arms of the gilt chair seemed to tighten their grip on him. It was obvious that Phoebe loved it here, loved the opportunity it afforded her of playing the poised young lady, Mr Griffin the consultant's daughter from Rathgar. Quirke watched her over the rim of his teacup, enjoying her enjoyment. She had taken off her hat and set it beside her plate, it looked like a table ornament, its feather languidly adroop. Her hair was so black the waves of it showed a bluish sheen in their hollows. She had her mother's vivid blue eyes. He thought she was wearing too much makeup—that lipstick was altogether too garish for a girl her age—but he made no remark. From an opposite corner of the room an elderly fellow of military bearing, with polished bald pate and a monocle, appeared to be regarding him with a fixed, affronted glare. Phoebe popped a miniature éclair whole into her mouth and munched it, widening her eyes, laughing at herself.

'How's the boyfriend?' Quirke said.

She shrugged, and swallowed mightily. 'He's all right.'

'Still at the law?'

'He'll be called to the Bar next year.'

'Will he, now? Well, that's simply spiffing.'

She threw a cake crumb at him, and he sensed an outraged flash of that monocle come flying at them from across the room.

'Don't be sarcastic,' she said. 'You're so sarcastic.' Her face darkened and she looked into her cup. 'They're trying to make me give him up. That's why I phoned you.'

He nodded, keeping a level look. 'Who's *they*?'

She tossed her head, her permed waves bouncing. 'Oh, all of them,' she said. 'Daddy, of course. Even Granddad.'

'And your mother?'

'Her?' she said, a derisive snort. She pursed her lips and put on a reproving voice. '*Now, Phoebe, you must think of the family, of your father's reputation.* Hypocrites!' She glared at him, then suddenly laughed, putting a hand over her mouth. 'Your face!' she cried. 'You won't hear a word said against her, will you?'

He did not respond to that, but said instead:

'What do you want *me* to do?'

'Talk to them,' she said, leaning forward quickly over the little table, her hands clasped at her breast. 'Talk to Daddy—or talk to Granddad, you're his white-headed boy, after all, and Daddy will do whatever Granddad tells him to.'

Quirke brought out his cigarette case and his lighter. Phoebe watched him tap the cigarette on his thumbnail. He could see her calculating if she dared to ask him for one. He blew a plume of smoke towards the ceiling and picked a flake of tobacco from his lower lip. 'I hope you don't seriously intend marrying Bertie Wooster?' he said.

'If it's Conor Carrington you mean, he hasn't asked me. Yet.'

'What age are you?'

'Twenty.'

'No, you're not.'

'I will be, soon.'

He leaned back in the low chair, studying her. He said: 'You're not planning to run away again, are you?'

'I'm considering *going* away. I'm not a child, you know. This is the nineteen fifties, not the Dark Ages. Anyway, if I can't marry Conor Carrington I'll elope with you.'

He sat back and laughed and the little chair gave a cry of protest. 'No, thanks.'

'It wouldn't be incest—you're only my uncle by marriage, after all.'

Something happened in her face then, and she bit her lip and looked down and began rummaging in her handbag. In consternation he saw a tear fall on the back of her hand. He glanced quickly in the direction of the man with the monocle, who had risen to his feet and was advancing between the tables with an air of grim purpose. Phoebe found the handkerchief she had been searching for and blew her nose juicily. The monocle was almost upon them now and Quirke braced himself for a confrontation—what had he done to provoke it?—but the fellow marched past the table, displaying an equine grin and extending a hand to someone behind Quirke's back and saying, 'Trevor! I *thought* it was you . . .'

Phoebe's face was blotched and there was an oily black pierrot-smear of mascara under one eye. 'Oh, Nuncle,' she said, a muted wail, 'I'm so unhappy.'

Quirke ground the stub of his cigarette into the ashtray on the table. 'Calm down, for heaven's sake,' he muttered; he still had a headache.

Phoebe scowled at him through her tears. 'Don't tell me to calm down!' she cried. 'Everyone is always telling me to calm down. I'm sick of it!' She snapped her bag shut and stood up, casting vaguely to right and left, as if she had forgotten where she was. Quirke, still in his chair, told her to sit down, for the love of God, but she ignored him. People at the tables round about were looking at her. 'I'm getting out of here,' she said, and strode away.

Quirke paid the bill and caught up with her on the hotel steps. She was dabbing the handkerchief to her eyes again. 'You're a mess,' he said. 'Go in and fix your face.'

Docile now, she went back into the hotel. Waiting for her, he stood in the railed-off area beside the glass door and smoked another cigarette. The day was almost done, the trees in the Green were throwing raked shadows along the street; it would not be long now until autumn. He was admiring the rich light on the brick façades of the houses over by Hume Street when Phoebe came out and stopped beside him and took his arm. 'Take me somewhere,' she said. 'Take me to some low dive.' She squeezed his arm against her side and laughed deep in her throat. 'I want to be *baad*.'

They strolled along the Green towards Grafton Street. People were out promenading, enjoying the last of the fine day that had started so badly. Phoebe walked close against him, her arm still linked in his; he could feel the warmth of her hip, the firmness of it, and, within, the smooth articulation of the joint. Then he thought of Christine Falls, waxen and wan on her bier. 'How are the studies?' he asked.

Phoebe shrugged. 'I'm going to switch,' she said. 'History is boring.'

'Oh? And what will you do instead?'

'Medicine, maybe. Join the family tradition.' Quirke made no comment. She pressed his arm again. 'I really am going to move out, you know. If they won't let me live my life, I'm off.'

Quirke glanced down at her and laughed. 'How will you manage?' he said. 'I can't see your father financing this life of bohemian freedom you're determined on.'

'I'll get a job. That's what they do in America. I had a pen-pal who was putting herself through college. That's what she wrote, *I'm putting myself through college.* Imagine.'

They turned into Grafton Street and arrived at McGonagle's. Quirke pulled open the big door with its red-and-green stained-glass panels, and a waft of beer fumes and cigarette smoke and noise came out to meet them. Despite the early hour the place was crowded.

'Huh,' Phoebe said, 'call this low?'

She followed after Quirke as he pushed his way through to the bar. They found two unoccupied high stools beside a square wooden column into which a narrow mirror was set. Phoebe hitched up her skirt to sit, smiling at him. Yes, Quirke told himself, she had Delia's smile. When they were seated he found that he could see his reflection in the mirror behind her shoulder, and had her change places with him; it always made him uneasy to look himself in the eye.

'What will you have?' he asked her, lifting a beckoning finger to the barman.

'What *can* I have?'

'Sarsaparilla.'

'Gin. I'll have gin.'

He raised his eyebrows. 'Oh, will you, now?'

The barman was elderly and stooped and of a priestly mien.

'The usual for me, Davy,' Quirke said, 'and a gin and

tonic for her ladyship here. More tonic than gin.' Mc-Gonagle's had been one of his watering-holes in the old days, the days of his serious drinking.

Davy nodded and sniffed and shuffled off. Phoebe was looking about the smoke-dimmed room. A large, florid woman in purple, holding a glass of stout in a beringed hand, winked at her and smiled, showing a mouthful of gapped and tobacco-stained teeth; the man with her was lean as a greyhound, with colourless, flat and somehow crusted hair.

'Are they somebody?' Phoebe asked, out of the side of her mouth; McGonagle's was famous as the haunt of self-appointed poets and their muses.

'Everybody is somebody here,' he said. 'Or think they are.'

Davy the barman brought their drinks. It was strange, Quirke reflected, that he had never got to like the taste of whiskey, or of any alcohol, for that matter; even in the wild times, after Delia had died, the sour burn of the stuff had always repelled him a little, though he had still managed to pour it into himself by the jugful. He was not a natural drinker; he believed there were such, but he was not one of them. That was what had kept him from destruction, he supposed, in the long, lachrymose years of mourning for his lost wife.

He lifted his glass and tipped it to the girl. 'Here's to liberty,' he said.

She was gazing into her drink, watching the ice cubes writhing amid the bubbles. 'You really are soft on Mummy, aren't you?' she said. *Mummy*. The word stopped him for a beat. A tall man with a high, smooth forehead went past, squeezing sideways through the crush. Quirke recognised him as the one from the hotel, the Trevor that the monocled old boy had crossed the room to greet. Small world; too small. 'You were sweet on her,' Phoebe said, 'years ago, and still are. I know all about it.'

'I was sweet on her sister—I *married* her sister.'

'But only on the rebound. Daddy got the one you wanted, and then you married Aunt Delia.'

'You're speaking of the dead.'

'I know. I'm awful, amn't I? But it's true, all the same. Do you miss her?'

'Who?' She struck him sharply on the wrist-bone with her knuckle, and the feather in her hat bobbed and the tip of it touched him on the forehead. 'It's twenty years,' he said, and then, after a pause, 'Yes, I miss her.'

Sarah sat down on the plush stool before the dressing-table and inspected herself in the looking-glass. She had put on a dress of scarlet silk but wondered now if it had been a mistake. They would study her, as they always did, pretending not to, searching for something to disapprove of, some sign of difference, some statement that she was not one of them. She had lived among them for—what? fifteen years?—but they had never accepted her, never would, the women especially. They would smile, and flatter her, and offer her tidbits of harmless chit-chat, as if she were an exhibit in a zoo. When she spoke they listened with exaggerated attention, nodding and smiling encouragement, as they would to a child, or a halfwit. She would hear her voice trembling with the strain of trying to sound normal, the sentences tottering out of her mouth and falling ineffectually at their feet. And how they would frown, feigning polite bafflement, when she forgot herself and used an Americanism. *How interesting*, they would say, *that you never lost your accent*, adding, *never, in all the years*, as if she had been brought back here by the first transatlantic buccaneers, like tobacco, or the turkey. She sighed. Yes, the dress was wrong, but she had not the energy, she decided, to change it.

Mal came in from the bathroom, tieless, in shirt-sleeves and braces, showing a pair of cufflinks. 'Can you do up these blessèd things for me?' he said, in plaintive irritation.

He extended his arms and Sarah rose and took the fiddly, cold links and began to insert them in the cuffs. They avoided each other's eye, Mal with his mouth pursed averting his face and looking vacantly into a corner of the ceiling. How delicate and pale the skin was on the under-sides of his wrists. It was the thing that had struck her about him when they had first met, twenty years ago, how soft he seemed, how sweetly soft all over, this tall, tender, vulnerable man.

'Is Phoebe home?' he asked.

'She won't be late.'

'She had better not be, on this of all nights.'

'You're too hard on her, Mal.'

He drew his lips tighter still. 'You'd better go and see if my father has arrived,' he said. 'You know what a stickler he is.'

When was it, she wondered, that they had begun to speak to each other in this stilted, testy way, like two strangers trapped in a lift?

She went downstairs, the silk of her dress making a scratching sound against her knees, like a muffled cackling. Really, she should have changed into something less dramatic, less—less declamatory. She smiled wanly, liking the word. It was not her habit to declaim.

Maggie the maid was in the dining room, laying spoons out on the table.

'Is everything ready, Maggie?'

The maid gave her a quick, frowning look, seeming for a moment not to recognise her. Then she nodded. There was a stain on the hem of her uniform at the back that Sarah hoped was gravy. Maggie was well past retirement age but Sarah had not the heart to let her go, as she had let go that other poor girl. There was a knocking at the front door.

'I'll get it,' Sarah said. Maggie did not look at her and only nodded again, squinting at the spoons.

When Sarah opened the door to him Garret Griffin thrust a bunch of flowers into her arms.

'Garret,' she said warmly. 'Come in.'

The old man stepped into the hall and there was the usual moment of helplessness as she wondered how to greet him, for the Griffins, even Garret, were not people who accepted kisses easily. He indicated the flowers where she held them against her; they were strikingly ugly. 'I hope they're all right,' he said. 'I'm no good at that kind of thing.'

'They're lovely,' she said, taking a cautious sniff of the

blossoms; the Michaelmas daisies smelled of dirty socks. She smiled; the daisies did not matter, she was happy to see him. 'Lovely,' she said again.

He took off his overcoat and hung it on the rack behind the door. 'Am I the first?' he asked, turning back to her and chafing his hands.

'Everyone else is late.'

'Oh, Lord,' he moaned, 'I'm always the same—always too early!'

'We'll have a chance to chat, before the others come and monopolise you.'

He smiled, looking down in that cumbersomely shy way he had. She thought again, with faint surprise—but why surprise?—how fond of him she was. Mal appeared on the stairs, solemn and stately in his dark suit and sober tie. Garret glanced up at him without enthusiasm. 'There you are,' he said.

Father and son stood before each other in silence. Sarah stepped towards them impulsively, and as she did so had the sense as of an invisible, brittle casing shattering soundlessly around her. 'Look what Garret brought!' she said, holding out the hideous flowers. 'Aren't they beautiful?'

Quirke was on his third drink. He sat sideways at the bar, leaning on an elbow, one eye shut against the smoke of his cigarette, half listening to Phoebe rehearsing her plans for the future. He had let her have a second gin, and her eyes glittered and her brow was flushed. As she talked, the feather in her little hat trembled in time to the beat of her excited chattering. The man next to them with the crusty hair kept shooting furtive glances at her, to the annoyance of his fat companion, though Phoebe appeared not to notice the fellow's fishy eye. Quirke smiled to himself, feeling only a little foolish to be so pleased at being here with her, in her summer dress, bright and young. The noise in the place was a steady roar by now, and even when he tried he could hardly hear what she was saying. Then there was a shout behind him.

'Jesus Christ in gaiters, if it isn't Dr Death!'

Barney Boyle stood there, flagrant, drunk and menacingly jovial. Quirke turned, assuming a smile. Barney was a dangerous acquaintance: Quirke and he had got drunk together often, in the old days. 'Hello, Barney,' he said warily.

Barney was in his drinking clothes: black suit crumpled and stained, striped tie for a belt, and a shirt, which had once been white, agape at the collar and looking as if it had been yanked open in a scuffle. Phoebe was thrilled, for this was the famous Barney Boyle. He was, she saw —she almost laughed—a scaled-down version of Quirke, a full head shorter but with the same barrel chest and broken nose and the same ridiculously dainty feet. He grabbed her hand and planted on it a lubricious kiss. His own hands, she noticed, were small and soft and endearingly chubby.

'Your niece, is it?' he said to Quirke. 'By God, Doc, they're making nieces nicer every day—and that, my darling,' turning his shiny grin on Phoebe again, 'is not an easy thing to get your tongue around, with a feed of porter on you.'

He called for drinks, insisting against Quirke's protests that Phoebe too must have another. Barney preened under the girl's eager gaze, rolling from heel to toe and back again, a pint glass in one hand and a sodden cigarette in the other. Phoebe asked if he was writing a new play and he swept the air with a deprecating arm. 'I am not!' he roared. 'I'll write no more plays.' He struck a histrionic pose and spoke as if addressing an audience: 'The Abbey Theatre from this day forth must make do without the fruits of my genius!' He took a violent draught of his drink, throwing back his head and opening his mouth wide, the cords of his throat pulsing as he swallowed. 'I'm writing poetry again,' he said, wiping his bulbous red lips with the back of his hand. 'In Irish, that lovely language that I learned in jail, the university of the working classes.'

Quirke could feel his smile slowly, helplessly congealing. There had been nights when he and Barney had stood here happily like this until closing time and long after, toe to toe, drink for drink, barging their pumped-up personalities at each other like a pair of boys fighting with balloons. Well, those days were long gone. When Barney attempted to order another round Quirke lifted a staying hand and said no, that they must be going.

'Sorry, Barney,' he said, stepping down from the stool and ignoring Phoebe's indignant glare. 'Another time.'

Barney measured him with a soiled eye, chewing his mouth at the side. For the second time that evening Quirke anticipated an assault, and wondered how best to avoid it—Barney, for all his diminutiveness, knew how to fight—but then Barney shifted his glare on to Phoebe.

'Griffin, now,' he said, screwing up one eye. 'Are you anything, by any chance, to Judge Garret Griffin, the Chief Justice and Great Panjandrum himself?'

Quirke was still trying to make Phoebe get down from the stool, tugging her by the elbow and at the same time gathering up his raincoat and his hat. 'Different family altogether,' he said.

Barney ignored him.

'Because,' Barney said to Phoebe, 'that's the boyo that put me away for fighting for the freedom of my country. Oh, yes, I was with the squad that set off them firecrackers in Coventry in 'thirty-nine. You didn't know that, did you now, Miss Griffin? The bomb, I can tell you, is mightier than the pen.' His forehead had taken on a hot sheen and his eyes seemed to be sinking back into his skull. 'And when I came home, instead of getting the hero's welcome I deserved, I was sent to the boys' jail for three years by Mr Justice Griffin, *to cool your heels*, as he put it, provoking laughter in the court. I was sixteen years old. What do you think of that, Miss Griffin?'

Quirke had begun determinedly to move away, trying to draw a still unwilling Phoebe after him. The man with the bad hair, who had been listening to Barney with interest, now leaned forward, a finger lifted. '*I* think—' he began.

'You fuck off,' Barney said, without looking at him.

'Fuck off yourself,' the woman in purple told him stoutly, 'you and your friend and your friend's tart.'

Phoebe giggled tipsily, and Quirke gave her a last, violent tug and she toppled forward from the stool and would have fallen but for his steadying hand under her arm.

'And now, I'm told,' Barney bellowed, loud enough for half the bar to hear, 'he's after being made a papal count. At least'—more loudly still—'I think *count* is the word.'

3

THERE WAS a low buzz of talk in the drawing room. The guests, a score or so, stood about in clusters, the men all alike in dark suits, the women bird-bright and twittering. Sarah moved among them, brushing a hand here, touching an elbow there, trying to keep her smile from slipping. She felt guilty for not being able to like these people, Mal's friends, mostly, or the Judge's. Apart from the priests—always so many priests!—they were business people, or people in the law, or in medicine, well-heeled, watchful of their privileges, of their place in the city's society, such as it was. She had acknowledged to herself a long time ago that she was a little afraid of them, all of them, not just the frightening ones, like that fellow Costigan. They were not the sort she would have expected Mal or his father to have for friends. But then, was there any other sort, here? The world in which they moved was small. It was not her world. She was in it, but not of it, that was what she told herself. She must not let anyone else know what she was thinking. *Smile*, she told herself, *keep smiling!*

All at once she felt faint and had to stop for a moment, pressing her fingers down hard on the drinks table for support.

Mal, watching from across the room, saw that she was having what Maggie the maid called, not without a touch of contempt, *one of her turns*. He felt a rush of something resembling grief, as if her unhappiness were an illness, one that would—he flinched to think it—kill her. He bowed his head and closed his eyes briefly, savouring for a moment the restful dark, then opened them again and turned to his father with an effort. 'I haven't congratulated you,' he said. 'It's a great thing, a papal knighthood.'

The Judge, fiddling with his tobacco pipe, snorted. 'You think so?' he said, with scornful incredulousness, then shrugged. 'Well, I suppose I have done the Church some service.'

They were silent, each wishing to move away from the other but neither knowing how to manage it. Sarah, recovered, turned from the table and approached them, smiling tensely. 'You two are looking very solemn,' she said.

'I was congratulating him—' Mal began, but his father interrupted him with angry dismissiveness:

'Arrah, he was trying to flatter me!'

There was another awkward silence. Sarah could think of nothing to say. Mal cleared his throat. 'Excuse me,' he murmured, and walked softly away.

Sarah linked her arm through the old man's and leaned against him fondly. She liked his staleish smell of tobacco and tweed and dry, ageing flesh. Sometimes it seemed to her he was her only ally, but that thought made her feel guilty too, for why and against whom did she need an ally? But she knew the answer. She watched as Costigan put out a hand and took Mal by the arm and began to talk to him earnestly. Costigan was a thickset man with heavy black hair swept straight back from his forehead. He wore horn-rimmed spectacles that magnified his eyes.

'I don't like that man,' she said. 'What does he do?'

The Judge chuckled. 'He's in the export business, I believe. Not my favourite, either, I confess, among Malachy's friends.'

'I should go and rescue him,' she said.

'No man more in need of it.'

She gave him a smile of rueful reproof and unlinked her arm from his and set off across the room. Costigan had not noticed her approaching. He was saying something about Boston and *our people over there*. Everything that Costigan said sounded like a veiled threat, she had noticed that before now. She wondered again how Mal could be friends with such a man. When she touched Mal's arm he started, as if her fingertips had communicated a tiny charge through the cloth of his sleeve, and Costigan smiled at her icily, baring his lower teeth, which were grey and clogged with plaque.

When she had got Mal away she said to him, smiling to soften it: 'Were you fighting with your father again?'

'We don't fight,' he said stiffly. 'I lodge an appeal, he delivers a judgment.' *Oh, Mal*, she wanted to say, *oh, my poor Mal!* 'Where's Phoebe?' he asked.

She hesitated. He had taken off his spectacles to polish them. 'Not home yet,' she said.

He halted. 'What—?'

With relief she heard, beyond the voices in the room, the sound of the front door opening. She walked away from him quickly, out to the hall. Phoebe was handing a man's hat and coat to Maggie. 'Where have you been?' Sarah hissed at the girl. 'Your father is . . .' Then Quirke turned from the door, with an apologetic smile, and she stopped, feeling the blood surge up from her breast and burn in her cheeks.

'Quirke,' she said.

'Hello, Sarah.' How youthful and gauche he looked, leaning down at her, still smiling; a big blond overgrown boy. 'I'm just delivering this black sheep home,' he said.

Mal came into the hall then. Seeing Quirke he stopped, with that pop-eyed glare that made it seem as if something had become stuck in his throat. Maggie, grinning mysteriously to herself, made off for the kitchen without a sound.

''Evening, Mal,' Quirke said. 'I'm not staying—'

'You most certainly are staying!' Phoebe cried. 'Since they wouldn't let me invite Conor Carrington I can at least have you!'

She glared defiantly from one of the adults to another, then blinked, her eyes swimming out of focus, and she turned, lurching a little, and stamped away up the stairs. Quirke was looking about for Maggie and his hat. 'I'd better go,' he muttered.

'Oh, but wait!' Sarah lifted a hand as if she would physically detain him, yet did not touch him. 'The Judge is here, he'd never forgive me if you leave before you've at least said hello.' Without looking at Mal she took Quirke's arm and turned him, mildly resisting, towards the drawing room. 'When is it you were last here?' she said, speaking in a rush so that he might not interrupt. '—Christmas, was it? It really is too bad of you, neglecting us like this.'

The Judge was standing with a group of guests, talking

volubly and gesturing with his pipe. When he caught sight of Quirke he gave an exaggerated start, throwing up his hands and opening wide his eyes. 'Well, will you look who's here!' he cried, and hurried forward, the abandoned guests smiling tolerantly after him.

'Hello, Garret,' Quirke said.

Sarah released him and took a step back, and the Judge tapped him on the breast fondly with a fist. 'I thought you couldn't come tonight, you rascal?'

Quirke rolled his shoulders, smiling and biting his lip. He was, the Judge could see, three sheets over, or two, anyway.

'Phoebe insisted,' Quirke said.

'Aye, she's a persuasive girl, that one.'

The two men surveyed each other, watched by Sarah, smiling, and Mal, expressionless.

'Congratulations, by the way,' Quirke said, with restrained irony.

The Judge flapped a hand before him bashfully. 'Go on out of that,' he said. 'You wouldn't want to take these things too seriously. Though, mind you, I'm hoping it will help my entry bid when I get to the Pearly Gates.'

Quirke was tapping a cigarette on this thumbnail. 'Count Garret Griffin,' he said. 'It has a ring to it.'

Mal coughed. 'It's Garret, Count Griffin. That's the proper form of address. Like John, Count McCormack.'

A brief silence followed this. The Judge twisted his lips in a sour smile. 'Malachy, my boy,' he said, and laid an arm about Quirke's shoulders, 'would you ever go and fetch this thirsty man a drink?'

But Sarah said she would get it. She was afraid that if she went on standing there she would break out in a shriek of hysterical laughter. When she returned with the whiskey Mal had moved away, and the Judge was telling Quirke a story about a case he had tried long ago when he was in the District Courts, something about a man selling a goat, or buying a goat, and falling down a well; she had heard the story before, many times, yet she could never remember the details. Quirke was nodding and laughing excessively; he too had heard the oft-told tale. He took the drink from her without offering thanks.

'Well,' he said, lifting the glass to the Judge, 'here's to the purple.'

'Oho!' the old man crowed. 'It's far from grand titles we were reared.'

Phoebe came into the room, looking pale and slightly dazed. She had changed into slacks and a black pullover that was too tight at the bust. Sarah offered her a drink, saying there was lemonade, but the girl ignored her and went to the drinks table and splashed gin into a tumbler.

'Well now, Malachy,' the Judge called across the room to his son, in a voice that was all innocence, 'I didn't know you were letting that young lady at the hard stuff?' Mal went a whiter shade of white as those around him fell silent and looked at him. The Judge ostentatiously put a hand to his mouth and said to Quirke sideways in a stage whisper, 'Indeed, by the look of her she's had a few already.'

Mal crossed the room and spoke to Phoebe in an undertone, but she turned aside from him as if he were not there. He hesitated a moment, clenching his fists—Mal was, Quirke thought, the kind of man who really does clench his fists—then whirled about and bore down grimly on Quirke and the Judge. Sarah made a movement as if to intercept him, and Quirke held up a hand. 'Yes, Mal, yes,' he said, 'I confess, I was the occasion of sin. She made me take her to McGonagle's.'

Mal, his forehead pale and glistening, was about to spit out a violent word but Sarah spoke up quickly. 'Shall we have something to eat?' she said, with desperate brightness. She turned to the guests, who had been watching avidly, while trying to seem not to, this little succession of familial confrontations. There was not always such rich entertainment to be had at the Griffins'. 'If everyone will step into the dining room,' Sarah said loudly, her voice cracking a little, 'we can start the buffet.'

But Mal persisted. 'Do you think,' he said to Quirke in quiet fury, 'that it's funny to bring a girl of her age to a pub?'

Quirke took a breath, but the Judge put an arm around his shoulders again and turned him firmly out of the line of Mal's anger, saying: 'McGonagle's, is it?' He chuckled. 'Lord, I haven't set foot in that den of iniquity since I don't know when . . .'

Quirke did not eat, but drank more whiskey instead. Suddenly he found himself in the kitchen, with Maggie. He looked about in dazed surprise. He seemed to have come to, somehow, just at that moment, leaning against the cupboard beside the sink, with his ankles crossed, nursing his whiskey glass to his midriff. What had happened to the intervening time, from when he was standing with the Judge to now? Maggie, bustling about, was speaking to him, apparently in reply to something he had said, though what it might have been he could not think. Maggie looked like the witch in a fairy tale, stooped and wizened, with a hooked nose and a tangled nest of steel-coloured hair; she even had a cackling laugh, on the rare occasions when she did laugh.

'Anyway,' Quirke said, thinking to start the conversation afresh, 'how are you getting on, Maggie?'

She paused by the stove and glanced at him, grinning archly at one side of her face. 'You're a terrible man,' she said. 'You'd drink it off a sore leg.'

He lifted the whiskey glass before his eyes and looked from it to her and back again with a mock-offended air, and she shook her head at him and went on with her work. She was cooking something in a steaming pot, into which she peered now, screwing up her face. *Grimalkin*, he thought: was that a witch's name? From the drawing room came the sound of the Judge's voice: he was making a speech to the company. '. . . *And I hope you'll believe me when I say that I consider myself unworthy of this great honour that the Holy Father has bestowed on me, and on my family. You all know where, and what, I came from, and how fortunate I've been, both in public and in private life . . .*'

Maggie gave a low, sardonic snort. 'I suppose you're here about the girl,' she said.

Quirke frowned. 'Phoebe?'

'No!' Maggie said, with another snort. 'The one that's after dying.'

There was a burst of applause outside as the Judge finished his speech. Sarah entered carrying a stack of used plates. Seeing Quirke she hesitated, then came and set the plates on the table among the other piles of washing-up waiting to be done. With weary forbearance she asked Maggie if the soup might be ready some time soon— 'They've eaten all the sandwiches, I'm afraid'—but Maggie, still bent over the steaming pot, only muttered something under her breath. Sarah sighed, and turned on the hot-water tap. Quirke watched her with a tipsily unfocused smile.

'I wish,' she said quietly, not looking at him, 'you wouldn't take Phoebe to places like McGonagle's. Mal is right, she's too young to be in pubs, drinking.'

Quirke put on a repentant expression. 'I shouldn't have come here either, I suppose,' he said, hanging his head, but looking up at her from a corner of his eye.

'Not straight from that place, no.'

'I wanted to see you.'

She turned a quick glance in Maggie's direction. 'Quirke,' she murmured, 'don't start.'

The hot water from the tap blurted into the sink, throwing up clouds of steam. Sarah put on an apron and took a soup tureen down from a shelf, shaking her head at the dusty state of it, and washed it with a sponge. Quirke was gratified to see how agitated she was. She carried the tureen to the stove and Maggie poured the soup into it. 'Will you serve it, Maggie, please?' Quirke lit another cigarette. The smoke, the smell of the soup, the whiskey fumes, all combined to promote in him a feeling of faint, sweet regretfulness. All this might have been his, had he done differently, he thought, this fine house, the band of friends, the family retainer, and this woman in her scarlet gown and elegant high-heeled shoes and those silk stockings with such straight seams. He watched her as she held the door for Maggie to pass through with the soup. Her hair was the colour of rain-wet wheat. He had chosen her sister, Delia Crawford; Delia the dark one; Delia who died. Or was it he who had been chosen?

'Do you know,' he said, 'what it was that struck me first about you, all those years ago, in Boston?' He waited, but she made no response, and would not turn to look at him. He whispered it: '*Your smell.*'

She gave a short, incredulous laugh. 'My *what*? My perfume, do you mean?'

He shook his head vigorously. 'No no no. Not perfume—you.'

'And what did I smell of?'

'I've told you—you. You smelled of you. You still do.'

Now she did look at him, smiling in a strained, unsteady way, and when she spoke her voice had a feathery quality, as if she were faintly in pain. 'Doesn't everybody smell of themselves?'

Again he shook his head, gently this time.

'Not like you,' he said. 'Not with that—that intensity.'

Quickly she turned her attention back to the sink. She knew she was blushing. She could smell *him*, now, or not smell but feel him, rather, the fleshy heat of him pressing against her like the air of a midsummer day thick with the threat of thunder. 'Oh, Quirke,' she said, with an effort at gaiety, 'you're just drunk!'

He swayed a little, and righted himself. 'And you're beautiful,' he said.

She closed her eyes for a second and seemed to waver. She was holding on to the rim of the sink. Her knuckles were white.

'You shouldn't talk to me like this, Quirke,' she said in an undertone. 'It isn't fair.' He had leaned so close to her from where he was standing that it seemed he might put his face into her hair at the side, or kiss her ear or her pale, dry cheek. He swayed again, smiling emptily. Suddenly she turned to face him, her eyes shining with anger, and he reared back from her unsteadily. 'This is what you do, isn't it?' she said, her lips whitening. 'You play with people. You tell them how nice they smell, and that they're beautiful, and all just to see their reaction, just to see if they'll do something interesting, to relieve your boredom.'

She began to weep, making no sound, big, shining tears squeezing out between her shut eyelids and her mouth clenched and dragged down at the corners. The door behind her opened and Phoebe stepped into the room and stopped, staring first at her mother's bowed back and then at Quirke, who, unseen by Sarah, lifted high his eyebrows and his shoulders in an exaggerated shrug of bewildered innocence. The girl hesitated a moment, a faint fear coming into her face, then soundlessly withdrew and as soundlessly closed the door.

The spectacle of another female in tears, the second this evening, was rapidly making Quirke sober. He offered Sarah his handkerchief but she fumbled in a pocket of her frock and brought out one of her own and held it up for him to see. 'I always keep a handkerchief handy,' she said, 'just in case.' She gave a congested laugh and blew her nose, then braced her hands on the sink again and lifted her face to the ceiling with a hoarse, infuriated groan. 'Look at me, my God! Standing in my own kitchen, crying. And for what?' She turned and contemplated him, shaking her head. 'Oh, Quirke, you're hopeless!'

Encouraged by her tearful smile Quirke lifted a hand to touch her cheek but she twitched her head aside, no longer smiling. 'Too late, Quirke,' she said, in a hard, tight voice. 'Twenty years too late.'

She tucked the handkerchief into the sleeve of her dress and took off the apron and set it on the sideboard and stood for a moment with her hand resting on the cloth as if on a child's head, her eyes downcast and blank. Quirke watched her; she was stronger than he was, in the end; far stronger. Again he moved to touch her but again she flinched from him and he let fall his hand. Then she gave herself a faint shake and turned and walked out of the room.

Quirke stayed where he was for a minute, gazing into his glass. It puzzled him, how with people nothing ever went as it seemed it should, or as it seemed it might. He sighed. He had the hot and guilty sense of having tinkered with something too delicately fine for his clumsy fingers. He put down his glass, telling himself to leave and not say another word to anyone. He was half-way to the door when it was pushed open brusquely and Mal came in. 'What did you say to her?' he demanded. Quirke hesitated, willing himself not to laugh; Mal looked so perfectly, so theatrically, the part of the irate husband. 'Well?' he snapped again.

'Nothing, Mal,' Quirke said, trying to sound both blameless and contrite.

Mal watched him narrowly. 'You're a trouble-maker, Quirke,' he said, in an unexpectedly mild and almost matter-of-fact tone. 'You come to my house, drunk, on this night when my father—'

'Look, Mal—'

'Don't *Look, Mal* me!'

He stepped forward and planted himself in front of Quirke, breathing loudly down his nostrils, his eyes bulging behind his spectacles. Maggie appeared in the doorway, in a repeat of Phoebe's appearance earlier. Seeing the two men confronting each other she, too, quickly withdrew, with a gleeful look.

'You have no place here, Quirke,' Mal said, speaking evenly. 'You may think you have, but you haven't.'

Quirke made to step past him but Mal put a hand against his chest. Quirke leaned backwards, teetering on his heels. He had a sudden vision of the two of them grappling clumsily, grunting and swaying, their arms thrown about each other in a furious bear-hug. The urge to laugh was stronger than ever. 'Listen, Mal,' he said, 'I was bringing Phoebe home, that's all. I shouldn't have taken her to the pub in the first place. I'm sorry. All right?' Mal was clenching his fists again; he now looked like the thwarted villain in a silent film. 'Mal,' Quirke said, trying to put conviction into his voice, 'you have no reason to hate me.'

'I'll be the judge of that,' Mal said quickly, as if he had known what Quirke was about to say, as if he had heard it said before. 'I want you to stay away from Phoebe. I'm not going to allow you to turn her into another version of yourself. Do you understand?'

There was silence between them then, a heavy, animal hush. Each man could hear the blood beating in his temples, Mal's from anger and Quirke's from the effect of too much whiskey. Then Quirke sidestepped his brother-in-law, saying, 'Goodnight, Mal,' in a tone of leaden irony. On his way to the door he stopped, and turned, and asked, in a deliberately light, conversational tone, 'Was Christine Falls your patient?'

Mal blinked, the glossy lids falling with a curious kind of languor over the swollen eyeballs. 'What?'

'Christine Falls—the one that died: was she your patient? Is that why you were down in the Department last night, poking in the files?' Mal said nothing, only stood and looked at him with that dull, protuberant stare. 'I hope you haven't been a naughty boy, Mal. Negligence cases can be very costly.'

He was in the hall, waiting for Maggie to bring his coat and hat. If he was quick he would make it to McGonagle's before closing time; Barney Boyle would still be there, drunker than ever, but he could handle Barney when there were just the two of them and no Phoebe to get Barney's dander up. He might find a woman there, too, and persuade her to come back with him to the flat, if he could sneak her past the unsleeping Mr Poole and his alertly deaf wife.

My life, he thought in drunken anger and self-pity. *My mess of a life.*

Maggie came with his things, mumbling to herself. She held his coat, and he enquired of her yet again, although he thought it was for the first time, how she was getting on, and she clicked her tongue in irritation and said he should go home now and sleep it off, so he should.

Something struck him, a hazed recollection. 'That girl you mentioned earlier,' he said. 'Who was that?'

She frowned at the collar of his coat as she handed it to him. 'What?'

He was struggling to remember.

'*The one that died*, you said. Who was she?'

She shrugged.

'Something Falls.'

He looked into the crown of his hat, the greasy darkness there. Falls, Christine. That name again. He was about to ask another question when a peremptory voice spoke behind him. 'And where do you think *you*'re going?'

It was Phoebe.

'Home,' he lied.

'And leave me with this crowd? Not on your nelly.'

Maggie made a sound that might have been a snigger. Phoebe, shaking her head in mock disbelief at Quirke's willingness to abandon her, took a shawl that was draped over the stair-post and wrapped it around her shoulders. Firmly she grabbed his hand. 'Lead on, big boy.'

Maggie grew suddenly agitated. 'What'll I say if they ask me?' she demanded, a rising whine.

'Tell them I've run away with a sailor,' Phoebe told her.

Outside, the night had turned chilly and Phoebe clung close to him as they walked along. Above the light of the street-lamps the massy beeches that lined the street had a spectral aspect, their leaves dryly rustling. All the drink that Quirke had drunk had begun to go stale in him in the night's chill, and he felt a clammy melancholy creeping along his veins. Phoebe, too, seemed despondent, suddenly. She was silent for a long while, and then asked: 'What were you and Mummy fighting about?'

'We weren't fighting,' Quirke said. 'We were having a conversation. It's what grown-ups do.'

She snickered. 'Oh, yes? Some conversation.' Eagerly she clutched his arm. 'Were you telling her you still love her, and that you're sorry you didn't marry her instead of her sister?'

'You read too many trashy magazines, my girl.'

She lowered her head and laughed. The night air breathed on him, and he realised how tired he was. It had been a long day. From the eager manner in which Phoebe was clinging to him he feared it was not over yet. He would have to cut down on his drinking, he told himself sternly, while another part of his mind laughed at him in mockery.

'Granddad really is fonder of you than he is of Daddy, isn't he?' Phoebe said, and then, when he did not answer, 'What was it like, being an orphan?'

'Smashing,' he said.

'Did they beat you in that place you were in, in Connemara—what was the name of it?'

'Carricklea Industrial School, so-called. Yes, they beat us. Why wouldn't they?'

Dull smack of leather on flesh in the grey light of morning, the huge, bare windows above him like indifferent witnesses looking down upon one more scene of hurt and humiliation. He had been big enough to defend himself against the other boys in the place, but the Brothers were another matter: there was no defending against them.

'Until Granddad rescued you?' Quirke said nothing. She joggled his arm. 'Come on. Tell me.'

He shrugged.

'The Judge was on the Board of Visitors,' he said. 'He took an interest in me, God knows why, and got me away from Carricklea and sent me to a proper school. Adopted me, as good as, him and Nana Griffin.'

Phoebe kept a thoughtful silence for the space of a dozen steps. Then she said:

'You and Daddy must have been like brothers.'

Quirke fairly cackled. 'He wouldn't care to hear you say it now.'

They stopped on a corner, under the grainy light of a lamp-standard. The night was hushed, the big houses behind their hedges shut fast, the windows dark in all but a few of them.

'Have you any idea who your parents were, the real ones?' Phoebe asked.

He shrugged again, and after a moment said:

'There are worse things than being an orphan.'

A light was flickering through the leaves above them. It was the moon. He shivered; he was cold. Such distances, such deeps! Then there was a blur of movement and suddenly Phoebe had thrown her arms around him and was kissing him full on the mouth, avidly, clumsily. Her breath tasted of gin, and something that he thought might be caramel. He could feel her breasts against his chest, and the springy struts of her underwear. He pushed her away.

'What are you doing?' he cried, and wiped a hand violently across his mouth. She stood before him staring in shock, her body seeming to vibrate, as if she had been struck. She tried to say something but her mouth slid askew, and with tears welling in her eyes she turned and ran back towards the house. He turned, too, and strode off drunkenly in the opposite direction, stiff-legged and snorting, his hurrying footsteps those of a man in flight.

4

QUIRKE LIKED McGonagle's best in the early evening, when there was no one in but a few of the regulars, that skinny type at the end of the bar poring over the racing pages and ruminatively scratching his crotch, or that slightly famous dipso poet, in cloth cap and hob-nailed boots, glaring at a spark of tawny light in the bottom of his whiskey glass. There was the memorials page in the *Evening Mail* to read—*O Mammy dear we miss you still, We did not know you were so ill*—and Davy the barman's awful, raspily murmured jokes to listen to. It was peaceful, sitting there on the stained, red-velvet banquette that smelled like a railway carriage, browsing and drowsing, soothed by whiskey and cigarette smoke and the prospect of the long, lazy hours until closing time. And so, when that particular evening he heard someone approach his table and stop, and looked up and saw that it was Mal, he did not know which he felt more strongly, surprise or irritation.

'Christ! Mal! What are you doing here?'

Mal sat down on a low stool without being invited and gestured at Quirke's glass. 'What's that?'

'Whiskey,' Quirke said. 'It's called whiskey, Mal. Distilled from grain. Makes you drunk.'

Mal lifted a hand and Davy approached, stooping mournfully and snuffling a silver droplet back up his nose. 'I'll have one of those,' Mal said, pointing again at Quirke's drink. 'A whiskey.' It might have been a bowl of sacrificial blood he was asking for.

'Right, boss,' Davy said, and padded away.

Quirke watched Mal looking about the place and pretending to be interested in what he saw. He was ill at ease. It was true, he usually was ill at ease, more or less, but these days he seemed like that all the time. When Davy brought the drink Mal delved in a pocket for his wallet but by the time he found it Quirke had paid. Mal took a sip gingerly and tried not to grimace. His wandering gaze came to rest on the copy of the *Mail* on the table. 'Anything in the paper?' he asked.

Quirke laughed and said:

'What is it, Mal? What do you want?'

Mal set his hands on his knees and frowned, pushing out his lower lip like a superannuated schoolboy being called to account. Quirke wondered, not for the first time, how this man had succeeded in becoming the country's most successful consultant obstetrician. It could not have been all due to his father's admittedly considerable influence—or could it?

'That girl,' Mal said suddenly, plunging in. 'Christine Falls. I hope you haven't been . . . talking about her.'

Quirke was not surprised. 'Why?' he said.

Mal was kneading the knees of his trousers. He kept his eyes fixed unseeing on the table and the newspaper. The evening sun had found a chink somewhere at the top of the painted-over window at the front of the bar and was depositing a fat, trembling gold lozenge of light on the floor carpet beside where they sat.

'She worked at the house,' Mal said, so quietly it was almost a whisper, and touched a finger to the bridge of his glasses.

'What—your house?'

'For a while. Cleaning, helping Maggie—you know.' Gingerly he took another sip of his drink and watched himself replace the glass on the round cork mat, positioning it just so. 'I don't want it talked about—'

'It?'

'Her dying, I mean, all that business. I don't want it discussed, around the hospital especially. You know what that place is like, the way the nurses gossip.'

Quirke leaned back on the banquette and surveyed his brother-in-law perched before him on the stool, heartsore and worried, his long neck stretched out and his adam's apple bouncing on its elastic. 'What's up, Mal?' he said, not harshly. 'You come in here, into a *pub*, and start knocking back whiskeys, and urging me not to talk about some girl who died . . . You haven't been up to any funny business, have you?'

Mal flared briefly at that. 'What do you mean, funny business?'

'I don't know, you tell me. *Was* she your patient?'

Mal gave a heavy shrug, half of helplessness and half of sullen annoyance.

'No. Yes. I was sort of . . . looking after her. Her family called me, from down the country. Small farmers—simple people. I sent an ambulance. By the time they got her up here she was dead.'

'Of a pulmonary embolism,' Quirke said, and Mal lifted his head quickly, staring. 'It was in her file.'

'Oh,' Mal said. 'Right.' He sighed, and drummed the fingers of one hand on the table, and began to cast about him vaguely again. 'You don't understand, Quirke. You don't deal with the living. When they die on you, especially the young ones, you feel . . . sometimes you feel that you've lost . . . I don't know. One of your own.' He fixed his gaze on Quirke again in anguished appeal, but still with that trace of annoyance, too—Mr Malachy Griffin was not accustomed to having to answer for his actions. 'I'm just asking you not to talk about it, at the hospital.'

Quirke returned him a level look and they sat like that for a long moment, facing each other, until Mal let drop his gaze. Quirke was not convinced by this account of Christine Falls's death, and wondered why it did not surprise him to find himself disbelieving it. But then, he had as good as forgotten about Christine Falls until Mal came in tonight to talk about her. She was, after all, only another cadaver. The dead, for Quirke, were legion.

'Have another drink, Mal,' he said.

But Mal said no, that he would have to be going, that Sarah was expecting him home, because they were invited out to dinner, and he had to change, and . . . His voice ran down and he sat gazing at Quirke helplessly with an expression of desperation and mild suffering, so that Quirke felt he should do something, should reach out and pat his brother-in-law's hand, perhaps, or offer to help him to his feet. Mal, however, seeming to sense what was going through Quirke's mind, withdrew his hands from the table and stood up hastily, and was as hastily gone.

Quirke sat thinking. It was true, he was not much concerned with the exact circumstances of the girl's death, but it interested him how much it obviously did concern Mal. And so, later that night, when Quirke left the pub, not sober but not quite drunk, either, he did not go home but instead went to the hospital, and opened up his office, and looked in the cabinet, intending to read again the file on Christine Falls. But the file was no longer there.

Mulligan the registry clerk was taking his elevenses. He sat tilted back in his chair with his feet on the desk; he was reading a newspaper and smoking a cigarette; a steaming mug of tea stood handily on the floor beside his chair. The paper was last Sunday's *People* and the story he was engrossed in was a juicy one about a tart in Bermondsey, wherever that was, and her sugar-daddy, who had done in some old one for her money. There was a photo of the tart, a big blonde in a little frock that her front was falling out of. She looked a bit like the nurse from upstairs that had left the other day to go to America, the one that was sweet on the boss—and be damned, but he was just thinking that when the boss himself came bursting in, full of piss and wind, as usual, and he had to get his feet off the desk and stub out the fag and stuff the paper in the desk drawer, all in the one smart go, while Quirke stood in the doorway with his hand on the knob, giving him the cold eye.

'An emergency case,' Quirke said. 'Name of Falls, Christine. A wagon was sent for her the other night. Wicklow, Wexford, somewhere down there.'

The clerk, all business now, went to the files and took down the current month's ledger and opened it flat on the desk and licked his thumb and began to turn over the pages. 'Falls,' he said, 'Falls . . .' He looked up. 'F-A-L-L-S, right?'

Quirke, still in the doorway, still watching him with that cod's cold eye, nodded.

'Christine,' he said. 'Dead on arrival.'

'Sorry, Mr Quirke. No Falls, not from down the country.' Quirke stood thinking, then nodded again and turned to go. 'Hang on,' the clerk said, pointing at a page. 'Here she is—Christine Falls. If it's the same one. Wasn't down the country, though—she was collected in the city. They picked her up at one fifty-seven a.m., Crimea Street, Stoney Batter. Number seventeen. Key-holder there is'— he peered more closely—'one Dolores Moran.'

He looked up with a smile of modest triumph—*one* Dolores Moran: he was proud of that—expecting at least a hint of gratitude for his alertness. But no thanks were forthcoming, of course. Quirke only took up a piece of paper and a pencil from the desk and had him repeat the address as he wrote it down, then turned again to go, but paused, eyeing the tea mug on the floor beside the chair.

'Busy, are you?' he asked mildly.

The clerk shrugged apologetically. 'Bit slow, this time of the morning.' And when Quirke was gone he slammed the door after him as violently as he dared. 'Sarky bastard,' he muttered. Who was this Christine Falls, he wondered, and why was the boss so interested? Some wagon, maybe, that he was banging. He chuckled: *a wagon to pick up a wagon*. He sat down at the desk and was about to resume

61

his reading of the paper when the door opened again and Quirke reappeared, filling the doorway.

'This Christine Falls,' he said, 'where was she taken to?'

'What?' the clerk snapped, forgetting himself. Seeing Quirke's look he scrambled to his feet. 'Sorry, Mr Quirke —what was it?'

'The body,' Quirke said. 'Where did it go?'

'City Morgue, I believe.' The clerk opened the ledger that was still on the desk. 'That's right—the Morgue.'

'Check if she's still there, will you? If the family haven't collected her, get her back.'

The clerk stared. 'I'll have to—I'll have to fill in the forms,' he said, although he did not know what forms they might be, since he had never before been told to fetch a stiff back from the morgue.

Quirke was unimpressed. 'You do that,' he said. 'You get the forms, I'll sign them.' Going out he stopped, turned back. 'Business picking up, eh?'

Afterwards he wondered why of the two junior pathologists it was Wilkins he had asked to stay on and assist, but the answer was not hard to find. Sinclair the Jew was the better technician, but he trusted Wilkins the Prod. Wilkins asked no questions, only looked at his fingernails and said with studied diffidence that he could do with an extra day off next weekend to go home to Lismore and visit his widowed mother. It was not an unreasonable demand, even though there was a backlog of scheduled work already, and of course Quirke had to concede, but the exchange sent Wilkins down a degree in his estimation, and he was sorry he had not asked Sinclair after all. Sinclair, with his sardonic grin and acid wit, who treated Quirke with a faint but unmistakable hint of disdain, would have been too proud to ask for time off in return for lending assistance in what must have seemed was likely to be no more than another of Quirke's whims.

As it turned out, Christine Falls was quick to give up her poor secret. The body was returned from the Morgue at six and it had still not gone seven when Wilkins had washed up and departed, in his usual flat-footed and somehow stealthy way. Quirke, still in his gown and green rubber apron, sat on a high stool by the big steel sink, smoking a cigarette and thinking. The evening outside was still light, he knew, but here in this windowless room that always reminded him of a vast, deep, emptied cistern it might have been the middle of the night. The cold tap in one of the sinks had an incurable, slow drip, and a fluorescent bulb in the big multiple lamp over the dissecting table flickered and buzzed. In the harsh, grainy light the cadaver that had been Christine Falls lay on its back, the breast and belly opened wide like a carpet bag and its glistening innards on show.

It sometimes seemed to him that he favoured dead bodies over living ones. Yes, he harboured a sort of admiration for cadavers, these wax-skinned, soft, suddenly ceased machines. They were perfected, in their way, no matter how damaged or decayed, and fully as impressive as any an ancient marble. He suspected, too, that he was becoming more and more like them, that he was even in some way becoming one of them. He would stare at his hands and they would seem to have the same texture, inert, malleable, porous, as the corpses that he worked on, as if something of their substance were seeping into him by slow but steady degrees. Yes, he was fascinated by the mute mysteriousness of the dead. Each corpse carried its unique secret—the precise cause of death—a secret that it was his task to uncover. For him, the spark of death was fully as vital as the spark of life.

He tapped his cigarette over the sink and a worm of ash tumbled softly into the drain, making a tiny hiss. The post-mortem had only confirmed a thing that, he now realised, he had already suspected. But what was he to do with this knowledge? And why, anyway, did he think he should do anything at all?

5

CRIMEA STREET was like all the other streets round about, two facing terraces of artisans' dwellings with low, lace-curtained windows and narrow front doorways. Quirke walked along in the late-summer dusk silently counting off the numbers of the houses. All was calm under a still-bright sky piled around the edges with copper-coloured clouds. Outside number twelve a fellow in a flat cap and a waistcoat shined with dirt and age was depositing a load of horse manure from the back of an upended cart on to the side of the pavement. The legs of his trousers were bound below the knees with loops of yellow baling twine. Why the twine, Quirke wondered—to keep rats from running up his legs, perhaps? Well, there were certainly worse livelihoods than pathology. As he came level with him the carter paused and leaned on the handle of his fork and lifted his cap to air his scalp and spat on the road in friendly fashion and observed that it was an *aisy oul' evenin'*. His little donkey stood stock-still with downcast eyes, trying to be elsewhere. The animal, the man, the light of evening, the warm smell of the smoking dung, all mingled to suggest to Quirke something he could not quite recall, something from the far past that hovered on the tip of his memory, tantalisingly beyond reach. All of Quirke's earliest, orphaned past was like this, an absence fraught with consequence, a resonant blank.

At the Moran woman's he had to knock twice before she answered, and even then she would only open the door a hand's breadth. She regarded him through the crack out of a single, hostile eye.

'Miss Moran?' he asked. 'Dolores Moran?'

'Who wants to know?' The voice had a hoarse rasp to it.

'My name is Quirke. It's about Christine Falls.'

The eye watched him for a beat unblinking.

'Chrissie?' she said. 'What about her?'

'Can I talk to you?'

She was silent again, thinking.

'Wait,' she said, and shut the door. A minute later she appeared again, carrying her handbag and her coat, and with a fox-fur stole around her neck that had the fox's sharp little head and little black paws still attached. She wore a flowered frock in a style too young for her and big white shoes with chunky high heels. Her hair was dyed a brassy shade of brown. He caught a whiff of perfume and ancient cigarette smoke. A lipstick mouth, the top lip a perfect Cupid's bow, was painted over her real one. Her eyes and the fox's were uncannily alike, small and black and shining. 'Come on then, Quirke,' she said. 'If you want to talk to me you can buy me a drink.'

She brought him to a pub called Moran's—'No relation,' she said dryly—a crumbling, cramped, dim dive with sawdust on the floor. Despite the mildness of the evening a tripod of turf sods was smouldering in the fireplace and

the air was fuggy with turf smoke, and at once Quirke's
eyes began to water. There was a handful of customers, all
men, all on their own, crouched over their drinks. One or
two looked up, with scant interest, when Quirke and the
woman entered. The barman, fat and bald, nodded to
Dolly Moran and gave Quirke a quick, appraising glance,
taking in his well-cut suit, his expensive shoes; Moran's
was not a house into which a consultant from the Holy
Family Hospital could easily blend, even one who was only
a consultant to the dead. Dolly Moran asked for gin and
water. They carried their drinks to a small table in a
corner. The three-legged wooden stools were low, and
Quirke looked at his doubtfully—it would not be the first
frail seat to give way under his weight. Dolly Moran took
off her fox-fur and laid it coiled around itself on the table.
When Quirke held his lighter to her cigarette she put a
hand on his and looked up past the flame at him with
what seemed a knowing, veiled amusement. She lifted her
glass. 'Bottoms up,' she said, and drank, and touched a
fingertip daintily to one corner and then the other of her
painted-on mouth. A thought occurred to her and she
frowned, an arch of wrinkles rising over one eye. 'You're
not a peeler, are you?' He laughed. 'No,' she said, picking
up his silver lighter from the table and weighing it in her
palm, 'didn't really think you were.'

'I'm a doctor,' he said. 'A pathologist. I work with—'

'I know what a pathologist is.' She bristled, but then
that veil of amusement fell again over her look. 'So, what's
your interest in Chrissie Falls?'

He ran a finger around the rim of his glass. The coiled
fox on the table regarded him beadily. He said:

'She was staying with you, wasn't she?'

'Who told you that?'

He shrugged. 'Born round here, were you?' he said. 'In this part of the city?'

The stool held, but it was much too small for him: he was overflowing it all round; too big for this world, too big and heavy and awkward. For some reason he thought of Delia, Delia his dead wife.

Dolly Moran was laughing at him now, silently. 'You sure you're not a detective?' she said. She finished her drink and held out her glass to him. 'Get me another and then tell me why you want to know about Chrissie.'

He turned her empty glass in his hand, studying the dim lights reflected in it from the fireplace. 'I'm just curious,' he said, 'that's all.'

'Pity you weren't curious about her before.' Her voice had suddenly gone hard. 'She might be alive yet.'

'I told you,' he said mildly, still studying the gin glass, 'I'm a pathologist.'

'Yes,' she said. 'Dead ones. No trouble there.' She crossed her legs impatiently. 'Do I get a drink, or not?'

When he came back from the bar she had taken another cigarette from the silver case he had left on the table and was lighting it with his lighter. She blew a stream of smoke towards the already kippered ceiling.

'I know who you are,' she said. He paused in the act of sitting down and looked at her in surprise. Her eyes, and the fox's, watched him unblinking, alert and shining. His expression of blank incomprehension seemed to gratify her. 'I used to work for the Griffins,' she said.

'Judge Griffin?'

'Him, too.'

'When was this?'

'Long time ago. First the Judge, then I was with Mr Mal and his missus, for a while, when they came back from America. I looked after the child, while they were settling in.'

'Phoebe?'

How was it, he wondered, that he did not remember her? She must have disappeared down the neck of a whiskey bottle, like so much else from that time.

Dolly Moran was smiling, recollecting the past. 'How is she, these days?'

'Phoebe?' he said again. 'Grown up. She'll be twenty, next year. Has a boyfriend.'

She shook her head. 'She was a terror, the same Miss Phoebe. But quite the lady. Oh, yes, quite the little lady.'

Quirke felt like a big-game hunter, cautiously parting the long grass, hardly daring to breathe—but what was it, exactly, that he was stalking? 'Is that how you knew Christine Falls?' he asked, keeping his tone vague and carefully casual. 'Through the Griffins?'

For a moment she did not respond, but remained lost in the past. When she roused herself it was with a flash of anger. 'Her name was Chrissie,' she snapped. 'Why do you keep calling her Christine? No one called her that. Chrissie. Chrissie was her name. And my name is Dolly.'

She glared at him, but he persisted. He said: 'Did Mr Griffin—Dr Griffin—Malachy—did he get you to look after her?'

She shrugged, turning aside. Her anger had turned to surliness. 'They paid for her keep,' she said.

'So he stays in touch with you, does he, Dr Griffin?'

A dismissive grunt. 'When I'm needed.'

She sipped her drink. He felt the momentum slipping.

'I did a post-mortem on her,' he said. 'On Chrissie. I know how she died.' Dolly Moran was folded into herself, her arms crossed on her breast and her face still turned to the side. 'Tell me, Miss Moran—Dolly—tell me what happened, that night.'

She shook her head, and yet she told him. 'Something went wrong. She was bleeding, the sheets were soaked. Jesus, I was terrified. I had to go three or four streets to the phone box. When I came back she was in a bad way.'

He put out a hand as if to touch her but withdrew it again. 'You phoned Dr Griffin,' he said, 'and he sent an ambulance.'

She straightened then, setting her hands on her thighs and arching her back and lifting up her head and taking in a deep draught of air through her nostrils. 'It was too late,' she said, 'I could see that. They took her away.' She shrugged. 'Poor Chrissie. She wasn't a bad sort. But who knows? Maybe it was for the best. What kind of a life would she have had, her, or the child?'

The three stacked logs of turf collapsed and a thick tongue of smoke rolled out from under the mantelpiece. Quirke took their glasses to the bar. When he came back he was clearing smoke from his throat.

'What happened to it, the child?' he asked.

Dolly Moran seemed not to have heard him.

'I knew a girl had a baby like that,' she said, looking at nothing. 'They took it off her, put it in an orphanage. She found out where. She used to go up there every day and stand outside the playground, looking in through the railings to see if she could recognise her boy, among all the others. For years and years she did that, until she heard he'd been moved, long before.' She sat in silence for a while, then stirred herself, and smiled at him, almost friendly suddenly. 'Do you see Mrs Griffin, ever?' she asked. 'Mrs Mal, I mean. How is she? I always liked her. She was decent to me.'

'I was married to her sister,' he said.

She nodded. 'I know.'

'She died too,' Quirke said. 'Mrs Griffin's sister. My wife. Delia. She died having a child, just like Christine.'

'Chrissie.'

'Chrissie, yes.' He reached out again and this time he did touch her, delivering the lightest of taps to the back of her hand, fleetingly feeling the texture of her ageing skin, papery and unwarm. 'Who was the father, Dolly? Of Chrissie's child, I mean—who was he?'

She drew back her hand and peered at it with a frown, as if expecting to find the mark of his fingers there, the indents. Then she looked about her, blinking, seeming to have forgotten suddenly what they had been talking about. Briskly she gathered her things together and stood up.

'I'm off,' she said.

The sky was dark by now except for a last, crimson streak low in the west that they could see repeated off at the end of each successive street that they passed by. The night air had an autumnal edge and Dolly Moran in her light dress clutched the fur stole to her throat and linked her arm in

Quirke's and walked along close up against him for warmth. She had been young, once. He thought of Phoebe, of her lithe body pressing against his as they walked along by Stephen's Green.

The front door of number twelve stood open on a narrow, lighted hallway. A man in shirtsleeves was forking dung from the load on the pavement on to a wheelbarrow. Sheets of newsprint were spread along the hall. Quirke took in the scene—the lighted doorway, the papers on the floor, the man bending with his fork to the manure—and again something spoke to him out of his lost past.

'I have it all written down, you know,' Dolly Moran said. Despite the odour of dung in the street he could smell the gin on her breath. 'About Chrissie, all that. Sort of a diary, you could call it. I have it safe.' Her tone darkened. 'And I'll know where to send it, if anything happens.' He felt the faint tremor that ran through her. 'I mean,' she said quickly, 'if there was someone that might want it, some day.'

They came to her door and she searched in her handbag for the key, squinting shortsightedly, suddenly old. He gave her his card. 'That's my number,' he said, 'at the hospital. And that one, see, is my home telephone.' He smiled. 'In case something might happen.'

She held the rectangle of pasteboard up to the light of the street-lamp and her eyes took on a strange shine and at the same time seemed to dim. '*Consultant pathologist,*' she read aloud. 'You've come a long way.'

She opened the door and stepped into the hall, but still he was not finished with her. 'Did you deliver the child,

Dolly—Chrissie's child?' She had not switched on the hall light and he could barely see her outline in the darkness.

'It wouldn't have been the first one I ever did.' He heard her sniff. 'Little girl, it was.'

He moved towards the doorway but stopped on the threshold, seeming to meet an invisible barrier. She had her back to him, still in the dark, and would not turn.

'What happened to her?' he said.

When she spoke her voice had hardened yet again. 'Forget the child,' she said. It had an almost sibylline ring to it, this voice speaking to him out of the gloom.

'And the father?'

'Forget him, too. Especially forget him.'

Firmly but with no violence she pushed the door against him and he stepped back and heard the lock click shut and the deadbolt sliding into place.

And in the morning he went to Registry and had Mulligan, the clerk there, write in his ledger that the ambulance had collected Christine Falls not in Stoney Batter but from her parents' house. Mulligan was reluctant at first—'It's a bit unusual, isn't it, Mr Quirke?'—but Quirke was firm. 'Need to keep your files in order, laddie,' he said briskly. 'Don't want inaccuracies. It wouldn't look good, if there was to be an inquiry.' The clerk nodded dully. He knew, and knew that Quirke knew, that there had been inaccuracies, to say the least, before now, when files had to be rewritten on the quiet. So with Mr Quirke looking over his shoulder he got to work with razor blade and steel-pen, and presently the record showed that Christine Falls had been collected at 1.37 a.m. on the 29th of

August from No. 7, St Finnan's Terrace, Wexford, and conveyed to the Holy Family Hospital in Dublin, where she was pronounced dead on arrival, having suffered a pulmonary embolism while staying at the family home.

6

Sunday morning was for Quirke a tiny interval of sweet redress for the oppressions of his childhood. When he was at Carricklea, and later, too, when the Judge got him away from there and sent him along with Mal to St Aidan's to board, the Sabbath morning was its own kind of torment, different from weekdays but just as bad, if not worse. During the week at least there were things to be done, work, lessons, the grinding rote of school, but Sundays were a desert. Prayers, Mass, the interminable sermon, and then the long, featureless day until Evening Devotions, with the Rosary and another sermon followed by Benediction, and then lights out, and the dread of Monday morning coming round again. Now his Sundays had other rituals, ones of his own devising, which he could vary, or ignore, or abandon, at his whim. The only constant was the Sunday papers, which he bought from the hunchback vendor on Huband Bridge and with which, when the weather was fine, he would settle down on the old iron bench there beside the lock and read, and smoke, his mind only half engaged by what was already yesterday's news.

He sensed Sarah's approach before he looked up and saw her walking towards him along the tow-path. She was wearing a burgundy-coloured coat and a Robin Hood hat with a feather, and was carrying her purse clutched in both hands against her breast.

She kept her eyes downcast as she walked, on the watch for puddles from last night's rain, but also because she was not ready yet to meet Quirke's surprised stare. She had known where he would be—Quirke was a creature of habit—yet she was already regretting coming to find him here. When she looked up at last she saw that he had guessed what she was feeling, and he did not rise to meet her as she drew near, only sat with the newspaper open on his knees and watched her with what seemed to her an ironical, even a faintly contemptuous, mocking smile.

'Well,' he said, 'what brings you down here, from the fastnesses of Rathgar?'

'I was at Mass, over in Haddington Road. I go there some Sundays, just for . . .' She smiled, shrugged, winced, all at the same time. '. . . Just for a change.'

He nodded, and folded the newspapers and stood up, as huge as ever, and as always she felt reduced a size or two, and leaned back involuntarily on her heels before him.

'Can I walk with you?' he asked, in that deliberately boyish way that he did, making it seem as if he were prepared to be refused. It was strange, she thought, to be in love with him still and expect nothing of it.

They went back along the path the way she had come, passing by stands of dried sedge. It was the first real day of autumn and the sky was a luminous mist that cast a milky reflection on the water. They were silent for a while, then Quirke said:

'That night of the party at your house—I'm sorry.'

'Oh, that seems an age ago, now. Besides, you were drunk. I always know you're drunk when you tell me how fond of me you are.'

'I wasn't apologising for that. I meant I shouldn't have taken Phoebe to the pub.'

She laughed unsteadily. 'Yes, Mal was terribly angry, at both of you, but you especially.'

He sighed his irritation.

'I brought her for a drink,' he said. 'I wasn't trying to sell her into the white slave trade.' Rebuked, she was silent. 'Anyway,' he said, softening his tone, 'what is all this about Mass? You weren't always so devout.'

'Perhaps it's desperation,' she said. 'Aren't people always supposed to turn to God in desperation?'

He did not answer, but turned his head and looked at her, and found that she was already looking at him, smiling distressfully with lips compressed, and it was as if they had come suddenly to a secret door and she had pushed it open a little way and turned to see if he would go with her into the darkness beyond. He felt himself draw back: there were places he would not enter. Two swans on the water came from behind and drew level with them, bearing aloft their strange, masked heads. He said:

'This young man of hers, this Conor Carrington—is she serious about him?'

'I hope not.'

'What if she is?'

'Oh, Quirke—is anyone serious at that age?

'We were.'

He said it so quickly, with such seeming conviction,

that it made her start. She looked down at the path. He was acting, she knew, but what a good actor he was; so good that on occasion, she felt sure, he managed to convince even himself.

'Please, Quirke,' she said. 'Don't.'

'Don't what?'

'You know very well.'

The swans were still swimming beside them, and now one made a sound deep in its breast, a subdued yet plaintive hoot; it seemed to Sarah a sound she might have made herself. They came to the bridge at Baggot Street. The sawmill on the opposite bank was shut because it was Sunday but still they caught a faint waft of its resinous smell. They stood below the bridge, side by side, facing the water. The swans, too, had paused in their progress.

'My father is very ill,' Sarah said. 'I thought of paying the priest at Haddington Road to say a Mass for him.' Quirke laughed briefly and she turned her serious eyes on him. 'Do you really not believe in God, Quirke?'

'I believe in the Devil,' he answered. 'That was one thing they taught us to believe in, at Carricklea.'

She nodded. He was acting again, now.

'Carricklea,' she said. 'I've heard you say that name so often, and always in the same way.'

'It's the kind of place that stays with you.'

She laid a hand on his arm, but he made no response and she took it back. What if he did pose and pretend? He had suffered, she was sure of that, even if his sufferings were long in the past.

'I came along this way on purpose,' she said, 'I suppose

you know that. I'm not good at covering up. Luckily, you don't change your habits.' She paused, gathering her words. 'Quirke, I want you to talk to Mal.'

He glanced at her, his eyebrows lifting. 'What about?'

She walked to the water's edge. The two swans turned and swam towards her, etching a closing V on the flawless surface of the water. They must think she had food, and why not? Everyone expected something of her.

'I want you and Mal to stop fighting,' she said. 'I want you to be . . . reconciled.' She laughed self-consciously at the word, the florid sound of it.

Still he looked at her, but he was frowning now, his brows drawn down. 'Did Mal ask you to come here?' he asked suspiciously.

Now it was her turn to stare. 'Of course not!' she said. 'Why would he?'

But Quirke would not relent. 'Tell him,' he said evenly, 'I've done all I can for him. Tell him that.'

The swans before her were turning from side to side slowly on their own reflections, growing impatient with her failure to produce whatever it was that her stopping and standing like this had seemed to promise, this woman in her blood-coloured coat and archer's hat. She paid the birds no heed. She was looking at Quirke, not understanding what he meant, and saw she was not expected to understand. But what could it be that Quirke had done for Mal, Quirke of all people, Mal of all people?

'I'm pleading with you, Quirke,' she said, appalled at herself, at the abjectness she was reduced to. 'I'm begging you. Talk to him.'

'And I'm asking you: what about?'

'Anything. Phoebe—talk about Phoebe. He listens to you, even though you think he doesn't.'

The swan again made its peculiar hoot, calling to her querulously.

'Must be the female,' Quirke said. Sarah, baffled, frowned. He pointed to the birds behind her. 'They mate for life, so it's said. She must be the female.' He smiled his crooked smile. 'Or the male.'

She shrugged aside the irrelevance. 'He's under a great deal of strain,' she said.

'What sort of strain?'

He was, she realised, becoming bored, she could hear it in his voice. Patience, tolerance, indulgence, these had never been among Quirke's anyway not numerous virtues. 'Mal doesn't confide in me,' she said. 'He hasn't, for a long time.'

Again she had pushed at that door into the darkness, again he declined her invitation to enter with her.

'You think he'd confide in me?' he said, with intended harshness.

'He's a good man, Quirke.' She lifted her hands to him in a gesture of pained supplication. 'Please—he needs to talk to someone.'

He in turn lifted his great shoulders, let them fall again. There were moments, such as when he flexed his great broad frame like this, that he seemed made not of flesh and bone but some more dense material, hewn and carved.

'All right, Sarah,' he said, in a voice cavernous with weary impatience. The swans, discouraged at last, turned and glided serenely, disdainfully, away. 'All right,' he said, a deeper fall. 'All right.'

He invited Mal to lunch at Jammet's. The choice, he was well aware, was a mild piece of mischief on his part, since fine food was not among the rich things that Mal coveted, and he was uncomfortable amid the restaurant's down-at-heel *splendeurs*. He sat vigilantly on a chair that was as spindly as his own frame, with his long neck protruding from his white shirt collar and the fingers of both hands —a strangler's delicate, shapely hands, Quirke always thought—clamped on the table edge as if he might leap up at any moment and hurry out of the place. He wore his habitual pinstripes and bow-tie. Despite the elegant cut of his clothes he never seemed quite squared up in them; it was as if someone else had dressed him with fussy care, as a mother would dress her unwilling son in his Confirmation suit. The maître d' descended on them flutteringly and offered *M'sieur Kweerk* and his guest an apéritif, and Mal sighed heavily and looked at his watch. Quirke enjoyed seeing him trapped like this: it was part of the payment, part of the recompense, that he exacted from his brother-in-law—his almost-brother—for the advantages he enjoyed, although what those advantages were, had he been challenged, Quirke could not have said, exactly, except that there was the obvious one, which was, of course, Sarah.

Quirke chose an expensive claret and made an ostentatious show of swirling a splash of it in his glass, sniffing, and tasting, and frowning in approval to the wine waiter, while Mal looked away, controlling his impatience. He would not take even a glass of the wine, saying he had work to do in the afternoon. 'Fine,' Quirke snapped. 'All the more for me, then.' The elderly waiter in his shiny black tailcoat tended them with the unctuous solemnity of an usher at a funeral service. After Quirke had ordered salmon in aspic and a roasted grouse, Mal asked for chicken soup and a plain omelette. 'For God's sake, Mal,' Quirke said, under his breath.

Their conversation was even more strained than usual. Only a couple of other tables in the place were occupied and everything above a murmur could be heard half-way across the room. They talked desultorily of hospital matters. Quirke's jaws ached from the effort of not yawning, and presently his mind, too, began to ache. He was both impressed and irritated by Mal's capacity to be engrossed, or at least to give a convincing impression of being engrossed, in the minutiae of the administration of the Holy Family Hospital, even the name of which, in all its bathos, always provoked in Quirke a shudder of embarrassment and loathing. Listening to Mal stolidly expounding on what he kept referring to as *the hospital's overall financial position*, he asked himself if he were lacking in an essential seriousness, but he knew, of course, that by asking this he was really only congratulating himself for not being dull and dogged like his brother-in-law. He found Mal to be a continuing mystery, but not thereby impressive. Mal was for Quirke a version of the Sphinx: high, unavoidable and monumentally ridiculous.

Yet what was he to make of this business of Christine

Falls? It could not be, he had decided, a question of professional negligence—Mal was never negligent. But what, then? Quirke would have had no doubt of the answer to that question had the man involved been anyone other than Malachy Griffin. Girls like Chrissie Falls were traps for the unwary, but Mal was the wariest man that Quirke had ever known. And yet, watching him now, plying his soup spoon with finical little swoops and lifts—those hands again, slow and somewhat clumsy despite their slender lines; in the delivery room he had a reputation for being too quick to reach for the forceps—Quirke wondered if throughout all these years he might have been underestimating his brother-in-law, or perhaps over-estimating would be the better word. What went on behind that bony, coffin-shaped face, those prominent, washed-blue eyes? What illicit hungers lurked there? No sooner had he begun to think this thought than his mind turned aside from it queasily. No: he did not want to speculate on Mal's secret predilections. The girl had died and he had covered up the sordid circumstances—surely that was all there was to it. These things happened, more often than was imagined. Quirke thought of Sarah standing on the canal bank, looking at the swans and not seeing them, her eyes brimming with troubles. *He's under a great deal of strain*, she had said; was the strain all to do with Christine Falls, and if so, did Sarah know about her? And what did she know? He had done, he told himself, the right thing: the Registry file was safely rewritten, and that coward Mulligan would keep his mouth shut. The girl was dead—what else was of consequence? And besides, he had an advantage on his brother-in-law, now. He did not think he would ever need or want to use it, but it gratified him to know that it was there, available to him, even though, knowing it, he felt the faintest twinge of shame.

The salmon was tasteless and faintly slimy in texture, and the grouse when it came was dry. A youngish, plump woman at the table nearest to them was looking at Mal and saying something about him to her companion; a patient, no doubt, another matron the great Mr Griffin would have had a hand in. Quirke grinned covertly, and then before he could stop himself he heard himself say:

'Sarah asked me to do this, you know.'

Mal, who had got on to the subject of budgets for the coming fiscal year, fell silent and sat quite still, gazing at the last forkful of omelette on his plate, his head inclined sideways a little as if he were hard of hearing or had water trapped in an ear.

'What?' he said, tonelessly.

Quirke was lighting a cigarette and had to speak out of the side of his mouth. 'She asked me if I would talk to you,' he said, blowing an accidental but perfect smoke ring. 'Frankly, it's the only reason I'm here.'

Mal laid aside his knife and fork with slow deliberation and again put his hands palm down on the table on either side of his plate in that way that made it seem he might be about to push himself violently to his feet. 'You've refused Sarah before now,' he said.

Quirke sighed. It had always been like this between them, this childish tussling, Mal dourly dogged and Quirke wanting to be offhand and gay but annoyed instead and blurting things.

'She thinks you're in trouble,' Quirke said shortly. He twiddled the cigarette irritably in his fingers.

'Did she say that?' Mal asked. He sounded genuinely curious to hear if it was so.

Quirke shrugged. 'Not in so many words.' He sighed again angrily, then leaned forward, lowering his voice for effect. 'Listen, Mal, there's something I have to tell you. It's about that girl, Christine Falls. I got her back from the Morgue and did a PM on her.'

Mal exhaled a long, silent breath, as if he were a large balloon that had been pricked by a tiny pin. The woman at the other table looked his way again and, seeing his expression, stopped chewing. 'Why did you do that?' he enquired mildly.

'Because you lied to me,' Quirke said. 'She wasn't down the country. She was lodging in a house in Stoney Batter—Dolly Moran's house. And she didn't die of a pulmonary embolism.' He shook his head and almost laughed. 'Honestly, Mal—a pulmonary embolism! Could you not have thought of something more plausible?'

Mal nodded slowly and turned his head aside again and, catching the eye of the woman at the next table, mechanically assumed for a second his blandest smile, the smile, it struck Quirke, more of an undertaker than that of a man whose profession it was to guide new life into the world.

'You've kept this to yourself,' Mal murmured, barely moving his lips, still looking not at Quirke but at the room.

'I told you,' Quirke said, 'I bear you no ill-will. I don't

forget that you did me a favour, once, and kept it to yourself.'

The funereal waiter—all was death today—came and removed the remains of their lunch. When he offered coffee neither man responded and he glided away. Mal sat sideways on the little chair with one leg crossed on the other, drumming his fingers again absently on the table-cloth.

'Tell me about the girl,' Quirke said.

Mal shrugged. 'There's precious little to tell,' he said. 'She was going out with some fellow and'—he lifted a hand and let it fall again—'the usual. We had to let her go, of course.' *We.* Quirke said nothing, and Mal went on, 'I arranged for the Moran woman to look after her. I got a call in the middle of the night. I sent an ambulance. It was too late.'

There was the sense between them on the table of something slowly falling, as Mal's hand had fallen, list-lessly, ineffectually.

'And the baby?' Mal's only reply was a faint shake of the head. There was a pause. 'You weren't tampering with Christine Falls's file that night,' Quirke said, with sudden certainty. 'You were *writing* it, weren't you? And then, after I challenged you, you took it away and destroyed it.'

Mal uncrossed his legs and turned back to the table with a low, weary grunt.

'Look—' he said, and stopped, and sighed. He had the jaded air of one compelled to explain something that should have been perfectly obvious. 'The fact is, I did it for the family.'

'What family?'

'The girl's. Bad enough they should lose a daughter, without having to know of the baby as well.'

'And what about the father?' Mal peered at him, perplexed. 'Her boyfriend,' Quirke said impatiently, 'the child's father.'

Mal cast about him, looking at the floor to one side of the table and then the other, as if the identity of Christine's missing seducer might somehow be written there plain for all to see. 'Some fellow,' he said, shrugging again. 'We didn't even know his name.'

'Why should I believe you?'

Mal laughed coldly. 'Why should I care whether you believe me or not?'

'And the child?'

'What about her?'

Quirke gazed at him for a moment in stillness.

'*Her?*' he said softly, and then, 'How did you know it was a girl, Mal?' Mal would not meet his eye. 'Where is she?'

'Gone,' Mal said. 'Stillborn.'

There seemed nothing more to say after that. Quirke, disconcerted and feeling obscurely confounded, finished the inch of claret in his glass and called for the bill. His head was buzzing from the wine.

In Nassau Street a pale sun was shining and the air was mild. Quirke's palate recalled the salmon with a qualm. Mal was buttoning his overcoat. He had an absent look, his mind already at the hospital, donning stethoscope and chivvying his students. Quirke was irritated all over again. He said:

'By the way, Dolly Moran has it all written down, you

know. Christine Falls, the child, who the father was, God knows what else.'

A bus trundled past in the street, swaying. Mal had gone very still, and his fingers paused in the act of doing up the last button of his coat. 'How do you know that?' he said, sounding, again, as if all this were a matter of only the mildest interest.

'She told me,' Quirke said. 'I went to see her and she told me. It seems she kept some sort of journal. Not her kind of thing at all, I would have thought, but there you are.'

Mal nodded slowly. 'I see,' he said. 'And what's she going to do with it, this journal?'

'She didn't say.'

Mal was still nodding, still thinking. 'I wish her well of it,' he said.

They parted then, and Quirke walked along to Dawson Street and turned up towards St Stephen's Green, glad of the sun's faint warmth on his face. There was work waiting for him, too, but he told himself a stroll would clear his head. In his mind he went back over the conversation with Mal, recalling it now in almost a skittish light, thanks, he supposed, to the continuing effect of the wine. What a wonder it would be, if old Mal had got a girl in the family way! Quirke had suffered through some scares himself in that quarter, and on one occasion had been forced to call on the services of an old medical-school pal who was working at a dodgy clinic in London; that had been a bad business, and the girl had never spoken to Quirke again. But he could not believe the same thing would have happened to Mal. Would he really have walked, as Quirke to his continuing discomfiture had done, into a trap that any first-year medical student would have known how to avoid? Yet the startling fact remained that Mal had falsified the records of a post-partum death. What was Christine Falls's family to him, that he would take such a risk—had he destroyed the original death cert, too, if there had ever been one?—to spare them the pain of a scandal no one but he and they was ever likely to know about? No, it must be himself Mal was saving, from something or other. Christine Falls must have been his patient—not his mistress, surely not!—and the mistake he had made must have been a medical one, despite all his professional diligence and care.

At the top of Dawson Street Quirke crossed the road and went through the side gate into the Green. Smells of leaves, grass, damp earth assailed him. He thought of his dead wife, so long gone under the ground and yet so vividly remembered. Strange. Perhaps he had cared for her more than he knew, had cared for what she was, that is, and not just for what she had been to him. He frowned: in his befuddlement he did not understand what he meant by that, but it seemed to mean something.

He would go and see Dolly Moran again. He would ask her once more what had become of the child, and this time he would force the truth out of her. He slowed his steps as he approached the gates of the university. Phoebe came out, among a band of students. Her coat was open, and she wore ankle socks and flat pumps and a tartan skirt fastened at the side with a giant safety-pin; her dark, lustrous hair—her mother's hair—was tied back in a ponytail. Not seeing him, she moved away from her companions, smiling back over her shoulder, then turned and set off swiftly across the road, head down, her books pressed to her breast. He was about to call out her name when he spotted on the opposite pavement a tall, slim young man in a dark suit and a Crombie overcoat stepping forward to meet her. Arriving, she nudged against him, catlike and shy-seeming, pressing the side of her cheek down into the hollow of his shoulder. Then they turned, arm in arm, and set off in the direction of Hatch Street, and Quirke, having watched them for a moment, turned too, in the opposite direction, and walked away.

7

DOLLY MORAN knew straight off who they were. She had seen them before. She had heard tell of them, too, around the neighbourhood, and knew what they did. She was sure, although she could not say why, that she was the reason they were there, standing at the corner of the street, pretending to be doing nothing. Were they waiting for it to be dark? She spotted them first when she started to go out for milk and the evening paper. She had her coat and hat on but stopped on the step when she saw them. One was thin, with dirty black hair coming down in a widow's peak on his forehead; his cheeks were a peculiar, high shade of red, and he had a huge hooked nose. The other one was fat, with a big chest and a bigger belly and a head the size of a football; a rough mop of hair hung down to his shoulders in rats'-tails. It was the one with the hooked nose that frightened her the most. They deliberately did not look in her direction, although there was not another soul to be seen in the street. She stood there, frozen, holding the door part-way open behind her. She did not know what to do. Should she shut the door and just walk down past them, not giving them a glance, showing them she was not afraid? But she was, she was afraid. She would retreat back inside—in her mind she saw herself, as if she were doing it already, slamming the door shut and locking it—and wait to see if they would go away.

She had not been surprised to see them; shocked, and frightened, too, but not surprised, not after Quirke had come knocking at her door again demanding to know what had become of Chrissie's child. She would not let him in—she thought he might be a bit drunk—and would only speak to him through the letterbox. She could not bear to see his face again. She knew she had said too much already, that day in the pub when he had poured all that gin into her and soft-soaped her into talking about Chrissie and the rest of it. Today he got angry when she would not tell him what he wanted to know. He thought the child had died, and asked her where it was buried. She would say nothing, standing behind the door with a knuckle pressed against her mouth, shaking her head to herself, her eyes squeezed shut. Had those two been there already, at the corner, had they seen him, had they heard him asking about the child? By then he was shouting at her, almost, and they would easily have heard what he was saying. In the end he gave up and went away, and after a while, when she was calm enough, she had started again to go to the shop for the bottle of milk and the paper and there they were, waiting for her.

Now she was upstairs, at the window in the front room, still in her coat and hat. She had to put her cheek right up against the casement and look out at the edge of the curtain to see down to the corner. They were still there. The fat one was holding a match cupped in his hands and the other one, the one with the nose, was leaning down to get a light from it for his cigarette. She could feel a pulse ticking in her temple. She heard herself breathing, with a flutter at the end of each breath that she could not control. She went downstairs, to the pokey kitchen where there was always a smell of damp and gas, and stood for a long time motionless beside the oilcloth-covered table, trying to get her mind to work, to concentrate, to tell her what to do. She took down an enamelled tin marked *Sugar* from a shelf behind the gas stove and opened the lid and extracted a rolled-up school jotter with a yellowy-orange cover, and took it into the front room and leaned down at the fireplace and put it into the grate. She could not find the matches. She closed her eyes for a moment, and in the dark behind her eyelids felt a sudden blaze of anger. No! She thought of poor Chrissie throwing her head from side to side on the pillow and crying for her Mammy, with blood and stuff everywhere, and no one to help her. No, she would not let Chrissie down a second time.

The post office closed at five, she knew she would have to hurry. She could find no envelope except the old one she kept her Tontine Society books in; it would do. The glue had worn off the flap and she had to seal it as best she could with a bit of sticking plaster. She could barely write the address, she was in such a rush and her hands were shaking so badly. For all her haste she was dreading the moment when she would have to open the front door again and step into the street. What would she do if that pair were still out there, loitering at the corner, pretending not to see her? She was not sure that she had the courage to walk past them. Maybe she could go the other way, up the street, away from the corner, and around by Arbour

Hill? But that would take longer, the post office would be shut when she got there, and anyway there was nothing to stop them following her still.

She drew open the door and stepped out, hardly daring to look in the direction of the corner. But they were gone. She scanned the street from end to end. There was no one, except the old Tallon one opposite, who opened her front door an inch and stuck out her nose, pretending to be looking to see what the weather was doing. Nice calm evening. That was the thing to be, calm, nice and calm. Ma Tallon withdrew inside and shut the door softly. Would she have seen the pair on the corner? Not much happened in the street that Ma Tallon missed. But so what if she had seen them? No help there. She bit her lip and tightened her grip on her bag. She saw the dung-stain on the path outside number twelve and remembered her walk home through the soft darkness when she had linked her arm with Quirke's. Should she call him, as he had urged her to do? For a second she considered it, her heart lifting. But no: Quirke was the last one she would call.

She got to the post office five minutes before it was supposed to close but the young fellow behind the grille was already shutting up shop, and scowled when she came in. He was like the rest of them around here, and she was used to being scowled at; sometimes they even called her names, muttering the words out of the sides of their mouths as she was going past. She did not care tuppence for any of them. When she put the envelope in the box it was a weight dropping from her conscience, and she felt better; it was like going to Confession, although she could not remember when she had last done that.

She decided she would go to Moran's and treat herself to a gin and water, just the one. She had three, however, in quick succession, and then another, more leisurely, and then a last one, for the road. As she walked home through the smoky dusk she began to feel a doubt: had she been too hasty in posting the envelope? Maybe those two were not who she thought they were, and even if they were, maybe it was not her they were watching. There were always things going on around here, thieving, and fights, and men found lying in the street with their teeth kicked in. If it was all no more than her imagination, Jesus, what had she done? Should she return to the post office and see if she could get back the envelope? But the place would be shut and the scowling clerk long gone, and anyway the post had probably been collected from the box by now. She belched, and a fiery tang of gin flooded the back of her throat. So what, anyway, if the thing was delivered? *Let them suffer a bit*, she thought, *let them see what life is like down here.*

Because of the gin she had drunk she had to search with the key for the keyhole. In the hall she felt a draught from the back of the house but took no notice. Even when she heard the wireless playing softly in the kitchen—the Inkspots crooning 'It's a Sin to Tell a Lie'—she supposed it must have been on when she went out and in her hurry she had forgotten to turn it off. She hung up her coat and went into the living room. Here, too, the air had an unaccustomed chill; she must think of getting an electric fire put in before the winter, one of those ones with the red light in them that looked like logs burning. She was on her knees on the hearth, stacking up kindling in the grate and wondering where she could have put those matches, when she heard them behind her. When she looked over her shoulder they were standing in the kitchen doorway. Everything slowed down suddenly, as if a huge engine that she was inside of had switched into its lowest gear. She was struck by the things she noticed—that the fat one's hair was a coarse, rusty colour in the electric light and that his shapeless jumper was hand-knitted, and that the one with the hooked nose was redder than ever in the face and that the cigarette he was holding between a tobacco-stained finger and thumb was a roll-up. She saw too, perfectly clearly, what she knew she could not be seeing, the smashed pane of glass in the corner of the back door just above the latch, and felt the cold black night air pouring in through the hole. And why had they turned on the wireless? For some reason that was the most frighten-ing thing, the wireless playing, those black fellows singing in their falsetto voices. ''Evening, Dolly,' the hooked-nosed one said affably, and she felt what was at first no more than a tickling sensation between her thighs, but then the sudden, scalding gush of liquid ran down the insides of her legs and spread its dark stain around her in the rug where she was kneeling.

The taxi was an ancient Ford that wheezed and shuddered. The ill-lit, smoky streets were silent. Quirke should have been used to this kind of thing, the late-night summons, the journey through the darkness, then the ambulance at the kerb, the slewed police cars, and the lighted doorway where large, vague men loomed. One of them, in a long raincoat and a slouch hat, stepped forward to greet him. 'Mr Quirke!' he said, sounding pleased and surprised. 'Is it yourself?'

Hackett. Inspector. Big, broad-shouldered, slow, with a merrily watchful eye. It was he who had telephoned.

'Inspector,' Quirke said, shaking a hand the size of a shovel. 'Is Miss Moran here?' he asked, flinching inwardly at the fatuous sound of it.

Hackett fairly twinkled. 'Dolly?' he said. 'Oh, she is, she is.'

He led the way into the hall, squeezing past two boffins from Forensics dusting for prints; Quirke knew them, but could not remember their names; they nodded to him, with that expression Forensics always had, po-faced and blank, as if they were covering up a private joke. The living room was a chaos of overturned chairs, spilt drawers, a disembowelled sofa, papers torn and strewn. A Guard in uniform and cap, young, with acne and a prominent, triangular adam's apple, was positioned by the kitchen doorway; he was a little green in the face. Beyond him there was more disorder, indecent in the glow of a single, bare bulb. The smell was so familiar Quirke barely registered it.

'There she is,' Hackett said, adding with a gleam of irony, 'your Miss Moran.'

She had been tied to a kitchen chair, bound at the ankles with her own stockings and at the wrists with lengths of electric wire. The chair had overturned and she lay on the floor on her right side. She had worked one arm free of its bonds. Quirke was struck by the pose, the flexed knees and upflung arm: another manikin.

'You called me at home,' Quirke said, still bending over the corpse with his hands on his knees. 'Did the hospital give you my number?'

Hackett showed the piece of white pasteboard, clipped by its four corners in the hollow of his palm like a conjuror's playing-card.

'It seems,' he said easily, 'you left your calling card, on some previous social visit.'

8

A YOUNG NUN with prominent teeth opened the door and stood aside and motioned her to enter. At the sight of the long, gaunt room something inside her shrank back, and for a moment she was a child again, quaking on the threshold of Mother Superior's office. Massive mahogany table, six high-backed chairs that no one had ever sat on, glass-fronted bookcases, a coatless coat rack; in a wall niche a three-quarters-life-sized statue of the Virgin stood disconsolate in pale blue and white, holding between two fingertips and a thumb, in an attitude of dainty misgiving, a large white lily, sign of her purity. At the other end, under a muddy picture of some sainted martyr, there was an antique desk with lamp and leather-bound blotter and two telephones—why two? Somehow, without her noticing, the young nun had left, shutting the door behind her without a sound. She stood in the midst of silence, the child in her arms asleep in its blanket. The trees outside the windows were unfamiliar, or did they only seem so? Everything here seemed strange to her, still.

Another door, one that she had not noticed, flew open as if a wind were behind it. What entered was a tall nun, high-shouldered as a man, with a narrow, stark, pale face.

She came forward quickly, both hands held out, her heavy black habit audibly displacing air, her face smiling and seeming at the same time surprised at itself, as if smiles were strangers to it. This was Sister Stephanus.

'Miss Ruttledge,' she said, taking Brenda's free hand in both of hers, 'welcome to Boston, and St Mary's.'

She had the usual nun's musty smell. Brenda could not stop herself recalling the stories that were told at the convent when she was a girl about the sisters being forbidden ever to be naked and having to wear a special sort of swimming costume in the bath.

'I'm very glad to be here, Sister,' she said, in a voice that annoyed her by its seeming meekness. She was no longer a child, she told herself, and this nun had no authority over her. She drew up her shoulders and stared back stoutly into the woman's coldly beaming face. 'Boston is very nice,' she added. That, too, sounded weak and silly. The baby kicked her in the side through its blanket, as if demanding to be introduced; quite the little miss already. The nun's brittle smile slid downwards.

'And this must be the baby,' she said.

'Yes,' Brenda said, and held aside the rim of the blanket with her finger to show the tiny, livid face with its rosebud mouth and permanently startled blue eyes. 'This is little Christine.'

II

1

CLAIRE STAFFORD was wondering if the dress she had chosen was suitable for the occasion. You never knew, with nuns. It was green, with white trimming on the hem, and a scalloped neckline, not low, but maybe showing too much of her throat and the freckled slope under her collarbone. She would keep the green scarf wrapped loosely around her neck, and even keep her coat on, if she was allowed. She had not wanted to ask Andy for an opinion; you never knew with Andy, either. Mostly he did not notice what she was wearing, then suddenly, when she least expected it, he would turn on her and say something, some mean remark, mostly. Once he had told her she looked like a whore. She would never forget it. They were living at the time in the rooming house on Scranton Street. She was wearing jeans and white mules and a scarlet blouse knotted at the waist. He had come in after a long drive down from Albany, looking hot and tired and mad, and walked right past her into the galley kitchen and grabbed a beer from the icebox and said it to her over his shoulder. 'Honey, you look like a ten-dollar whore.' He pronounced it *hoor*, just like her Daddy did. She would not let herself cry, that would have made him even madder. Even in her hurt she saw yet again how beautiful he was, leaning against the icebox in his boots and work pants and stained white sweatshirt, his rodeo-rider's forearms gleaming and that lock of hair black as a crow's wing falling across his forehead. The most beautiful boy she had ever known.

Today he was wearing a pair of pressed dark pants over his cowboy boots, white shirt with a woollen knit tie, and a sport jacket in tan check with broad lapels. She had told him he looked nice but he had scowled and said he felt like Bozo the Clown. Now as they walked up the driveway to St Mary's he kept running a finger around the inside of his shirt collar and jerking up his chin and sighing. He was nervous, she could see that. He had talked non-stop in the cab, complaining about the pay he was losing by having to come here with her, but now he was silent, squinting up through the fall sunlight at the high, flat front of the orphanage that seemed to grow steadily higher the nearer they got to it. She, too, was a little scared, but not of the place. For she knew St Mary's, knew it like a home.

The door was opened by a young nun she did not recognise. Her name was Sister Anne. She would have been pretty but for her buck-teeth. She led them across the wide entrance hall and down the corridor toward Sister Stephanus's office. The familiar smells—floor polish, carbolic soap, institutional cooking, babies—stirred in Claire an excited mixture of emotions. She had been happy here, or not unhappy. Somewhere high above a choir of children was singing a hymn in ragged unison.

'You used to work here, didn't you?' Sister Anne asked. She had a South Boston accent. She had avoided looking at Andy, made shy, Claire guessed, by his cowboy's good looks. 'How do you like being a lady of leisure?' It was said good-naturedly.

Claire laughed. 'Oh, I really miss the place,' she said.

Sister Stephanus looked up as they entered. She was seated at her desk, with a stack of papers before her. Claire suspected the pose was deliberate, but then chided herself for the bad thought.

'Ah, Claire, here you are. And Andy, too.'

'Good morning, Sister.'

Andy said nothing, only nodded. He had put on a sulky look that was supposed to cover up his anxiousness. Despite herself, Claire experienced a brief surge of exultation: this was her place, not his; her moment.

Sister Stephanus invited them to sit, and Andy brought up a second chair from the six around the table.

'You must be very excited, both of you,' the nun said, leaning forward with her clasped hands resting on the papers on the desk. She smiled brightly from one of them to the other. 'It's not every day you become a parent!'

Claire smiled and nodded, her lips pressed tight. Beside her Andy shifted his legs, making the chair creak. She was not sure how she was expected to take the nun's words. Such a strange thing to say, straight out like that. In all the years she had spent here—first as an orphan after Ma died and her daddy had run off, then working in the kitchens and later in the nursery—she could never figure out Sister Stephanus, or the other nuns, either, for that matter, never could quite get on to their way of thinking. They had been good to her, though, and she owed them everything—everything except Andy, that is: him she had got by herself, this black-eyed, drawling, dangerous, lean-limbed young husband of hers. Trying not to, she pictured him as she had glimpsed him in the mirror while he was getting dressed that morning, the neat, unblemished, honey-coloured back and the taut line of his stomach where it ran down into darkness. Her man.

Sister Stephanus opened flat before her on the desk a brown cardboard file and put on a pair of wire-framed spectacles, pushing the ear-pieces in at the stiff sides of the wimple almost as if, Claire thought, she were giving her face a double injection. Claire blushed a little; the strange things that came into her head! The nun riffled through the papers in the file, now and then stopping to read a line or two, frowning. Then she looked up, and this time fixed on Andy.

'You do understand the position, Andy, don't you?' she said, speaking slowly and separating the words carefully, as if she were talking to a child. 'This is not an adoption, not in the official sense. St Mary's, as Claire can tell you, has its own . . . arrangements. The Lord, I always say, is our legislator.' She glanced between them with eyebrows lifted, awaiting acknowledgement of the quip. Claire smiled duti-fully, and Andy shifted his legs again, crossing them first one way and then the other. He had not said a word since they had come into the room. 'And you understand too, both of you,' the nun continued, 'that when the time comes it will be Mr Crawford and his people who will decide on what education is suitable for the child, and so forth? You'll be consulted, of course, but all those decisions will be theirs, in the end.'

'We understand, Sister,' Claire said.

'It's important that you do,' the nun said, in the same grave, unrelenting voice that sounded like a voice on the radio, or something that had been recorded. Although she was from South Boston she had an Englishwoman's accent, or what Claire thought an Englishwoman's accent would be, refined and crisp. 'All too often we find that young people forget where their child came from, and who it is that has the final say in his or her upbringing.'

There was silence then in the room for a long, solemn moment. Faintly from outside came the children's voices, singing. *Sweet heart of Jesus, fount of love and mercy!* Claire felt her mind begin to fidget in that way it did sometimes, when her thoughts seemed to be flying asunder like the parts of a machine breaking up under pressure. *Please, God*, she prayed, *don't let me have one of my headaches.* She forced herself to concentrate. She had already heard all these things that Sister Stephanus was saying. She supposed they had to make sure that everything was clear so no one could come back later and say the conditions that they laid down had not been properly explained. The nun was reading in the file again and now she turned once more to Andy.

'There was something else I wanted to mention,' she said. 'Your work, Andy. It must take you away from home for long periods?'

Andy looked at her warily. He began to speak but had to clear his throat and start again. 'It can be a few days,' he said, 'on a run up to the border, a week or more if I go across to the Lakes.'

The nun was impressed. 'That far?' she said, sounding almost wistful.

'But I make sure to call home every day,' Andy said.

'Don't I, sweetheart?' While he was saying it he turned his face full toward Claire, boring his eyes into hers, as if he thought she might deny it. She would not think of denying it, of course, even though it was not strictly true. She loved the way that Andy spoke—*Doanah, sweet-hawt?*—like she imagined the winds out on the western plains would sound.

Sister Stephanus too seemed to have caught that lovely, lonesome note in his voice, and now it was she who had to clear her throat. 'All the same,' she said, not so much turning to Claire as turning away from Andy, 'it must be hard for you, sometimes?'

'Oh, but it won't be, any more,' Claire said in a rush, and then bit her lip; she knew she should have denied ever having found life with Andy anything less than sweet and easy; she hoped he would not pick up on it, later. 'I mean,' she finished lamely, 'with the baby, for company.'

'And when we get the new place she'll have a whole passel of new friends,' Andy said. He had found his confidence now, and was playing up the cowboy act and the crooked, John Wayne smile—after all, the nun was a woman, Claire found herself thinking, with a faint sourness, and there was nothing Andy could not do with a woman, when he put his mind to it.

'Yet I wonder,' the nun said thoughtfully, as though speaking to herself, 'if there might not be a possibility of some other kind of work, some other kind of driving. A taxi cab, for instance?'

That put a stop to Andy's smiling, and he sat up as if he had been stung.

'I wouldn't want to stop working for Crawford Transport,' he said. 'With Claire giving up her job here, and then the baby . . . well, we'll need all the cash we can get. There's the overtime, and bonuses for them long draws up to Canada and the Lakes.'

Sister Stephanus leaned back in her chair and made a steeple of her fingertips and studied him, trying to judge, it seemed, if his tone was one of genuine concern or guarded threat. 'Yes, well,' she said, with a faint shrug. Her eyes drifted to the file again. 'Perhaps I might speak to Mr Crawford about it . . .'

'That'd be real good,' Andy said, too eagerly, he knew, and she gave him a quick, sharp glance, which made him blink and sit back in his chair. He forced himself to relax then and resumed his cowpoke's easy grin. 'I mean, it'd be good if I had a job nearer home and the baby, and all.'

Sister Stephanus went on studying him. The silence in the room seemed to creak. Claire realised that all this time she had been clutching a handkerchief, and when she opened her fist now it was stuck there, a damp lump in her palm. Then Sister Stephanus shut the file with a snap and stood up.

'All right,' she said. 'Come along.'

She led them briskly to the door and out.

'You haven't been down here before, have you?' she said to Andy over her shoulder, stopping at the end of a corridor and throwing a door wide to reveal a long, low room, painted a dazzling white, with rows of identical cribs facing each other along two walls. Nuns in white habits moved about, some bearing swaddled babies in the crooks of their arms with a sort of cheery, practised negligence. Something fierce and zealous came into Sister Stephanus's smile. 'The nursery,' she announced. 'The heart of St Mary's, and our pride and joy.'

Andy stared, impressed, and barely stopped himself producing a whistle. It was like something out of a science-fiction movie, all the little aliens in their pods. Sister Stephanus was looking at him expectantly, her head thrown back.

'Lot of babies,' was all he could say, in a faint voice.

Sister Stephanus gave a ringing laugh that was supposed to be rueful but sounded a little crazed instead. 'Oh,' she said, 'this is only a fraction of the poor mites in the world in need of our care and protection!'

Andy nodded doubtfully. It was something he did not like to think of, all those lost and abandoned kids screaming for attention and shaking their fists and kicking their legs in the air. The nun had led them into the room, and Claire was looking about eagerly in that jerky, rabbity way he hated; it even seemed to him sometimes when she was excited that the edges of her pink and nearly transparent nostrils twitched.

'Is . . . ?' she said, and did not know how to finish.

Sister Stephanus nodded and said: 'She's having a last check-up before she starts out on her new life.'

'I wanted to ask,' Claire began tentatively, 'if the mother—' but Sister Stephanus held up a long, white hand to silence her and said: 'I know you'd want to know something about the baby's background, Claire. However—'

'No, no, I was only going to ask—'

But the nun was unstoppable. '*However*,' she continued,

in a voice edged like a saw, 'there are certain rules we must abide by.'

The wadded handkerchief in Claire's fist was hot and hard as a boiled egg. She had to persist. 'It's only that,' she said, and took a gulping breath, 'it's only that when she's growing up I won't know what to tell her.'

'Oh, well,' the nun said, closing her eyes briefly and giving her head a dismissive little shake, 'you must decide, of course, when the time comes, whether she should know you're not her natural parents. As for the details . . .' She opened her eyes and this time for some reason it was Andy she addressed. 'Believe me, in certain matters not knowing is best.—But ah, here's Sister Anselm now!'

A short, square-shaped nun was approaching. There was something wrong with her right side, and she walked with a wrenching movement, dragging her hip after her like a mother dragging a stubborn child. Her face was broad, her expression stern but not unkind. A stethoscope hung about her neck. She had a baby in her arms, wrapped like a larva in a white cotton blanket. Claire greeted her in a rush of relief—Sister Anselm was the one who had looked after her from her earliest days here at St Mary's.

'Well now,' Sister Stephanus said with forced brightness, 'here we are, at last!'

Everything seemed to pause then, as in the Mass when the priest lifts the Communion host, and from a distance somehow Claire saw herself reach out, it might have been across a chasm, and take the baby in her arms. How solid a weight it was, and yet no weight at all, no earthly weight. Sister Stephanus was saying something. The baby's eyes were the most delicate shade of blue, they seemed to be looking into another world. Claire turned to Andy. She tried to speak but could not. She felt fragile and in some wonderful way injured, almost as if she were really a mother, and had really given birth.

Christine, that was what Sister Stephanus was saying, *your new little daughter, Christine.*

When she had seen the Staffords off at the front door Sister Stephanus walked back slowly to her office and sat down behind the desk and lowered her face into her hands. It was a small indulgence she allowed herself, a moment of weakness and surrender and of rest. Always after another child had gone there was an interval of empty heaviness. She was not sad, or regretful in any way—in her heart she knew she had no very deep feeling for these lost creatures that passed so briefly through her care—only there was a burdensome hollowness that took a little time to fill. Drained, that was the word: she felt drained.

Sister Anselm came in, without bothering to knock. She limped to the window nearest Sister Stephanus's desk and sat back on the sill and fished in a pocket under her habit and brought out a pack of Camels and lit up. Even after all these years the nun's habit fitted her ill. Poor Peggy Farrell, one-time terror of Sumner Street. Her father had been a longshoreman, Mikey Farrell from the County Roscommon, who drank, and beat his wife, and knocked his daughter down the stairs one winter night and left her maimed for life. *How vividly I recall these things*, Sister Stephanus thought, *I, who have trouble sometimes remembering what my own name used to be.* She hoped Peggy—Sister Anselm—had not come to deliver one of her lectures. To forestall the possibility she said:

'Well, Sister, another one gone.'

Sister Anselm expelled an angry jet of smoke toward the ceiling. 'Plenty more where that one came from,' she said.

Oh, dear. Sister Stephanus turned her attention pointedly to the papers on her desk. 'Isn't it well, then, Sister,' she said mildly, 'that we're here to take care of them?'

But Sister Anselm was not to be put off so lightly. This was the Peggy Farrell who had overcome all handicaps to win a first-class medical degree and take her place among the men at Massachusetts General before Mother House ordered her to St Mary's. 'I must say, Mother Superior,' she said, putting an ironical emphasis on the title, as she always managed to do, 'it occurs to me that the morals of the girls of Ireland today must be very low indeed, considering the number of their little mistakes that come our way.'

Sister Stephanus told herself to say nothing, but in vain: Peggy Farrell had always known how to provoke her, starting back in the days when they had played together, the small-time lawyer's daughter and Mikey Farrell's girl, on the front stoop in Sumner Street. 'Not all of them are *little mistakes,* as you call them,' she said, still pretending to be absorbed in her paperwork.

'By the Lord Harry, then,' Sister Anselm said, 'the mortality rate among mothers over there must be as high as the unmarried ones' morals are low, to produce that number of orphans.'

'I wish, Sister, you wouldn't talk like this.' Sister Stephanus kept her voice low and even. 'I wouldn't want,' she continued, 'to have to institute disciplinary procedures.'

There was silence for a long moment, then Sister Anselm with a grunt pushed herself away from the sill and came forward and stubbed out her cigarette in the cut-glass ashtray on the desk and heaved herself across the room to the door and was gone. Sister Stephanus sat motionless and stared at the hastily squashed cigarette butt, from which there poured upward a thin and sinuous thread of heaven-blue smoke.

2

In the Pathology Department it was always night. This was one of the things Quirke liked about his job—the only thing, in fact, he often thought. Not that he had a particular taste for the nocturnal—*I'm no more morbid than the next pathologist*, he would insist in the pub, to raise a groaning laugh—but it was restful, cosy, one might almost say, down in these depths nearly two floors beneath the city's busy pavements. There was, too, a sense here of being part of the continuance of ancient practices, secret skills, of work too dark to be carried on up in the light

Quirke had given the Dolly Moran job to Sinclair, he was not sure why—certainly he entertained no squeamish scruples about cutting up the corpse of someone he had briefly known. Sinclair had assumed he was only to assist but Quirke had pressed the scalpel into his hands and told him to get on with it. The young man was suspicious at first, fearing he was being put to a test or led into a professional trap, but when Quirke went off into his office muttering about paperwork that needed catching up on he set himself to the task with enthusiasm. In fact, Quirke ignored the pile of papers requiring his attention, and sat for an hour with his feet on his desk, smoking and thinking, while he listened to Sinclair out in the dissecting room, whistling as he plied the knife and saw.

Quirke had decided to assume, for reasons most of which he did not care to examine, that Dolly Moran's murder had no connection with the business of Christine Falls. True, it was suspiciously coincidental that she had died only a few hours after his second visit to Crimea Street. Had she known she was in danger? Was that why she had refused to let him in? Something she had said to him through the door kept slithering through his mind like an insistent worm. Not caring how foolish he might look to anyone watching from that row of lace-curtained windows on the other side of the street, he had leaned down to speak to her through the letterbox, demanding, out of an anger for which he could not quite account— true, he had been a little drunk still from the wine at Jammet's—that she tell him about Christine Falls's child and what had become of it. '*I'll tell you nothing,*' Dolly Moran had hissed back at him—her voice, it struck him now, might have been coming through a vent in the lid of a coffin—'*I've said too much already.*' But what was it she had told him, in the smoky pub that evening, that would have constituted the *too much* she seemed to think she had revealed? While he was leaning there, shouting into the letterbox, had he been watched? he wondered now.

No, he told himself, no: he was being fanciful and ridiculous. In his world, the world he inhabited up in the light, people did not have their fingernails broken or the soft undersides of their arms scorched with cigarettes; the people whom he knew were not bludgeoned to death in their own kitchens. And what had he known of Dolly

Moran, except that her tipple was gin and water and that she had worked for the Griffin family long ago?

He stood up and paced the narrow length of floor behind his desk. This office was too small—everywhere was too small, for him. He had an image of his physical self, half comic and half dispiriting, as a huge spinning-top, perilously suspended, held upright by virtue of an unrelenting momentum and liable at the merest touch to go reeling off in uncontrollable wobblings, banging against the furniture, before coming helplessly to rest at last in some inaccessible corner. His excessive size had always been a burden to him. From boyhood on he had been built like a bus, and thus had been a natural challenge first to the orphanage toughs, then schoolyard bullies, then rugby types at dances and drunks in pubs at closing time. Yet he had never been involved directly in serious violence, and the only blood he had ever spilled had been at the dissecting table, although there had been rivers of that.

The scene in Dolly Moran's kitchen had affected him peculiarly. In his time he had dealt with countless corpses, some more abused than hers, yet the pathos of her predicament, lying there on the stone floor bound to a kitchen chair, her head lolling in a gluey puddle of her own gore, had provoked in him a rolling wave of anger and something like sorrow that had not subsided yet. If he could get his hands on whoever had done this terrible thing to her, why, he would . . . he would . . . But here his imagination failed him. What would he do? He was no avenger. *Yes. Dead ones,* Dolly had said. *No trouble there.*

Sinclair came to the glass door and knocked and entered. He was a meticulous cutter—*You could eat your tea off of Mr Sinclair*, one of the cleaners had once assured Quirke—and there was hardly a smear on his rubber apron and his green lab boots were spotless. From the back of a drawer in the filing cabinet Quirke brought out a bottle of whiskey and splashed a tot of it into a tumbler. It was a ritual he had instituted over the years, the post-post-mortem drink. By now the little occasion had taken on something of the solemn atmosphere of a wake. He handed the glass to Sinclair and said: 'Well?'

Sinclair was waiting for him to produce a glass for himself, but Quirke did not care to drink to the memory of Dolly Moran, whose remains he could plainly see, if he glanced through the glass door, glimmering palely on the steel slab out there.

Sinclair shrugged. 'No surprises,' he said. 'Blunt-force trauma, intra-dural haematoma. Probably she wasn't meant to die—fell sideways on the chair, smacked her head on the stone floor.' He looked into his drink, which he had hardly touched, held back no doubt by Quirke's unwonted abstemiousness. 'You knew her, did you?' he said.

Quirke was startled. He did not recall having said anything to Sinclair about his dealings with Dolly Moran, and was not sure how he should answer. His dilemma was solved by the appearance in the glass of the doorway at Sinclair's back of a bulky figure in hat and mackintosh. Quirke went to the door. Inspector Hackett wore his usual expression of mild merriment, and came sidling in like a theatregoer arriving late at a farce. He was as broad as Quirke but a good half a foot shorter, which seemed to trouble him not at all. Quirke was accustomed to the stratagems that people of normal stature adopted for dealing with him, the backward-leaning stance, the vigorous straightening of the shoulders and the craning of the neck, but Hackett went in for none of this: he looked up at Quirke with a sceptically measuring eye, as if he and not Quirke were the one with the advantage, the one with the loftier if slightly laughable eminence. He had a large rectangular head and a slash for a mouth and a nose like a pitted and mildewed potato. His soft brown eyes resembled the lenses of a camera, leisurely scanning everything, taking everything in. Under his glance Sinclair hastily put the glass down on the desk, the whiskey half undrunk, and murmured something and left. Hackett watched him as he crossed the dissecting room, discarding his apron as he went and, hardly breaking his stride, flinging a sheet over Dolly Moran's corpse with an expert flick of the wrist before passing on and exiting through the green swing doors.

Hackett turned to Quirke. 'Delegated the job, did you?'

Quirke was searching in the desk drawer for cigarettes. 'He needed the practice,' he said.

There were no cigarettes in the drawer. The detective produced a packet and they lit up. Quirke pushed the ashtray forward on the desk. He felt as if he were embarking on a chess match in which he would be both a player and a piece. Hackett's easy manner and Midlands drawl did not deceive him—he had seen the detective at work before now, on other cases.

'Well,' Hackett said, 'what's the verdict?'

Quirke told him Sinclair's findings. Hackett nodded, and perched himself on one broad ham on the edge of Quirke's desk. He had not taken off his hat. For a moment

Quirke hesitated and then sat down too, behind the desk, in his swivel chair. Hackett was contemplating Sinclair's whiskey where the young man had left it on the corner of the desk; a tiny star of pure white light was burning in the bottom of the glass.

'Will you take a drink?' Quirke offered.

Hackett made no reply, and asked instead: 'Was she interfered with?'

Quirke gave a short laugh. 'If you mean, was she sexually assaulted, then no, she wasn't.'

Hackett gazed at him expressionlessly for a moment, and the atmosphere in the room tightened, as if a screw holding something vital in place had been given a small, effortful turn. 'That's what I meant, all right,' the detective said softly; he was not a man to be laughed at. The light shining upwards from the desk lamp made his face a mask, with jutting chin and flared nostrils and pools of empty darkness in the eye sockets. Quirke saw again, with a clarity that shook him, the woman on the floor, the burn marks on her arms, and the blood that was almost black under the ceiling's single, bare bulb. 'So they weren't there for fun, then,' Hackett said.

Quirke felt a stab of irritation.

'Did you think they were?' he said sharply. Hackett shrugged, and Quirke went on, 'What do you mean by *they*—how many of them were there?'

'Two,' Hackett said. 'Footprints in the back garden, before you ask. No one in the street saw or heard anything, of course, or so they say, even the old biddy opposite, who I'd imagine could hear a sparrow fart—but people like to mind their own business. It would have taken two of them to get poor Dolly trussed up like that. We're assuming she was conscious all the time. Not easy to tie a woman by the legs, if you've ever attempted it. Stronger than you'd expect, even the no-longer young ones, like Dolly.' Quirke tried to discern an expression in that shadowed mask but could not. 'Would you have any idea as to what they were after?' Hackett continued, almost musingly. 'Must have been something worth finding, for they tore the place apart.'

Quirke had finished his cigarette and Hackett offered another, and after the briefest of hesitations he took it. Smoke rolled along the top of the desk like a fog at night on the sea. Quirke heard Dolly Moran's voice again: *I have it all written down.* He coughed, giving himself a moment.

'I've no idea what they might have been looking for,' he said, his voice sounding unnaturally loud in his own ears. Hackett was watching him again, his face more mask-like than ever. From somewhere far above them, in the upper floors of the hospital, there came a muffled crash. How strange, Quirke thought, with vague inconsequence, the inexplicable noises that the world makes. As if the sound from above had been a signal Hackett rose from the desk and walked to the door and stood leaning against the jamb, looking out at Dolly Moran's sheeted corpse. The white light falling from the great lamps in the ceiling seemed to vibrate minutely, a colourless, teeming mist.

'So anyway,' Hackett said, returning to the earlier part of their exchange as if there had been no break, 'Dolly knew this girl . . . what was her name?'

'Christine Falls,' Quirke answered, too quickly, he realised.

Hackett nodded, and did not turn. 'That's right,' he said. 'But tell me this, now, would you normally give your telephone number to somebody who was a friend of somebody that died?'

Quirke did not know how to answer, yet had to. He heard himself say:

'I was interested in her—in Christine Falls, I mean.'

Still Hackett did not turn but went on looking out through the glass of the door as if there were something of great interest occurring in the other, empty room.

'Why?' he said.

Quirke shrugged, even though the detective was not to see him do it. 'Curiosity,' he said. 'It goes with the job. Dealing with the dead, you sometimes find yourself wondering about the lives they led.'

He heard the contrivance in the words but could do nothing to correct it. Hackett turned with his easy half-smile. Quirke had an almost irresistible urge to tell him to take off, for God's sake, that damned hat.

'And what did *she* die of?' Hackett asked.

'Who?'

'This girl, this Falls girl.'

'Pulmonary embolism.'

'What age was she?'

'Young. It happens.'

Hackett stood gazing down at his boots, with the wings of his mackintosh pushed back and his hands in the jacket pockets of his tightly buttoned, shiny blue suit. Then he looked up. 'Right,' he said, and moved to the door, 'I'll be off.'

Quirke, surprised, pushed his chair back on its castors

and stood up. 'You'll let me know,' he said, sounding faintly desperate, 'you'll let me know, I mean, if you find out anything?'

The detective turned back, the smile broadening on his smudged features, and said in a tone of jovial good humour:

'Oh, we'll *find out* plenty of things, no doubt of that, Mr Quirke. Plenty of things.'

And still smiling he turned again to the door and was through it and had shut it after him before Quirke had time to come forward from behind the desk. Hardly noticing what he was doing Quirke picked up Sinclair's glass and drank off the whiskey in it, then lumbered to the filing cabinet and fished out the bottle again and poured himself another go. *Mal Griffin*, he thought savagely, *you'll never know how much you owe me.*

3

IT WAS NOT exactly what Claire had been hoping for, the top half of a two-family house on Fulton Street, but it was a world away from the places they had been living in since they were married, places that were not much better than flop-houses, and she knew she could turn it into a home; best of all, it was hers—theirs—for it was all paid for, with nothing owing to the bank, and they could fix it up whatever way they liked. It was grey clapboard with a steep roof and a nice porch at the front with a swing. They had the three rooms upstairs, as well as a kitchenette and bathroom. The living room was full of light, and there was an arched window in the gable end, like the window in the alcove of a church, that looked right into the heart of an old walnut tree growing at the side of the house where squirrels hopped and skittered. Mr Crawford's man had sent over the painters from the body shop in Roxbury, and she had been allowed to choose the colours herself, buttercup yellow in the living room, white for the kitchen, of course, and a cool, pale blue for the bathroom. She had not been sure about the shade of candy-pink she had picked for the baby's room, but it looked fine, now that it had dried. The store had promised to deliver the crib this morning, and Andy had arranged for their things to be brought over from the old place on a flatbed by one of his buddies in the afternoon. For now she was enjoying the look of the rooms before they were filled up. She liked the emptiness, the space, the way the sun fell slanting on the wall here in the living room, the way the polished maple floor rang clean and solid under her heels.

'Oh, Andy,' she said, 'isn't it just the prettiest place? And to think, it's all ours!'

He was on one knee in a corner, jiggling a loose power socket in the wall there.

'Yeah,' he said without turning, 'old Crawford has a real big heart.'

She went and stood behind him, leaning her hips against his back and draping her arms around his shoulders, savouring his strong, metallic smell that she always thought of as blue, the jukebox-blue of spilled machine oil or a sheet of pliant milled steel.

'Come on,' she said, reaching down past his shoulders and patting his chest with her two hands, 'don't be such a sourpuss.'

She was about to speak again, to tell him how handsome he looked in the dark pants and the sport jacket, but just then the baby in her carry-cot behind her woke up. Claire was secretly thrilled at the way the baby's—Christine, she must get used to thinking of her by her name—at the way Christine's thin, rising wail, like the sound of a flute or some high instrument like that, already affected her, causing something to move in her stomach and making her heart beat faster and more heavily, as though it was a fist thumping softly inside her chest. 'What's wrong with baby then, hmm?' she whispered. 'What's the matter? Don't you like our nice new housey?'

She wished her mother could be alive to see her now. Daddy would only laugh, of course, and wipe the back of his hand across his mouth, as if to wipe away a bad taste.

She smiled at Andy and snuffed up a deep breath through her nostrils. 'Smell that,' she said. 'Fresh paint!'

Andy was balancing on one leg, pulling on a boot. 'I'm hungry,' he said. 'Let's go get a hamburger.'

She said all right, although she did not want to leave yet, wanted to stay and get used to the place, to let it soak into her. There was a short hall beside the kitchenette with a sort of french door at the end of it that opened on to a set of rickety wooden stairs leading steeply down into the yard at the side; this would be their front door. Andy went first, descending the stairs sideways and holding her by the elbow to steady her as she followed with the baby in her arms. This was one of the things she loved most about him, the easy, graceful way he had of being helpful, not just to her but others, too, women in stores, children, the one-armed old man at the gas station out on the turnpike who looked after the pumps; sometimes negroes, even.

The backyard was brown after the dry summer and the grass crackled under their feet and gave off dust that smelled like wood ash, and crickets the same colour as the grass clicked their hinged back legs and sailed away from them on all sides. There was nothing in this part of the yard, only a gnarled peach tree, its leaves gone already, and an old dug patch where someone must have raised vegetables, overgrown long ago.

'Well,' Claire said, with a rueful laugh, 'this is going to take some rethinking.'

'What gives you the idea it's going to be ours to rethink?' Andy said.

He was looking past her toward the house, and she turned and saw a tall, thin-faced woman standing on the porch, watching them. Her no-colour hair was pulled back and tied in a tight ball at the back of her neck. She wore a brown apron.

'Why, hello there,' Claire said, going forward with the baby in one arm and a hand outstretched. It was a strategy she had devised for meeting new people, always to make a move right away, before her shyness had time to stop her. The woman on the porch ignored the hand she was offering and she quickly took it back. 'I'm Claire Stafford,' she said.

The woman looked her up and down and was obviously unimpressed with what she saw. 'Bennett,' she said. When she shut her mouth her lips made a straight, colourless line.

She must be thirty-five, Claire guessed, but she gave an even older impression. Claire wondered if Mr Bennett was about, or if there was a Mr Bennett. 'Pleased to meet you,' she said. 'We're moving in today. We were just up there, getting the feel of the place.'

The woman nodded. 'I heard the baby.'

Claire held out the bundle in her arms. 'This is Christine,' she said. The woman ignored the baby: she was squinting at Andy standing back in the dry grass with his hands in the seat pockets of his jeans and his head on one side, and the look in her eye warmed a half a degree or so,

Claire noted. 'That's my husband, Andy,' Claire said. She lowered her voice to a woman-to-woman level. 'He's a mite put out,' she said. 'I think he thinks the place is on the small side.'

She knew at once it had been the wrong thing to say.

'That right?' the woman said coldly. 'Guess he's used to grander quarters, is he?'

Andy must have seen from the angle of Claire's back that she needed rescuing. He came forward with his widest grin.

'Howdy there,' he said, 'Miss . . . ?'

'Bennett,' the woman said. 'Mrs.'

'No!' He lifted a hand in mock amazement and opened wide his velvety brown eyes. Claire watched him with an amusement in which there was only the faintest touch of jealousy. His charm knew no shame, and always worked, however obvious the lies he told. 'Well,' he said to the woman, 'I'm mighty glad to make your acquaintance.'

He stepped up on the porch and she let him take her hand, having wiped it first on her apron.

'Likewise, I'm sure,' she said.

Claire saw how he held her fingers in his a moment before releasing them, and how her tight lips twitched into a smile.

There was silence then between the three of them. Faintly, like the rumbling of far-off thunder, Claire felt the first beats of a headache starting up. The baby flexed its arm, pressing out the blanket as if it—she—Christine— also wanted to reach out to this hard-faced, long-boned woman. Claire drew the warm bundle more tightly to her breast.

Andy slapped his hands against his hips. 'Well,' he said, 'I guess it's about lunchtime.' He waited a second, but if he expected the Bennett woman to invite them in then he was disappointed. 'Let's go get something to eat, honey,' he said. 'I'll fetch my billfold.'

He went off up the wooden stairway two at a time. Claire smiled at Mrs Bennett and turned to follow him. The woman said:

'I hope that baby ain't a bawler. Noise carries easily, in these tiny little houses.'

4

QUIRKE COULD NOT remember the last time he had been in the hospital chapel, and he was not sure what he was doing there now. The doors, giving off the corridor that led to Radiology, struck an incongruous note, with their fancy handles and the two narrow panels of stained-glass that some rich old lady had paid to have installed a couple of years previously in memory of her married daughter who had died. The air in here was always cold, with a special sort of cold not to be felt elsewhere, but which Quirke associated, unaccountably, with the vase of lilies that had stood every summer on the altar of the chapel in Carricklea—he used to believe it was always the same bunch, miraculously undying—into the bell of one of which he had one day dared to put his hand, and the chill, clammy, flesh-like feel of which he had never forgotten. The Holy Family chapel was small, without pillars or side alcoves, so that there was no avoiding the beady eye of the little oil lamp with the ruby-red globe that burned perpetually before the tabernacle. It was there at noon that Quirke found Mal, kneeling with hands joined and head bowed before a statue of St Joseph. He went forward quietly and sat down in the seat beside where Mal knelt.

Mal did not turn, and gave no sign to acknowledge his presence, but after a minute or two he crossed himself and sat back on the seat with a sigh. They were both silent for a time, then Quirke lifted a hand and made a gesture indicating the statue, the sanctuary lamp, the altar with its gold-embroidered white cloth, and said:

'Tell me, Mal, do you really believe in all this?'

Mal considered. 'I try to,' he said. He looked sidelong at his brother-in-law. 'And you—what do you believe in?'

'I was cured of believing in things a long time ago.'

Mal gave an amused little sniff. 'You love to hear yourself saying things like that, don't you?' he said. He took off his spectacles and rubbed a finger hard into one eye and then the other and sighed again. 'What do you want, Quirke?'

Now it was Quirke's turn to consider. 'I want you to tell me about Dolly Moran's death.'

Mal registered no surprise. 'I know less about it than you, seemingly,' he said. 'I'm not the one going about poking my nose into places where it's liable to get cut off.'

Quirke gave an incredulous laugh. 'Is that a *threat*, Mal?'

Mal gazed before him stonily.

'You may think you know what you're doing, Quirke,' he said, 'but believe me, you don't.'

'I know Christine Falls didn't die of an embolism,' Quirke said, quietly at first, 'as you claimed she did, in that false file you wrote up. I know she died having a child, and that her child was stillborn, as you told me, but that it disappeared, or was disappeared, without a trace. I know I told you Dolly Moran kept a diary and that the next day she was tortured and had her head smashed open. Tell me these things are not connected, Mal. Tell me my suspicions are groundless. Tell me you're not up to your neck in trouble.'

Quirke was surprised at himself. Where did it come from, all this anger? And what injustice was he protesting—the one done to Dolly Moran, or to Christine Falls or Christine Falls's child, or to himself? But who had been unjust to him, or injured him? It was not he who had died amid the blood and screams of childbirth, or had his flesh burned or his head cracked open. Mal was obviously unimpressed. He made no reply, only gave a brisk nod, as if something had been confirmed, and stood up. In the aisle he genuflected, and rose again and turned to go, but paused. The sombre suit gave him a faintly ecclesiastical aspect; even the dark-blue bow-tie might have been the elaborate neckwear of a prelate of some ultramontane faction of the Church. His expression when he looked back at Quirke was one of cold amusement mingled with a pitying contempt.

'I'll tell you this, Quirke,' he said. 'Stay out of it.'

Quirke, still seated, shook his head. 'I can't,' he said. 'I'm in it, up to my neck, just like you.'

Mal walked out of the chapel. After a while Quirke stood up. The red eye before the altar flickered and seemed to wink. He shivered a little. *The cold heaven . . .*

5

ANDY STAFFORD liked the night runs best. It was not just that the rate of pay was better or that there was less traffic on the highway. Something about that high dome of darkness all around him and the headlights of the big twelve-wheeler cutting through it made him feel in control of more than just this Crawford Transport truck with its load of roof shingles or auto parts or pig iron. What all he did out here was up to nobody but himself. There was only him and the road and some heartsick hillbilly on the cab radio twanging away about hound dogs and lonesomeness and love. Often, standing in the forecourt of a deserted gas station or stepping out of the late-night smoke and fry-smells of a roadside hamburger joint, he would feel the breeze on his face and seem to smell clean, sage-scented air coming to him like a message just for him all the way from out West, from New Mexico or Colorado, Wyoming, maybe, or even the high Rockies, all those places he had never been to, and something would well up in him, something sweet and solitary-seeming and full of promise for the day to come, the day that was already laying down a thin line of gold on the horizon before him.

He got on to the turnpike, then ran through Brookline

and down across the deserted south city. When he turned into Fulton Street he cut the engine and let the rig run smooth and silent down the soft incline of the road to the house, the freewheeling tyres warbling under him on the asphalt. Mrs Bennett—'*You can call me Cora*'—had already started making comments about him parking the truck outside the house, only to Claire, of course, never to him. He swung down from the cab, the muscles in his arms and across the saddle of his shoulders aching and the seam of his jeans wedged like a hot wet lariat rope between his legs. All the houses in the street were dark. Someone's dog started a half-hearted baying but soon shut up. It was still an hour to dawn and the air had a bite but he sat down anyway on the porch swing to rest a minute and look up at the stars, his hands clasped behind his neck that was already tingling and beginning to unstiffen. The swing creaked on its chains and made him think of nights in Wilmington when he was a kid, sprawled on the porch like this to smoke a cigarette stolen from the pack in the bib pocket of his old man's overalls, the smoke harsh and cutting in the cool night air and tasting of all forbidden things, racetrack beer and sour-mash whisky and girls' juices, the very taste of what it would be like to be grown-up and all the hell away from Wilmington, State of Delanowhere. He laughed to himself. When he was there he dreamed of being somewhere like here, now he was here and dreamed of being back there. That was how it always was with him, satisfied noplace, always hankering after other towns, other times.

He stood up and walked around by the side of the house, past what he knew was Cora Bennett's bedroom, and climbed the wooden stairs and let himself in at the french door. There was still that damned smell of new paint that sometimes almost made him sick to his stomach; he thought he could catch the baby's smells, too, the usual milk and damp cotton, and the poop that stank like horse feed. He had not bothered to turn on the light and a sort of greyish mist was seeping in from the eastern sky, and he could see the thin, mean-looking spire of St Patrick's church over on Brewster Street outlined against the dawn with the morning star, the only one remaining now, sitting plumb on top of the weathervane. His mood was growing darker the more the morning got light. He wondered, as he had begun to do lately, how long he could stay in this town before the itch to move on got so bad he would have to scratch it.

He sat down in the living room and eased himself out of his boots, then tore off his work-shirt. With his arms still lifted he sniffed his armpits; pretty high, but he did not want to bother with a shower; besides, Claire always said she liked his smell. He went on tiptoe in his socks into the bedroom. The shades were pulled, allowing in no chink of dawn light. He could make out Claire's form in the bed but could not hear her breathing—he liked it that she was a quiet sleeper, when she slept and her headaches were not keeping her awake. Feeling his way about the still unfamiliar room and trying not to make a sound, for he did not want her to wake yet, he got out of the last of his clothes with impatient haste and naked approached the bed and carefully lifted the covers.

'*Hey there,*' he whispered, putting one knee on the side of the mattress and leaning down to the form lying there, '*how's my baby girl?*' There were two, separate stirrings, and two voices, one of them Claire's, which murmured a blurred 'What . . . ?' and the other making an urgent, wet, sucking sound. He reared back. 'Jesus Christ!'

It was the kid, of course, lying beside Claire and sucking on its fist. Claire pulled the child from her and sat up, confused and half frightened. 'Is that you, Andy?' she said, and had to clear her throat.

'Who the hell did you think it was?' He was lifting the sopping, hot infant out of her arms. 'You expecting somebody else?'

She realised what he was doing, and made a grab for the baby. 'She was crying,' she said plaintively, 'I was just getting her back to sleep.'

But he was already on his way out of the room, moving through the darkness like a glimmering ghost. She fell back on the pillow, moaning faintly, and thrust a hand into her hair. She tried to see what time it was but the clock on the bedside cabinet was turned away. The baby's diaper must have leaked, and there was a big wet patch on the front of her nightshirt. She knew she should take it off but she did not want to be naked when Andy came back. It was too late, or too early, for what she knew he would want, and she was tired, for the baby had woken her twice already. But Andy did not notice, or ignored, the wet spot and the faint ammoniac smell, and took the nightshirt off her himself, making her sit up and lift her arms and pulling it roughly over her head and throwing it behind him on the floor.

'Oh, honey,' she began, 'listen, I'm—'

But he would not listen. He stretched himself on top

of her, forcing her legs apart—his kneecaps were icy—and was suddenly inside her. He smelled of beer, and his lips were still greasy from something he had eaten. She felt chilled, and reached out beside her and found the edge of the bed covers and pulled them over his rhythmically arching back. She could hardly feel him, she was so tired and distracted, but even so she started to slip and slide along with him, and had that familiar, faintly panicky sensation, as if she were sinking slowly, languorously, under water.

'Honey,' he whispered in her ear, in a hoarse, distressed, lost voice that made her hold him more tightly to her, 'oh, honey.'

She heard it before he did, the baby winding out into the dark like a party streamer her thin, demanding, unignorable cry. Andy went still, and lay on her, rigid, his head lifted.

'Jesus,' he said again, and smacked a fist hard into the pillow beside where her head was. 'Jesus H. Christ!'

And then, just as she was becoming afraid, he began to laugh.

In the morning he was still in a funny mood. She was hanging sheets on the clothesline he had rigged up temporarily for her between a thick branch of the walnut tree and the newel post at the top of the wooden staircase—Mrs Bennett had said nothing yet about this arrangement; she had some kind of a newfangled electric dryer herself—when he came creeping up behind her and grabbed her around the waist with a whoop and lifted her high off her feet and swung her in a circle. She would have been glad to see him happy but she was not sure this was happiness. He had kind of a wild look in his eye, as if he had been running real hard and had just now come to a stop. When he set her down she was out of breath herself. With the fingers of one hand he pushed aside the collar of her shirt. 'Hey,' he said softly, 'what's this here?' There was a hickey the size of a silver dollar on the side of her neck. 'Now where did that come from?'

'Oh,' she said, turning away from him to hang another sheet, 'some big old brute came sneaking into my bed sometime around dawn—didn't you hear him?'

'Why, no. I slept like a baby. You know me, honey.' He put his arms around her again from behind and ground his hips slowly against her. His arms were like two hot steel cables. 'Tell me,' he whispered, his mouth hot too against her ear, 'what else he do to you, this big old brute?'

She turned, laughing in her throat, and he slipped his arms higher and put his hands on her shoulder blades and pulled her hard against his chest, and she put her open mouth to his and he drank her sweet breath and their tongues touched. A breeze came from somewhere, maybe the faraway Rockies again, and caught the wet sheet on the clothesline and wrapped it briefly around them. Kissing, they did not see, in a downstairs window of the house, a thin-lipped face and a pair of cold eyes, watching them.

6

THE AUTUMN NIGHT was closing in as Quirke walked up Raglan Road. There were haloes of fog around the street-lamps and smoke was rolling down from the chimneys high above him and he could taste coal grit on his lips. He was rehearsing in his mind the conversation—the word *confrontation* hovered worryingly—which he was already sorry he had sought. He could avoid it, even yet, if he wanted. What was to stop him turning on his heel and walking away, as he had walked away from so many things in his life—what made this one any different? He could find a telephone—in his head he heard Dolly Moran saying, *I had to go three or four streets to the phone box*—and call and make some excuse, say that the matter he had wanted to talk over had solved itself. But even as he was thinking these thoughts his legs carried him on, and then he was at the gate of the Judge's house. In the dark the autumn garden gave off a rank, wet smell. He climbed the worn steps to the front door. There was a dim light in the transom but none in the tall windows on either side and he found himself hoping the old man might have forgotten their appointment and gone out to the Stephen's Green Club for the evening, as was his habit. He worked the bell-pull and heard the bell jangle echoingly within and his hopes rose further, but then there came the unmistakable sound of Miss Flint's footsteps approaching along the hall. He prepared his face, forcing on to it the makings of a smile: Miss Flint and he were old adversaries. When she opened the door he had the impression that she was barely keeping in check a smirk of distaste. She was small and sharp-faced and wore her coarse ungreying hair in a helmet shape that made it look like a wig, which it might be, for all Quirke knew.

'Mr Quirke,' she said, in her driest voice and with the barest hint of an unwelcoming exclamation mark. She was scrupulously, vengefully polite.

''Evening, Miss Flint. Is the Judge in?'

She stepped back, opening wider the door. 'He's expecting you.'

The air in the hall was dead and there was a trace even here of an old man's musty smell. The bulb in the light fixture dangling from the high ceiling was sixty watts or less, and the shade resembled what he imagined dried skin would look like. His heart contracted. He had been happy here, when Nana Griffin was alive. Shouts in this hall, and Mal on the stairs dodging the rugby ball that Quirke was punting at him, the two of them in short trousers and school ties, their shirttails hanging out. Yes, happy.

Miss Flint took his hat and coat and led him off into the heart of the house, the thick rubber soles of her prison warder's shoes squeaking on parquet and tile. As so often Quirke found himself wondering what things she might know, what family secrets. Did she watch Mal, too, with that searching, lopsided stare, on his rare visits to his father's house?

The Judge had heard the bell and had come to the door of what he called his den. When Quirke saw him standing there in his slippers and his old grey cardigan, nearly as tall as Quirke but stooped a little now, peering anxiously out of the shadows, it occurred to him that the day could not be far off when he would knock at the front door and be met by Miss Flint with a mourning band on her arm and her eyes red-rimmed. He stepped forward briskly, once again making himself smile.

'Get in here, man,' the Judge said from the doorway of the room, making shooing motions with his arm, 'this hall is like a refrigerator.'

'Will you be wanting tea?' Miss Flint asked, and the Judge said, 'No!' shortly and put a hand on Quirke's shoulder and drew him into the room.

'Tea!' he said, shutting the door behind them with a thud. 'I declare to God, that woman . . .' He led Quirke to the fireplace and an armchair beside it. 'Sit down there and thaw yourself out, and we'll have a drop of something stronger than tea.'

He went to the sideboard and busied himself with glasses and the whiskey bottle. Quirke looked about him at familiar things, the old leather-covered chaise, the antique writing desk, the Sean O'Sullivan portrait of Nana Griffin as a young wife, calmly smiling, marcel-waved. Quirke had been one of the few people the Judge would permit to enter this room. Even as a boy, half wild still from the years at Carricklea, he was allowed the run of the

Judge's den, and often of a winter afternoon, before he and Mal went off to board at St Aidan's, he would perch here, in this same chair, beside a banked coke fire that might have been this one, doing his sums and his Latin prep, while the Judge, still a barrister then, sat at his desk working on a brief. Mal, meanwhile, did his homework at the white deal table in the kitchen, where Nana Griffin fed him wholemeal biscuits and warm milk and quizzed him about his bowels, for Mal was considered to be delicate.

The Judge brought their whiskeys and handed Quirke his and sat down opposite him. 'Have you had your dinner?' he asked.

'Yes, I'm fine.'

'Are you sure?' He peered at Quirke closely. Age had not dulled the old man's keen ear, and he had heard the discomforted note in Quirke's voice when he had telephoned and asked if he could come and talk to him. They drank in silence for a minute, Quirke frowning into the fire while the Judge watched him. The coke fumes, sharp as the smell of cat-piss, were stinging Quirke's nostrils.

'So,' the Judge said at last, large-voiced and forcedly hearty, 'what's this urgent matter you need to discuss? You're not in trouble, are you?'

Quirke shook his head. 'There was this girl . . .' he began, and stopped.

The Judge laughed. 'Uh-oh!' he said.

Quirke smiled faintly and again shook his head. 'No, no, nothing like that.' He looked into the shivering red heart of the fire. *Get it over with.* 'Her name was Christine Falls,' he said. 'She was going to have a child, but she died.

She was being looked after by a woman called Moran. After Christine Falls's death the Moran woman was murdered.' He stopped, and drew a breath.

The Judge blinked a few times rapidly, then nodded. 'Moran,' he said, 'yes, I think I read something about it in the paper. The poor creature.' He leaned forward and took Quirke's glass, seeming not to notice that there was a finger of whiskey undrunk in it, and rose and went again to the sideboard.

Quirke said:

'Mal wrote up a file on her—on Christine Falls.'

The Judge did not turn. 'How do you mean, wrote up a file?'

'So as to leave out any mention of the child.'

'Are you saying'—he looked at Quirke over his shoulder—'are you saying he falsified it?'

Quirke did not reply. The Judge stood there, still with his head turned and still looking at him, and suddenly opened his mouth slackly and uttered a quavering sound that was half-way between a moan of denial and a cry of anger. There was the squeak of glass sliding off glass and the glugging of whiskey spilling freely from the neck of the bottle. The Judge grunted again, cursing his trembling hand.

'I'm sorry,' Quirke said.

The Judge, having righted the bottle, bowed his head and remained motionless for fully a minute. There was the sound of the spilled whiskey dripping on to the floor. The old man was ashen-faced. 'What are you telling me, Quirke?' he asked.

'I don't know,' Quirke said.

The Judge came with their topped-up whiskeys and sat down again. 'Could he be struck off?' he asked.

'I doubt it would come to that. There's no real question of malpractice, that I know of.'

The Judge gave a sort of laugh. 'Malpractice!' he said. 'By the Lord, there's a pun in bad taste.' He ruminated angrily, shaking his head. 'What connection did he have with this girl, anyway? I suppose she was his patient?'

'I'm not sure what she was. He was taking care of her, was how he put it. She had worked at the house for a while.'

'What house?'

'Sarah took her on as a maid, to help out Maggie. Then she got in trouble.' He looked at the Judge, who sat with eyes downcast, still slowly shaking his head, the whiskey glass forgotten in his hand. 'He says he rewrote the file to spare the family knowing about the child.'

'What business was it of his to be sparing people's feelings?' the Judge broke out hoarsely. 'He's a doctor, he swore an oath, he's supposed to be impartial. Bloody irresponsible fool. What did she die of, anyway, the girl?'

'Post-partum haemorrhage. She bled to death.'

They were silent, the Judge scanning Quirke's face, just as, Quirke thought, an accused before the Bench in the old days might have scanned the Judge's face, looking for leniency. Then he turned aside. 'She died at Dolly Moran's house, is that so?' he asked. Quirke nodded. 'Did Mal know her, too?'

'He was paying her to look after the girl.'

'A fine set of acquaintances my son has.' He brooded,

his jaw muscles working. 'You spoke to him about all this, obviously?'

'He won't say much. You know Mal.'

'I wonder do I.' He paused. 'Did he say anything about this business with the people in Boston?'

Quirke shook his head. 'What business is that?'

'Oh, he has a charity thing going out there, him and Costigan and that Knights of St Patrick crowd, helping Catholic families, supposedly. Your father-in-law, Josh Crawford, funds it.'

'No, Mal said nothing about that.'

The Judge drank off the whiskey in his tumbler in one quick go. 'Give us here your glass, I think we need another stiffener.' From the sideboard he asked, 'Does Sarah know about all this?'

'I doubt it,' Quirke said. He thought again of Sarah by the canal that Sunday morning, looking at the swans and not seeing them, asking him to talk to her husband, the *good man*. How could he say what knowledge she might or might not have? 'I only know about it because I stumbled on him while he was writing up the file.'

He got to his feet, feeling suddenly overcome by the heat of the room, the fumes from the fire, the smell of the whiskey the Judge had spilled and the raw, scorched sensation on the surface of his tongue from the alcohol. The Judge turned to him in surprise, holding the two glasses against his chest.

'I've got to go,' Quirke said shortly. 'There's someone I have to meet.'

It was a lie. The old man looked put out, but made no

protest. 'You won't . . . ?' He held up Quirke's whiskey glass but Quirke shook his head, and the old man turned and put both glasses back on the sideboard. 'Are you sure you've eaten? I think you're not taking care of yourself.'

'I'll get something in town.'

'Flint could rustle you up an omelette . . . ?' He nodded ruefully. 'No, not the most tempting of offers, I grant you.' At the door a thought struck him and he stopped. 'Who killed her, the Moran woman—do they know?'

'Someone got into the house.'

'Burglars?'

Quirke shrugged. Then he said:

'You knew her.' He watched the old man's face. 'Dolly Moran, I mean. She worked for you and Nana, and then later on for Mal and Sarah, taking care of Phoebe. That was how Mal knew where to go for help, with Christine Falls.'

The Judge was looking to one side, frowning and thinking. Then he closed his eyes and gave a cry as he had done earlier, softer but more sorrow-laden. 'Dolores?' he said, and seemed about to falter on his feet, and Quirke reached out a hand to him. 'Merciful God—was it Dolores? I never made the connection. Oh, no. Oh, God, no. Poor Dolores.'

'I'm sorry,' Quirke said again; he seemed to have been saying it since he had arrived. They went into the hall, the Judge walking as if in a daze, his arms hanging stiffly before him, and for a moment Quirke saw his likeness to Mal. 'She was very loyal, Dolly was,' Quirke said. 'Any secrets she had, she kept them. Mal should be grateful to her.'

The old man seemed not to have heard him. 'Who's in charge of the case?' he asked.

'Fellow called Hackett. Detective Inspector.'

The Judge nodded. 'I know him. He's sound. If you're worried, I can talk to him, or get someone to drop a word . . . ?'

'I'm not worried,' Quirke said, 'not for myself.'

They had reached the front door. Suddenly it came to Quirke that what he was feeling most strongly was a sort of shamefaced pleasure. He recalled an occasion when he and Mal were boys and the Judge had summoned him into the den and made him stand by the desk while he questioned him about some minor outrage, a window broken with a stone from a catapult or a stash of cigarette butts found hidden in a cocoa tin in the linen cupboard. Who had fired the stone, the Judge demanded, who had smoked the cigarettes? At first Quirke had insisted that he knew nothing, but in the end, seeing clearly how much of his authority the Judge had invested in this cross-examination, he had admitted that Mal was the culprit, which most likely, he thought, the Judge already knew, anyway. The feeling he had now was like what he had felt then, only now it was much stronger, a hot mixture of guilt and glee and defiant self-righteousness. The Judge that time had thanked him solemnly and told him he had done the right thing, but Quirke had detected in his eye a faint, evasive look of—of what? Disappointment? Contempt?

Now Quirke said:

'The business with the file, all that: I'm the only one who knows about it. I said nothing to Hackett, or anyone.'

The Judge once more was shaking his head. 'Malachy

Griffin,' he muttered, 'you're a bloody fool.' He laid a hand heavily on Quirke's shoulder. 'I understand your interest in the Falls girl, of course,' he said. 'You were thinking of Delia, the same way that she went.'

Quirke shook his head. 'I was thinking of Mal,' he said. 'I was thinking of all of us—of the family.'

The Judge seemed to be only half listening. His hand was still on Quirke's shoulder. 'I'm glad you told me,' he said. 'You did the right thing.' *You're a good boy.* 'Do you think I should speak to him?'

'To Mal?' Quirke shook his head. 'No, best to leave it, I think.'

The Judge was watching him. 'And you,' he said, 'will *you* leave it?'

Quirke did not know what he would have answered, for at that moment Miss Flint came forward squeakingly, impassive of expression, bringing Quirke's coat and hat. How long, he wondered, had she been standing there, listening?

7

THE THING THAT Andy wanted was a car. Not any old car, that some nigger with too much cheap liquor in his veins had finished bolting together one rainy Monday morning in Detroit. No, what he had set his heart on was a Porsche. He knew the very model, too, a Spyder 550 coupé. He had seen one, over near the Common where Claire had dragged him with the baby to take a walk one day. In fact, he heard it before he saw it, a growling roar that for a thrilling moment turned the Common to savannah and a stand of pin oaks into tropical palms. He turned, all his instincts prickling, and there the beast was, throbbing under a red light at the intersection of Beacon Hill and Charles Street. It was small to be making so much noise, jelly-bean scarlet, with tyres a foot thick, and so low to the road it was a question how any normal-sized person could get in behind the wheel. The top was down; he wished, later, for the sake of his peace of mind, it had been left up. The driver was just some Boston guy trying to look like one of those Englishmen in the magazine ads, slick-haired and cissyish, wearing a blue blazer with two rows of brass buttons and a loosely tied gold-coloured silk scarf inside the open collar of his white sport shirt. But the girl beside him, she was a knockout. She had kind of an indian profile, with high cheekbones and a nose that came down in a straight line from her forehead. She was no indian, though, but pure Boston Brahmin, honey-skinned, with big blue wide-apart eyes, a cruel red mouth the same shade as the paintwork of the car, and a heavy mane of yellow hair that she pushed aside from her forehead with a sweep of one slender, pale arm, letting Andy see for a second the delicate blue shadow in her shaved armpit. She felt his hungry eyes on her and gave him a look, amused, mocking, and about a hundred miles distant, a look that said, *Hey, pretty boy, you get yourself a college education, a rich daddy and an income of a couple of hundred grand a year and a car like this one, and who knows? A girl like me might let you buy her a Manhattan some evening over there at the Ritz-Carlton.*

That Saturday he had been out to Cambridge to a used-auto place where there was a Porsche for sale, not a Spyder but a 365. It had looked good, all polished up like a shiny black evil beetle, crouched there among a fleet of chrome-encrusted jalopies, America's finest, but two minutes under the hood had told him it was no good, that someone had driven the heart out of it and that it had probably been in a wreck. Anyway, who did he think he was fooling?—he did not have the dough to buy it even if they offered it to him at a tenth of the asking price. The trip across the river had taken two bus rides there and two back again, and now he was home and in no mood for entertaining callers.

When he turned into Fulton Street, footsore and mad as hell, he saw the Olds parked at the kerb outside the house. It was no Porsche, but it was big and new and shiny, and he had never seen it before. He was looking it over with a critical eye when Claire appeared around the side of the house with a red-haired priest carrying his hat in his hand. Andy did not know why he fixed first of all on the hat, but it was the thing about the priest that he least liked the look of: it was an ordinary black homburg, but there was something about the way that he carried it, holding it by the crown, like a bishop or a cardinal holding that four-cornered red flowerpot thing that they wore saying Mass—he could not remember the name of it but it sounded like the name of a hand-gun, Italian, maybe, but he could not remember that, either, and was irritated all the more. Andy did not like priests. His folks had been Catholics, sort of, and at Easter time his Ma would lay off the gin for the day and take him and the rest of the kids on the bus down to Baltimore to go to High Mass there in the Cathedral of Mary Our Queen. He had hated those trips, the boredom on the Greyhound, the baloney sandwiches that were all they would have to eat until they got home again, and the crowds of fat-cat harps in the cathedral making the place stink of bacon and cabbage, and the crazy-sounding guys chanting and moaning up on the altar in their weird robes that looked like they were made of metal, some sort of silver or gold, with purple letters and crosses and shepherd's crooks embroidered on them, and everyone being so holy it would make you want to puke and muttering along with the prayers in Latin that they did not understand a word of. No, Andy Stafford did not care for priests.

This one was called Harkins, and he was bog-Irish to

the roots of his oily red hair. He shook hands with Andy and meanwhile gave him the once-over, all smiles and stained teeth but the little yellowish-green eyes cold and sharp as a cat's.

'Pleased to meet you, Andy,' he said. 'Claire here was just telling me all about you.' She was, was she? Andy tried to catch her eye but she kept her gaze fixed firmly on the Mick. 'I was just passing,' Harkins went on, 'and thought I'd drop in.'

'Sure,' Andy said. If he had just dropped in, how come Claire was in her best green dress with her hair all done up?

'The baby's going to have a special blessing from the Holy Father,' Claire said brightly. She was still having trouble meeting his eye. What had this sky-pilot been saying to her?

'You going to bring her over there to Italy, are you?' Andy said to Harkins, who laughed, those green eyes of his flickering.

'It'll be a case of Muhammad coming to the mountain,' he said, 'although I'm not sure the Archbishop would appreciate the comparison—His Grace will dispense the blessing on the Pope's behalf.' Andy was about to speak again but the priest turned to Claire, cutting him off, and showing him he was cutting him off. 'I'd best not dally,' he said, 'for I've a few other calls to make.'

'Thanks for dropping in, Father,' Claire said.

Harkins went to the car and opened the door and threw his hat on the passenger seat and got in behind the wheel.

'God bless, now,' he said, and to Andy, 'Keep up the good work!' whatever that was supposed to mean, and slammed the door and started up the engine. Firing on only six cylinders, as Andy heard with satisfaction. As the car pulled away from the kerb—burning oil, too, by the look the exhaust smoke—Harkins lifted a hand from the wheel and made a rapid movement with his fingers, as if he were sketching something—was that a blessing? The Archbishop would have to do better than that.

Andy turned to Claire. 'What'd he want?'

She was still waving goodbye. She shivered, for the day was misty and chill. 'I don't know, really,' she said. 'I guess Sister Stephanus might have asked him to call in.'

'Doesn't trust us, huh?'

She heard what he was really saying—honestly, he was jealous of everyone!—and she sighed and gave him a look. 'He's a priest, Andy. He was just paying a visit.'

'Well, I hope he don't visit too often. I don't like priests in the house. My old Ma always said it was bad luck.'

There were quite a few things Claire could say about Andy's old Ma, if only she dared.

They went round the side of the house and climbed the wooden stairway. Claire told him Mrs Bennett was out. 'She called up to ask if there was anything I needed at the store.' She smiled over her shoulder at him teasingly. 'Of course, I'm sure it was you she was hoping to see.'

He said nothing. He had been watching Cora Bennett. She was no beauty, with that bony face and mean mouth, but she had a good figure, behind the apron she never seemed to take off, and a hungry eye. He had dropped a few enquiring hints as to the whereabouts of Mr Bennett but had got no response. Run off, probably; if he had been dead she would likely have said so—widows tended to be real fond of their late husbands, Andy always found, until someone turned up who looked a candidate to take the sainted one's place.

In the house he walked into the kitchenette, wanting to know what there was for dinner. Claire said she had not thought about it yet, what with Father Harkins visiting and all, and anyway she wished he would say *lunch*, which is what folk ate in the middle of the day, not dinner, which sounded so low-class.

'So *Irish*, I guess you mean,' he said over his shoulder, opening a cupboard door and letting it slam shut again.

'No, that is *not* what I meant, and you know it.' Claire had grown up in a village south of Boston, with picket fences and white-frame houses and a white church spire pointing up past the maples, all of which she seemed to think gave her a right to her New England airs, but he knew what she came from—German hog farmers who had lost their few acres to the banks in the hard times and moved upstate to try their hand at running a feed store until that failed too. Now in the kitchenette she walked up behind him and had him turn to her and took him by the wrists and made him put his arms around her waist, and then laid her fists on his chest and smiled up into his face. 'You know that's not what I meant, Andy Stafford,' she said again, softly, and kissed him lightly on the lips, a bluebird's peck.

'Well,' he said, putting on his slow drawl, 'I guess if there's nothing to eat I'm just going to have to eat *you*.'

He was leaning down to kiss her when he looked past her shoulder and saw the bassinet on the table in the living room, and the blanket in it stirring. 'Shit,' he said, and pushed her away from him and stalked to the table and violently picked up the bassinet by its handles and headed for the baby's room.

'She's asleep!' Claire cried. 'She's . . .'

But he was gone. When he came back he pointed a shaking finger in her face. 'I told you, girl,' he said, in a quiet voice, 'the kid has her own room, and that's where she stays when she's asleep. Right?'

She could see how angry he was: his mouth was twitching at the side and he had that flecked look in his eye. He was still mad over Father Harkins being here—could he really be jealous of a priest? 'All right, honey,' she said, making her voice very slow and calm. 'All right, I'll remember.'

He went to the icebox and got a beer. She could never decide which was more scary, his rages, or the way they suddenly ended, as if nothing had happened. He knocked the cap off the bottle and threw back his head and took a series of long swallows, his adam's apple bobbing in a rhythm that made her think, blushing inside, of being in bed with him.

'That guy,' he said, 'the priest—did he say if what's-her-name spoke to old man Crawford yet?' She looked blank and he waggled the bottle impatiently. 'Sister . . . you know . . .'

'Stephanus?'

'Yeah, her. She said she'd talk to Crawford about a job for me.'

The baby was trying out a few exploratory squeaks, that sounded to Claire like the sounds a blindman would make feeling at something shiny with his fingertips; Andy seemed not to hear. 'I thought,' she said cautiously, 'you weren't interested in other work?'

'I'd kind of like to hear what he has to offer.'

Claire stood, half of her listening anxiously for the baby, who seemed to have changed her mind and gone back to sleep, and the other half considering the possibility of Andy not being on the trucks any more. They would be like an ordinary couple—*normal* was the first word that came to her mind—but it would be the end of their happy nights alone together, just the two of them, her and little Christine.

8

Sarah hated the smell of hospitals, summoning up as it did vivid memories of a childhood tonsillectomy. She could detect the smell even on Mal's clothes, a mixture of ether and disinfectant and what she thought must be bandages, that no number of dry-cleanings could remove. She had never complained or even mentioned it—a fine thing it would be for a doctor's wife to admit she disliked the smell of doctoring!—but he must have seen her once or twice wrinkling her nose, for nowadays he would vanish upstairs to change as soon as he was in the door. Poor Mal, trying to look after everyone, to take care of everything, and getting no thanks. Yet his side of the wardrobe reeked for her of that moment of childhood terror and pain under the doctor's knife.

When she walked into Reception at the Holy Family, carrying her gloves, the smell hit her at once and it was so strong she thought for a moment she would have to turn around and walk out again. But she forced herself forward to the desk and the dragon lady there—why would anyone choose to wear spectacles with pale-pink, translucent frames?—and asked if Dr Quirke might be available. '*Mr* Quirke, is it?' the dragon snapped. Sarah knew of course it should be Mr, and serve her right for her patronising assumption that she would not be understood if she did not ask for him as Dr. She would never master the rules, never.

She sat on a hard bench by the wall and waited. Quirke had told the dragon to say he would come up right away. She watched the usual procession of the halt and the maimed, the accident cases, the bandaged children, the shock-faced old, the mothers-to-be struggling along in the wake of their enormous stomachs, being bullied already by the unborn. She wondered how Mal could face these women, day after day, year after year. Quirke's clients at least were conveniently dead. She chided herself: her thoughts were all of an unrelieved bleakness in these days.

Quirke was loosely gowned in green. He apologised for the delay: one of his assistants was off sick, the place was in chaos. She said it was not important, that she could come back another time, yet wondered silently how there could be such urgency to his work—the dead would stay dead, surely? No, he was saying, no, she must stay, now that she was here. She could see him wondering why she *was* here; Quirke had always been a calculator.

They sat at a plastic-topped table beside a dusty window in the hospital canteen. Down at the serving end there was a counter with rumbling tea urns and glass cases containing triangular sandwiches curled at the tips, and miniature packets of biscuits, and what were called, with what she thought of as stark aptness, rock cakes. Why was it, she wondered idly, when Quirke had gone off to the fetch their tea, that hospitals here were so run-down and dingy and uniformly miserable? The window beside the table where she sat looked out on a blockhouse built of bricks the colour of old blood, the flat roof of which, apparently made of asphalt, sported at one corner a crooked stove-pipe chimney with a cowl, from which smoke was pouring sideways, flattened by the strong October wind. Without her wanting it to, her mind speculated on what in a hospital could require burning that would produce a smoke so dense and black. Quirke returned, bearing mugs of pre-sugared, milky tea, which she knew she would not be able to bring herself to drink. She felt it coming on, that increasingly familiar sense of weakness, of lightness, as if she were somehow floating up out of herself, as if her mind were detaching itself and floating free of her. Was this what they meant in the old books when they spoke of *the vapours*? She wondered how worried she should be about her health. But would not death, she thought, be a solution to so many things? Though she did not really imagine she would escape that easily, or that soon.

'So,' Quirke said, 'I suppose this is about Mal?'

She looked at him searchingly. How much did he know? She wanted to ask, she dearly wanted to ask, but she could not bring herself to speak the words. What if he knew more than she did, what if he was privy to things even more terrible than she had learned of? She tried to concentrate, grasping at her scattering thoughts. What had he asked her? Yes: if it was about Mal that she had come. She decided to ignore this. She said:

'Phoebe wants to marry that young man.' She touched the handle of the mug with her fingertips; it felt slightly sticky. 'It's impossible, of course.'

Quirke frowned, and she could see him readjusting his

thoughts, his strategies: Phoebe, then, not Mal. 'Impossible?' he said.

She nodded. 'And needless to say, there's no talking to her.'

'Tell her to go ahead and do it,' he said. 'Tell her you're all for it. Nothing more likely to put her off the idea.'

She thought it best to disregard this also. 'Would you speak to her?'

He leaned back in the chair and lifted high his head and looked at her along one shallow side of his flattened nose, nodding slowly, grimly. 'I see,' he said. 'You want to persuade me to persuade Phoebe to give up her inconvenient boyfriend.'

'She's so young, Quirke.'

'So were we.'

'She has all her life before her.'

'So had we.'

'Yes,' she said, pouncing, 'and look what mistakes we made!' The fierceness was gone as quickly as it had come. 'Besides, it wouldn't work. They'd make sure of that.'

Quirke raised an eyebrow. 'They? You mean Mal? Would he really want to destroy her happiness?'

She was shaking her head before he had finished speaking, her eyes cast down. 'You don't understand, Quirke. There's a whole world. You can't win with a whole world against you, I know that.'

Quirke looked out of the window. Clouds the colour of watered ink were roiling on the far horizon; it would rain. He was silent a moment, studying her with narrowed eyes. She looked away. 'What is it, Sarah?' he said.

'What?' She tried to be offhand and airy. 'What's what?'

He would not let go; she felt like the quarry borne down on by a single, relentless, huge hound.

'Something's happened,' he said. 'Are you and Mal—?'

'I don't want to talk about Mal,' she said, so fast it might have been not a sentence but a single word. She put her hands on the table before her, beside her gloves, and looked at them. 'Then there's my father,' she said. He waited. She was still frowning at her hands, as if they had suddenly become an object of fascination. 'He's threatened to cut her out of his will.'

Quirke wanted to laugh. Old Crawford's will, no less— what next? Then he had a sudden, unnervingly clear image of horse-faced Wilkins his assistant waiting for him in the lab—Sinclair was having one of his strategic bouts of 'flu— and shivered at this glimpse of the world of the dead, his world.

'What about the Judge?' he said. 'Why not get him to talk to Phoebe, or to Mal—to your father, maybe, too? Surely he'd knock sense into them all and make them solve it?' She gave him a pitying look. He said, 'There will have to be a solution, one way or the other, in the end. I say it again: tell her she can marry him, urge her on. I bet she'll give Bertie Wooster the old heave-ho.'

Sarah would not smile. 'I don't want Phoebe to be tied down in an early marriage,' she said.

He laughed incredulously. 'An early marriage? What's this? I thought it was because Carrington is a Prod?'

She was shaking her head again, her eyes on the table. 'Everything is changing,' she said. 'It will be different in the future.'

'Oh, yes, in a hundred years' time life will be beautiful.'

She shook her head stubbornly. 'It will be different, in the future,' she said again. 'Girls of Phoebe's generation, they'll have a chance to escape, to be themselves, to'—she laughed, embarrassed by what she was about to say—'to live!' She lifted her eyes to his and shrugged one shoulder, abashed. 'I wish you'd speak to her, Quirke.'

He sat forward so abruptly her gloves on the table seemed to shrink back from him, clasping each other. How lifelike they looked, Sarah thought, a pair of black leather gloves. As if some otherwise invisible third person at the table were wringing her hands.

'Listen,' he said impatiently, 'I have no time for that chinless wonder Phoebe has set her heart on, but if she's determined to marry him, then good luck to her.' She made to protest but he held out a hand to silence her. 'However, if you were to ask me to speak to her, for you—not for Mal, or your father, or anyone else, but for you—then I would.'

In the silence they heard the rattle of raindrops blown against the window. She sighed, then rose and picked up her gloves, banishing that other, invisible, anguished sharer of her troubles. As if to herself she said, ruefully, 'Well, I tried.' She smiled. 'Thank you for the tea.' The two mugs stood untouched, a crinkled wafer of scum floating on the faintly quaking surface of the grey liquid. 'I must go.'

'*Ask me*,' Quirke said.

He had not risen, but sat sideways at the table, poised and tense, one hand on the back of his chair and the other flat on the smeared table-top. How could he be so cruel, playing with her always like this?

'You know I can't,' she said.

'Why can't you?'

She gave a laugh of mild exasperation. 'Because I'd be in your debt!'

'No.'

'Yes!' she said, as vehement as he. 'Do it, Quirke. Do it for Phoebe—for her happiness.'

'No,' he said again, flatly. 'For you.'

9

It was Saturday, it was the middle of the afternoon, and Quirke was wondering if he should find another pub to drink in. A dry October storm was sweeping through the streets and he had ducked into McGonagle's with his coat collar up and a newspaper under his arm. The place was almost empty but he had no sooner settled himself in the snug than Davy appeared at the hatch and handed in a glass of whiskey. 'Compliments of the gent in the blue suit,' he said, jerking a thumb behind him towards the bar and giving a sceptical sniff. Quirke put his head out at the door and saw him, perched on one haunch on a stool at the bar: suit of a shiny, metallic blue, horn-rimmed specs, black hair swept back from a lumpy forehead. He lifted his glass to Quirke in a wordless salute and smiled, baring his lower front teeth. He was vaguely familiar, but from where? Quirke drew in his head and sat with his hands on his knees and contemplated the whiskey as if expecting it to foam up suddenly and overflow with rancid whorls of smoke.

After a moment the blue suit appeared in the doorway. 'Mr Quirke,' he said, holding out a hand. 'Costigan.' Quirke gingerly shook the proffered hand, which was square, blunt-fingered and slightly damp. 'We met at the Griffins', the day of the party for the Chief Justice. The day the honour from the Pope was announced?' He pointed to the place beside Quirke. 'May I?'

A coincidence, of a sort: Quirke had been thinking about Sarah, her face like Ophelia's floating up pale but insistent out of the newspaper pages and their quag of reported grim goings-on—the Yanks testing a bigger and better bomb, the Reds rattling their rusty sabres, as usual. He was wondering still why she had come to him at the hospital and what it was exactly that she wanted of him. People seemed forever to be asking him for things, and always just the things he could not give them. He was not the man they took him for, Sarah, and Phoebe, even poor Dolly Moran; he had no help for them.

He often recalled the first unsupervised post-mortem he had performed. He was working in those days with Thorndyke, the State Pathologist, who was already going gaga, and Quirke that day had been called on at short notice to stand in for the old boy. The cadaver was that of a large, silver-haired, antiquated gentleman who had died when the car in which he had been a passenger had skidded on a patch of ice and toppled into a ditch. His daughter had been bringing him back after a day out from the old folks' home where he was living; she was elderly herself, the daughter, and had been driving cautiously because of the freezing conditions, but had lost all control of the machine when it began its sedate slide across the ice. She had escaped without injury, and the car was hardly damaged, but the old boy had died, instantly, as the newspapers liked to put it—who could say, he often asked himself, how long that instant might seem to the one who was doing the dying?—of simple heart failure, as Quirke was able quickly to establish. When the dissecting-room assistant had begun to undress the corpse, with the usual rough adroitness, there had slipped out of the fob of the waistcoat an old and beautiful pocket watch, an Elgin, with Roman numerals and a second hand in an inset dial. It had stopped at five twenty-three exactly, the moment, Quirke was certain, when the old man's heartbeat, too, had stopped, heart and watch giving up the ghost together in sympathetic unison. So it had been with him, he believed, when Delia died: an instrument that he carried at his breast, one that had been keeping him aligned and synchronised with the rest of the world, had stopped suddenly and never started up again.

'A lovely day, that was,' Costigan was saying. 'We were all so happy for the Judge, happy and proud. A papal knighthood, that's a rare honour. I'm a knight myself'—he pointed to a pin in his lapel, in the form of a little gold staff twined about by a gold letter P—'but of a humbler order, of course.' He paused. 'You never thought of joining us, Mr Quirke? I mean the Knights of St Patrick. You've been asked, I'm sure. Malachy Griffin is one of us.'

Quirke said nothing. He found himself fascinated, almost hypnotised, by the steady, omnivorous regard of Costigan's magnified eyes, suspended like two deep-sea creatures in the fishbowl lenses of his spectacles.

'Lovely people, the Griffins,' Costigan went on, un-deterred by Quirke's wordless and resistant stare. 'Of course, you were married into the family, weren't you?'

He waited. Quirke said:

'My wife was Sarah's—Mrs Griffin's—sister.'

Costigan nodded, assuming now an expression of unctuous solemnity. 'And she died,' he said. 'In childbirth, wasn't it? Very sad, a thing like that. It must have been hard for you.'

Quirke hesitated again. Those under-sea eyes seemed to be following his very thoughts. 'It was a long time ago,' he said, maintaining a neutral tone.

Costigan was nodding again. 'Still and all, a hard loss,' he said. 'I suppose the only way to cope with a thing like that would be to try to forget it, to put it out of your mind altogether. Not easy, of course. A young woman dead, a child lost. But life must go on, mustn't it, Mr Quirke?' There was the sense of some large, dark thing stirring soundlessly between them in the little space where they sat. Costigan pointed to the whiskey glass. 'You haven't touched your drink.' He glanced down at another lapel pin, declaring him a member of the Pioneer Total Abstinence Association. 'I'm strictly TT, myself.'

Quirke leaned back on the bench seat. Davy the barman hovered by the serving hatch, polishing a glass and eavesdropping.

'What exactly is it you're saying to me,' Quirke asked, 'Mr . . . What was the name again?'

Costigan ignored the second question, smiling tolerantly, as at a childish ruse. 'I'm saying, Mr Quirke,' he said softly, 'that some things are best forgotten about, best left alone.'

Quirke felt his forehead go hot. He folded the newspaper and clamped it under his arm and stood up. Costigan watched him with what seemed a lively interest and even a touch of amusement. 'Thanks for the drink,' Quirke said. The whiskey sat untasted in the glass. Costigan nodded again, briskly this time, as if something had been said that demanded his assent. He was still seated, but Quirke, towering over him, felt that somehow it was he who was on the inferior level.

'Good luck, Mr Quirke,' Costigan said, smiling. 'I'll see you around, I'm sure.'

In Grafton Street gusts of wind were swooping more strongly than ever and the Saturday-evening shoppers were hurrying homewards with their heads down. Quirke was aware of his quickened breathing and a thick, hot sensation in his chest that was not fear, exactly, but a kind of dawning alarm, as if the smooth, empty little island on which he had been happily perched had given a preliminary heave, and would presently reveal itself to be not dry land at all but the humped back of a whale.

10

Andy Stafford knew he was not the sharpest tool in the box. It was not that he was stupid, but he was no genius, either. This knowledge did not trouble him. In fact, he considered that he was pretty much of a good balance. He had known guys that were all brawn, and one or two that were all brain, and both kinds had been a mess. He was between the two extremes, like the kid standing in the middle of the seesaw, having a good time without the effort of all that swinging up and down. So he just could not understand why it had not struck him, before he had agreed to Claire taking the kid, what the consequences might be for his reputation. It was in Foley's one night that he first heard, behind his back, that particular laugh he would come to hear often, too often.

He had arrived in from a night and most of a day on the road, and had stopped to drink a beer before going home to the house that these days seemed to smell of nothing else but baby things. Foley's was crowded and noisy, as it always was on Friday night. On his way to the bar he passed a table of five or six guys, truckers like him, most of whom he knew, sort of. One of them, a big meaty fellow with sideburns the size of lamb chops, name of

M'Coy, known as Real—ha ha, big joke—said something as he went past, and that was when he heard it, the laugh. It was low, it was dirty, and it seemed to be directed at him. He got his beer and turned and stood with his elbows behind him on the bar and one boot heel hitched on the brass footrail and lazily surveyed the room, not looking at M'Coy's table but not avoiding it either. Be cool, he told himself, be easy. Besides, he did not know the laugh well enough yet to be absolutely sure it was him they had been laughing at. But it was him M'Coy was grinning at, and now he called out:

'Hello, stranger.'

'Hello, M'Coy,' Andy answered. He would not call him Real, it sounded so dumb, even for a nickname, though M'Coy himself was proud of it, as if it really did make him someone special. 'How's it going?'

M'Coy took a drag from his cigarette and shoved his big gut against the table and pushed himself back, and leaned up his face and blew a fan of smoke at the ceiling, settling in for some fun. 'Don't see much of you, these days,' he said. 'Gotten too good for us, now that you've moved out to Fulton Street?'

Easy, Andy told himself again, nice and easy. He shrugged. 'You know how it is,' he said.

M'Coy, grinning wider, gave him a measuring look, while the others at the table, grinning too, waited for what was coming next.

'I was telling the boys here,' M'Coy said, 'I heard you had a miracle over at that new place of yours.'

Andy let a beat or two pass by. 'How's that?' he said, making his voice go soft.

By now M'Coy was almost laughing outright. 'Didn't your old lady have a kid without ever being knocked up?' he said. 'I call that miraculous.'

A heave of suppressed merriment passed along the table. Andy looked at the floor, his lips pursed, then sauntered forward, carrying his beer glass. He stopped in front of M'Coy, who was wearing a checked lumberjack shirt and denim overalls. Andy had gone chill all over, as if he was breaking out in a cold sweat, although his skin was dry. It was a familiar feeling, there was almost a kind of joy in it, and a kind of happy dread that he could not have explained. 'Better watch your mouth, pal,' he said.

M'Coy put on a look of innocent surprise and lifted his hands. 'Why,' he said, 'what'll you do, give me the one you can't give your old lady?'

The others were still scrambling out of the way when Andy with a quick spin of the wrist threw the beer from his glass into M'Coy's face and broke the rim of the glass against the table edge and thrust the crown of jagged spikes against the side of the fat man's fat soft throat. The quiet spread outward from the table like fast, running ripples. A woman laughed and was abruptly silenced. Andy had a clear picture in his head of the barman directly behind him reaching down cautiously for the baseball bat he kept slung on two coat hooks behind the bar.

'Put down the glass,' M'Coy said, trying to sound tough but his eyes showing just how scared he was. Andy was trying to think of something good to say in reply, maybe something about M'Coy not seeming so Real now, when from behind him someone's fist swiped him clumsily along the side of the head, making his ear sing. M'Coy, seeing him stunned, gave a shout of terror and reared away from the spikes of glass, and his chair tipped over and dumped him backwards on the floor, and despite the hurt to his ear Andy almost laughed at the thud of the man's big head as it banged on the boards and the soles of his boots came flying up. There were three or four of them behind him, and he tried to turn and defend himself with the glass but already they had him, one clasping him about the waist from behind while a second one got both hands on his wrist and wrenched it as if it was a chicken that was being choked, and he dropped the glass, not from the pain but from fear that he would gash himself. M'Coy was on his feet again, and advanced now with a shit-eating smile smeared on his fat face and his left fist bunched and lifted—Andy with a sort of dreamy interest was wondering why he had never noticed before that M'Coy was a southpaw—while the others held him fast by the arms so that M'Coy could take leisurely aim and sink the first, sickening punch into his belly.

He came to in a narrow concrete passageway that smelled of sour beer and piss. He was lying on his back, looking up into a strip of sky with stars and rags of flying cloud. He tasted blood and puke. Pains in various parts of his body were competing for his attention. Someone was leaning over him, asking him if he was okay, which seemed to him pretty funny in the circumstances, but he decided not to risk letting himself laugh. It was the barman, Andy could not remember his name, a decent guy, family man, kept the place quiet, mostly. 'You want me to call you a cab?' he asked. Andy said no, and got himself to a sitting position, and then, after a pause, and with the barman's help, succeeded in hauling himself by stages to his feet. He said his truck was out front, and the barman shook his head and said he was crazy to think of driving, that he could be concussed, but he said he was all right, that he should get home, that his wife would be worrying, and the barman—Pete, that was his name, Andy suddenly remembered it, Pete Somebody—showed him a steel door at the end of the passageway that led out into an alley along by the side of the bar to the deserted street and the lot across the way where his rig was parked. The rig looked accusing, somehow, like a big brother who had waited up late for him. His brain seemed swollen a size bigger than his skull, and his stomach muscles where M'Coy had landed that first punch were clenched on themselves like a bagful of fists.

It was midnight when he coasted the rig down Fulton Street and drew to a squeaking stop outside the house. The upstairs was dark, and there was only a faint line of light under the blind in the window of Cora Bennett's bedroom; he suspected lonesome Cora slept with the light on. He got himself down from the cab, jangling all over with pain but feeling still the excitement of the fight, a tingle like foxfire all along his nerves. The fall night air was chill and he had only his windbreaker to wear but he did not feel like going inside yet. He climbed the porch steps, dragging a leg—someone had kicked him on the ankle—and sat down on the swing, careful not to set it going and make the chains creak: he did not want Claire coming down in her night things and fussing over him, not just yet, anyway. His head ached, his left knee as well as his ankle was aching, his mouth was all cut up at one side and a molar there was loose, but he was surprised not to have been more badly hurt. He had done a deal of damage himself, had landed a few good punches, and kicked M'Coy in the nuts and got his thumb up someone's nose and tore it half off, before one of them, he did not see who it was, came up behind him and cracked him over the skull with what must have been a chair leg. He leaned his head back on the swing and eased out a long sigh, holding his aching chest in both hands. It was gusty, and clouds were racing across a sky black and shiny as paint, and the walnut tree at the side of the house was rattling its dry leaves. There was a full moon, peering in and out of the clouds; it looked like M'Coy's grinning fat face. *A miracle*, M'Coy had said. Some miracle. He lit a cigarette.

He was thinking over it all, or thinking at least how much figuring he had to do about it all—it had simply not occurred to him before tonight that everyone would know the kid was not his; how dumb can you be?—when he heard the porch door opening behind him. He did not turn, or move at all, just went on sitting there, looking at the sky and the clouds, and for a moment he saw the whole scene as if from outside it, the windy street, the moonlight coming and going on the yard, the porch all in shadow, and him there, hurting and quiet, and Cora Bennett standing behind him with an old coat pulled on over her nightshirt, saying nothing, only raising her hand slowly to touch him. It was like one of those scenes in a movie when the whole audience knows exactly what is going to happen yet holds its breath in suspense. He did not flinch when her fingers found the knot on his skull where the chair leg had landed. Then, instead of sitting down beside him on the swing, she came round in front of him and knelt down on both knees and put her face close up against his. He smelled the sleep on her breath and the stale remains of the day's face powder. Her hair was untied and hung in trailing strands like a slashed curtain. He flicked the last of his cigarette into the yard, it made a red, spiralling arc. 'You're hurt,' she said, 'I can feel the heat from your face.' She touched with her fingertips the bruises on his jaw and the swollen place at the side of his mouth, and he let her, and said nothing. When she leaned closer still her face framed by her hair was shadowed and featureless. Her lips, cool and dry, were nothing like Claire's, and when she kissed him there was none of Claire's eagerness and anxiety: it was like being kissed in a ceremony, by some kind of official; it was as if something was being sealed. 'Hnn,' she said, drawing away, 'you taste of blood.' He put his hands on her shoulders. He had been wrong: she was not wearing a nightshirt, but was naked under the coat.

It was strange. Cora was, he guessed, ten years older than he was, and her stomach had marks on it that made him guess she must have had a child herself at some time in the past. If so, where was the kid, and where was the kid's father? He did not ask. The only photograph he saw, in a fancy silver frame on the night table beside her bed, was of a dog, a Yorkshire terrier, he thought it was, wearing a bow around its neck and sitting up on its hind legs and grinning with its tongue out. 'That's Rags,' she said, reaching out a bare arm and picking up the frame.

'God, did I love that mutt.' They were sitting on her bed, she at the top end, naked, with a pillow on her lap, and he at the foot, leaning back against the wall, wearing only his shorts and drinking a beer. The bruises on his ankle and knee and all around his ribcage were coming up blue already; he could imagine what his face looked like. The only light was from a shaded lamp on the night table, and in it everything in the room seemed to droop downward, as if the whole place was wilting in the rank heat of the steam radiator humming and hiccuping under the window. He had hardly spoken in the hour he had been here, and then only in a whisper, uneasily aware of his wife's sleeping presence somewhere close overhead. He could see his nervousness amused Cora Bennett. She watched him now with a faint, sceptical smile through the smoke of her cigarette. Her breasts were flat along their fronts, adroop like everything else in the place; they gleamed, amber-coloured in the lamplight; she had pressed his throbbing face between them, and a drop of her sweat had run into his mouth and stung his burst lip. He had never been with a woman as old as she was. There was something excitingly shameful about it; it had been like sleeping with his best friend's mother, if he had a best friend. At the end, when the fierce storm they had whipped up between them was over, she had cradled him against her, nursing his bruised and burning body, as he had sometimes seen Claire hold the child. He could not remember his own mother ever holding him like that, so tenderly.

Then he found himself telling her about his plan, his big plan. He had never spoken of it to anyone else, not even Claire. He sat with his bare back against the bedroom wall, nursing the beer bottle between his knees—the beer was warm by now but he hardly noticed—and laid it all out for her, how he would get hold of a top-class auto, a Caddy or a Lincoln, and set up a limo service. He would borrow the money from old man Crawford, who liked to think of himself as John D. Rockefeller, the help of the working man; he was sure he would have the loan repaid inside a year, with maybe enough over to start thinking of a second limo and another driver. In five years there would be a fleet of cars—he wrote the title on the air with a sweep of a flattened palm: *Stafford Limo Service, A Dream of a Drive*—and he would be sitting behind the wheel of a crimson Spyder 550, driving west. Cora Bennett listened to all this with a thin smile that in any other circumstances would have made him mad. Maybe she thought it was just a truck driver's dream, but there were things she did not know, things he had not told her, for instance that Mother Superior's promise to talk to Josh Crawford about getting him off the trucks and into some other, better-paid work. She had mentioned a taxi cab, but he would never drive a lousy cab. All the same, maybe the nun could fix a meeting for him with Josh Crawford. He was sure he could persuade the old man, one way or another, to advance him the cash. They did not know, Sister What's-her-name or Josh Crawford or any of them, just how much he knew about this thing they had going with the babies. He saw himself at the Crawford place down there in North Scituate, sitting at his ease over a cup of fine tea in a big room with palms and a glass wall, and Josh Crawford before him in his wheelchair with a blanket over his knees, ashen-faced, his hands shaking, as Andy calmly told him how much he had found out about the baby smuggling, and that a check for, say, ten grand would be a great help to him in keeping his mouth shut . . .

Cora Bennett had moved down in the bed and now her foot came out from under the sheet and started trying to wriggle its way into his shorts. He got up and put on his shirt and pants. He was sitting on the end of the bed pulling on his boots when she scrambled to her knees and waded forward and draped herself over his back, the way Claire liked to do, and he could feel her naked breasts and belly pressing against him. 'It's late,' he said, trying not to sound irritated, which he was. She breathed a hot, low laugh into his ear, her hands reaching down to his crotch. He had to admit, she certainly was something. That thin mouth of hers could do some special things, things no one, certainly not Claire, had ever done for him before. She asked when she would see him again but he said nothing, only turned and kissed her quickly and stood up, buckling his belt. 'So long then, Tex,' she said, with that smile again, kneeling there on the bed naked in the lamplight, with those flat breasts, the nipples dark and shiny like his bruises. Tex, she was calling him. He did not think he liked that. It felt as if she was laughing at him.

He went out by the front door and round by the side of the house—something skittered in the boughs of the walnut tree—and hauled himself up the wooden stairs and through the french door. The place was silent, and still there were no lights burning, he was relieved to see. He was bone tired, and his knee and his cut mouth hurt like hell. He limped into the bedroom, making hardly a sound, but of course Claire woke up. She raised herself on an elbow and peered at the luminous hands of the clock beside her. 'It's late,' she said, 'where were you?' and he said, 'Nowhere,' and she said his voice sounded funny, and when he did not answer she switched on the lamp. When she saw his cut mouth and the swelling on his cheekbone she jumped up from the bed like she had been scalded, and then there was the usual palaver. What happened? Who did it? Was there a fight? He stood motionless in the middle of the floor, arms hanging and eyes cast down, waiting for her to finish. Did women really feel all this stuff, he wondered, or were the fluttering and squeaking and hand-wringing just their way of getting through the first minute of a crisis while they figured out what to do? She soon calmed down and went off to the bathroom and came back with wads of cotton wool and Lysol or something and warm water in an enamelled bowl. She made him sit down on the side of the bed and began dabbing at him with the disinfectant, which stung. He thought of Cora Bennett, lying below in the dull yellow light of the lamp beside her bed, and his anger flared again. He felt weakened, as if he had let her take something away from him, something inside him that no one should ever even be let see. Yet what angered him most was not the memory of what they had done together in her bed and how it might have affected him, but the fact that he had told her his plan for Stafford Limos.

'What happened?' Claire said again, calm now that she had something to be busy at. 'Tell me,' she said, almost commanding, 'tell me what you were fighting about.'

She was standing over him, pressing a pad of wet cotton against his face; he could feel the blanket-warmth of her body. Her hands were capable and strong, surprisingly strong for such a skinny girl. He was being, he realised, mothered, for the second time that night, but how differently this time, with none of Cora's hot tenderness. Claire put her hand to the back of his head to make him sit steady and pressed the swelling there and he flinched. Suddenly it came to him, out of nowhere, that it was not one of M'Coy's buddies who had whacked him with a chair leg, but the barman, Pete the goddamned barman, with his baseball bat! He recalled him in the passageway, a tough little harp with a boxer's nose, leaning over him and asking him if he was okay. Of course, it had to have been him: he would naturally have sided with M'Coy and the others. Andy clenched his fists on his knees. Somehow this betrayal was the thing that made him most angry now, angrier even than he had been when he broke the beer glass and stuck it at M'Coy's throat. He could just see Pete, the little bastard, sidling out from behind the bar and taking up a batter's stance, hefting the bat in his hands, waiting for just the right moment to give it to him across the back of the head. Well, he would get his, would Pete: some night at closing time after he had locked up and was stepping out by that steel door into the alley on his way home to his harp wife and his harp kids Andy would be there, waiting for him, with a tyre iron—

Claire had taken the cotton pad away from his forehead and was leaning down to look into his face. 'What is it, Andy?' she said. 'What's wrong?'

He stood up quickly, a red flare of pain exploding in his gut, and pushed her aside and limped to the window. 'What's wrong?' he said, with a furious laugh. 'What's *wrong*? Half of goddamned Boston is laughing behind my back—that's what wrong. Andy Stafford, the poor schmuck who can't get it up!'

Claire gave a little mousey cry. 'But that's . . .' She faltered. 'How can they say that?

He glared out at the walnut tree where it stood shivering in the wind. She knew, he had heard it in her voice, she knew what they had been saying about him; she had known all along how it would be, how they would talk about it, and distort it, and laugh at him behind his back, and she had not warned him. For all his anger there was a part of him that was ice cold, standing off to the side, calculating, judging, thinking what to do next, thinking what to think next. It had always been like this with him, first the rage and then the icy chill. He thought of Cora Bennett again and another wave of anger and resentment rolled over him, resentment at Cora, at Claire and the baby, at this house, at South Boston, at his job, right back all the way to Wilmington and his lowlife family, his old man who was not much more than a hobo and his mother in her brown apron like Cora Bennett's, smelling of cheap booze and menthol cigarettes at nine o'clock in the morning. He wanted to put his fist through this window pane, he could almost feel it, the glass smashing, slicing his flesh, cutting down to the clean, white bone.

Claire was so quiet behind him he had almost forgotten she was there. Now in that little-girl voice that set his teeth on edge she said:

'We could try again. I could see another doctor—'

'—Who'll tell you the same thing the other one did.' He had not turned from the window. He gave a bitter laugh. 'I should do up a sign to hang it round my neck. *It's not me, folks, I'm not the dud one!'*

He heard her quick intake of breath, and was glad.

'I'm sorry,' she whispered.

'Yeah,' he said. 'I'm sorry, too. Sorry I ever let you persuade me to take in that kid. Whose is it, anyway? Some Irish whore's, I suppose.'

'Andy, don't . . .' She came and stood behind him and put up a hand to massage the back of his neck, as he sometimes let her do. Now he jerked his head away, and then was sorry he had, but only because of the pain, which had a liquid feel, as if his skull was filled part-way to the top with some sluggish, oily stuff that swayed sickeningly at every sudden movement he made. A car passed by in the street, going slowly, its headlights dimmed; a Studebaker, light green, it looked to be, with a white top. Who would be driving down this street at four in the morning? 'Come to bed,' Claire said softly, her voice heavy with weariness, and he turned, suddenly exhausted, and followed her meekly. As he was taking off his shirt he wondered if she would smell Cora Bennett on him, and realised he did not care, not at all.

11

Quirke did not consider himself to be a brave man, maybe not even a courageous one. The fact was, his physical courage or otherwise had never been tested, and he had always assumed it never would be. Wars, murders, violent robberies, assaults with blunt instruments, the newspapers were full of such things, but they seemed to take place elsewhere, in a sort of parallel world ruled and run by a different, more violent, altogether more formidable and vicious species of human being than the ones he normally encountered. True, casualties from this other place of strife and blood-letting were brought to his expert attention all the time—often it seemed to him that he was in a field hospital far behind the front line, a hospital to which never the wounded but only the dead were delivered—but it had not occurred to him that one day he might himself be wheeled into the dissecting room on a trolley, bloodied and broken, like poor Dolly Moran.

When the two toughs materialised behind him out of the fog that autumn evening he knew at once that they were from that other world, the world that up to now he had only read about in the papers. They had an air of jaunty relentlessness; they would stick at nothing, these two. Early rage or hurt or unlovedness had hardened for them into a kind of indifference, a kind of tolerance, almost, and they would beat or maim or blind or kill without rancour, going about their workaday task methodically, thinking of something else. They had a smell, flat, sweetish yet stale, which was familiar to Quirke but which for the moment he could not place. He had stopped on the corner of Fitzwilliam Street to light a cigarette and suddenly they were there, on either side of him, the thin, red-faced one on his left, on his right the fat one with the large head. The thin one grinned and touched a finger to his forehead in a sort of salute. He looked uncannily like Mr Punch, with those chafed red cheeks and a nose so hooked the sharp tip of it almost touched his lower lip.

''Evening, Captain,' he said.

Quirke glanced from one of them to the other and without a word set off swiftly across the road. The two came with him, still to right and left, keeping pace effortlessly, even the fat one, whose globular head was prodigiously huge and set with tiny eyes like glass beads; his coarse hair hung about his face like the strings of a mop; he was Judy to the other's Mr Punch. Quirke commanded himself not to hurry, and to walk as normal—but what was normal? In a conversational tone the red-faced one said:

'We know you.'

His fat friend agreed. 'That's right, we do.'

Gaining the corner of Mount Street Quirke halted. Office workers were passing by, hunched against the misty air—*witnesses*, Quirke thought, *innocent bystanders*—but Punch and Judy seemed oblivious of them.

'Look,' Quirke said, 'what do you want? I have no money on me.'

This seemed to amuse Mr Punch greatly. He leaned his head forward to look past Quirke at fat Judy.

'He thinks we're beggars,' he said.

Fat Judy laughed and shook his huge head incredulously.

Quirke thought it necessary to maintain an air merely of irritation and exasperated bafflement; after all, he was a citizen returning home from work, and this impudent pair were keeping him from the blameless pleasures of the evening. He looked about. The twilight was much further advanced than it had been a minute ago, and the fog was much more dense.

'Who are you?' he demanded. He had aimed for righteous indignation but it came out sounding merely peevish.

'We're a caution,' Mr Punch said, 'that's what we are,' and he laughed again, pleased with himself; pleased as Punch.

Quirke gave an angry grunt and threw away his cigarette—he had forgotten about it, and it had gone out—and strode off along the pavement in the direction of his flat. It was like the moment in McGonagle's that day after he had realised the true import of what Costigan had said to him: he was not exactly frightened, being in a public place and so near to home and shelter, but he had a sense of something being about to shift enormously and send him sprawling. All efforts at flight seemed unavailing, as in a dream, for no matter how he hastened, still Punch and Judy easily kept pace with him.

'We've seen you, hanging around,' Mr Punch said. 'Not advisable, in this sort of weather.'

'You could get a cold,' the fat one said.

Punch nodded, his hooked nose going up and down like a sickle.

'You could catch your death,' he said. He glanced past Quirke at his companion again. 'Couldn't he?'

'You're right,' fat Judy said. 'Catch his death, definitely.'

They came to the house and Quirke halted; only with an effort did he keep himself from scampering up the steps.

'This your gaff?' Mr Punch asked him. 'Nice.'

Quirke wondered wildly if the two intended to come inside with him, to climb the stairs and elbow their way through the door into the flat and . . . and what? By now he really was afraid, but his fear was a kind of lethargy, hampering all thought. What should he do? Should he turn and run, should he burst into the hall and shout for Mr Poole to call the police? At that moment the two at last moved away from him, stepping backwards, and the red-faced Mr Punch made that salute again, tipping a finger to his forehead, and said, 'So long, then, Captain, we'll be seeing you,' and suddenly they were gone, into the gloom and the fog, leaving behind only the faintest trace of their smell, which Quirke at last identified. It was the smell, stale, flat, spicily sweet, of old blood.

He woke with a shock to the shrilling of the doorbell. He had fallen asleep in an armchair beside the gas fire. He had dreamed of being pursued through a version of the city he had never seen before, down broad, busy avenues and under stone arcades, through sunlit pleasure gardens with statues and fish ponds and crazily elaborate topiary. He did not see his pursuers but knew that he knew them, and that they were relentless and would not stop until they had run him down. When he woke he was sprawled in the chair with his head askew and his mouth open. He had kicked off his shoes and peeled off his socks. A spill of rain clattered against the window. He squinted at his watch and was surprised to find that it was not yet midnight. The bell rang again, two sustained, angry bursts. He could hear not only the sound of the bell but the electric whirring of the little clapper as it vibrated, beating on the metal dome. *Why arcades? Why topiary?* Widening his eyes and blinking, he got himself up and went to the window and drew up the sash and put his head out into the tempestuous night. The fog was gone and all was wind and rain now. Below, Phoebe stood in the middle of the road, clutching herself about the shoulders. She was wearing no coat.

'Let me in!' she cried up at him. 'I'm drowning!'

He fetched a key from a bowl on the mantelpiece and dropped it down to her. It spun through the darkness, flashing, and rang on the roadway with a money sound, and she had to scramble to retrieve it. He shut the window and went and stood in the doorway of the flat and waited for her, not willing to go down and risk an encounter with the unsleeping Mr Poole. The yoke of his shirt had got wet when he leaned out of the window and was damp across his shoulders. It made a pleasant coolness, and his bare feet too were cool. He heard the front door open and a moment later a faint breath of the night came up the stairs and wafted against his face. He always found affecting the air's little movements, draughts, breezes, the soughing of wind in trees; he was, he realised, still half in a dream. There were voices briefly below—that would be Poole accosting Phoebe—then the sound of her uneven footsteps ascending. He went down to the return to meet her. He watched her rise towards him, a Medusa head of wet hair and a pair of naked, glistening shoulders; she was barefoot, like him, and carried a shoe dangling from each hand, hooked by a back strap on an index finger, and had her purse under her arm. She wore a frock of midnight-blue satin. She was very wet. 'For God's sake,' Quirke said.

She had been to a party. A taxi had brought her here. She thought she must have left her coat behind. 'The fact is,' she said, moulding her lips with difficulty around the words, 'I'm a bit drunk.'

He walked her to the sofa, the satin of her dress rustling wetly, and made her sit. She looked about, smiling inanely.

'For God's sake, Phoebe,' he said again, wondering how he might get rid of her, and how soon.

He went down to the bathroom on the return and fetched a towel and came back and dropped it in her lap. She was still gazing about her blearily. 'I'm seeing two of everything!' she said, in proud delight.

'Dry your hair,' he said. 'You're ruining the furniture.'

She spoke with her head inside the towel. 'I'm only wet because you left me standing out there so long. Plus the fact that I got out of the cab in Lower Mount Street by mistake.'

He went into the bedroom in search of something for

her to wear. When he returned to the living room she had dropped the towel to the floor, and sat blinking and frowning, more of a gorgon than ever, with her towelled hair standing on end.

'Who was that man downstairs?' she said.

'That would be Mr Poole.'

'He was wearing a bow-tie.'

'He does.'

'He asked me did I know where I was going. I said you were my uncle. I think he didn't believe me.' She snickered. 'Oo,' she said, 'I have a drip,' and wiped her nose on the back of her hand. Then she asked for a drink.

He went into the kitchen and filled the coffee machine and put it on the gas to brew. He laid out a tray with cup, sugar, milk jug. 'Where was this party?' he called to her.

Her answer came back muffled. 'None of your business.'

He went and glanced through the crack of the kitchen door into the living room but drew back when he saw her standing in her underwear with her arms lifted, pulling the blue frock over her head. She had the slightly thick waist of the Crawford girls, her mother and her aunt, and their long, shapely legs. The coffee was rumbling in the pot but he delayed a while before he brought it in, waiting for her to be finished changing.

He carried the tray into the living room. Phoebe, wearing the pullover and clownishly outsized slacks he had given her, was fiddling with the wooden manikin.

'Stop that,' he said sharply. She let her hands fall from the doll but did not turn, and stood with her head bowed and her arms hanging at her side, herself a slack-stringed marionette. 'Come on,' he said, less sharply, 'here's your coffee.' She turned then and he saw the big, childish tears sliding down her cheeks. He sighed, and put the tray on the floor in front of the sofa and went and took her, gingerly, in his arms. Limply she allowed herself to be held, and put her face against his shoulder and said something. 'What?' he said, trying to keep the harsh edge from his voice—how was it that women, all women, wept so much? 'I can't hear you.'

She drew away from him and spoke through burbling sobs. 'They won't let me marry him! They won't let me marry Conor Carrington!'

He turned from her and crossed to the fireplace and took a cigarette from the antique silver box on the mantelpiece. The box had been a wedding present from Sarah and Mal.

'They say I can't marry him because he's a Protestant!' Phoebe cried. 'They say I'm not to see him any more!'

His lighter was empty of fuel; he patted his pockets; he had used his last match to light the gas fire. He went to the marble-topped sideboard where there was a copy of yesterday's *Evening Mail* and tore a strip from the bottom of a page, revealing a theatre advertisement on the page underneath. He returned and lit the slip from the gas-flame. His hands were quite steady, quite steady. The cigarette tasted stale; he must remember to put fresh ones in the box.

'Well?' Phoebe said behind him in consternation, indignantly. 'Are you not going to say anything?'

Punch and Judy, the advertisement had said, *the new hit comedy!—last three performances!* Oh, Mr Punch, what have you done?

'Tell me what you'd like me to say,' he said.

'You could pretend to be shocked.'

She had stopped crying, and gave a great sniff. She had not expected much from him in the way of support but she had thought he would at least be sympathetic. She studied him with an indignant eye. He looked even more remote than usual from the things around him. He had lived in this flat for as long as she remembered—when she was a child her mother used to bring her with her on visits here, as a chaperone, she had suspected even then—but he seemed no more at home in it now than he had in those days. Padding barefoot about the floor, all shoulders and little feet and big, broad back, he had the look of some wild animal, a bear, maybe, or an impossibly beautiful, blond gorilla that had been captured a long time ago but still had not come to understand that it was in a cage.

She went and stood beside him, facing the fireplace, with her elbows resting on the high mantelpiece, which he was leaning back against. She was not drunk any more—she had not really been drunk in the first place, but had wanted him to think she was—only sleepy, and sad. She studied the framed photographs on the mantelpiece.

'Aunt Delia was so lovely,' she said. 'Were you there when . . . ?' Quirke shook his head. He did not look at her. His profile, she thought, was like the profile of an emperor on an old coin. 'Tell me,' she urged softly.

'We had a fight,' he said, flat and matter-of-fact and a touch impatient. 'I went out and got drunk. Then I was in the hospital, holding her hand, and she was dead. She was dead, and I was still drunk.'

She went back to studying the photographs in their expensive silver frames. She touched the one of the foursome in their tennis whites, tracing their faces with a fingertip: her father, and Sarah, and Quirke, and poor, dead Delia, all of them so young, smiling, and fearless-seeming. She said:

'They looked really alike, didn't they, even for sisters, Mummy and Aunt Delia? Your two lost loves.' To that he would say nothing, and she shrugged, tossing her head, and walked to the sideboard and picked up the newspaper and pretended to read it. 'Of course,' she said, 'you don't care that they won't let me marry him, do you?'

She threw down the paper and crossed to the sofa and sat down and folded her arms angrily. He came and knelt on one knee and poured the coffee for her. 'I meant a real drink,' she said, and turned her face away from him in childish refusal. He replaced the coffee pot on the tray and went and took another cigarette and then tore another spill from the newspaper—tore the theatre advertisement itself, this time—and leaned down and touched it to the gas-flame.

'Do you remember Christine Falls?' he said.

'Who?'

She made it into a rebuff. She still would not look at him.

'She worked for your mother for a while.'

'You mean Chrissie the maid? The one that died?'

'Do you remember her?'

'Yes,' shrugging. 'I think Daddy was soft on her. She was pretty, in a washed-out sort of way. Why do you ask?'

'Do you know what she died of?' She shook her head. 'A pulmonary embolism. Know what that is?'

Things were stirring in him like mud at the bottom of

a well. Who had sent those two thugs to frighten him? *We're a caution, that's what we are.*

'Something to do with the lungs?' Phoebe said. Her voice was growing drowsy. 'Did she have TB?'

She drew up her legs beside her on the sofa and lay down and leaned her cheek on a cushion. She sighed.

'No,' Quirke said. 'It's when a blood clot finds its way into the heart.'

'Mnn.'

'Saw a remarkable case of it only the other day. Old chap, bedridden for years. We opened him up, sliced along the pulmonary artery, and there it was, thick as your thumb and a good nine inches long, a huge great rope of solid blood.' He paused, and glanced at her, and saw that she had fallen asleep, with the curtness of youth. How frail and vulnerable she looked, in his ragged pullover and corduroy bags. He took a rug that was folded on the back of the armchair by the fireplace and draped it over her carefully. Without opening her eyes she drew in a quivery breath and rubbed a finger vigorously under her nose and mumbled something and settled down again, snuggling into the warmth of the rug. Quirke returned to the fireplace and stood with his back against the mantelpiece again and contemplated her. Although he tried to resist it, the thought of Christine Falls and her lost child entered his mind like a knife blade being forced between a door frame and a locked door. Christine Falls, and Mal, and Costigan, and Punch and Judy . . . 'Mind you,' he said softly to the sleeping girl, 'that's not what poor Chrissie died of at all, a pulmonary embolism. That's only what your daddy, who was soft on her, wrote in her file.'

He went to the window on which it was his habit never to draw the curtains. The rain had stopped; when he put his face close to the glass he could see a speeding moon and the livid undersides of clouds lit by the lights of the city. He glanced again at Phoebe, and went and opened the sequined purse she had left on the table and found in it the calf-bound red address book he had given her on her last birthday and riffled through the pages; then he went to the telephone and picked up the receiver and dialled.

He was still at the window when Conor Carrington arrived, and he opened the window and dropped the key down to him, too, before he could ring the bell, for even from three floors away Mr Poole, unlike his wife, had the hearing of a bat. Phoebe, on the couch, was still asleep. He had draped her things, her frock, her slip, her stockings, on a chair in front of the gas fire to dry. He had to shake her hard by the shoulder before she would wake up, and when she did she looked at him hare-eyed in terror and seemed as if she would leap from under the rug and take to her heels.

'It's all right,' he said brusquely. 'Young Lochinvar has come to rescue you.'

He gathered her clothes from the chair while she got herself upright and sat a moment with her head hanging and then rose shakily to her feet. Licking her lips, which were dry from sleep, she took the bundle of clothes in her arms and let him steer her towards the bedroom.

Conor Carrington was, Quirke noted, the kind of person who enters sideways through a doorway, slipping rather than stepping in. He was tall and sinuous with a long, pale face and the hands, slender and pliant and white, of the phthisic heroine of one of the more mournfully romantic novels of the Victorian era. Or at least that was the view of him Quirke took in his jaundiced fashion. In reality, Quirke had to admit, Carrington was a goodlooking if somewhat meagre young man. In his turn Carrington obviously disapproved of Quirke, but he was, too, Quirke could see, not a little nervous of him. He wore a shortie tweed overcoat over a dark, pinstriped suit that would have been worthy of the man who was not now, it seemed, likely to be his father-in-law, and carried a trilby hat, holding it by the curled brim in the fingers of both hands; he had the look, Quirke thought, of a man arriving unwillingly at the wake of someone with whom he had been barely acquainted. He handed the door key to Quirke, who also took the trilby from him, noting the hesitancy with which the young man relinquished it, as if he feared he might not get it back.

Entering the living room, on the bias, again, Carrington glanced about enquiringly, and Quirke said:

'She'll be ready in a minute.'

Carrington nodded, pursing lips that were unexpectedly full and rosy-tinted; a hand-reared boy. 'What happened?' Carrington asked.

'She was at a party, not with you, evidently. You should keep a closer eye on her.' Quirke pointed to the tray on the floor. 'Cup of coffee? No? Just as well—it'll be cold by now. Cigarette?' Again the young man shook his head. 'No vices at all, eh, Mr Carrington? Or may I call you Conor? And you can call me Mr Quirke.'

Carrington would not take off his coat. 'Why did she come here?' he said peevishly. 'She should have phoned me. I waited up all evening.'

Quirke turned aside to hide his curled lip; what time was the fellow usually in the habit of going to bed at? He said:

'She tells me they won't let her marry you.' Carrington stared at him. They appeared to be of almost an equal height, the broad man and the slim, but that was only, Quirke thought with satisfaction, because he was barefoot. 'They don't like your crowd, I'm afraid,' he said.

Carrington's brow had taken on a pinkish sheen. 'My crowd?' he said, and delicately cleared his throat.

Quirke shrugged; he saw no profit in continuing along that line. He said:

'Have you actually popped the question?'

Again Carrington had to cough softly into his fist. 'I don't think we should be having this conversation, Mr Quirke.'

Quirke shrugged. 'You're probably right,' he said.

Phoebe came in from the bedroom. At the sight of her Conor Carrington raised his eyebrows and then frowned. Her hair was still kinked from the rain and the skirts of her frock clung damply to her legs. In one hand she carried her stockings, which were still greyly wet at heel and toe, and in the other her high-heeled slingback shoes; Quirke's corduroy trousers were draped over her arm. 'What are you doing here?' she said.

Carrington gave her back a baleful look. 'Mr Quirke telephoned me,' he said. It came out flat and ineffectual-sounding. He dropped his voice to a huskier level. 'Come on, I'll take you home.'

'Oh, will you, now?'

'Please, Phoebe,' he said to her, in a brusque, reproving murmur.

Quirke had positioned himself by the fireplace again and was regarding each in turn, like a spectator at a tennis match. He said:

'I'd put her in a taxi, if I were you, old boy. Won't go down too well *chez* Griffin when you pull up in the old roadster at three in the morning with Honoria Glossop here slumped beside you drunk and singing.'

Phoebe gave him a quick, sly, complicitous smile.

'Come on,' Carrington said to Phoebe, his voice shrill again and a little desperate, 'put on your shoes.'

But Phoebe was already putting them on, standing unsteadily stork-like on one leg with the other crossed and supported on her knee, her face going through contortions of discomfort and vexedness as she worked her foot into the wetly resistant leather. Carrington took off his overcoat and laid it over her shoulders, and Quirke, despite himself, was touched by the tender solicitude of the gesture. Where was it Carrington was from—Kildare? Meath? Rich land down there, rich heritage. Probably when he had played at the law for a few years he would return happily to tend the ancestral acres. True, he was young now, but that would be remedied presently. There were, Quirke considered, worse choices that Phoebe could make.

'Conor,' he said. The couple stopped and glanced back in unison, two clear, young, expectant faces. Quirke lifted an admonishing finger. 'You should fight them,' he said.

12

QUIRKE HAD ARRANGED to meet Barney Boyle at Baggot Street bridge. They strolled along the tow-path where Quirke had walked with Sarah that Sunday that seemed so long ago now. It was morning, and a vapid sun was struggling to shine through the November mist, and there was a ghostly silence everywhere, as if the two men were alone in all the city. Barney wore a black overcoat that reached almost to his heels; beltless and buttonless, it swirled about his short fat legs like a heavy cloak as he toddled along. Outdoors, in daylight, he had a slightly dazed and bashful air. He said it was a long time since he had seen the world in the morning, and that in the interval there had been no improvement at all that he could make out. He coughed raucously. 'Too much fresh air for you,' Quirke said. 'Here, have a cigarette.' He struck a match and Barney leaned forward and cupped a babyish fist around the flame, his fingertips touching the back of Quirke's hand, and Quirke was struck as he always was by this peculiar little act of intimacy, one of the very few allowed among men; it was rumoured, he recalled, that Barney had an eye for the boys.

'Ah, Jesus,' Barney breathed, blowing a trumpet of

smoke into the mist, 'that's better.' Barney, the people's poet and playwright of the working class, in fact lived, despite those rumours of queer leanings, with his long-suffering wife, a genteel watercolourist and something of a beauty, in a venerable white-walled house in leafy Donny-brook. But he still had his contacts in the old, bad world that had produced him. Quirke wanted information and Barney had been, as he put it, asking around the place.

'Oh, all the brassers knew Dolly Moran,' he said. Quirke nodded. Brassers were whores, he assumed, but how? Brass nails, rhyming with tails, or was it something to do with screws? Barney's slang seemed all of his own making. 'She was the one they went to when they were in trouble.'

'What sort of trouble?'

'Up the pole—you know.'

'And she'd fix it for them? Herself?'

'They say she was a dab hand with the knitting needle. Didn't charge, either, apparently. Did it for the glory.'

'Then how did she live?'

'She was well provided for. That's the word, anyway.'

'Who by?'

'Party or parties unknown.'

Quirke frowned ahead into the mist.

'Look at them fuckers,' Barney said, stopping. Three ducks were paddling through the sedge, uttering soft quacks of seeming complaint. 'God, I hate them yokes.' He brightened. 'Did I ever tell you the one about my Da and the ducks?'

'Yes, Barney, you did. Many times.'

Barney pouted. 'Oh, well, excuse me.' He had finished his cigarette. 'Will we go for a pint?' he said.

'For God's sake, Barney, it's eleven o'clock in the morning.'

'Is it? Jesus, we better hurry up, then.'

They went to the *47* on Haddington Road. They were the only customers at that hour. The stale stink of last night's cigarette smoke still hung on the sleepy air. The barman in shirtsleeves and braces leaned on his elbows on the bar reading the sports pages of yesterday's *Independent*. Barney ordered a bottle of porter and a ball of malt to chase it. The porter reek and the stinging scent of the whiskey made Quirke's nostrils flinch.

'And the pair that came after me,' he said, 'did you manage to find out anything about them?'

Barney lifted his baby's little red mouth from the rim of his glass and wiped a fringe of sallow froth from his upper lip. 'The one with the nose sounds like Terry Tormey, brother of Ambie Tormey's that used to be with the Animal Gang.'

Quirke looked at him. 'Ambie?'

'Short for Ambrose—don't ask me.'

'And the other one?'

'Name of Callaghan—is it Callaghan? No: Gallagher. Bit slow, not the full shilling. Dangerous, though, when he gets going. If it's the same fellow.'

Now he lifted the whiskey glass with a dainty flourish, a stiff little finger stuck out, and drank off the whiskey in one gulp, grimaced, sucked his teeth, set down the glass and looked at the barman. '*Arís, mo bhuachalín*,' he said. Slow-moving, mute, the barman poured another go of the amber liquor into a pewter measure and emptied it, tinkling, into the tumbler. The two watched in silence the little ceremony, and Quirke paid. Barney told the barman to leave the bottle. He said, 'I'd rather a bottle in front of me than a frontal lobotomy,' and gave Quirke a quick, shy, sideways glance; by now all Barney's jokes were second-hand. The thought came to Quirke: *He's Falstaff grown inconvenient*, which did not, he knew, make himself the King. He ordered what was called a coffee, hot water and a dollop of tarry syrup from a square bottle: *Irel, the Irish Coffee!* He stirred into the brew three heaping spoonfuls of sugar. *What am I doing here?* he asked himself, and Barney, as if he had read his mind, turned on him a quizzical eye and said, in his Donnybrook voice: 'Bit out of your depth here, aren't you, Quirke? Terry Murphy and his loony pal, that crowd—Dolly Moran that got murdered. What are you up to?'

It was another misty morning when Quirke, in his black coat and carrying his hat, stepped out of the front door of the house in Mount Street and encountered Detective Inspector Hackett, also hatted and in his policeman's gaberdine, loitering on the footpath, smoking a cigarette. At the sight of the policeman, with his big flat face and deceptively affable smile, Quirke's heart gave a guilty joggle. Three young nuns on high black bicycles went past, three sets of shrouded legs churning demurely in unison. The wettish morning air reeked of smoke and the fumes of car exhausts. It was winter, Quirke gloomily reflected, and he was on his way to cut up corpses.

'Good morning, Mr Quirke,' the detective said heartily, dropping the last of his cigarette and squashing it under his boot. 'I was just passing, and thought I might catch you.'

Quirke descended the steps with measured tread, putting on his hat. 'It's half past eight,' he said, 'and you were just passing.'

Hackett's smile broadened into a lazy grin. 'Ah, sure, I've always been an early riser.'

They fell in step and turned in the direction of Merrion Square.

'I suppose,' Quirke said, 'you used to be up at five to milk the cows when you were a boy.'

Hackett chuckled. 'Now, how did you know that?'

Quirke, thinking to get away, was covertly scanning the street for a taxi. He had been in McGonagle's the night before and did not trust himself or know what he might be led into saying, and Hackett was at his most insinuatingly friendly. But there were no taxis. At Fitzwilliam Street they found themselves among a crowd of mufflered office workers making their way towards Government Buildings. Hackett was lighting another cigarette. He coughed, and Quirke closed his eyes briefly at the sound of the strings of mucus twanging in the fellow's bronchioles.

'Have there been any developments in the Dolly Moran case?' Quirke asked.

For a moment Hackett was silent and then began to laugh wheezily, his shoulders shaking. The tall, high-windowed house-fronts seemed to peer down upon him in surprise and cold disapproval. 'Ah, God, Mr Quirke,' he said, with rich enjoyment, 'you must go to the pictures an awful lot.' He lifted his hat and with the heel of the same hand wiped his brow and resettled the hat at a sharper angle. 'Developments, now—let me see. We have a full set of fingerprints, of course, and a couple of locks of hair. Oh, and a cigarette butt—Balkan Sobranie, I recognised the ash straight away—and a lucky monkey's paw dropped by a person of Oriental origin, a Lascar, most likely.' He grinned, showing the tip of his tongue between his teeth. 'No, Mr Quirke, there have been no developments. Unless, of course, you'd call it a development that I've been directed to drop the investigation.' Quirke stared at him and he tapped a finger to the side of his nose, still smiling. 'Orders from on high,' he said softly.

Before them was the domed bulk of the parliament building; it had to Quirke's eye suddenly a malignant aspect, squatting behind its gates, a huge stone pudding.

'What do you mean,' he said, and swallowed—'what do you mean, orders from on high?'

The detective only shrugged. 'Just what I say.' He was looking at his boots. 'You're on your own, Mr Quirke, in the matter of Dolly Moran, deceased. If there are to be *developments in the case*, as you call them, then somebody else will have to do the developing, I'm afraid.'

They came to the corner of Merrion Street. From across the road the policeman guarding the parliament gates was eyeing them with lax curiosity where they had halted in the midst of the morning crowd of functionaries and typists hurrying to their desks. He had probably recognised Hackett, Quirke thought, for Hackett was famous in the Force.

'I wonder, Mr Quirke, have you anything you might want to tell me?' the detective said, squinting off to the side. 'For the fact is, you seem to me a man burdened with a secret.' He swivelled his eyes and fixed them on Quirke's face. 'Would I be right?'

'I've told you all I know,' Quirke said, sounding almost sulky, and looked away.

'Because here's the thing,' Hackett went on. 'Before I was called off the case—and maybe, for all I know, it was the reason I was called off it—I discovered that Dolly Moran used to work for the family of Chief Justice Griffin himself. It's something you omitted to mention, when we had our little talk at the hospital that day, but I'm sure it just slipped your mind. Anyway, now here you are, that used to be married into that same family, asking after developments in the investigation of Dolly's murder. Not at all elementary, I'd say, Dr Quirke. Eh?' He smiled. 'But I'll let you get on to your work, now, for I'm sure you're a busy man.' He made to move away, stopped, turned back. 'By the bye,' he said in a conversational tone, 'did Dolly Moran mention anything to you about the Mother of Mercy Laundry?' Quirke shook his head. 'Place up in Inchicore. They take in girls that have got themselves in trouble and work them till they've—what's the word? —expiated their sin. There was some talk of Dolly Moran being connected with the place. I had a word with the head nun up there, but she swore she'd never heard of anyone of that name. I'm ashamed to say I was almost inclined to disbelieve the holy woman.'

Quirke cleared his throat. 'No,' he said, 'Dolly didn't say anything about a laundry. In fact, she said very little. I think she didn't trust me.'

Hackett, his head on one side, was studying him with the careful but detached attention of a portrait painter measuring up his subject. 'She was good at keeping secrets, all right, it seems,' he said, and sighed. 'Ah, God rest her, poor old Dolly.'

He nodded once and turned and strolled away in the direction in which they had come. Quirke watched him go. Yes, poor old Dolly. A gust of wind caught the skirts of the detective's overcoat and made them flap around him like furling sails, and for a moment it was as if the man inside the coat had vanished, vanished entirely.

'. . . I'm sorry, Mr Quirke,' the nun said, 'but I can't help you.' Her look was distracted and flickering, and she kept passing an invisible set of rosary beads agitatedly through her fingers, which were bony and tapered, like pale twigs. He had been startled to see, despite the wimple, that she was, or had once been, beautiful. She was tall and angular of frame, and the floor-length black habit that she wore, falling from her waist in fluted folds like a classical column, gave her an aspect of the statuesque. Her eyes were blue and so clear it seemed that if he peered deeply enough he would see all the way through into the narrow white chamber of her skull. She was called Sister Dominic; he wondered what her own, her given, name had been. 'You tell me that she died,' she said, 'this girl?'

'Yes. In childbirth.'

'How very sad.' She drew her lips together until the blood was pressed out of them. 'And what became of the child?'

'I don't know. That's one of the things I would like to find out.'

They were standing in the icy stillness of a checkerboard-tiled hallway. From within the body of the building he could feel rather than hear the rumble of hand-operated machinery and the raucous voices of women at work. There was a wet smell of heavy, woven things, wool, cotton, linen.

'And Dolores Moran,' he said, 'Dolly Moran, she was never here either, you say?'

She looked down quickly, shaking her head. 'I'm sorry,' she said again, hardly more than a murmur.

A young woman, short, thick-waisted, with a shapeless mop of bright-red hair, came along the corridor pushing an enormous cane basket on wheels. The basket must have been full of laundry for she had to use all her strength to propel it along, leaning into the effort with her arms stretched out straight before her and her head down and her knuckles white on the worn wooden handles. She was dressed in a loose grey smock, and grey stockings that were concertinaed around her thick red ankles, and what looked like a man's hobnailed boots, laceless and several sizes too big for her. Not seeing Quirke and the nun she came on steadily, the wheels of the basket squealing in a repeated, circular protest, and they had to step back and press themselves against the wall to allow her to pass by.

'Maisie!' Sister Dominic said sharply. 'For goodness' sake, watch where you're going!'

Maisie stopped, and straightened, and stared at them. It seemed for a moment that she might laugh. She had a broad, freckled, almost featureless face, with nostrils but hardly any nose to go with them and a little raw mouth that looked as if it had been turned inside out. 'Sorry,

Sister,' she said, but seemed not sorry at all. She regarded Quirke with a lively interest, scanning his herringbone tweed suit, his expensive black overcoat, the soft felt hat he was holding in his hands. One of her eyelids flicked—was it a tic, he wondered, or had she actually winked at him?

'Get on, now,' Sister Dominic said, not without a certain softening of tone; Sister Dominic, Quirke thought, appeared not entirely suited to the work here, whatever that work was, exactly.

'Right-oh, Sister,' Maisie answered, and giving Quirke another humorously big-eyed look, she bent to the basket and trundled off with it.

Sister Dominic, increasingly anxious to be rid of him, was edging along the wall towards the stained-glass vestibule through which he had been admitted. Following after her, he turned the brim of his hat slowly in his fingers, as she had turned the invisible rosary in hers. He was convinced, despite the nun's denial, that Christine Falls had been here at least for some time before Dolly Moran took her to the house in Stoney Batter. He pictured the girl trailing along these corridors in a mouse-grey smock like Maisie's, her dyed yellow hair turning back to its original nondescript brown, her knuckles red and broken, and the child already stirring restlessly inside her. How could Mal have condemned her to such a place?

'As I say,' Sister Dominic was saying, 'we had no Christine Falls here. I would remember. I remember all our girls.'

'What would have happened to her baby, if she'd had it here?'

The nun kept her gaze directed in the vicinity of his

knees. She was still sidling towards the exit and he was forced to keep moving in her wake. 'She wouldn't have,' she said.

'What?'

'This is a laundry, Mr Quirke, not a lying-in hospital.'

Spirited for a moment she allowed herself to look him defiantly in the face, then lowered her eyes again.

'So where *would* it have been born?'

'I'm sure I don't know. The girls who come to us have . . . they have already . . . given birth.'

'And what would have become of the babies they would have left behind them when they were sent here?'

'They would have been gone to an orphanage, of course. Or often they—' She stopped herself. They had arrived at the glass door of the vestibule and with undisguised relief she pushed it open and stood back to let him go through. He paused in the doorway, however, and stood facing her. He tried by staring hard at her to make her yield, to make her give him something, however little it might be, but she would not. 'These girls, Mr Quirke,' she said coldly, 'they find themselves in trouble, with no one to help. Often the families reject them. Then they are sent to us.'

'Yes,' he said dryly, 'and I'm sure you are a great comfort to them.'

The transparent azure irises of her eyes seemed to whiten for a moment, as if a gas had formed briefly behind them. Was it anger that was flaring there? The stained-glass panels of the door at her back had the look of a lurid, storm-riven sky, and he was startled and not a little appalled to find himself picturing her naked, a stark white impassioned figure by El Greco.

'We do our best,' she said, 'in the circumstances. It's all any of us can do.'

'Yes, Sister,' he said, in a forced contrite voice, embarrassed as that conjured image of her nakedness hovered still, refusing to fade. 'I understand.'

Once outside he turned and made his way down the hill in the direction of the river. The sky was heavy with a seamless weight of putty-coloured cloud that looked to be hardly higher than the rooftops of the houses on either side of the road, and flurries of heavy wet snow scudded before the wind. He turned up his coat collar and pulled low the brim of his hat. Why was he persisting like this? he asked himself. What were they to him, Christine Falls, or Christine Falls's bastard, or Dolly Moran who was murdered? What was Mal to him, for that matter? And yet he knew he could not leave it behind him, this dark and tangled business. He had some kind of duty, he owed some kind of debt; to whom, he was not sure.

13

Moss Manor's famous Crystal Gallery could accommodate three hundred people and still not seem overcrowded. The Irish millionaire who had built the house, back in the 1860s, had handed his architect a picture of the Crystal Palace in London torn from an illustrated magazine and ordered him to copy it. The result was a huge, ungainly construction of iron and glass, resembling the eye of a giant insect, fixed to the south-eastern flank of the house and glaring out across Massachusetts Bay toward Provincetown. Within, the great room was steam-heated by a latticework of underfloor piping, and palms grew in profusion, and dozens of species of orchid, and nameless, dark-green creepers that wound their tendrils around the iron pillars that were themselves moulded in the shape of slender tree trunks shooting up dizzyingly to spread in sprays of metal fronds under the gleaming canopy of glass a hundred feet above. Today, long trestle tables were set up under the palms, bearing heaping platters of festive food, sliced turkey and ham and goose, and silver tubs of potato salad, and thick slices of fruitcake, and glistening plum puddings shaped like anarchists' bombs. Bowls of fruit punch were ranged at intervals along the tables, and there were ranks of bottled beer for the men. From a stage at one side a band of musicians in white tuxedos was blaring out show tunes, and couples were dancing restrainedly between the tables. Sprigs of plastic holly were tucked incongruously among the palm leaves, and streamers of coloured crêpe paper were strung from trunk to trunk and from pillar to metal pillar, and above the stage a white satin banner pinned with red block letters wished all the staff of Crawford Transport a Merry Xmas. Outside, the already darkening afternoon was dense with frost-smoke and the ornamental gardens were hidden under snow and the ocean was a leaden line in front of a bank of lavender-tinted fog. Now and then a pane-sized square of snow would slide from the roof and burst into powder and cascade in eerie silence down the glass wall and disappear into the drifts that had already built up at the edges of the lawn, white into white.

The party had hardly been going an hour and already Andy Stafford had drunk too many bottles of beer. Claire as usual had wanted to be at a table at the front, to see everything that was going on, but he had insisted on getting as far away as he could get from that band—Glenn Miller types, average age a hundred or so—and now he was sitting on his own, glowering at his wife where she was dancing with that son-of-a-bitch Joe Lanigan. The baby was in her bassinet at his feet, though he did not understand how she could sleep with all the noise going on. Claire had said he would get used to the kid in time, but the months had passed and he still felt that his life had been invaded. It was like when he was a kid himself and his Cousin Billy came to live with them after his old man blew his brains out with a hunting rifle. The baby was always there, just like cousin Billy had been, with his farm-boy's big hands and straw-coloured eyelashes, watching and listening and breathing on everything.

Joe Lanigan was a trucker like Andy, a big, freckle-faced Irishman with a boxy head and arms as long as an ape's. He danced like a hillbilly, lifting his knees high and lunging down sideways until his fist with Claire's hand folded in it almost banged on the floor. Andy eyed them sourly. Claire was talking non-stop—what about?—and grinning in that way she did when she was excited, showing her upper gums. The number came to an end with a brassy shout from the trumpet, and Lanigan stepped back and made an exaggerated, sweeping bow, and Claire pressed her clasped hands to her breast and put her head to one side and batted her eyelashes, like she was some heroine out of the silent movies, and she and Lanigan both laughed. Lanigan went back to his table, where that sidekick of his whose name Andy could not remember, a little fat guy with slicked-back hair who looked like Lou Costello, was sitting with a couple of pizza-waitress types. As Lanigan sat down he glanced back over his shoulder at Claire making her way between the tables toward Andy, smiling to herself, and he said something, and the fat guy and the two broads laughed, and the fat guy looked across at Andy with what seemed a pitying sort of grin.

'Oh, I'm dizzy!' Claire said, arriving at the table.

She sat down opposite him and swung her knees in under the table and lifted a hand to touch her hair, still being the movie star. She did not seem dizzy to him. Her blouse had damp patches under the arms. He stood up, saying he was going to get another beer, and she asked in her sweetest little voice if he did not think that maybe he should take it easy, and even though she made herself smile as she said it he scowled at her. Then she said that since he was up he could get her a glass of punch. As he was walking away she leaned forward eagerly and peered into the bassinet with another one of those loony smiles of hers.

He knew he should not do it, but when he had got the drinks he made a detour that would bring him past Lanigan's table. He stopped and said hello. Lanigan, whose back was to him, made a show of being surprised, and swivelled his big square head and looked up at him, and asked him how he was doing, and called him *pal*. Andy said he was doing all right; he was being friendly, not making any big point about anything. The others, the two women and the fat guy—Cuddy, that was the little creep's name, suddenly he remembered it—were watching him from across the table; they seemed to be trying not to grin. Cuddy's womany little pursed-up mouth twitched at one side.

'Hey, Cuddy,' Andy said, still keeping it light, keeping it calm. 'See something funny, do you?' The fat man raised his eyebrows, which were heavy and black and looked painted on. 'I said,' Andy repeated, making his voice go hard, 'do you see something funny?'

Cuddy, too near to laughter to risk answering, looked at Lanigan, who answered for him. 'Hey, hey,' he said, lightly laughing himself, 'take it easy, Stafford. Where's your Christmas spirit?'

One of the women giggled and leaned sideways to the

other one until their shoulders met. The one who had laughed was large and blowsy, her big front teeth flecked with lipstick; the other was thin and Spanish-looking, showing a bony expanse of broiled chicken-breast in the loose V-shaped neck of her blouse.

'I'm just asking the question,' Andy said, ignoring the women as if they were not there—'do either of you guys see anything funny around here?'

People at nearby tables had turned and were staring at him, all of them smiling, thinking he was making some joke. He heard someone say, *Look, it's Audie Murphy*, and someone else gave a stifled shout of laughter.

'Listen, Stafford,' Lanigan said, starting to sound nervous, 'we don't want any trouble, not here, not today.'

Where, then, Andy was about to ask, *and when?* but felt a touch on his arm and turned quickly, defensively. Claire was beside him, smiling. In her bright little baby-doll voice she said:

'That punch is going to be warm before I get to taste it.'

He did not know what to do. People three tables away were looking at him now. He saw himself as they would see him, in his white shirt and jeans and cowboy boots, with that glass of pink stuff in his hand and a nerve jumping in his cheek. Lanigan had turned sideways on his chair and was looking up at Claire, signalling to her silently to take her little man away and keep him out of trouble.

'Come on, honey,' she murmured. 'Let's go.'

When they were back at their table Andy's left knee began to twitch up and down very fast, making the table vibrate. Claire was pretending nothing had happened.

She sat with her chin propped on a crook'd finger, watching the dancers and humming, and weaving her shoulders to the rhythm. He imagined himself snatching the punch glass from her hand and breaking it on the edge of the table and thrusting the shattered rim into her defenceless soft white throat. He had done it once before, long ago, when he slashed the face of that high-school prom queen who had laughed at him when he had asked her to dance, which was another reason for him never to go back to Wilmington.

Josh Crawford was in almost a light-hearted mood today. He liked to savour the fruits of his success, and the sight of his staff disporting themselves amid the greenery in this glass pleasure dome was sweet to him, he who these days had to taste so much of bitterness. He knew there would be few more such occasions; this might even be, for him, the last. The air around him grew thinner by the day; he sucked at it in a kind of slow panic, as if he were slowly sinking under water with only a tube to breathe through that was itself becoming increasingly fine, like one of those glass tubes he remembered from his schooldays, few and long ago though his schooldays had been—what were they called, those tubes? He found in a strange way comical the process of his accelerating dissolution. His lungs were so congested he was swelling up and turning blue, like some species of South American frog. The skin on his legs and feet was as taut and transparent as a prophylactic; he joked with the nurse when she was cutting his nails, warning her to be careful not to puncture him with the scissors or they might both end up in trouble. Who would have thought that time's betrayal would strike him as funny, at the end?

He rapped his knuckles now on the arm of the wheel-chair to make the nurse stop pushing and attend him. When she leaned down from behind him and put her face beside his he caught her pleasing, starchy smell; he supposed it must in part be a smell he was remembering from his long-dead and long-forgotten mother. So much of his concern now was for the past, since there was so little of the future left to him.

'What's the name of those things that chemists use,' he said hoarsely, 'those thin glass tubes that you put your finger on the top of to keep the liquid held inside—what do you call them?'

She gave him that sceptical, half-smiling, sidelong look that she did when she suspected he was teasing her. 'Tubes?' she said.

'Yes, glass tubes.' His patience was fraying already, and he beat again at the arm of the chair. 'You're a nurse, damn it, you're supposed to know these things.'

'Well, I don't.'

She straightened, disappearing behind him, and began to push him forward again. He could not stay angry at her for long. He liked people who stood up to him, although with her, he believed, it was less a case of courage than of stupidity: she did not seem to realise just how dangerous he was, or how vindictive he could be. Or maybe she did know, and did not care? If no man is a hero to his valet, he thought, then maybe no man is a monster to his nurse. On her first day at the house he had offered her a hundred dollars to show him her breasts. Fifty bucks apiece! She had stared at him and then laughed, and, stung, and unexpectedly discomfited, he had tried to bluster his way out of it, telling her it was something he asked all his female staff to do, by way of a test, which by refusing she had passed. That was the first time he had seen that archly mocking, faint smile of hers. 'Who says I'm refusing?' she said. 'I might have shown you them for nothing, if you'd asked me nicely.' But he never did ask, again, nicely or otherwise, and she had not repeated the offer.

The couples at the edge of the dance floor had noticed him by now, and they had stopped dancing and stood watching his approach, awkwardly together, two by two, like children, he thought contemptuously, in their gaudy party outfits. Unlike the nurse, they knew his reputation, and what he could do, and had done, when provoked. One of the women began tentatively to applaud, then her partner joined in, and then so did the rest of the stalled dancers, and after a few moments the great glass hall was filled with a storm of clapping. It was a sound he hated; it made him think of penguins, or was it seals? He lifted a hand in a limp, papal gesture, nodding acknowledgement to one side and then the other, wishing they would stop this awful racket, in which the band members now joined, rising to their feet and launching with their instruments into a string of farts and whistles that he dimly recognised as a parody of 'Hail to the Chief'. At length, when the last, would-be ingratiator had let fall his or her hands, and the band had sat down again, he made an attempt to address the crowd, to wish them the happiness of the season, but of course his voice failed him, and then he began to cough, and soon he was doubled over on himself, almost falling forward out of the chair, gasping and shuddering and dribbling mucus on the blanket covering his knees, and the nurse was fumbling with the stopcock of the oxygen tank that was slung under the chair between the wheels, and then a hand was laid on his shoulder and a voice said:

'You called, dear?'

Rose Crawford was a handsome woman, and she knew it. She was tall and slim with narrow shoulders and a narrow waist and a panther's stalking stride. Her eyes were large and black and lustrous and her cheekbones high—it was rumoured she had indian blood—and she looked down upon the world in general with undisguised, sardonic amusement. Josh Crawford liked to boast that she was his most prized possession, and joked that he had swapped a Rembrandt for her, though there were some who thought it might not be entirely a joke. She had appeared in his life seemingly out of nowhere, sporting a ring on her wedding finger with a diamond set in it that was surely the size, someone had said, of Josh's prostate. There had been a previous Mrs Crawford—two, in fact, the first of whom had died—but she had been bundled away into a fancy nursing-home and now no one could remember clearly what she had looked like, the memory of her eclipsed entirely by the far more ritzy Rose. It seemed something out of a fairy tale, or maybe one of those stories out of the Bible, more like, the union of this hard but beautiful woman and the bad old man. People looked at Josh Crawford looking at his so much younger wife and were reconciled for a moment to being not as rich as he was or as good-looking as she.

Rose took the plastic face-mask brusquely from the nurse's hands and pressed it over Josh's nose and mouth. The hiss of oxygen in the rubber pipe always made her think of snakes—with brittle affection she often called Josh her old cobra. Today, crouched hugely in the wheelchair with rounded shoulders and gasping into the muzzle of the mask, he resembled more a wounded moose. The interrupted dancers had been gaping at him with anxious interest as he struggled for breath—he was their meal ticket, after all, she reflected, though he certainly did not over-feed them—but at one sweeping glance from those inky eyes of hers they turned hastily away.

Josh tore the mask from his face and flung it aside. 'Get me out of here!' he snarled, gasping. He was furious at being seen like this by the workers. The nurse made to take the handles of the chair but he twisted about and swung a fist at her. 'Not you!' There was white froth on his lips. Rose smiled at the nurse in her blithe, bland way and turned the chair about and set off toward the archway that led into the house proper. Josh was scrabbling now with his nails at the leather armrests of the chair and muttering to himself some word that sounded like *pipit*. Birds, Rose asked herself—why was he talking about birds? From the dropsical caverns of his chest he produced a deep, rolling rumble that she recognised as laughter. When he spoke again she had to lean forward and put her face beside his, as the nurse had done earlier.

'Not a bird!' he croaked. He had heard what she was thinking, as he so often did; it impressed and alarmed her, in equal measure, this uncanny telepathic knack he had. 'A pipette,' he said, 'that's what it is, the thing that chemists use.'

'Whatever you say, darling,' she answered, with a sigh, 'whatever you say.'

When Claire got Andy on to the floor he would not dance, could not, he was that drunk. The room was spinning around him and everywhere he looked there were faces shiny and red from laughing. Claire, worried at what he might do—the expression in his half-closed eyes was truly scary now—drew him by the hand back to their table, making sure to keep on smiling so no one around her would see how she was really feeling. Little Christine had woken up and the woman at the next table had her on her knee and was talking to her. The baby was dressed in the white satin christening robe that a young nun at St Mary's had made for her; she had nearly grown out of it by now, but it was long in the skirt and hung down sideways like, Claire thought, the tail of a star. She took her, her little shooting star, her little angel, and sat down with her on her own knees, and thanked the woman for minding her, and then felt bad for she guessed from the look the couple exchanged, smiling but sad, that they were childless themselves, and she knew how *that* felt. She pretended not to notice Andy standing over her, breathing heavily and swaying a little and glaring, she was sure, at the child, as he always did when he had drunk too much. He grabbed a beer bottle by the neck and threw back his head and poured the beer into his open mouth; the look of him as he swallowed made her think this time not of being in bed with him, but of a mule her father had had on the farm that used to hold up its head like that and hee-haw, because it was lonesome for love, or so her brother Matty told her with a leer, Matty who years later was to die in a helicopter crash in Korea. Poor Andy, she thought, lonesome, too, because no one had loved him until she came along, to which although she tried not to she heard herself adding, *too late*.

Somebody Andy knew, one of the drivers he worked with, had promised them a ride back to town. They went to look for him, Claire moving ahead quickly with the baby in her arms and Andy slouching after her in a beer sulk, belching and muttering to himself and lugging the empty bassinet. They had to go through the double-doors that led out of the Crystal Gallery into a high stone hall with a huge fireplace with a bearskin in front of it and animal heads and old brown paintings on the walls. The place was noisy and crowded with people putting on storm coats and galoshes and calling goodbye and wishing each other a merry Christmas. Claire, looking back to make sure Andy was still following her, bumped into someone who had stepped backward into her path, and gave a little cry, afraid she would let the baby fall, which she might have done had the other person not put out a strong hand to steady her. Claire recognised Mr Crawford's nurse. She had a real Irish face, wide and friendly, from which her reddish hair was pulled back in two shells that covered her ears and were pinned under her cap at either side. She had been talking to one of the young truckers, flirting with him, by the look of it, for there were spots of colour on her cheekbones and she was still smiling when she turned and put a hand instinctively under Claire's arm that was holding the baby. *Oh, sorry!* both women said at the same time, and both looked down at little Christine where she was watching them in her puzzled, inquisitive way out of the folds of the pink blanket she was wrapped in. The nurse was about to say something more but Andy pushed forward, breathing his beer breath, and the trucker the nurse had been talking to moved aside, seeing that Andy was drunk and not caring to be in his way, for Andy had a reputation, and Claire said thanks to the nurse and they smiled at each other and Claire and Andy moved on, Andy squeezing Claire's arm hard to make her move faster.

When they had gone past, Brenda Ruttledge stood frowning to herself a moment, then shook her head and turned back to look for the trucker, but he had disappeared into the crowd.

Claire had not known she was asleep until the crying from the baby's room wakened her. She had been dreaming she was still at the party and the dream had been so real it had seemed she was really there and not here, at home, in her own bed, in glimmering snow-light, with nothing to disturb the huge hush coming in from the snowy streets all around except the baby's familiar, coughing cry that always made her heart beat faster the way she knew it was only supposed to do if she was the natural mother. Natural! What could be more natural than the love she lavished on her little Christine? She put out a hand and felt only a warm but already cooling space beside her where Andy should have been. He must have heard the baby before she had and got up to see to her. She could hear his voice, talking, and saying *ssh, ssh!* She must have fallen back to sleep then for a minute. When she woke again it was the silence that awakened her, a silence that had something wrong with it. She did not leap up straight away, as she knew she should, but lay there motionless, fully alert, all senses a-tingle. She thought afterward that she must have known, known without knowing, that these were the last few moments of innocence and peace that she would have on earth.

She was not conscious of running, of her legs carrying her, of her feet striking the floor, but only of moving, effortlessly and unhindered—*like the wind*, those were the very words that came to her—across the bedroom, and the passage outside, and into the open doorway of the baby's room, where she stopped. The light was not switched on in the room, yet she saw the scene as if lit like the film sets there were sometimes pictures of in movie magazines, with a harsh, unreal brightness. Andy was standing beside the baby's crib, motionless, his shoulders hunched, knees bent, his eyes shut and eyebrows lifted, as if, she thought, as if he were waiting for a sneeze to arrive. What he was holding in his hands might have been a wadded-up sheet, but she knew, of course, that it was not. They remained like that for an impossibly long time, she in the doorway and he by the crib, and then, hearing her, or maybe just sensing her there, he opened his eyes and blinked two or three times like a hypnotised person coming out of a trance and gave her a guilty, furtive look, frowning, trying, she could see, to think of something to say.

It was all so strangely calm. She walked to him and he handed her the bundle he had been holding, pushed it into her arms almost as if it were a gift he was presenting her with, a bunch of flowers, say, that he had grown tired of holding while he waited for her. The baby was in her sleepsuit, a limp, warm weight lying in her hands. Claire cradled the head in her palm, feeling the familiar texture of the skin, like a patch of velvet, loose over the skull.

'Oh, Andy,' she said, as if he and not what she was holding were the child. 'What have you done?'

An accident, he said it was. An accident. He kept saying it over and over, it might have been something he had been set to learn by heart. They were in their own room now, and she was sitting on the side of the bed, upright, her back very straight, with the baby laid out unmoving across her knees. Andy was pacing in front of her, running a hand repeatedly through his hair from his forehead all the way to the back of his neck. He was in his jeans and undershirt—when they came home he had started to undress and then, too drunk to finish, had collapsed into bed in his clothes—and a pair of white, ankle-high socks. She could smell the stale beer on his breath. Yet he seemed so young, in that undershirt and the little socks. She stopped looking at him; she wished, in a weary, wistful way, that she might never have to look at him again. The baby's eyelids were not quite closed, she noticed, and something glittered between them. *Dead.* She spoke the word to herself as if it were a word in a foreign language.

'She was crying,' Andy was saying. 'She was crying and I shook her.' He spoke in a low, urgent voice, not to her but not to himself, either: he was like an actor desperately trying to memorise the lines that presently, when the curtain went up, he would have to deliver with such force and sincerity that the whole house would be convinced. 'It was an accident. A terrible accident.'

She felt a prickle of impatience. 'Phone St Mary's,' she said.

He stopped, stared. 'What?'

She was so tired, suddenly; so tired. 'Sister Stephanus,' she said, speaking again in a slow, distinct voice, again as if to a child; perhaps, she thought, from now on she would never be able to talk any other way, to anyone. 'At St Mary's. Phone her.'

He narrowed his eyes suspiciously, as if suspecting a trick. 'What will I tell her?'

She shrugged, and at the movement little Christine's lifeless arm lolled sideways, her tiny fat hand upturned, as if she, too, were about to ask a question, demand guidance, plead for help.

'Tell her,' Claire said, in a tone of sudden, harsh sarcasm, 'tell her it was an accident.'

Then something broke in her, she felt it like the snapping of a bone, and she began to weep.

He left her there, sitting on the bed in her cotton nightdress with the baby lifeless on her splayed knees and the tears running down her face. There was something about her that scared him. She looked like a stone figure some Red Indian or Chinaman might worship. He threw a coat over his shoulders and hurried down the outside stairs. Ridges of frozen snow on the steps were glass-hard under his bare feet. The storm had cleared and the sky was high and clear and hung all over with glistening stars. Cora Bennett was awake—did she ever sleep?—and let him in at the back door. The telephone, he told her before she could speak, he needed to use the telephone. She had thought he had come for something else but when she saw his face and heard the way he spoke she just nodded and gestured toward the front hall, where the telephone was. He hesitated. She wore a slip and nothing else. He could see the goose-bumps on her forearms.

'What happened?' she said.

He told her there had been an accident and she nodded. How come, he wondered, women never seemed surprised when things went wrong? Then he saw something in her eyes, a light, an eager flash, and he realised she thought it was Claire the accident had happened to.

He had to look up the number of the orphanage in the phone book. There were dozens of churches, convents, schools, all called St Mary's. The telephone was the old-fashioned kind, a spindle with a dial and mouthpiece, and a receiver slung on a hook at the side. Again he hesitated. It was the middle of the night—would anyone be awake there to answer his call? And even if there was, what chance was there that he would be put through to the Mother so goddamned Superior? He began to dial the number, then stopped, and stood with his finger resting in the little hole, feeling with vague satisfaction how tensely the sprung dial pressed itself against the side of his nail. Cora came up silently and stood beside him. He had never noticed before how much taller than him she was. He never minded when women were taller, even liked it, in fact. She asked who he was calling but he did not answer.

The coat had slipped from one of his shoulders and she lifted it and set it tenderly back in place. Her fingers brushed his neck. He closed his eyes. He could not remember picking up the kid from her crib. She had been crying, and would not stop. He had not shaken her hard, he knew that, but how hard was hard? There must have been something wrong with her, some weakness in her head, it would have shown up sooner or later. It had been an accident. It was not his fault. He put the receiver back on the hook and turned to Cora wordlessly with his head bowed and she took him in her arms, pressing his face to her cold breast.

14

AFTERWARDS QUIRKE tried to put it all back together in his mind like a jigsaw puzzle. It would never be complete. The bits he remembered most clearly were the least significant, such as the smell of the drenched laurel behind the railings in the square, a street-lamp's rain-pocked reflection in a puddle, the cold, greasy feel of the area steps under his desperately scrabbling fingers. There was, throughout, a sense of deep embarrassment—that must have been the reason he did not cry out for help. Embarrassment, and a kind of incredulity. Such things simply did not happen, yet this one did, he had the wounds to prove it. He had thought, when he reached the bottom of those steps, in the wet, glistening darkness there, that he was going to die. An image had flashed before him of his pallid corpse laid out on the dissecting table under merciless lights and Sinclair his assistant standing over him in his green apron, flexing his rubber-gloved hands like a virtuoso about to set to at the piano. Pain had come flying at him from all directions, sharp, black, angular, and he thought of another image, of rooks at nightfall wheeling and spinning above bare trees against a winter sky. Or no, that was what he thought of afterwards, when he was reassembling the bits and pieces of what had happened. At the time he was not aware of his mind working at all, except to register trivial things, wet laurel leaves, the lamp's reflection, the slimed steps.

It had seemed at first an absurd instance of events repeating themselves, and in the confusion of the initial moments he had thought a joke was being played on him. It was the end of twilight and he was walking homewards along the square. There had been a Christmas-drinks party at the hospital in the afternoon, a staid and wearying affair, which Malachy had presided over with uneasy bonhomie, and although Quirke had drunk no more than a few glasses of wine he felt blurred and heavy-limbed. A half-hearted wind was blowing, and it was raining in a desultory way, and smoke from chimneys was flying this way and that in the sky above the square. Just as they had done the previous time, and at just the same place, the two appeared as silently as shadows out of the gloom and fell easily into step on either side of him. They were bare-headed and wore cheap, transparent plastic raincoats. The thin one, Mr Punch himself, gave him a regretfully reproving smile. 'Compliments of the season, Captain,' he said. 'Out in the damp and the dark again, are you? Didn't we warn you about that?'

'We did, we warned you,' fat Judy agreed, nodding vigorously his great round head on which a fine sprinkling of raindrops sparkled.

They had begun to crowd in on him from either side, shoulder to shoulder, squeezing him between them. They were shorter than he was and surely not as strong, yet pincered like this he felt helpless, a great, soft, helpless child. Mr Punch was making tut-tutting noises. 'You're a very inquisitive man, do you know that?' he said. 'A real Nosy Parker.'

It seemed imperative to Quirke that he should not speak, for if he did it would give them an advantage, he was not sure how, but he knew it was so. They came to the corner of the square. A few motor cars went past, their tyres on the wet roadway making a sound like the sound of frying fat. One slowed for the turn, its lighted orange trafficator sticking out. Why did he not call to the driver, wave his arms, or run forward, even, and jump on to the running-board and be borne away to safety? But he did nothing, and the car continued down the square, trailing grey exhaust smoke.

The three of them crossed the street to the other corner. Quirke had a sense of almost comic inadequacy. He thought what a trio they must make, the two hunched in their smoke-coloured plastic coats and him huge in his old-fashioned tweed ulster and black hat. Those two student types passing along on the other side, would they notice, would they remember, would they be able to describe the scene to the coroner's court, *in their own words*, as they might before long be asked to do? Despite the chill of the ending day Quirke felt the sweat along his hairline under the band of his hat. He was afraid, but at one remove, as if his fear had conjured up another version of him for it to inhabit, and he, the original he, was obliged to attend to this other, fearing self and be concerned for it, as he would be, he imagined, for a twin, or a grown-up son. Crazily the thought came to him that he might be dead already, that he might have died of fright back there on the corner, and that this big body stumping along helplessly between its captors was only the mechanical remnant of the self that was out here observing the sad end of his life with pity and shame. Death was his professional province yet what did he know of it, really? Well, it seemed that now he was about to receive first-hand instruction in that dark knowledge.

It was lightless at the bottom of the area steps and smelled of urban weeds and wet masonry. Quirke was aware of a barred basement window and at his back a narrow door that he felt sure had not been opened for many a year. He had a moment almost of peace, sprawled there with his legs twisted under him, looking up at the railings, each one with an identical, liquid smear of light down its side from the nearest street-lamp, and above them the soiled sky, faintly lit too, with the sickly radiance of the city. The fine cool rain prickled on his face. Seen from this angle his assailants looked almost comic as they came clattering down the steps after him, two jostling, foreshortened figures, their knees and elbows working like piston rods and their plastic raincoats crackling. They began kicking him, in wordless concentration, hampered by the narrow space where he had lodged after the fall. He turned himself this way and that as best he could, trying to protect his vital organs, his liver, his kidneys, his instinctively retracted genitals, knowing what these parts of him would look like when Sinclair opened him up. The pair laboured on him with skill and expertise, the thin one displaying an almost balletic finesse while the fat one did the heavier work. He was aware, however, of a certain angry restraint in their efforts—they confined their kicks to his legs and his upper torso and avoided his head when they could—and it came to him that they had been ordered that he was not to die. He greeted this realisation with an indifference that was almost disappointment. Pain was what mattered now, more, even, it seemed, than survival itself; pain, and how to bear it, how to—the word came to him—how to accommodate it. In the end his consciousness found the solution for him by letting itself lapse. As he passed out he seemed to see a face, round and rocky as the invisible moon, floating above the railings and regarding him with dispassion, a face he recognised yet could not identify. Whose? It troubled him, not to know.

It was still there, that face, when he came to the first time. The darkness was different now, softer, more diffuse, and it was not raining. Everything, in fact, was different. He did not understand where he was. It was Mal who was leaning over him, frowning and intent. But how had Mal known where to find him? Someone seemed to be holding his hand, but when he turned his head to see who it was a wave of nausea rose in him and he hastily shut his eyes. When he opened them, no more than a moment later, so it seemed to him, Mal was gone, and the darkness had changed again, was no longer darkness, indeed, but a greyish mistiness with something throbbing slowly and hugely at the heart of it—it was he, he was what was throbbing, in dull, vast, hardly believable pain. Cautiously this time he turned his eyes to the side and saw that it was Phoebe who was holding his hand, and for a moment in his drugged, half-dreaming state he thought she was his dead wife Delia. She was sitting beside him, on the area steps, was it? Something like fog lay between them, or a bank of cloud, but solid enough for his hand in hers to rest on. For a giddy moment he was afraid he was going to burst into tears. It was not fog, but a white sheet with a blanket under it.

Sleep, he must sleep.

When he next awoke it was daylight, and Mal was there again, and Sarah was sitting beside the bed where Phoebe had sat, and off behind her there were other people, moving, speaking, and someone laughed. There were coloured paper shapes strung across the ceiling.

'Quirke,' Sarah said. 'You've come back.' She smiled. It seemed to cost her an effort, as if she, too, were in some pain.

Mal, standing, took a deep breath grimly in through his nostrils. 'You're in the Mater,' he said.

Quirke shifted, and his left knee buzzed like a beehive. 'How bad is it?' he asked, surprised to find that his voice worked.

Mal shrugged. 'You'll live.'

'I meant my leg,' Quirke said. 'My knee.'

'Not so bad. They put a pin in it.'

'Who did it?'

Mal's eyes skittered off to the side. 'The Guards don't know,' he said, mumbling. 'They're assuming it was an attempted robbery.'

Quirke's aching ribs would not allow him to laugh. 'The pin, Mal,' he said. 'Who put in the pin?'

'Oh.' Mal looked sheepish. 'Billy Clinch.'

'Billy the butcher?'

The sheepish look turned cold. 'He was on a skiing holiday. We got him to come back specially.'

'Thanks.'

A big red-headed nurse approached. 'There you are,' she said to Quirke, in a broad accent—Cork, was it, or Kerry? 'We thought you were never going to wake up at all.'

She took his pulse and went away, her departure leaving the three of them somehow more at a loss than they had been before. Mal screwed up his lips and put his hands into the pockets of his tightly buttoned jacket with his thumbs outside and studied the toecaps of his shoes. He had not looked at Sarah once, nor she at him. Mal's suit was light blue, and he wore a yellow bow-tie. How incongruous on him they looked, Quirke thought, these festive glad-rags.

'You'll come to us, of course, when they let you out?' Sarah said.

But they both knew she did not mean it.

The Judge visited him the next afternoon. By then he had been moved from the accident ward to a private room. The red-headed nurse ushered the old man in, impressed and excited by the coming of so eminent a visitor. She took his overcoat and hat and offered him tea, which he declined, and she said she would leave them in peace, so, but added, addressing the Judge, that if he, meaning Quirke, got any way obstreperous, Your Honour had only to give a call and she would be here in a tick. 'Thank you, Nurse,' the Judge said, with his crinkliest smile, and she beamed at them both and departed. The old man looked at Quirke and arched an eyebrow. 'Is that the way it is?' he said. 'It's true what they say, a doctor can't afford to get sick.' He sat down on a chair beside the bed. Behind him a tall window looked out on a confusion of roofs and smoking chimneys and a sky filled with the flying debris of snow clouds. 'Merciful God, Quirke,' he said, 'what happened to you at all?'

Quirke, propped against a bank of pillows, gave a ruefully apologetic grimace. 'Fell down a set of steps,' he said.

Outlined under the bedclothes his left leg, encased in plaster, was the size of a log.

'They must have been steep, the same steps,' the Judge said. In the window behind his shoulder a flock of small black birds spurted raggedly from behind the rooftops and twirled about the tattered sky, then fell back in ones and pairs to wherever it was they had come from. 'Are you all right?' The old man shifted awkwardly on the chair, chafing his squarish, liver-spotted hands. 'I mean, is there anything you need?'

Quirke said no, and added that the Judge was good to come. At the top of his nose and between his eyes he had again that tremulous, hollow sensation of incipient weeping, an effect, he assumed, of delayed shock—his system, after all, would be in turmoil still, working desperately to fix itself, and why would he not want to weep?

'Mal and Sarah were here,' he said. 'Phoebe, too, at some stage, when I was still half comatose.'

The Judge nodded. 'Phoebe is a good girl,' he said, with a faint note of insistence, as if to forestall an objection. He moulded his hands against each other again in a washing motion. 'She's going to America, did she tell you?'

Quirke felt a breathless, lifting sensation in the region of his heart. He said nothing and the Judge went on: 'Yes, to Boston, to her Grandfather Crawford's.' He was looking everywhere except at Quirke. 'A holiday, only. Or vacation, as I believe they say out there.'

He fished in the pocket of his jacket and brought out his tobacco pipe and pouch and busied himself with them, plugging the damp dark strands into the bowl with the discoloured ball of his thumb. Quirke watched him from the bed. The afternoon light was failing fast in the room. The old man struck a match and put it to the pipe and smoke and sparks flew up. Quirke said:

'So the boyfriend has been given his final marching orders, has he?'

The Judge was looking about for an ashtray in which to deposit the spent match. Quirke made no attempt to help, but lay and watched him, unblinking.

'These mixed marriages,' the Judge said, trying to sound unconcerned, 'they never work.' He leaned forward and placed the match carefully on a corner of the wooden locker beside the bed. 'Besides, she's . . . What is she?'

'Twenty, in the new year.'

At last the Judge looked at him, the glimmer from the window making his faded blue eyes seem paler still. He said:

'A life is easily ruined, at that young age.'

Without lifting his head from the pillows Quirke put down a hand beside the bed and tried gropingly to open the locker, but in the end the Judge had to help him, and found his cigarettes for him and gave him one and struck a match. Then Quirke rang the nurse's bell and the nurse came and he told her to fetch an ashtray. She said he should not be smoking but he ignored her, and she turned to the Judge and threw her eyes to heaven and asked him if he did not think Quirke was *a holy terror*, but went back into the corridor and a moment later returned with a tinfoil pie-plate and said that would have to do them for it was all she could find. When she had gone they smoked in silence for a while. The old man's pipe had fouled the air and Quirke's cigarette tasted to him of burning card-board. The last of the daylight was dying away into the shadowed corners of the room but neither man made a move to switch on the lamp beside the bed.

'Tell me,' Quirke said, 'about this Knights of St Patrick business that Mal is involved in.' The Judge put on a puzzled frown but Quirke saw that he was feigning. 'The thing in America, with the Catholic families, that Josh Crawford funds.'

The old man took from his pocket a smoker's penknife and used the blunt end of it to tamp the tobacco in his pipe, sucking away meanwhile at the mouthpiece and blowing out busy clouds of blue smoke.

'Malachy,' he said at last, with heavy emphasis, 'is a good man.' He looked Quirke directly in the eye. 'You know that, don't you, Quirke?'

Quirke only looked back at him. He recalled yet again Sarah saying the same thing: *a good man.* 'A young woman died, Garret,' he said. 'Another woman was murdered.'

The Judge nodded. 'Are you suggesting,' he enquired, as if he had no more than the mildest interest in hearing what the reply might be, 'that Mal was involved in these things?'

'He was—he is. I told you so. He arranged for Christine Falls to—'

The old man waved a hand wearily. 'Yes, yes, I know what you told me.' In the gloom now, with the window behind him, his face was a featureless mask. Quirke could see the burning dottle in the pipe-bowl flare and fade, flare and fade, a slow, fiery pulse. 'He's my son, Quirke. If he has things to tell me, he'll tell me, in his own time.'

Quirke reached out cautiously and crushed the last of his cigarette in the tin plate on the locker, the stub exhaling its final, bitter fume. The nicotine had reacted with whatever the painkillers were they had given him and his nerve-ends were fizzing. The old man went on:

'When I was a boy I used to go to school with my boots tied around my neck to spare the shoe leather. Oh, I'm telling you—they laugh about that sort of thing these days, saying people of my generation are exaggerating, but I can tell you, it's no exaggeration. The boots around the neck, and a roasted spud and a bottle of milk with a bit of paper for a stopper and that was our rations for the day. Josh Crawford and myself, two lads from the same townland. Half the time we had no backsides to our trousers.'

'And look at you now,' Quirke said, 'you the Chief Justice and him a Boston millionaire.'

'We were the lucky ones. People talk about the good old days, but there was precious little that was good about them, and that's the sad truth.' He paused. The room was almost in darkness now, the lights of the city coming on and twinkling fitfully afar in the window. 'We all have a duty to try to make the world a better place, Quirke.'

'And the likes of Josh Crawford are out to make a better world?'

The Judge chuckled. 'When you think of the material God has to work with,' he said, 'you have to feel sorry for Him, sometimes.' Again he paused, as if to test what he would say before he said it. 'You're not much of a believer, are you, Quirke? You realise it's a great disappointment to me, that you left the Church.'

The effect of the cigarette had worn off and Quirke was sinking again into a dull fatigue. 'I don't know,' he said, his voice growing thin, 'that I was ever in it.'

'Ah, but you were—and you'll come back, sooner or later, don't you mistake it. The Lord stamps His seal on every soul'—he gave a coughing laugh—'even one as black as yours.'

'I've cut up a lot of corpses in my time,' Quirke said, 'but I've never found the place where the soul might have been.'

Feeling himself rebuked, the Judge fell huffily silent. Quirke did not care; he wanted to be left alone now, so that he might sleep. Pain was a pyramid, heavy and dull at the bottom and excruciatingly sharp at the top, the top being his shattered kneecap. The Judge upended the bowl of his pipe and knocked it on the pie-plate. He was shaking his head.

'You and Mal,' he said. 'I thought you'd be like brothers.'

Quirke had a sensation of drifting into himself, a self

that had grown cavernous and dark. 'Mal was always jealous,' he murmured. 'So was I. I wanted Sarah and got Delia.'

'Aye, and were sorry you did, I know that.' The Judge stood up and reached above Quirke's head and pressed the nurse's bell. He waited in the dark, looking down at what he could see of Quirke, the great white-swathed bulk of him laid out corpselike on the narrow bed. 'I realise, Quirke,' he said, 'that your life didn't go as you hoped it would, and as it should have, if there was any justice. You made too many mistakes—we all did. But go easy on Mal.' He leaned down closer to the supine form. But Quirke, he saw, was asleep.

15

For Quirke the year ended and a new one began in a blur of days each one of which was hardly distinguishable from its predecessors. The gaunt hospital room reminded him of the inside of a skull, with that high ceiling the colour of bone and the window beside him looking out like an unblinking eye on the wintry cityscape. Phoebe on one of her visits had brought him a miniature plastic Christmas tree complete with plastic ornaments; forlornly festive, it stood a little lopsided in the deep embrasure of the window, growing increasingly incongruous as that seemingly interminable first week dragged itself painfully towards New Year. Barney Boyle came to see him, furtive and lightly sweating—'Christ, Quirke, I hate hospitals'—bringing two naggins of whiskey and an armful of books. When he asked what had happened to him Quirke said what he had said to everyone else, that he had fallen down the area steps in Mount Street. Barney did not believe him, but made no mention of Ambie Tormey's brother or of Gallagher who was not the full shilling; Barney knew when to mind his own business.

On New Year's Eve the staff held a party somewhere in the upper regions of the building. The night nurse when she came with his sleeping pill was half-way tipsy. He listened to the city's bells at midnight crazily ringing in the new year and lay back against the pillows and tried not to feel sorry for himself. Billy Clinch, a fierce little sandy-haired terrier, had come to tell him, with a certain relish, Quirke could see, that his leg would never be right—'*The patella was in bits, man!*'—and that most likely he would have a limp for life. He took the news calmly, even with a certain indifference. He went over and over in his mind those minutes—he knew it must have been no more than minutes—at the dank bottom of the area steps. There was something in it, in what had happened there, a lesson, not the one that Mr Punch and fat Judy had been out to teach him, the nature of which he more or less understood, but one that was at once more profound and more common-place. As they toiled over him with their blunt toecaps the two had been, it seemed to him now, like a pair of common labourers, coal-heavers, say, or butchers manoeuvring an awkward carcase, vengefully resentful of the job in hand, grunting and sweating and getting in each other's way and wanting to be done. He had thought he was going to die and was surprised at how little he feared the prospect. It had all been so shabby and shoddy, so *ordinary*; and that, he now realised, would be the manner of his real death, when it came. In the dissecting room the bodies used to seem to him the remains of sacrificial victims, spent and inert after the frightful, bloody ceremony of their souls' leaving. But he would never again view a cadaver in that lurid light. Suddenly for him death had lost its terrifying glamour and become just another bit of the mundane business of life, although its last.

And day after day his drug-dimmed thoughts circled upon the question of who it was who had set those two on his trail. He kept doggedly posing the question, he knew, only so that he would not have to answer it. He told himself it was impossible that Mal could have done such a thing—imagine Mal on the step of a dark doorway in Stoney Batter handing out their instructions to Mr Punch and his fat partner!—yet the vistas that stretched beyond that impossibility were murkier still. When he summoned to mind the image of the face he had seemed to see hovering gloatingly above the area steps that night, watching as he was beaten, its features began to shift and rearrange themselves—or was it he who was shifting and rearranging them?—until it was no longer Mal's long, unmoonlike countenance, but one squarer and more roughly hewn. Costigan. Yes. But those dim, faceless others crowding in turn behind him, who were they?

Phoebe paid him a visit on New Year's Day. A fitful wind was driving sleet like spittle against the window, and the smoke from the city's chimneys no sooner appeared than it was blowsily dispersed. Phoebe wore a black beret pulled down at one side and a black coat with a fur collar. She seemed slimmer than when he had last been awake enough to look at her, and her face was pale, and the cold had given a raw, pink edging to the wings of her nose. There were other changes, less easily identified. He seemed to detect in her manner a certain watchfulness, and a sense of willed restraint, that had not been there before. He supposed this new hardness in her, if that was what it was—he looked at her knuckles, the white shine of them where the small bones were pressing up under the flesh—must be the result of the loss of Conor Carrington, of all the suppressed violence and anger at that loss, against which she had honed herself like a knife against a stone. But then he thought, no, it was not losing him that had embittered her, but the taking of him from her. She had been bested, and she was furious for it. He found her presence, in her grown-up's coat and ironically tilted Left Bank beret, faintly unnerving. The girl who had been was suddenly a woman.

She did not want to talk about the trip to America, she said. When Quirke mentioned it he shunted her mouth sideways and shrugged her shoulders in faint, listless impatience. 'They're getting rid of me,' she said. 'They want a rest from my accusing eye following them everywhere, as they imagine. Actually, I don't care about any of that any more.'

'Any of what?' he asked.

She shrugged again, and scowlingly regarded the Christmas tree on the window sill, then suddenly turned her eyes to his and, coldly and calculatedly mischievous, said:

'Why don't you come with me?'

He had noticed that his damaged knee inside its cast seemed to have taken on the task of alerting him at moments of surprise or alarm, moments which he in the narcotic haze in which he was still afloat could not register with sufficient force or instantaneity, so that the pinned-up joint of his leg must bring them to his attention by way of a twinge, a sort of pinch, such as a sadistically jolly uncle might give, meant to be playful but leaving a bruise. Phoebe took his indrawn gasp of pain now for a dismissive laugh and turned her vexed face again to the window. She unclasped her little black handbag—he thought: *All women look the same looking into their handbags*—and took from it a slim silver cigarette case and a matching lighter. So now she was a smoker in her own right. He made no comment. She opened the case with a flick of her thumb and middle finger and held it towards him spread upon her palm. The cigarettes, fat and flat, were ranked in an overlapping file, like oval organ pipes.

'Passing Cloud,' he said, taking one. 'My my, such sophistication.'

She held the lighter for him. When he leaned forward from the bank of pillows he caught from under the lifted sheet a whiff of his new, hospital smell, warm and raw, a meaty stink.

'All we need now is a little drink,' Phoebe said, with brittle gaiety. 'A couple of gin and tonics would be just the thing.' She twirled her cigarette with inexpert insouciance.

'How is it at home?' he asked.

'How is what at home?' Saying it, she was briefly a girl again, snappish and defiant. Then she sighed, and put the tip of her little finger between her teeth and nibbled on the nail. 'Awful,' she said, out of the side of her mouth. 'They hardly speak to each other.'

'Why is that?'

She let her finger go and took an angry drag at her cigarette and glared at him. 'How do I know? I'm not supposed to know anything, I'm a child.'

'And you,' he said, 'do *you* talk to *them*?' She looked at her shoes, a slow, deep frown gathering between her eyebrows. 'They might need you, you know.'

She decided not to hear that.

'I want to go away,' she said. She looked up. 'I want to *get* away. Oh, Quirke'—in a rush now—'it's terrible, terrible, they're like, I don't know what, it's as if they hate each other, as if they were strangers trapped together in a cage. I can't stand it, I have to get out.'

She stopped, and something dark crossed the window, the shadow of a bird, or something else, passing in the sky. She had lowered her face again and was watching him from under her eyelashes, trying to judge, he could see, how much of her distress he believed in, how much he would help her in her plan to escape. She was a simple creature, after all. He asked her:

'When do you go to Boston?'

She drew her knees tightly together and gave a shiver of annoyance. 'Oh, it's not for ages—weeks and weeks. The weather is too bad there, or something.'

'Yes, they get blizzards at this time of year.'

'Huh,' she said—'blizzards!'

He shut his eyes and saw Delia and Sarah in snow boots and Russian-style fur hats walking arm and arm out of an ice storm towards him, an impossible sun that was shining from somewhere making thousands of miniature rainbows around them, the rims of their nostrils pinkly translucent, like Phoebe's now, and their perfect teeth agleam—Quirke had never before known such white, such pristine, teeth: they seemed the very promise of all that might await him in this easeful and sleekly appointed land. They were on the Common, Mal was there too. They could hear the myriads of tiny slivers of ice tinkling against each other as they fell. It was—what? 1933?—the hard times were starting to ease and the bad news from Europe seemed no more than rumours, not to be credited. How innocent they had been, the four of them, how full of eagerness and assurance, how impatient for the future. Wearily he opened his eyes: *And here it is,* he thought, *the future we were so impatient for.* Phoebe, brooding, sat hunched forward with her knees crossed and one hand under an elbow and the other under her chin. The end of her cigarette was stained with lipstick, the smoke ran up by the side of her face. She hefted the cigarette case lightly in her hand.

'That's nice,' Quirke said.

'This?' She looked at the silver trinket. 'It was a present. From him'—she dropped her voice to a comical bass boom—'my lost love.' She sketched a regretful laugh, then rose and crushed the last of her cigarette into the tin plate that was still acting as an ashtray. 'I'll go,' she said.

'So soon?'

She did not look at him. What was it really that she had come to him in need of? For he knew she had come looking for something. Whatever it was he had been unable to supply it. Perhaps she was unclear herself as to what it was.

The afternoon was waning.

'You should think of it,' she said. 'You should think of coming with me, to Boston.'

Then she was gone, leaving a faint wraith of cigarette smoke on the air, the pallid blue ghost of herself.

Alone, he watched vague flakes of snow flickering down

into the lighted window like moths, then spinning away quickly into the darkness. He speculated again as to what it was she had wanted of him; he could not let it go. She should have known she was wasting her time, for what had he ever given her?—what had he ever given anyone? He shifted uneasily, his huge leg tugging at him like a surly, intractable child. He began a kind of reckoning, unwillingly; it made him squirm inside himself. There was Barney Boyle, poor Barney, burnt-out and steadily drinking himself to death: what sympathy or understanding had he ever given him? Young Carrington, fearful of the damage Mal Griffin and his father the Chief Justice might do to his career: why had he mocked him, and tried to make him appear a coward and a fool in front of Phoebe? Why had he gone to the Judge and planted suspicions in his mind about the son who was already a painful disappointment to him, the son who as a child was sent to be with his mother in the kitchen while Quirke the cuckoo sat in the Judge's den toasting his shins at the fire and sucking toffees from the brown-paper bag the Judge kept specially for him in a drawer of his desk? And Nana Griffin: what regard had he granted her, who had to invent a delicate constitution for Malachy her son in the hope of winning for him a little of his father's love or even a moment of his full attention? There were so many, suddenly, so many to be reckoned with; they crowded in upon him, and he shrank from them, but in vain. Sarah, whose tender affections he played on for his amusement, Sarah with her dizzy spells and her loveless marriage; Mal, floundering in God knows what deeps of trouble and sorrow; Dolly Moran, done to death for the keeping of a diary; Christine Falls and Christine Falls's child, both lost and soon to be forgotten; all of them, all scorned by him, unvalued, ignored, betrayed, even. And then there was Quirke himself, the Quirke he was taking grim measure of: Quirke dodging into McGonagle's of an afternoon to drink his whiskey and laugh at the memorials in the *Mail*—what right had he to laugh, how much better was he than the joxer scratching his balls over the racing pages or the drunken poet contemplating his failures in the bottom of a glass? He was like this leg, cocooned in the solid plaster of his indifference and selfishness. Again that face with the black-rimmed glasses and the stained teeth rose before him in the darkness of the window like a malign moon, the face, he realised, that would be with him always, the face of his nemesis.

16

FEBRUARY BROUGHT a false spring and, allowed free at last, Quirke ventured out on walks by the canal in the pale, chill sunlight. On the day that he left the hospital the red-headed nurse, whose face was the first thing he had seen when he woke briefly after Billy Clinch had finished working on his leg, and whose name was Philomena, had given him a present of a blackthorn stick, which she said had belonged to her late father—'Big brute of a thing he was, like you'—and with this stout aid he punted himself cautiously along the tow-path from Huband Bridge to Baggot Street and back again, feeling ancient, his knuckles white on the knob of the stick and his lower lip gripped between his teeth, mewling in pain like an infant and swearing at every lurching step.

The walking-stick was not the only gift that green-eyed Philomena had given him. The day before he was to be discharged, when she was on the afternoon shift, she had come into his room and shut the door and wedged a chair under the handle, and turned and shrugged off her uniform with dazzling ease—it unbuttoned handily down the front—to reveal a complicated armature of ribbed and boned pale-pink underwear, and approached the bed with a playful, ducking smile that gave her a double chin suggestive to Quirke's suddenly inflamed imagination of other, nether folds, and laughed in her throat and said:

'God, Mr Quirke, you're a terrible man—look what you have me doing.'

She was a big girl, with strong limbs and big broad freckled shoulders, but she accommodated herself to his encased leg with tender inventiveness. She had left on her suspender belt and her stockings, and when she set herself astride him, a flame-haired Godiva, the taut nylon of the stockings chafed his flanks like fine, warm emery paper. He realised how long a time it was since he had held a woman in his arms and heard her laugh. He wished he, too, might laugh but something held him back, not just his throbbing knee but some mysterious new access of woe and foreboding.

Next day she put on, merely for his sake, he knew, a sad but stoical face, saying she supposed he would forget her as soon as he was outside the hospital gates. She walked him down the corridor to the main exit, with a hand under his arm to support him and letting her breast brush with fond negligence against his sleeve. He asked for her address, being dutiful in his own way, but she said there was no point, that she only had a room in the nurses' quarters at the hospital and went home at the weekends, home being somewhere still unspecified down in the deep south. He thought of other country girls, of that other nurse Brenda Ruttledge and, less willingly, of Christine Falls, poor, pale Christine who was fading steadily from his remembering, every day a little more gone of the little of her that had been there in the first place. 'And anyway,'

Philomena said, with a sigh, 'I have a fella down there.' She lowered her voice to a husky whisper. 'Though he never gets what you got.'

He had told no one the date of his leaving, unable to bear the thought of finding Sarah waiting for him at the gate, bravely smiling like a war bride, or Phoebe with her new, hard-eyed manner, or even, God forbid, Mal, lugubrious in his secret torment that he wore like a penitent's sackcloth. The anger he had not felt through all the weeks in hospital had suddenly boiled up in him, out of nowhere, so it seemed, and as he lurched along the canal path on Philomena's father's blackthorn stick in the eerie silence of those unseasonably sunlit afternoons, with the moorhens scuttling among the reeds in a deluded mating fever, he busied himself devising all manner of vengeful stratagems. He was surprised at the violence of these fantasies. He imagined in almost erotic detail how he would search out Mr Punch and fat Judy one by one and hurl them down the same area steps in Mount Street where they had hurled him and beat them with his fists until their flesh burst, their bones splintered, their blood gushed from ruined mouths and punctured eardrums. He saw himself snatching off Costigan's glasses and plucking the Pioneer pin from his lapel and plunging it into his undefended eyes, first one, then the other, feeling the fine steel spike sinking into the resistant jelly and savouring Costigan's howls of agony. There would be others to be dealt with, the ones whose identities he could as yet only guess at, standing in a huddle behind Costigan and Mal and Punch and Judy. Oh, yes, they, too, the faceless Knights, would have to be called out and skewered with their own lances. For Quirke knew by now that all that had happened, to Christine Falls and Dolly Moran and to him, was more than a matter of Mal and his poor, dead girl, that it was a wide and tangled web in which he had become enmeshed.

And so, one day not long after leaving hospital, he found himself manoeuvring his stiff and still strapped-up leg out of a taxi at the gates of the Mother of Mercy Laundry. The day was clammily cold with the sun shining whitely through the morning mist. It was Saturday and the front of the place was shut and silent like a clenched mouth. He started towards the entrance, intending to ring the bell and wait however long it took for it to be answered, but veered off instead and made his way around the side of the building, not knowing what it was he was hoping to find. What he found was the young woman with the shapeless red hair who on his previous visit had almost run into him in the corridor with the laundry basket. She was standing by a drain emptying a basin of soapy water. She looked different in a way that he could not make out at first. She wore the same grey smock she had worn the last time and the same hobnailed boots. He saw her thick ankles, the skin swollen tight and shiny and diamond-mottled. He could not remember her name. When she saw him she stepped back and looked at him with her head to one side, clutching the emptied basin before her in both hands like a breastplate. In the middle of that featureless face she had Philomena the nurse's startlingly pellucid green eyes. At first he could not think what to say, what to ask, and they stood for a long moment in silent, baffled regard.

'What is your name?' he said at last.

'Maisie,' she said stoutly, as if in answer to a challenge. Her frown deepened and then cleared. 'I remember you,' she said. 'You're the one that was here that day.' She looked at the walking-stick, at the scars on his face. 'What happened to you?'

'A fall,' he said.

'You were talking to Her Holiness, asking about the Moran one.'

Quirke felt a sort of rapid inward slide, as if he were on board a ship that had listed suddenly. *The Moran one.*

'Yes,' he said carefully. 'Dolly Moran, yes. Did you know her?'

'And the old hake telling you she never heard tell of her!' She gave a short laugh that made her button nose wrinkle and lifted her upper lip. 'That's a good one, and her here every second week, collecting the babbies.'

Quirke, taking a deep breath, produced his cigarettes. Maisie eyed the packet hungrily. 'I'll have one of them,' she said.

She held the cigarette clumsily between two fingers and a thumb and bent to the flame of the lighter that Quirke was offering. He asked carefully:

'So Dolly Moran came here, to collect babies?'

The smoke of their cigarettes was a deep, dense blue in the misty air.

'Aye,' she said, 'for sending off to America.' Her look darkened. 'They won't get mine, that's for sure.'

Of course! That was the change in her: the swollen stomach. 'When are you due?' he asked.

She wrinkled her nose and her rabbit's lip was drawn upwards again. 'When am I what?'

'The baby,' he said, 'when will it be born?'

'Oh.' She shrugged, glancing aside. 'In a few months.' Then she looked at him directly again, a sharp light dawning in those pale green eyes. 'Why, what's it to you?'

He peered beyond her down the grey length of the yard; how long could he manage to keep her here before suspicion and fear drew her away?

'Would they take your baby from you?' he said, trying to make his voice sound like the voices of the do-gooders who would occasionally turn up at Carricklea, asking about *diet*, and *exercise*, and how often the boys *received the sacraments*.

Maisie gave another snort. 'Wouldn't they half!'

He had not succeeded in deceiving her, any more than the do-gooders had deceived him. He said:

'Tell me, how did you come to be here?'

She gave him a pitying look. 'My Da put me in.'

As if everyone should know that simple fact.

'Why did he do that?'

'He wanted me out of the way, like, in case I might tell on him.'

'Tell what?'

Her eyes grew purposely vague. 'Ah, nothing.'

'And the baby's father?' She shook her head quickly and he knew he had made a mistake. He hastened on. 'You say you won't let them take the baby—so what will you do?'

'I'll run away, so I will. I have money saved.'

He noted again, with a pang of pity, the laceless boots and bare, mottled legs, her work-roughened hands with their raw knuckles. He tried to picture her making her desperate escape but all he could conjure were images out of Victorian melodrama, of a shawled, stricken-faced girl hurrying along a snowy, rutted road with her precious bundle clutched to her breast and watched by a robin on a twig. The reality would be the mailboat and a rented room down a back-street in some anonymous English city. If she got that far, which he very much doubted. Most likely she would not get beyond the gates of this place.

He was about to speak again but she put up a hand to silence him and lifted her head to the side, listening. Somewhere a door creaked on its hinges and slammed shut. Hastily, with an expert flick of her thumb, she knocked the burning tip from her cigarette and hid the unsmoked half inside her smock and turned to go.

'Wait,' he said urgently. 'What's wrong? Are you frightened?'

'You'd be frightened,' she said darkly, 'if you knew them crowd.'

'What crowd?' he said. '*What* crowd, Mary?'

'*Maisie.*' Her eyes were chips of glass now.

He put a hand to his forehead. 'Sorry, sorry—Maisie.' Again he scanned the long yard behind her. 'It's all right,' he said in desperation, 'look, there's no one.'

But it was too late, she was already turning away. 'There's always somebody,' she said simply. The distant, unseen door opened again, creaking. Hearing it, she crouched in stillness, a sprinter on the blocks. He fumbled the packet of cigarettes from his pocket and held it out to her. She threw him a look, cold and bleak and almost contemptuous, and snatched the cigarettes from his hand and stowed them in the pocket of her smock and was gone.

17

HE WANTED TO GO to the mountains. Every day on his walks he looked longingly at them: they seemed to be just beyond the bridge at Leeson Street, snow-clad and as if afloat, like mountains in a dream. It was Sarah who offered to drive him there, and arrived at his door one afternoon in Mal's leather-upholstered Jaguar. To Quirke's nose the car inside had what he was sure must be its owner's smell, thin, sharp and medicinal. Sarah drove with nervous intensity, pressing her back against the seat and holding the steering-wheel at arms' length, her hands clamped close together on the top quadrant; on left turns she leaned so far to the side that Quirke felt stray tendrils of her hair touch his cheek like filaments of charged electric wire. She was quiet, and he could sense her brooding on something, and he was conscious of a stirring in him of unease. She had said on the telephone that she wanted to talk to him. Was she going to tell him what she knew about Mal? For by now Quirke was certain that she did know, that she had somehow found Mal out. Or perhaps he had broken down and confessed all to her. But whatever all was, Quirke did not want her to tell it to him, did not want to hear those things, in her mouth, did not want to have to sympathise, did not want to take her hand and look into her eyes and tell her how much he cared for her; that was gone, now, there would be no more hand-holding, no more soulful gazing into her eyes, no more of anything. He had gone beyond Sarah, into another, darker place, a place of his own behind another doorway like the doorway through which often in the past she had invited him, in vain, to enter with her.

They went by way of Enniskerry and Glencree. The high bogs were hidden under snow but already there were newborn lambs on the slopes, spindly, dazed-looking scraps of white and black with stumpy, clockwork tails; even through the rubber-sealed windows of the car their plaintive bleatings could be thinly heard. The mountain roads had been cleared but there were patches of black ice, and on a steep bend approaching a narrow stone bridge the back end of the big car slewed sideways and with cowlike stubbornness refused to straighten until they were across the bridge, the parapet of which the left mudguard missed by what Quirke, wildly looking back, saw had been no more than an inch or two. Sarah steered the machine to the side of the road and stopped, and closed her eyes and leaned her forehead in the space between her hands on the rim of the steering-wheel.

'Did we hit anything?' she murmured.

'No,' Quirke said. 'We would have known, if we had.'

She gave a low, groaning laugh. 'Thank God,' she said. 'His precious car.'

She switched off the ignition and they sat for a while listening to the cooling engine ticking and plinking.

Gradually the wind, too, made itself heard, faint and fitful, whistling in the car's front grille and thrumming in the limp strands of rusted barbed wire beside the road. Sarah lifted her head from the wheel and leaned it on the seat-back, still with her eyes closed. Her face was drawn and paper-pale, as if the blood had all drained out of it; this could not be solely the effect of the near-miss on the bridge. Quirke's unease deepened. His leg, too, began to ache, because of the thinned air up here, he supposed, or the cold that was seeping into the car now that the heater was off, or perhaps just because of the cramped position he had been forced to hold it in during the journey up from the city. He suggested that they should get out and walk a little, and she asked if he would be able, and he said impatiently that of course he would, and was already opening the door and lowering his leg with grunts and curses to the ground.

They had stopped on the edge of a long, shallow sweep of mountainside at the foot of which there was a black lake, its surface an unmoving sheet of steely shards. Beside them was a low, rounded hill, snowed over, and seeming to crouch, somehow, against a stone-dark sky. Snared tufts of soiled wool fluttered on the barbed wire, and here and there a gorse bush or a clump of heather showed starkly through the snow. A turf-cutter's track led slantwise up the hill, and this they followed, Quirke on his stick stepping cautiously over the ice-ribbed, stony ground with Sarah at his side, her arm firmly linked in his. The cold burned in their nostrils and made their lips and eyelids feel glassy. Half-way up the track Sarah said they should turn back, that they must be mad, coming up here, him with his leg in a cast and she in these ridiculous shoes, but Quirke set his jaw and went on, tugging her with him.

He asked after Phoebe.

'She goes to Boston next week,' Sarah answered. 'Her ticket is booked. She'll fly to New York, then on by train.' She spoke with a willed calmness, keeping her eyes fixed on the track.

'You'll miss her,' he said.

'Oh, dreadfully, of course. But I know it will be good for her. She needs to get away. She's furious about Conor Carrington. I'm afraid what she might do. I mean,' she went on quickly, 'she might make some awful mistake—girls often do, when they're thwarted in love.'

'Thwarted?'

'You know what I mean, Quirke. She could throw herself at the next young guy who comes along, and lose everything.' She was silent for a moment, walking along with her arm in his and holding her wrist with her other hand. She wore black silk gloves, and the shoes, slimly elegant, that were so incongruous in this wild place. 'I wish,' she said suddenly, hurrying the words, 'I wish you'd go with her, Quirke.' She glanced at him, smiling tensely, then looked away again.

He watched her profile. 'To Boston?'

She nodded, setting her lips tight together. 'I'd like to think,' she said, choosing the words carefully, 'that there was someone there to look after her.'

'She'll be with her grandfather. She won't be throwing herself at any young men with old Josh there to frighten them off.'

'I meant, someone I could trust. I don't want her to—I don't want her to become one of them.'

'Them?'

'My father, all that. Their world.' She twisted her mouth into a bitter smile. 'The Crawford clan.'

'Then don't let her go.'

Her grip on his arm tightened. 'I'm not strong enough. I can't fight them, Quirke. They're too much for me.'

He nodded. 'What about Mal?' he said.

'What about him?' Suddenly there was the coldness of steel in her voice.

'Does he want Phoebe to go?'

'Who knows what Mal wants? We don't discuss these things. We don't discuss anything, any more.'

He stopped, and made her stop with him. 'What's wrong, Sarah?' he said. 'Something has happened. You're different. Is it Mal?'

Her answer this time came like the snap of a tautened wire. 'Is *what* Mal?'

They walked on. Quirke felt the ice under his feet, the treacherous smoothness of it. What if he were to slip and fall here? He would not be able to get himself to his feet again. Sarah would have to go for help. He might die. He entertained the thought with equanimity.

They came to the crest of the hill. Before them was another long valley the floor of which was hidden under a haze of frost. They stood and gazed into that glowing grey immensity as if it were the very heart of desolation.

'*Will* you go to America?' Sarah asked, but before he could answer a shiver ran through her; he felt the force of it in her arm that was still linked in his, and with a sort of swooning sigh she let all her weight collapse against him, so that he thought his knee might give way. 'Oh, God,' she whispered, in distress and terror. Her eyes were closed, the lids fluttering like moth-wings.

'Sarah,' he said, 'what is it?'

She took a deep, trembling breath. 'Sorry,' she said, 'I thought I . . .' He wedged the walking-stick under his elbow for support and held both of her hands in his. Her fingers were icy. She tried to smile, shaking her head. 'It's all right, Quirke. I'm fine, really.'

He led her away from the track, the frozen snow snapping like glass under their shoes, to a large, round rock standing in self-conscious isolation on the barren hillside. He brushed the snow from the top of the rock and made her sit. A little colour was coming back into her face. She said again she was all right, that it was just her dizzy feeling. She laughed weakly. 'One of my *turns*, as Maggie calls them.' A nerve in her cheek twitched, giving her a bitter aspect. 'One of my turns,' she said again.

Nervously he lit a cigarette. At this high altitude the smoke cut into his lungs like a flung handful of blades. A large grey crow with a sharpened chisel of a beak alighted near them on a fence post and uttered a derisive croak.

Sarah was looking at her hands clasped in her lap. 'Quirke,' she said, 'I have something to tell you. It's about Phoebe. I don't know how to say it.' In her distress she lifted her hands, still clasped, and shook them before her in a curious gesture, like a dice player preparing to throw but knowing the throw will fail. 'She's not mine, Quirke. She's not Mal's, either.' Quirke stood so still he might have been made of the same stuff as the stone on which she sat. Sarah shook her head slowly from side to side in a kind of disbelieving amazement. 'She's yours,' she said. 'Yours and Delia's. You didn't know she lived, but she did. Delia died and Phoebe lived. The Judge, Garret, he phoned us in Boston that night, to tell us Delia was dead. I couldn't believe it. He asked if Mal and I would look after the baby—for a while, he said, until you were over your shock. There was a nun coming out from Dublin. She brought Phoebe with her.' She sighed, and cast about her as if vaguely in search of some way by which she might escape, some passageway or hollow in the snow down which she might drop. 'I shouldn't have kept her,' she said, 'but told myself it was for the best. You were already drinking so much, because of Delia, because she wasn't what you had hoped she'd be. And then she was dead, and there was Phoebe.' He turned, a stone man, and took some steps over the snow, leaning his weight on his stick, and stopped, looking away from her, down again into the frozen valley far below. The bird on the post ducked its head and flexed one wing and this time gave a low, rattling squawk that might have been of entreaty, or mildly regretful deprecation. Sarah sighed again. 'I wanted something of you, you see,' she said, to Quirke's enormous, hunched back. 'Something that was yours. Terrible of me, I know.' She laughed briefly, as if amazed again, at herself, at what she was saying. 'All these years . . .' She rose to her feet, clenching her fists and holding them at her sides. 'I'm sorry, Quirke,' she called to him, making her voice loud, for it seemed to her that when she had stood up the air had somehow grown too thin to carry mere words, and that anyway he was, over on that bare mountain rim, almost beyond hearing her. He would not turn, only stood there in his crow-black coat with his back to her and his head bowed. 'I'm sorry,' she said again, and this time it was as if she were saying it to herself.

III

1

ANDY STAFFORD felt like he was on trial. They were in Sister Stephanus's office, he and Claire, sitting side by side on two straight chairs in front of the big oak desk behind which Sister Stephanus was seated. At her back, standing, was the red-haired priest, Harkins, the one who had called to the house that day to spy on them. Another nun, he could not remember her name, she was a doctor, she had a stethoscope around her neck, was standing by the window looking out at the brilliant day, her face lit by the light reflected from the snow. He had explained to them, again, what had happened, how he had found the baby having a fit or something and had given her—he just managed in time to stop himself saying *it*—a shake to try to get her to snap out of it, and how she had died instead. It was all a misunderstanding, an accident. He had been drunk, he had not tried to deny it; that was probably part of the reason why it had happened, that the kid had died. So yes, he admitted it, it was sort of his fault, if an accident could ever be anyone's fault. Even though she was sitting down, Sister Stephanus looked taller than everyone else in the room. At last she stirred herself, and sighed and said:

'You must try as best you can, both of you, to put this

terrible thing behind you. Little Christine is with God now. It was His will.'

The other nun turned from the window and looked at Claire, who gave no response. The young woman had not moved or said a word since they had sat down. She was white-faced and hunched, as if she were cold, and her hands, the palms turned upward, lay lifeless in her lap. Her gaze was fixed on the floor in front of the desk, and she was frowning in concentration, trying to make out, it seemed, something in the pattern of the carpet.

Sister Stephanus went on:

'Andy, your task now is to help Claire. You've both had a loss, but hers is the greater. Do you understand?'

Andy nodded vigorously, to show how eager he was, and how determined, to try to undo what had been done. 'I understand, Sister,' he said, 'yes, I understand. Only . . .' He jerked his chin up and ran a finger around the inside of his shirt collar. He was wearing his tan check sport jacket and dark pants, and he had even put on a tie, to make a good impression.

Sister Stephanus was watching him with her wide-open, glistening, slightly staring eyes, eyes that looked as if they had been frozen. 'Only?' she said.

Andy took a heavy breath, lifting his chin again. 'I was wondering if you'd talked to Mr Crawford about a job for me. I mean a different job, one that would keep me nearer home.'

Sister Stephanus glanced over her shoulder to where the priest was standing. He lifted his eyebrows but said nothing. The nun turned back to Andy. 'Mr Crawford is very ill,' she said. 'Gravely ill.'

'Sorry to hear that,' Andy said, a little too slickly, as he realised. He hesitated, getting himself ready. Now was the moment. 'Must be tough,' he said in his slow drawl, 'Mr Crawford being sick and all. I suppose the rest of you'— he looked from her to Harkins and back again—'have to take up the slack. Funny, a big operation like the one you have going, yet you never see anything about it in the newspapers.'

There was another silence, then the priest said in that twangy harp accent of his: 'A lot of things don't get into the newspapers, Andy. Even serious accidents aren't reported, sometimes.'

Andy ignored him. 'Trouble is, see,' he said to the nun, 'I'll have my hands full helping Claire here to get over her loss. Have to turn down those long runs up to Canada and the Lakes. There's the overtime, I'll lose that.'

The nun glanced at Harkins again and again all he did was raise up his eyebrows. She turned back to Andy. 'All right,' she said, 'we'll see what can be done.'

'The point is, Andy,' Harkins put in, 'we have to keep these matters between ourselves. We have our own way of doing things here at St Mary's, and often the world doesn't understand.'

'Right,' Andy said, and allowed himself the ghost of a sneer. 'Right.'

Sister Stephanus rose abruptly, the black stuff of her habit making a busy, crumpling sound. 'Very well, then,' she said. 'We'll be in touch. But, Andy, I want you to be clear on one thing. Claire's welfare now is our first concern—ours, and yours.'

'Sure,' he said, deliberately offhand this time, just to

show them, 'sure, I understand.' He too stood up, and turned to Claire. 'Come on, honey. Time to go.'

She did not respond, but continued staring at the carpet. Sister Anselm came from the window and put a hand gently on her shoulder. 'Claire,' she said, 'are you all right?'

Claire blinked, and with an effort lifted her head and looked at the nun, struggling to concentrate. Slowly she nodded.

'She's fine,' Andy snapped, and could not keep an edge of menace out of his voice. 'I'll take care of her. Right, sweetheart?'

He gripped her by the elbow and made her stand. When she was on her feet it seemed for a moment that she might fall over but he held her steady with an arm around her shoulders and turned her to the door. Sister Stephanus came from behind her desk and led them out.

When the three of them were gone, Sister Anselm said: 'That young woman is not well.'

Father Harkins eyed her worriedly. 'Do you think she might . . . ?' He let the question hang.

'I think,' the nun said, with angry emphasis, 'her nerves are in a bad way—a very bad way.'

Sister Stephanus came back into the room, shaking her head. 'Dear Lord,' she said wearily, 'what a business.' She turned to the priest. 'Did the Archbishop . . . ?'

He nodded. 'I spoke to his office. His people will have a word with the Commissioner—there'll be no need for the police to get involved.'

Sister Anselm made a sound of disgust. Sister Stephanus turned her tired gaze on her. 'Did you speak, Sister?'

She turned and limped out of the room. Sister Stephanus and the priest looked at each other, and then away. They said nothing.

There was ice on the front steps and Andy kept an arm around Claire's shoulders so she would not slip. Since the accident with the kid he had not known what to do with his wife, she was so silent and withdrawn. She spent her time sitting around the house half in a trance, or watching the kiddies' programmes on TV, *Howdy Doody* and *Bugs Bunny* and the one with the two talking crows. It gave him the creeps to hear the way she laughed at those cartoons, a sort of gurgling in her throat, just the way, he supposed, her Kraut cousins would laugh, *hurgh hurgh hurgh*. At night when she lay unsleeping beside him he could feel her thoughts turning and turning in her head, turning on the same damned thing that she could not let go of. She would just about answer when he spoke to her, otherwise she said nothing. One night he came home late and tired out after a run down from Buffalo and the house was in darkness with not a sound to be heard. He searched the place and found her in the kid's room, sitting by the window with the kid's baby-blanket pressed in her arms. He had shouted at her, not so much because he was sore but because of the scare she had given him, sitting there like a ghost in the weird, bluish glow that came up from the snow-covered yard. But even when he yelled she only turned her head a little way toward him, frowning, like a person who has heard someone calling from a long, long way off.

Cora had been the only good thing for him in all of this. She had calmed him down on the night of the accident and helped him to get his story straight. Sometimes now during the day she came up and sat with Claire, and more than once he had arrived home to find her preparing his dinner, while Claire, wearing the housecoat that she had not changed out of since morning, red-eyed and with a handkerchief pressed to her mouth, lay on her front on their bed with her feet hanging over the side. There was something about her feet, white on the instep and discoloured and callused on the undersides, that gave him a nauseous feeling. Cora's feet were long and tanned, and narrow at the heel and broad and rounded where the toes started. Cora wanted nothing from him but his hard brown body. She never asked him to tell her he loved her, or worried about the future, or what would happen if Claire found out about the two of them. Being with Cora was like being with a man, except when they were in bed, and even then she had almost a man's brutal appetite.

They were walking down the driveway of the orphanage when they met Brenda Ruttledge coming in at the gate. She was wearing a big alpaca coat and a woollen hat and fur-trimmed boots. Andy did not remember her from when Claire had bumped into her when they were leaving the Christmas party at Josh Crawford's place—in fact, there was not much he did remember about that afternoon—and Claire, of course, was too wrapped up in herself to know whether she recognised someone or not.

But Brenda remembered them from the party, the pale young woman with the baby and her baby-faced little husband flushed and in a rage from having drunk too much beer. The young woman looked terrible today. She was grey and gaunt, as if she were in shock, or sick with dread, or grief. Brenda watched them as they passed her by, the wife walking stiff-legged and the husband guiding her with his arm tense around her shoulders.

Brenda had expected America to be different from home, the people happier, more forward-looking, friendlier, but they were just the same as her own folk, just as angry and petty-minded and afflicted. Or maybe it was only Boston that was like that, with so many Irish here, still with their race-memories of the Famine and the death ships. But she did not like to think of these things: of her being here and lonely, and home so far away.

The door was opened by the same young nun with the prominent teeth who had opened it the last time she was here, when she had brought the baby. She thought of asking her name but did not know if it was allowed to ask such a thing; anyway it would not be her own name but that of some saint Brenda had never heard of before. She had a nice face, small and round and jolly-looking; well, they would soon knock the jollity out of her, in this place. The nun, too, like the couple on the drive, showed no sign of remembering Brenda. But then, probably she had opened the door to hundreds of people since Brenda had last been here.

'I wonder if I could see Sister Stephanus?'

She was afraid the nun would ask her what her business was, but instead she invited her to step into the hall and said she would go and see if Mother Superior was in. When she smiled her teeth stuck out and two babyish dimples appeared in her fat little cheeks. She was gone for what seemed a long time, then came back and said Sister Stephanus was not in at present. Brenda knew she was being lied to. Embarrassed, she avoided the young nun's not unkindly eye.

'I just wanted to ask about—about one of the babies,' she said. 'Christine is her name.'

The young nun answered nothing, only stood with her hands clasped one upon the other at her waist, smiling politely. Brenda supposed she was not the first courier— would that be the word?—to come back here to St Mary's enquiring after a baby. She recalled the cockney purser on the boat when she was coming over who had warned her about getting attached to the child. He had barely glanced at their papers, hers and the baby's, then sat back in his chair behind his desk and looked at her bosom with the hint of a weasely leer and said, 'Believe me, I've seen it happen, time and again, girls going out, some of them hardly out of school. By the time they hit Stateside they think the baby's their own.' But it was not that she felt an attachment, exactly, she thought now, walking back down the driveway, only she still found herself thinking about little Christine, and remembering the funny feeling in her insides when she first took the baby in her arms that evening on Dun Laoghaire pier. The couple she had met here on the drive, where was their baby today? she wondered. She saw again the woman's shocked white face and dead eyes, and she shivered.

2

PHOEBE HAD SLEPT for most of the flight over, while Quirke with bitter determination had got drunk on complimentary brandies liberally plied to him by a frisky-eyed stewardess. Despite the five hours they had saved flying westwards it was dark when they arrived aboard the Clipper, and Quirke was resentful of the whole day he seemed to have missed out of his life, a lost day that was nonetheless more significant now than so many others he had lived through. From the airport they took a taxi to Penn station, slumped away from each other against their respective windows, both groggy in their own way. The train was new and sleek and fast, although it smelled much the same as an old steam train. In Boston they were met at the station by Josh's driver, a dark, slight young man who looked more like a boy got up in a chauffeur's uniform, a smart grey affair complete with leather leggings and a cap with a shiny peak. He smelled of hair oil and cigarettes. His name, he said, when Quirke asked, was Andy.

An icy rain was falling, and as they drove across the city Quirke peered through the murk at the lighted streets, looking for remembered landmarks and finding none. It was twenty years, and seemed a thousand, since he had last been here, he and Mal, two tyro medical men work-ing—masquerading, more like—as interns for a year at Massachusetts General thanks to the strings that had been pulled for them by the Judge's old pal Joshua Crawford, a freeman of this city and father of two lovely and marriage-able daughters. Yes, more like a thousand years.

'Tender memories stirring?' Phoebe enquired slyly from her side of the car. He had not realised that she had been watching him. He said nothing. 'What's the matter?' she asked, in a different tone. She was fed up with his moodiness; he had been in some kind of sulk the whole way over.

Quirke turned his eyes to the window again and the shining city sliding past. 'What do you mean, what's the matter?' he said.

'You're different. No jokes any more. I'm the one who's supposed to be in a mood. Is it that fall you took?'

He was silent for a time and then said:

'I wish we could . . .'

'What?'

'I don't know. Talk.'

'We are talking.'

'Are we?'

She shrugged, giving up on him. He could feel the driver's eye watching him in the mirror.

They crossed South Boston and out on to the highway. Scituate, where Josh Crawford had his mansion, was twenty miles down the coast, and soon after Quincy they were on narrow back roads where the sea mist hung under the trees and the lighted windows of isolated houses shone yellow and mysterious in the darkness. There had been snowdrifts still in Boston but down here, on the sea's edge, even the verges were clear. They passed by a white-steepled church standing on a rise, ghostly and somehow anguished in its empty-windowed solitude. No one spoke, and Quirke, the brandy glow now turned to an ashen burn, had again the eerie sense of detachment that came over him so often these days: it was as if the big car, wallowing effortlessly around these bends on its plush suspension, had left the road and was being borne aloft on the dense, wet darkness towards some secret place where its passengers would be lifted from it and spirited silently away without trace. He pressed a finger and thumb to his eyes. His mind was not his own, tonight.

When they turned in at the gates of Moss Manor a pack of penned dogs began to howl somewhere in the grounds. Approaching along the drive they saw that the great front door of the house was standing open and someone was in the doorway, waiting to greet them. Quirke wondered how the precise time of their arrival had been made known to the household. Perhaps the car had been heard, or its lights seen, as it rounded some bend up the road. Andy the driver rolled the big machine in a sweeping half-circle on the gravel and stopped. The person in the doorway, Quirke saw, was a woman, tall and slim, wearing a sweater and slacks. Phoebe and he stepped out of the car, the driver holding the door for Phoebe. A miasma of exhaust smoke lingered in the heavy, damp night air, and from far off came the hollow moan of a foghorn. The dogs had fallen silent.

'Welcome, voyagers,' the woman called to them, in a tone of dry amusement. They walked forward and she reached out and took both of Phoebe's hands in her own. 'My,' she said, in her low, husky, Southern-accented drawl, 'look at you, all grown-up and pretty as a picture. Have you got a kiss for your wicked step-grandmother?'

Phoebe, delighted, kissed her swiftly on the cheek. 'I don't know what to call you,' she said, laughing.

'Why, you charming girl, you must call me Rose. But I suppose I mustn't call you a girl.'

She had deliberately delayed turning to Quirke, giving him time, he guessed, to admire her flawless profile and the swept-back wings of her auburn hair, the high, unmarred brow, the noble line of the nose, the mouth turned down at the corners in an ironically regal, lazy smile. Now at last she delivered to him languidly a slim, cool hand, a hand, he noted, that was not as youthful-seeming as the rest of her. 'You must be the famous Mr Quirke,' she said, letting her eye wander over him. 'I've heard a great deal about you.'

He sketched a swift, half-serious bow. 'Good things, I hope?'

She smiled her steely smile. ''Fraid not.' She turned to Phoebe again. 'My dear, you must be exhausted. Was it a dreadful journey?'

'I had Mr Cheerful here to keep my spirits up,' Phoebe said, with a grimace of comical disgust.

They moved into the wide, high hall, and Andy the driver came in behind them with their bags. Quirke looked about at the animal heads on the walls, the broad staircase of carved oak, the dark-beamed ceiling. The atmosphere in the house had a faintly tacky feel, as if many coats of varnish had been applied a long time in the past and had not quite dried yet. Twenty years ago he had been impressed by the mock-Gothic awfulness of Moss Manor; now that ghastly splendour had to his eye a certain dinginess—was it the result of the wear and tear of time, or just his general disenchantment, that had dimmed the former grandeur of the place? No, it was the years: Josh Crawford's house had grown old along with its owner.

A maid in a dark-blue uniform appeared; she had mousey hair and mournful Irish eyes.

'Deirdre here will show you to your rooms,' Rose Crawford said. 'When you're ready please come down. We'll have a drink before dinner.' She laid a hand lightly on Quirke's sleeve and said, with what seemed to him a smiling sarcasm, 'Josh can't wait to see you.'

They moved to the foot of the staircase, the maid padding before them; Andy the driver had already gone ahead with their suitcases.

'How *is* Grandpa?' Phoebe asked.

Rose smiled at her. 'Oh, dying, I'm afraid, dear.'

The upper floors of the house were less oppressive and self-consciously grand than the downstairs. Up here the hand of Rose Crawford was evident in the dark-pink walls and Empire furnishings. After they had deposited Phoebe in her room the maid led Quirke to his. He recognised at once where he was, and faltered on the threshold. 'My God,' he muttered. On a chest of drawers of inlaid walnut stood a silver-framed photograph of Delia Crawford as a girl of seventeen. He remembered that picture: he had made her give him a copy of it. He lifted a hand to his forehead and touched the scars there, a habit he had developed. The maid was watching with some alarm his reactions of surprise and dismay. 'I'm sorry,' he said to her, 'this used to be my wife's room, when she lived here.' The photograph had been taken at some debutante ball or other and Delia wore a tiara, and the high collar of her elaborate gown was visible. She was looking into the camera with a kind of amused lasciviousness, one perfect eyebrow arched. He knew that look: all through those love-drunk Boston months it used to spark in him such extremes of desire for her that his groin would ache and his tongue would throb at the root. And how she would laugh at him, as he writhed before her in his blissful anguish. They had thought they had all the time in the world.

When the maid had gone, shutting the door soundlessly behind her, he sat down wearily on the bed, facing the chest of drawers, his hands hanging limply between his knees. The house was silent around him, though his ears were humming even yet from the relentless grinding drone of the aircraft's engines. Delia's sardonically tolerant eye calmly took him in, her expression seeming to say, *Well, Quirke, what now?* He brought out his wallet and took from it another photograph, much smaller than the one of Delia, badly creased and torn along one edge. It was of Phoebe, taken when she, too, was seventeen. He leaned forward and tucked it into a corner of the silver frame, and then sat back, his hands hanging as before, and gazed for a long time at the images of the two of them, the mother, and her daughter.

When he came down he followed the sound of voices to a vast, oak-floored room that he remembered as Josh Crawford's library. There were high, glass-fronted bookcases filled with leather-bound volumes that no one had ever opened, and in the middle of the floor a long reading-table with a top that sloped on either side, and a huge, antique globe of the world on a wooden stand. In the fireplace that was the height of a man a wood fire was blazing on a raised, black metal grating. Rose Crawford and Phoebe were sitting together on a leather-covered couch. Opposite them, on the other side of the fireplace, Josh Crawford was slumped in his wheelchair. He wore a rich silk dressing-gown and a crimson cummerbund, and Oriental slippers embroidered with gold stars; a shawl of Persian blue wool was draped over his shoulders. Quirke looked at the bald, pitted skull, the shape of an inverted pear, to the sides and back of which there clung yet a few lank strands of hair, dyed a pathetic shade of youthful black; at his loosely hanging, raw pink eyelids; at the gnarled and rope-veined hands fidgeting in his lap, and he recalled the vigorous, sleek and dangerous man that he had known two decades before, a latter-day buccaneer who had made a rich landfall on this still piratical coast. He saw that what Rose Crawford had said was true: her husband was dying, and rapidly. Only his eyes were what they had always been, shark-blue and piercing and merrily malignant. He lifted them now and looked at Quirke and said: 'Well, well, if it isn't the bad penny.'

'Hello, Josh.'

Quirke came forward to the fire and Josh noted his limp and the bunched dead patch of flesh under his left eye where one of Mr Punch's or fat Judy's steel-tipped toecaps had left its mark.

'What happened to you?'

'Had a fall,' Quirke said. He was growing weary of that same old pointless lie.

'Oh?' Josh grinned on one side of his leathery face. 'You should be more careful.'

'So everyone tells me.'

'So why don't you take everyone's advice?'

Rose, Quirke could see, was entertained by this little tussle. She had changed into a sheath of scarlet silk and matching scarlet shoes with three-inch heels. She blew cigarette smoke towards the ceiling and lifted her glass and waggled it, making the ice cubes chuckle.

'Have a drink, Mr Quirke,' she said, rising from the couch. 'Whisky?' She glanced at Phoebe. 'What about you, my dear? Gin and tonic? If, that is'—turning to Quirke—'it's permitted?'

'Why are you asking him?' Phoebe said airily, and put out the tip of her tongue at Quirke. She, too, had changed, into her formal blue satin dress. Quirke said to Rose:

'Thank you for putting me into Delia's room.'

She looked back from the table where the drinks were, glass and bottle in hand. 'Oh, dear,' she murmured vaguely, 'was that hers?' She gave a shrug of regret that was patently fake, and then frowned. 'There's no ice, again.' She went to the fireplace and pressed the button of a bell that was set into the wall.

'It's fine,' Quirke said, 'I don't need ice.'

She handed him the whisky and lingered a moment, standing close in front of him. 'My goodness, Mr Quirke,' she murmured, so that only he could hear, 'when they told me you were big they did not exaggerate.' He smiled back at her smile, and she turned away with an ironical little twitch of her hips and went to the drinks table again and poured a gin for Phoebe, and another bourbon for herself. Josh Crawford from his wheelchair greedily watched her every movement, fiercely smiling. The maid came and Rose requested her brusquely to fetch more ice. It was plain the girl was terrified of her mistress. When she had gone Rose said to Crawford:

'Honestly, Josh, these waifs and strays you make me take in.'

Crawford only laughed. 'Good Catholic girls,' he said. He winced at something happening inside him, then scowled. 'This damned fire's too hot—let's go into the glasshouse.'

Rose's mouth tightened and she seemed about to protest, but meeting her husband's look—the scowling jaw, those cold, fish eyes—she put her bourbon aside. 'Whatever you say, darling,' she said, making her voice go soft and silky.

They progressed, the four of them, along corridors cluttered with expensive, ugly furniture—oak chairs, brass-studded trunks, rough-hewn tables that might have come over on the *Mayflower* and, Quirke thought, most likely had—Quirke pushing Crawford in his chair and the two women following behind.

'Well, Quirke,' Crawford asked, without turning his head, 'come to see me die, have you?'

'I came with Phoebe,' Quirke said.

Crawford nodded. 'Sure you did.'

They arrived at the Crystal Gallery and Rose pressed a switch and banks of fluorescent lights high above them came on with a series of faint, muffled thumps. Quirke looked up past the lamps at the weight of all that darkness pressing on the huge glass dome that was stippled now with rain. The air in here was heavy and sultry and smelled of sap and loam. He thought it strange that he did not remember this extraordinary place, yet he must have seen it, must have been in it, when he was first here with Delia. All around, polished leaves of palms and fern and unblossoming orchids hung motionless, like so many large, intricately shaped ears attending to these intruders. Rose drew Phoebe aside and together they drifted away among the crowding greenery. Quirke pushed the wheelchair into a clearing where there was a wrought-iron bench and sat down, glad to rest his knee. The metal was clammy to the touch and almost warm. Keeping this space heated over a winter, he reflected idly, probably cost the equivalent of what he earned in a year.

'I hear you've been interfering with our work,' Josh Crawford said.

Quirke looked at him. The old man was watching the spot among the palms where the two women had gone from sight. 'What work is that?'

Josh Crawford sniffed, making a sound that might have been a laugh. 'You afraid of death, Quirke?' he asked.

Quirke reflected for a moment. 'I don't know. Yes, I suppose. Isn't everyone?'

'Not me. The nearer I get to it the less afraid I am.' He sighed, and Quirke heard the rattle in his chest. 'The only good thing about old age is that it gives you the opportunity to even up the balance. Between the bad and the good, I mean.' He swivelled his head and looked at Quirke. 'I've done some wicked things in my time'—a chuckle, another rattle—'even made people take falls, but I've done a lot of good, as well.' He paused a moment. 'What they say is right, Quirke. This is the New World. Europe is finished. The war and all that followed saw to that.' He pointed the yellowed nail of a long, knobbled finger at the concrete floor. 'This is the place. God's country.' He sat nodding, his jaw working as though he were gnawing on something soft and unswallowable. 'I ever tell you the history of this house? Scituate, here, this is where the Famine Irish came to, back in the black eighteen forties. The Prods, the English, the Brahmins, they'd settled the North Shore, no Irish need apply up there, so our people came south. I often imagine them, picture them in my mind'—tapping his forehead with a fingertip—'skin-and-bone wildmen and their scrawny red-headed women, trailing the coast with their litters of unkillable kids. Shit-poor the lot of them, starved at home and then starved here. This was rough country then, cliffs, rocks, salt-burned fields. Yes, I see them, clinging by their fingernails along this shore, scratching in the shallows for crabs and clams, afraid of the sea like most of us Irish, afraid of the deeps. A few fisher-families, though, had settled Second and Third Cliffs down there'—he jerked a thumb over his shoulder—'Connemara people, slick as otters, used to hard water and running the channels. At low tide they spotted it on the rocks: the red moss. They knew it from home, you see. *Chrondus crispus*, and another kind, *Gigartina mamillosa*—how's your Latin, Quirke? Carragheen moss. Red gold, it was, in those days. A thousand uses for the stuff, everything from blancmange to wallpaper size to printer's ink. They started gathering it, out in dories at low tide with their rakes, dry it on the beach, ship it off to Boston by the cartload. Within ten years there were moss millionaires down here—oh, yes, millionaires. One of them built this house, William Martin McConnell, otherwise known as Billy the Boss, a County Mayo man. The Boss and his moss. Moss Manor—see? Then the railroad arrived. Eighteen seventy-one the first trains came through. Hotels went up all along North Scituate, fancy holiday cottages at Egypt Beach, Cedar Point. Fire chiefs, police captains, the lace-curtain Irish, businessmen from over at Quincy, from as far away as Worcester, even, they all came here. Cardinal Curley had a house in ... I forget where. All kinds of people, taking their bite of the country, sinking their teeth into this rich coast. The Irish Riviera, it was called, and still is. They built golf courses, country clubs—the Hatherly Beach Playground Association!' He cackled phlegmily, his frail head wobbling on its stringy stalk of a neck. He was tickled at the thought of the shit-poor Irish and their pretensions, their outrageous successes. This was his sustenance, Quirke realised, this was what was keeping him alive, a thin bitter gruel of memories and imaginings, of malice and vindictive amusement. 'You can't beat the Irish, Quirke. We're like the rats, you're never more than six feet away from one.' He began to cough again, and thumped a fist repeatedly, hard, into his chest, and slumped back exhausted in the chair. 'I asked you, Quirke,' he said, in a hoarse whisper, 'why did you make this trip? And don't say you came for the girl's sake.'

Quirke shrugged, and moved his aching leg to ease it; the iron of the seat was growing cold under him. 'I ran away,' he said.

'From what?'

'From people who do wicked things.' Josh smiled and, smiling, looked away. Quirke watched him. 'What's this business of yours I've been interfering in, Josh?'

Crawford lifted his eyes and scanned vaguely the tall panes of gleaming black glass all around them. In this vast place with its artificial atmosphere they might have been a hundred leagues under the ocean or a million miles out in empty space.

'Know what I am, Quirke?' Crawford said. 'I'm a planter. Some people plant grain, others plant trees—me, I plant souls.'

The women had paused by a terracotta pot containing a leafless rose bush with long, many-thorned thin branches that reminded Phoebe of the clawing hands of a fairy-tale witch. 'It's called after me,' Rose said. 'Isn't it crazy? Josh paid a fortune to some fancy grower in England, and there it is, *Rose Crawford*. The flowers when they come out are a nasty shade of crimson, and have no scent.' She smiled at the girl trying dutifully to seem interested. 'You don't care for horticulture, I can see. It doesn't matter. To be honest, neither do I, but I have to pretend, for Josh's sake.' She touched a hand to Phoebe's arm and they turned back the way they had come. 'Will you stay here for a while?' she said.

Phoebe stared at her in surprise and faint alarm. 'In Boston?' she said.

'Yes. Stay with us—with me. Josh thinks you should.'

'What would I do?'

'Whatever you like. Go to college—we can get you into Harvard, or Boston College. Or just do nothing. See things. Live—you know how to do that, don't you?'

In fact, she suspected that was one of the things— the main thing—the girl had not yet learned how to do. Behind the lipstick-thin veneer of worldliness she was, Rose could see, a sweet little thing, untried, uncertain, hungry for experience but not sure that she was ready for it yet, and worried as to what frightening form it might take. There were so many things that Rose could teach her. She rather liked the idea of having a protégée.

Ducking under a tropical climbing plant the entwined, shaggy tendrils of which reminded Phoebe of the legs of a giant spider, they came in sight again of Quirke and Josh Crawford.

'Look at them,' Rose said softly, pausing. 'They're talking about you.'

'About me? How do you know?'

'I know everything.' She touched the girl's arm again. 'You'll think over what I said, yes, about staying?'

Phoebe nodded, smiling with her lips pressed tight together and her eyes shining. She felt giddy and excited. It was the same feeling that she used to have on the garden swing when she was a child. She loved it when her father pushed her higher and higher until it seemed she would go right over in a complete circle. There was an instant at the highest point of the arc when everything would stop and the reeling world would hang suspended over a huge emptiness of air and light and thrilling silence. That was how it was now, except that the instant was going on and on. She knew she should not have said yes when Rose offered her that gin—although it was only ten o'clock here it was really the middle of the night for her—but she did not care. One moment she had been sitting motionless on the swing, a good little girl, then a hand had pushed her in the small of the back and here she was, higher than she had ever been before.

They went forward to where the men were sitting. Quirke's damaged face was swollen from the effects of travel tiredness and drink and the knotted lump of flesh under his left eye was a dead white colour. Josh Crawford looked up at Phoebe and smiled broadly. 'Here she is,' he said, 'my favourite granddaughter!'

'That's not much of a compliment,' Phoebe said, smiling back at him, 'since I'm the only granddaughter you have.'

He took her by the wrists and drew her towards him. 'Look at you,' he said, 'a woman already.'

Quirke watched the two of them, marvelling with bitter amusement at how quickly Phoebe had forgiven her grandfather for siding with the others against her determination to marry Conor Carrington.

Rose in her turn was watching Quirke, registering the haggard sourness of his look. 'Where do they go to,' she said lightly, 'the years, eh, Mr Quirke?'

Brenda Ruttledge appeared, in her nurse's uniform and neat little hat, bearing a phial of pills and a glass of water on a silver tray. Seeing Quirke she faltered and her mouth went loosely sideways for a second. He, too, was faintly shocked to see her; he had forgotten that she would be at Moss Manor.

'Time for your pills, Mr Crawford,' she said, in a voice that cost her an obvious effort to hold steady.

Quirke gave her his weary smile. 'Hello, Brenda,' he said.

She would not, could not, meet his eye. 'Mr Quirke.' She smiled glancingly at Phoebe, and they both nodded, but no one bothered to introduce them.

Rose cast a sharp look from the nurse to Quirke and back again. Josh Crawford, too, caught the frisson of acknowledgement that had passed between them, and grinned, baring his side teeth. 'Know each other, do you?' he said.

Quirke did not look at him. 'We were colleagues, in Dublin,' he said.

There was a brief quiet as the echoes of that word, *colleagues*, reverberated incongruously. Crawford took the glass of water and Brenda shook three large tablets from the phial into his palm. He clapped them into his mouth, and drank, and grimaced.

Rose brought her hands soundlessly together. 'Well,' she said, gently brisk, 'Phoebe, Mr Quirke, shall we have dinner . . . ?'

Later, Quirke could not sleep. Over dinner in the funer-eally candle-lit dining room conversation had been scant. Glistening slabs of beef were served, and hickory-brown roast potatoes and minced cabbage and heat-shrivelled carrots, all seeming to be slathered over with a sticky coating of the ubiquitous household varnish. More than once Quirke had felt his mind swimming away from him into a dim, twittering place that was neither here nor elsewhere. He had stumbled on the stairs coming up, and Phoebe had put a hand under his arm and laughed at him and said he was obviously missing his beauty sleep. For a while he lay on the bed in his room, Delia's room, without undressing—he had not unpacked yet—and even though he turned Delia's photograph to the wall she was still unsettlingly present. Or no, not she, exactly, but a remem-brance of her, rancid with resentment and old anger. He tried to keep it from his mind but could not. It was the night of the going-away party Josh Crawford had given for him and Mal, twenty years before. Delia had drawn him aside, a finger to her mischievously smiling lips, and brought him up here and lain with him on the bed in her party frock. At first she would not let him make love to her, would not let him do anything, and kept pushing away his importunately questing hands. He could still hear her laughter, soft, mocking, provocative, and her voice hoarse in his ear as she called him her big buffalo. When he was about to give up, however, she shucked off her dress, with a practised ease the acknowledgement of which afterwards slipped like a heated knife blade into his unwilling consciousness, and lay back smiling and opened her arms and took him so deeply inside her he knew he would never quite find his way out again.

He got up from the bed now and had to stand a moment with his eyes closed, waiting for the dizziness to pass. He had drunk too much whisky and then too much wine at dinner and had smoked too many cigarettes and the inside of his mouth seemed to be lined with a gossamer-thin integument of warm, smooth, seared meat. He put on his jacket and left the room and went down through the silent house. He had the sense that others, too, were awake: he seemed to feel their presence around him in the gaunt air, jadedly attending him. Cautiously he negotiated the wide, oaken staircase, carrying his walking-stick under his arm and gripping his strapped and still bandaged leg in both hands and swinging it awkwardly from one step to the next. He did not know where he was going. The atmosphere was watchful, hostile, even, as if the place itself and not just its inhabitants were aware of his presence, aware of him, and resentful, somehow. Doors as he opened them clicked their tongues in annoyed unwelcome and, when he was leaving, closed behind him sighingly, glad of his quittance.

He thought he was heading in the direction of the Crystal Gallery and its silent plant life, hoping the company for a while of living but insensate things might soothe his mind and drive him back to his bed and sleep at last, but try as he would he could not locate it. Instead he found himself in a space almost as lofty, housing a long, shallow swimming-pool. The lights were set in hooded niches under the lip of the pool, the stealthily shifting surface of which cast wallowing reflections on to the sheer marble walls and the ceiling that was a segmented dome of pale plaster moulded in the shape of the roof of a Bedouin chieftain's tent. Here, too, the artificially heated air was cottony and cloying, and as Quirke approached the edge of the pool he felt the sweat gathering between his shoulder blades and on his eyelids and his upper lip. There came again the blarings of distant foghorns; they sounded to him like the forlorn and hopeless calls of great wounded animals crying in pain far out at sea.

He heard himself catch his breath. There was a body in the water.

It was a woman, wearing a black bathing suit and a rubber bathing cap. She was floating on her back with her eyes closed, her knees flexed a little and her arms outspread. The rim of the tight black cap blurred her features and at first he did not know her. He thought of slipping quietly away—his heart was still thumping from the start the sudden sight of her had given him—but just then she turned on to her front and began to swim with slow breast strokes towards the edge where he was standing. Seeing him towering above her on his stick she drew back in fright with a frog-like thrashing of arms and legs, making the water churn. Then she came on again, with her chin lifted, ruefully smiling. It was Brenda Ruttledge. 'God almighty,' she said, grasping the sides of the metal ladder and flipping herself up out of the water with a buoyant little bound, 'you gave me an awful fright.'

'You frightened me, too,' he said. 'I thought you were a corpse.'

'Well,' she said, laughing, 'I imagine you of all people should know the difference.'

When she stepped from the ladder they found themselves facing each other in closer proximity than either of them had expected. He could feel the watery chill emanating from her flesh and even the blood heat behind it. Around them on the walls the water-lights pranced and wallowed. She pulled off the bathing cap and shook her hair. 'You won't tell, will you?' she said half seriously. 'They don't like the staff to use the pool.'

She stepped past him and bent to pick up her towel. It struck him he had not seen this much of her ever before. She was broad-hipped, with short, rather thick, shapely legs. A country girl, built for child-bearing. He felt old suddenly. She would still have been in her cradle when he was frolicking here with the lovely Delia Crawford. One kiss, he reminded himself, that was all that was between them, him and this girl, one stolen, tipsy kiss at a party the night he had first heard the name Christine Falls. She came back with the towel, drying her shoulders. The look of a woman's face washed of its makeup never failed to affect him. When she lifted her arm he saw the little smudge of dark wet hair underneath.

'What happened to your face?' she said. 'I noticed earlier. And you're limping.'

'Took a tumble.'

She gazed into his face; he could see her not believing him. 'Oh,' she said suddenly, 'I've a drop on my nose!'

She sniffed, and laughed, and buried her face in the towel. Quirke thought: *All this has happened before somewhere.*

At the pool's edge there were two cane armchairs on either side of a low bamboo table. Brenda put on a white terry-cloth robe and they sat down. The cane crackled like a fire of thorns under Quirke's weight. He offered Brenda a cigarette but she shook her head. The reflections from the pool, calmer now that the water had calmed, moved in dreamy arabesques on wall and ceiling, reminding him vaguely of blood cells pressed between the glass slides of a microscope. Brenda said:

'What are you doing up, anyway, at this hour?'

He shrugged, and the chair made another loud complaint. 'Can't sleep,' he said.

'I was like that for ages, when I first came. I thought I would go mad.'

He seemed to hear a rasping something in her voice, a sorrowing catch. 'Homesick, are you?' he asked.

Again she shook her head. 'I was sick of home, that's why I left.' She gazed before her, seeing not here but there, not now but then. 'No,' she went on, 'it's the place I can't get used to. This house. Those bloody foghorns.'

'And Josh Crawford?' he said. 'Have you got used to him?'

'Oh, I can handle the likes of Mr Crawford.' She turned to him, lifting her legs and tucking her feet under her and stretching the robe over her smooth, round knees. He imagined putting his face between her thighs, his mouth finding the cold wet lips there and the burning hollow within. 'I was surprised,' she said, 'when I heard you were coming.'

'Were you?'

Their voices travelled out over the water and struck faint, marine echoes from the walls. She was still studying him. 'You've changed,' she said.

'Have I?'

'You're quieter.'

'*No more jokes.*' He smiled glumly. 'It's something Phoebe said.'

'She seems nice, Phoebe.'

'Yes. She is.'

They were silent, and the echoes fell. Distantly in the house a clock struck a single, silver note, and an instant later from farther off there came another chime, and yet another, farther off still, and then the silence settled again. Quirke said:

'Tell me, what do you know about this charity work that Josh does?'

'You mean the orphanage?'

He looked at her. 'What orphanage,' he asked slowly, 'is that?'

'St Mary's. It's out in Brookline. He gives money to it.' A tremor of unease touched her like the tip of a needle. What was he after? To change the subject she said, 'Mrs Crawford has taken a shine to you.'

He raised his eyebrows. 'And how do you know that?'

'I just know.'

He nodded. 'Your female intuition, is it?'

She flinched at the sudden cold mockery in his tone.

She stood up and pulled the robe tight around her and walked away amid the capering, ghostly lights, dangling the black bathing cap by its strap from her finger.

'Your niece was right,' she threw back over her shoulder. 'No more jokes.'

3

HEAVY WAVES, boxy and thick, rolled in slow motion past the lighthouse on its offshore rock and broke against the beach, lacing the air with ice-white spume. The coast sloped steeply here, diving off towards Provincetown and the vast Atlantic distances beyond. Quirke and Phoebe stood side by side on the concrete slipway, looking out to the horizon. A hard wind roaring in from the sea blew spray into their faces and whipped the flaps of their overcoats against their legs. Phoebe said something but Quirke could not hear her for the wind and the slushy clatter of the shingle rolling under the waves. He cupped a hand to his ear and she leaned close and shouted again, 'I feel if I put out my arms I'd fly!' How young she was; the long and tedious journey from Ireland seemed not to have affected her at all, and her eyes sparkled and her cheeks glowed. Josh Crawford's big Buick was parked behind them at an angle on the sandy track, humped and shining, like something huge that had slithered its way up out of the sea. Andy Stafford in his chauffeur's greatcoat stood beside it, watching them narrowly, holding his smart peaked cap at his side, his oiled black hair blowing straight back and plastered against his skull. Slight of form in field-grey outfit and polished leggings, he had the look of a boy soldier facing into the wind of battle.

Quirke and Phoebe turned and set off walking along the sandy pathway in the lee of the low dunes. A few clapboard holiday homes stood some way back from the sea, their paint peeling and windows hazed over from the salt winds. Quirke on his walking-stick had to go gingerly for the ground was uneven and shifting in places and the marram grass looked tough and wiry enough to wrap itself around his ankles and send him sprawling. Despite having to stump along clumsily like this he felt so giddily light in the head it seemed he, too, might be plucked up by the wind and whirled away into the tumultuous sky. He stopped and brought out his cigarettes but the wind was too strong and his lighter would not light. They went on.

'I used to come here with Delia,' he said, and regretted it at once, for Phoebe pounced, of course.

'What was she like, Delia?' she asked greedily, putting a hand on his arm and squeezing it. 'I mean, really. I want to know, now that I'm here. I can almost feel her presence, in the house.'

'Oh, exciting, I suppose.'

Was it true? She had been wholly without scruple of any kind—her father's daughter—and that had certainly excited him. But he had hated her, too. Curious, loving and hating, the two sides of the precious coin she had so casually handed him. Phoebe was nodding solemnly as if he had uttered a profound insight. This eagerness of hers to know what Delia had been *really like*—did she have some unconscious inkling of who Delia really was? She said:

'I thought Mummy was supposed to be the exciting one.'

'We were all different, then.' He sounded to himself like a fond old fool, maundering over the lost years. It occurred to him that he was sick of being Quirke, but knew there was no one else he could be. 'I mean,' he said quickly, irritated, 'we were all someone else, your father, Sarah, me—' He broke off. 'Look, let's go back. This wind is making my head ache.'

But it was not only the wind that was tormenting him. When Phoebe spoke Delia's name now he felt as an adulterer might feel when his wife makes casual mention of the family friend who is his secret lover. He knew that he should tell his daughter—his daughter!—the truth, should tell her who her real parents were, but he did not know how to say it. It was too enormous to be put into words, a thing outside the commonplace run of life. It would not square, he told himself, with what they had been to each other up to now, the easy tolerance there had been between them, the freedom, the untaxing gaiety. It was absurd—how could he begin to be a father to her, after all these years, the so many years that made up the entirety of her life? Yet even as he went along here with her hand tugging at his arm he was convinced that he could feel the loss of her, the absence of her, from whatever hollow place it was in his heart that she would have filled, in those years. Since the moment in the mountains when Sarah had made her confession to him there had been gathering steadily in him, like a head of water behind a dam, something that if he released it would swamp his life and drown his peace of mind, and so he limped along, and smiled, and entertained his oblivious daughter's chattering enquiries about the woman she did not know was her mother. Some day, he told himself, with almost a vindictive satisfaction, some day he would suffer for this laxity, this laziness of spirit, this cowardice. For that was what it was—plain funk. He might make all the excuses he wished, might talk of the *tolerance there had been between them*, the *freedom* and the *gaiety* that he must not put at risk, but he knew it was just an alibi he was attempting to construct, a front behind which he could go on as he had always done, in peace, being nobody's father.

Andy Stafford had climbed into the car and was just about to light a cigarette. He put it away hastily when he saw them turn back, Quirke swivelling abruptly on his stick like some sort of huge mechanical toy man. In the rear-view mirror Andy caught a glimpse of his own reflection and was startled by what he saw, the somehow grimacing face with its dark, furtive eye. He studied Phoebe through the windshield as she approached, the wind moulding her coat against her form. When she had got into the car he had tried to spread the tartan lap-rug over her knees but she had taken it from him without giving him even a glance and tossed it over her shoulder into the back window space. Now he listened idly to the two of them talking behind him as the car lurched down the track away from the dunes on its voluptuously squashy suspension.

'How did you meet up,' Phoebe was asking, 'the four of you?'

Quirke, his hands set atop his stick, was watching the dwindling shore through the side window. 'Your grandfather had fixed for Mal and me to work at the hospital,' he said. 'Just for a year, with a view to something more permanent, if it worked out, which it didn't, for various reasons.'

'Delia being one of them?'

He shrugged. 'I might have stayed. Big bucks, even in those days. But then . . .' He let it drift away. He had the feeling that he was lying even though he was not; the secret that he carried was suddenly infecting everything. 'Your grandmother was there, being treated, at the hospital. Sarah came to see her. She didn't know her mother was dying. I was the one who told her. I think she was glad—to be told, I mean. Then we were a foursome for a while, Sarah, Delia, Mal, me.'

He stopped. *Big bucks. A foursome.* What was it—was he hoping the momentum of mere talk would lead him to blurt out another, altogether different word, would lull him into telling her without his intending it the things he had not the nerve to utter straight out, the things it was her right to know? He saw she was no longer listening to him, but was gazing out blankly through the window on her side as the car gained the main road and turned in the direction of North Scituate. Quirke studied the back of Andy Stafford's head, sleek as a seal's and narrow at the neck, and pondered how unmistakable it was, the physiognomy of the poor, the low, the dispossessed. Phoebe's voice startled him.

'Rose wants me to stay here.' She spoke in a sort of sighing fall, pretending weary indifference.

'Here?' he said.

She glanced at him archly. With his hands folded like that on the handle of the walking-stick he had the distinct look of Grandfather Griffin. 'Yes,' she said, 'here. In America. In Boston.'

'Hmm.'

'What do you mean, *hmm*?'

He looked again at the back of the driver's head, uncannily motionless in the moving car. He lowered his voice but spoke with a deliberate emphasis. 'I don't think that's a good idea.'

'And why not?' she enquired.

He thought for a moment. What was he to say? After all, why should she not stay here? Why should she not do anything she wanted? Who was he to advise her on how to live her life?

'What about home?' he said. 'What about Conor Carrington?'

She made a wry face and turned to look out of her window again. There was the church with the white spire they had passed by last night in the mist-hung darkness; today it looked ordinary and even a little sheepish, as if its ghostly nocturnal springing up were a prank it was ashamed to be reminded of in daylight.

'Home,' Phoebe said quietly, 'feels very far away, here. I don't mean just in miles.'

'It *is* far away,' Quirke said, 'in miles and everything else. That's the point.' He paused, floundering, then tried again: 'I promised your—I promised Sarah I'd look after you. I don't think she'd want you to stay here. In fact, I know she wouldn't.'

'Oh?' she said, turning again to stare at him superciliously down her nose, and for a second he saw how she would look when she was middle-aged, a slightly less hard-eyed, less imperious Delia. 'Just how do you *know* she wouldn't?'

He felt a pressure inside his chest—was it anger?—and had to pause again. He was acutely aware now of the back of Andy Stafford's head: it seemed to have become a bulbed and shiny listening device. He made his voice go lower still. 'There are things you don't know, Phoebe,' he said.

She was still fixing him with that ingenuously haughty stare. 'What things?' she said scoffingly. 'What sort of things?'

'About your mother. About your parents.' He looked away. 'About me.'

'Oh, you,' she said, softening suddenly, and laughed. 'What's there to know about you?'

When they came into the village he told Andy Stafford to stop and levered himself on his stick out of the car, saying there was a place he wanted to find, a bar, where he used to drink when he first came here. Phoebe said she would come with him but he waggled his stick impatiently and told her no, that she should go on to the house and send the car back for him in an hour, and he slammed the door. She watched him lurch away, his long coat billowing and his hat in his hand and his hair shaking in the icy wind. Andy Stafford said nothing, letting the engine idle. The quiet in the car seemed to broaden, and something unseen began to grow up out of it and spread its indolent fronds.

'Take me somewhere,' Phoebe said crisply. 'Anywhere.'

He palmed the gearshift and she felt a greased meshing

as he let in the clutch and the car glided away from the kerb with an almost feline stealth, purring to itself. She had turned aside to look out of her window but she could feel him watching her in the mirror, and she was careful not to let her eye meet his. They whispered along the empty broad main street of the icebound village—*Joe's Diner, Ed's Motors, Larry's Tackle and Bait*: it seemed the men owned everything here—and then they were on the coast road again, from which despite its designation she could catch only occasional glimpses of the sea, iron-blue and somehow tilted up towards the horizon. She did not like the sea, its unnatural uniform flatness, its worrisome smells. Untidy, track-like roads led down to it, the continent petering out along this ragged eastern coastline. She experienced a sudden flush of weariness, and for a second her head nodded unstoppably and her eyelids came down like two curved, leaden flanges that had suddenly been attached to her eyes. She snapped herself upright, blinking. The driver was looking at her again in the mirror —should she tell him please to concentrate on the road? She wondered if his eyes, small and glossy brown, like a squirrel's, she thought, and much too close together, were particularly lacking in expression, or if everybody's eyes looked like that in isolation from the face's other features. She leaned forward to check her own reflection but quickly sat back again, shaken by the sight of their two faces in the glass, suddenly beside each other but in different perspectives.

'So,' he said, 'how do you like Boston?'

'I haven't seen it, yet.' She had been determined to maintain a frosty distance, and was disconcerted to hear herself adding, 'Maybe you'd take me there some time.' She faltered, and sat upright quickly, clearing her throat. 'I mean, you might take Mr Quirke and me, to see the sights, some afternoon.' She told herself: *Shut up, you dope!* 'If my grandfather can spare you, that is.' She could feel him being amused.

'Sure thing,' he said easily. 'Anytime.' He paused, calculating how much he might risk. 'Mr Crawford don't have much use for the car, him being sick and all, and Mrs Crawford, well . . .' The very back of his head seemed to smirk. She wondered what that *well* might mean and thought it was probably best not to enquire. 'You want to go to New York,' he said. 'Now there's a real town.'

She asked his name. 'Stafford?' she said. 'That's Irish, isn't it?'

He shrugged a shoulder. 'I guess.' He did not much care for the idea of being Irish, even though she was not like any of the Irish over here that he knew.

She asked him where he was from—'Originally, I mean. Where were you born?'

'Oh, out West,' he lied, in a voice he made purposely vague and dry, wanting to suggest sagebrush and shimmering deserts and a silent man solitary on his horse, gazing off from the rim of a mesa toward distant, rocky peaks.

They turned inland. She wondered, a little uneasily, where he was taking her. Well, it was what she had told him, to take her anywhere. And despite that eye of his in the mirror it was not unpleasant, rolling leisurely along these country roads that did not look all that much different from the roads at home.

The engine was running so smoothly he could hear the

quick little hiss of nylon against nylon when she crossed her legs.

'Do you have to drive at such a slow speed?' she said. 'I mean, is it the rule, here?'

'It's standard with Mr Crawford. But'—carefully—'I don't always stick to it.'

'Yes,' she said, 'I'm sure.'

She brought out her oval cigarettes and lit one. The smoke snaked over Andy Stafford's shoulder and he sniffed the unfamiliar flat dry papery odour of the tobacco and asked if they were Irish cigarettes. 'No,' she said, 'English.' She considered offering him one but thought she had better not. She held the slim silver case lightly in her palm and with her thumb clicked the catch open and shut, open and shut. She had suddenly begun to feel the effects of the air journey, and everything seemed to her to have a beat of its own, precise, regular, yet to be part, too, of a general ensemble, a sort of drawn-out, untidy, complexly rhythmic chord, which she could almost see in her mind, undulant, flowing, like a bundle of wires pulsing and twitching inside a pouring column of thick oil. The urge to sleep was like oil too, spreading over her mind and slowing it. She closed her eyes and felt the gathering momentum of the car as Andy Stafford increased the acceleration, gradually, or stealthily, as it even seemed—was he afraid she would tell on him for breaking the Crawford limit?—but the cushioned churning of the wheels underneath her feet seemed more like something that was happening inside her, and gave her a horrible, lurching sensation and she hastily opened her eyes and made herself focus on the road again. They were going very fast now, the car bounding along effortlessly with a muted roar, seeming to exult in its own tigerish power. Andy Stafford was tensed forward at the wheel. She noted his leather driving gloves with holes punched in the backs of them; he was just the type who would wear that sort of thing, she told herself, and then felt a little ashamed for thinking it. They were on a long straight stretch of narrow road. Tall marsh grasses growing on either side leaned forward languorously even before the car was abreast of them, its momentum somehow reaching a yard or two ahead and folding the air inwards. Phoebe stubbed out her cigarette and braced her hands flat on either side of her on the seat. The leather was stippled and warmly pliant under her palms. There was some kind of barrier in the road away in front of them, with an upright wooden pole and a white signboard with a black X painted on it. She felt rather than heard a drawn-out wail that seemed to come from far off, but a moment later there was the railroad train, bullet-nosed and enormous, hurtling forward at a diagonal to the road. Clearly, calmly, as if from high above the scene, she saw the X of the sign resolve itself into a diagram of the twin trajectories of car and train, speeding towards the level crossing. Now the upright wooden pole ahead quivered along its length and began jerkily to descend. '*Stop!*' she cried, and was startled—it had sounded more like a shout of glee than a cry of panic. Andy Stafford ignored her and on the car sped, seeming to sweep together all the countryside behind and whirl it with it into the funnel of its headlong rushing. She was sure they would hit the descending barrier—she could hear already the crash of metal and shattering glass and timber. In the corner of her eye she saw a snapshot, impossibly detailed and exact, of the crossing-keeper standing in the doorway of his wooden hut, his long-jawed face and his mouth open to call out something, a shapeless felt hat pushed to the back of his head and one buckle missing from the bib of his dungarees. A little black car, squat and rounded like a beetle, was approaching from the other side of the crossing, and at the sight of them surging forward it veered in fright and seemed for a moment as if it would scurry off the road altogether to hide among the marsh grass. Then with a rumble they went bounding over the tracks and Phoebe turned about quickly to see the barrier fall the last few feet and stop with a bounce, and a moment later the train thundered through, sending after them a long, accusatory bellow that dwindled quickly into the distance and died. They flashed past the little black car, which sounded at them its own little bleat of protest and reproof. She realised that she was laughing, laughing and hiccuping, and her hands were clutching each other in her lap.

They went on until the road took them around a bend and then stopped. There was a sensation of gliding, and settling, as if they had landed gently out of the air. Phoebe put three fingers over her mouth. Had she really laughed? 'What did you think you were doing?' she cried. 'We could have been killed.' He did not turn to her, only slid himself forward at the hips with a luxuriating sigh and rested his head on the back of the seat. He put on his chauffeur's cap, too, and tipped it over his eyes. She sat up very straight and glared at him, at the little she could see of him, in the almost horizontal angle he was sprawled at. 'And why have you stopped?'

'Catch our breath,' he said, his voice coming up relaxed and amused from under the peak of his cap. She could think of nothing else to say. He reached up and adjusted the mirror and his eyes sprang at her again, seeming set more closely together than ever and cut across half-way by the shiny cap-brim. He said in a low, insinuating sort of drawl, 'Think I could try one of them English cigarettes?'

She hesitated. She could hardly refuse, but honestly—! She felt distinctly giddy still. She snapped open the silver case and offered it over the padded back of the bench seat. He reached his left hand lazily across and took a cigarette, making sure his fingertips brushed against her hand. She could have done with another cigarette herself—she was beginning to understand why people smoked—but she knew obscurely that she must not seem to be joining him in anything that smacked of intimacy. She shut the case and returned it to her handbag—or purse, she must remember to say purse, in this country—and took out her lipstick instead, and peered into the little mirror of her compact. She could see clearly the two spots of bright pink on her cheekbones and the unsuppressible, almost wild light in her eyes. Well, at least she was not sleepy any more.

But when she had fixed her lips and put the lipstick and the compact away there seemed nothing else to do except sit with her hands in her lap and try not to look prim. The invisible thing that had sprouted earlier out of the silence between the two of them was turning rank now.

Abruptly Andy Stafford stirred himself and rolled his window down a little way and threw out the unsmoked three-quarters of the cigarette. 'Tastes like rawhide,' he said. He settled down as before, with his arms folded and his cap tipped over his eyes.

'Are you intending to stay here all day?' Phoebe demanded.

He waited a moment, and then said, putting on now the lazy, good-old-boy version of his drawl:

'Why don't you come and sit up here in front, with me?'

She gave a little gasp. 'I think,' she said, with all the weight and command she could muster, 'that you should take me home.'

It was peculiar, talking to him like this, ridiculous, really, since all she could see of him was the crown of his cap. He snickered and said:

'Home? That's a long way, even for a car as fancy as this one.'

'You know very well what I mean,' she snapped. 'Come on, drive—and not as if we're in a race.'

He straightened, taking his time, and started up the engine. At the next crossroads he steered them back in the direction of the coast. They did not speak now, but she could sense how pleased he was with himself. Had he really said that, about her coming into the front seat with him? Yet for all the indignation she was forcing herself to feel she was aware of another, altogether involuntary feeling, a sort of buzzing, burning sensation at the front of her mind that was uncomfortable and yet not entirely unpleasant, and her cheeks stung as if she had been slapped in a hard yet playful, provocative way. And when they arrived at the house and he made a little prancing leap out of the car in order to open the door for her before she had even begun to reach for the handle he gave her a look that was at once mocking, intimate and enquiring, and she knew he was asking her wordlessly if she intended to tell the others—Quirke, Rose, his employer—of all that had taken place in this past, fraught hour—but what was it, exactly, that had taken place?—and try not to as she might she responded to his silent query with a silent reply of her own. No, she would not tell, and they both knew it. Blushing, her forehead and cheeks fairly on fire by now, she brushed past him, not daring to look into his eyes again, saying only, and trying to make it sound brusque and offhand, that he had better go back to the village and collect Mr Quirke.

The man was waiting for him on a corner of the village's main street. He looked like a big old storm-tossed crow, leaning there on his stick with his black coat blowing out sideways in the wind and his black hat tilted down over his face. Andy got out and made to open the passenger door, hoping Quirke would sit beside him, but Quirke had already opened a rear door and was climbing into the back seat. There was something about Quirke that Andy liked, or that at least he respected—he guessed that was the word. Maybe it was just Quirke's size—Andy's father had been a big man—and they had hardly got under way again when he started to tell him about his plan for Stafford Limos. As he talked, the plan came to seem more and more possible, more and more real, so that after a while it was almost as if Stafford Limos was already in operation.

Quirke did not say much but that was all right since Andy, as Andy realised, was really talking to himself.

He was about to turn off the road and head for Moss Manor when Quirke interrupted him—he had got on to the Porsche that he was going to buy with his first six months' profits from the limo scheme—and said that he wanted to go to Brookline.

'A place called St Mary's,' Quirke said. 'It's an orphanage.'

Andy said nothing, only turned the car. He felt a trickling sensation down his spine. He had thought he would never again find himself anywhere near the place and now here was this guy wanting to be taken there. Why? Was he one of the Knights of whatever-it-was, over from Ireland to do some checking up on the facilities, see how the kids were being cared for, if the nuns were behaving themselves? And was he going to go there without telling Mr Crawford? Andy began to relax. That must be it: Quirke was a snoop. That was fine. He even liked the idea of Quirke getting the goods on old man Crawford, and that bitch Stephanus—what kind of a name was that anyway?—and the harp priest Harkins. There was a thing or two Andy himself could have told Quirke, if it was not for the business with the kid. Again he felt that trickle along his backbone. What if Quirke found out about the kid dying? What if? But no. How would he find out, and who would tell him? Not Stephanus or the priest, and old Crawford probably knew nothing about the accident, and had probably even forgotten about the kid itself, since there were so many at St Mary's and at the other places all over the state. For everyone, little Christine was history, and her name was likely never going to be mentioned again. Still, it was a pity he could not let Quirke know just what sort of a joint St Mary's was—unless, of course, he knew already.

4

QUIRKE HAD NOT expected a reception party. When he telephoned St Mary's from a bar in the village he had been kept waiting on the line for a long time, feeding dimes into the phone and listening to his own breathing making sounds like the sea in the mouthpiece, before he was put through to the Mother Superior. In a crisply cold voice she tried to establish who exactly he was and what his business with her might be. He told her his name, and fancied he heard a quick indrawing of her breath. The more evasive he became the more suspicious she sounded, but in the end, and with lingering reluctance, she had agreed that he might come to Brookline.

When he stepped inside the high, arched doorway of St Mary's he caught at once the unmistakable smell of the past and the years fell away like the leaves of a calendar and he was an orphan again. He stood in the silent hallway and looked at the statues in their niches of Mary and Jesus and Joseph—gentle Joe held what seemed to be a wood-plane in his improbably pale hands and looked both resentful and resigned—until a young nun with front teeth so prominent they seemed almost prehensile led him along soundless corridors and stopped at a door and knocked softly and a voice spoke from within.

The Mother Superior, when she stood up behind her desk, was tall and gaunt and grimly handsome. It was the priest with her, however, who spoke first. He was potato-pale with pale-red hair and green eyes that were sharp yet muddy; Quirke knew the type, remembered it, from Carricklea days, and nights. The cleric came forward, smiling unctuously with his mouth only, a hand outstretched. 'Mr Quirke,' he said. 'I'm Father Harkins, chaplain here at St Mary's.' His eyelashes, Quirke saw with almost a shiver, were almost white. He took Quirke's hand but instead of shaking it he drew him by it gently forward to the desk. 'And this is Sister Stephanus. And Sister Anselm.'

Quirke had not noticed the other nun, standing off to his right, beside a vast, empty fireplace of marble and polished brick. She was short and broad, with a sceptical yet not, he thought, unsympathetic look. The two nuns nodded to him. Father Harkins, who seemed to have taken it on himself to be the spokesman, said:

'You're Mr Crawford's son-in-law? Mr Crawford is a great friend of ours—a great friend of St Mary's.'

Quirke was conscious of Sister Stephanus's keen eye scanning him, like a fencing opponent, searching out his weak spots. The priest was about to speak again but the nun said:

'What can we do for you, Mr Quirke?'

Hers was the voice of authority, and its tone told him who was really in charge here. Still she gazed at him, cool, candid and even, it might be, a little amused. He fumbled his cigarettes from his pocket and lit one. Sister Stephanus, who had taken her seat again, pushed a large, crystal ashtray to the front edge of the desk where he might more easily reach it. He asked about the child, saying her name would probably be Christine and that if she had a surname it was likely to be Falls. 'I think she was brought here from Ireland,' he said. 'I have reason to believe she came to St Mary's.'

The silence that fell in the room was more eloquent than any words. Sister Stephanus touched lightly in succession a number of objects set out before her on the desk—a fountain pen, a paper-knife, one of two telephones—taking care not to move any of them from their places. This time when she spoke she did not look at him. 'What was it you wanted to know about this child, Mr Quirke?'

This child.

'It is,' he said, 'a personal matter.'

'Ah.'

There was another silence. The priest looked from the nun to Quirke and back again but had no word to offer. Suddenly, from where she stood by the fireplace, the other nun, Sister Anselm, coughed and said:

'She died.'

Father Harkins whirled on her with a look of panic, drawing a hand up sharply as if he might run forward and strike her, but Sister Stephanus did not flinch, and continued to regard Quirke with that cool, measuring gaze, as if she had heard nothing. The priest looked at her and licked his lips, and with an effort resumed his bland smile. 'Ah, yes,' the priest said. 'Little Christine. Yes, now I . . .' His tongue snaked over his lips again, his colourless eyelashes beating rapidly. 'There was an accident, I'm afraid. She was with a family. Very unfortunate. Very sad.'

This left yet another, trailing silence, into which Quirke said:

'What family?' Father Harkins lifted his eyebrows. 'The family the child was with—who were they?'

The priest gave a breathy laugh and this time lifted both his hands as if to catch an invisible, tricky ball that Quirke had lobbed at him. 'Oh, now, Mr Quirke,' he said in a rush, 'we couldn't be giving out information of that nature. These situations call for great discretion, as I'm sure you'll—'

'I'd like to find out who she was,' Quirke said. 'I mean, where she came from. Her history.'

The priest was about to speak again but Sister Stephanus drew in a slow breath through her nostrils and he glanced at her uncertainly and was silent. The nun's smile deepened. She said softly:

'Don't you know, Mr Quirke?'

He saw at once that he had blundered. If he knew nothing, they need not tell him anything. What did he have, other than a name?

Abruptly Sister Stephanus rose from her chair with the brisk finality of a judge delivering a verdict. 'I'm sorry, Mr Quirke, that we cannot help you,' she said. 'As Father Harkins says, these matters are delicate. Information of the kind you ask for must be kept in the strictest confidence. It is our covenant, here at St Mary's. I know you'll understand.' She must have pressed a bell under the desk for Quirke heard the door behind him open, and she looked past him and said, 'Sister Anne, please show Mr

Quirke out.' She held out a hand to him and he had no choice but to rise too and take it. 'Goodbye, Mr Quirke. So nice to have met you. Please give our kind regards to Mr Crawford. We hear he's not in the best of health.'

Quirke, irritated by her queenly plurals, had to admire the deftness with which she had brought the encounter to a close. As he turned away he glanced at Sister Anselm, but she was gazing grim-faced into a far corner of the ceiling and would not return his look. Father Harkins stepped forward, glistening with relief, and walked with him to the door. He seemed about to put a friendly hand on his shoulder but thought better of it. He said: 'You're not one of the Order yourself, I take it, Mr Quirke?' Quirke looked at him. 'The Knights, I mean? Of St Patrick? Mr Crawford is a lifelong member, I believe. In fact, if I'm not mistaken, a founding member.'

'No,' Quirke said dryly, 'I'm sure you're not mistaken.'

The buck-toothed nun opened the door for him and, swinging himself forward on his stick, he yanked himself from the room, like an angry parent dragging away a stubbornly recalcitrant child.

Seeing him come stumping down the steps Andy Stafford took his knees from the dashboard of the Buick and sat up hastily and donned his chauffeur's cap. Quirke got into the car without a word, refusing his help. He seemed mad. Andy did not know what to think about that. What had happened in there? He could not get the suspicion out of his head that Quirke's coming here was something to do with the kid. It was crazy, he knew, but there was still that feeling in his spine, like something cold rolling down inside it.

They were on the driveway when Quirke tapped him on the shoulder and told him to stop. He had been looking back and had seen through the bare trees Sister Anselm come out by a side door of the orphanage. 'Wait here,' he said, and got himself out of the car, grunting.

Andy watched him poling himself back up the drive on his stick, and the nun stopping to wait for him, and the two of them turning and setting off along a path under the trees, the two of them limping.

At first the nun would tell Quirke nothing, yet he was sure she had not appeared from that doorway by chance. They walked along together in silence, their breath misting in the winter air. They had acknowledged, with no words but only from each of them simultaneously an ironic, diagonally directed glance, the melancholy comedy of their like conditions, his smashed knee, her twisted hip. There were ragged patches of snow under the trees. The path was paved with wood-chips. The sharp, resinous odour of the chips reminded him of the pine woods behind the big stone house at Carricklea. All around them quick, brown birds, seemingly unfrightenable, were pecking busily among the dead leaves. Grackles, were they? Choughs? He knew so little about this country, not even the names of its commonest birds. The sky among the tracery of branches was the colour of dulled steel. His knee had begun to ache. The nun wore no coat over her habit. 'Are you not cold, Sister?' he asked. She shook her head; she had her hands folded before her, using the broad sleeves of her habit as a muff. He tried to guess her age. Fiftyish, he thought. Her limp was not so much a limp as a toppling, sideways heave at every other step, as if the pivot that held her upright had suffered a corkscrew twist half-way along its length.

'Please,' he said, 'tell me about the child. I've no intention of doing anything. I simply want to hear what happened.'

'Why?'

'I don't know. I honestly don't know.'

'You're a doctor, right? Were you involved in the birth?'

'No. That is, not directly. I'm a pathologist.'

'I see.'

He doubted that she did. He scuffed at the wood-chips with the tip of his blackthorn stick. Out of nowhere a picture came to him of Philomena the nurse astride him in the wan light of a Dublin afternoon. To have been there, and then here; these things, he thought, that seem so straightforward and are not.

'Tell me at least who the family was,' he said, 'the family that adopted her.'

The nun snorted.

'Adopted!' she said. 'We don't bother with such legal niceties here at St Mary's.' She stopped on the path and turned to face him. Her lips were blue from the cold and her angry eyes were red-rimmed and teary. 'How much do you know of what goes on here, Mr Quirke?' she asked. 'I mean here, and where you come from, too—the whole thing.'

He braced the walking-stick at an angle to the ground and gazed at it. 'I know,' he said measuredly, 'that Joshua Crawford finances a scheme for children from Ireland to be brought out here. I suspect Christine was one of them.'

They walked on.

'A scheme, yes,' she said. 'A scheme that has been going on for twenty years—did you know that? Yes, twenty years. Can you imagine how many children that is? How many babies taken over here and handed out like . . . like . . . ?' She could find no word sufficiently encompassing. 'They call it charity, but that's not what it is. It's power, just naked power.'

Somewhere behind them a bell began to clang with a hectic urgency.

'Power?' Quirke said. 'What kind of power?'

'Power over people. Over their souls.'

Souls. The word had a ring to it, urgent and dark like the peals of the bell. *A planter of souls*, Josh Crawford had said.

They did not speak for the space of half a dozen paces. Then the nun said:

'They care nothing for the children. Oh, they think they do, but they don't. Their only interest is to see them grow up and take their place in the structure they've devised.' She paused, and gave a meagre laugh. 'St Mary's, Mr Quirke, is a forcing house for the religious. The children are delivered to us, some no more than a few weeks old. We make sure they're healthy—that's my job, by the way, I'm a physician'—again she laughed thinly—'and then they're . . . distributed.' The bell had stopped. The birds, at some sound in the aftermath of the pealing that only they could hear, flew up in a flock, their wings whirring, then quickly settled again. 'We hand them out to good Catholic homes, people we can trust—the respectable poor. Then when the children are old enough they are taken back and put into seminaries and convents—whether they want to be or not. It's a machine for making priests, for making nuns. Do you see?'

She looked at him sidelong. He was frowning.

'Yes,' he said, 'I see. Only . . .'

She nodded. 'But it doesn't seem so bad, right? Taking in orphans, finding them good homes—'

'I was an orphan, Sister. I was glad to get out of the orphanage.'

'Ah,' she said. They had come again in sight of the Buick; the engine was going, and pallid wisps of smoke were trailing from the exhaust pipe. They stopped. 'But you see, it's unnatural, this thing, Mr Quirke,' the nun said. 'That's the point. When bad folk take it on themselves to do what are supposed to be good works it makes a sulphurous smell. I think you've had a whiff of it, that smell.'

'Tell me about the child,' he said. 'Tell me about Christine Falls.'

'No. I've told you too much already.'

He thought: *Just like Dolly Moran did.*

'Please,' he said. 'Things have happened, wicked things.' She cast a glance enquiringly at the walking-stick. 'Yes, this,' he said, 'but worse, too. Far worse.'

She looked down. 'It's cold, I have to go back.' Yet still she stood, gazing at him thoughtfully. Then she came to a decision. 'What you should do, Mr Quirke,' she said, 'is ask the nurse, the one who looks after Mr Crawford.'

'Brenda?' He stared. 'Brenda Ruttledge?'

'Yes, if that's her name. She knows about the child, about little Christine. She can tell you, some of it, anyway.

And listen, Mr Quirke.' She was looking past him to where the Buick waited on the drive. 'Watch out for yourself. There are people—there are people who are not what they seem, who are more than they seem.' She smiled at him, this huge man standing stooped before her, asking his awkward questions. *Yes*, she thought: *an orphan*. 'Goodbye, Mr Quirke,' she said. 'I wish you well. From the little I've seen of you, I think you're a good man, if only you knew it.'

5

Moss Manor, when Quirke got back to it, gave the impression of having been flung wide open, like a door. There was an ambulance outside and a pair of automobiles, and in the entranceway two grave, sober-suited men were engaged in a hushed conversation: they paused and looked at him with curiosity as he entered but he ignored them and went through into the house and lurched from room to room. He was angry again, he was not sure why, exactly, for what he had learned from Sister Anselm had not been news to him, not really. He had begun to consider the possibility that this unfocused anger would be the condition of his life from now on, that he would have to keep bouncing along before it helplessly for ever, like a piece of litter buffeted by an unceasing wind. In the main drawing room he came upon the mousey maid, he could not remember her name, arranging dried flowers in a vase on the lid of the grand piano on which he was certain no one had ever played a note. A great fire of logs was burning in the fireplace. The maid quailed before him. He asked her where Miss Ruttledge was. She looked blank. 'The nurse,' he said, beginning to shout, and thumping his stick on the floor, 'Mr Crawford's nurse!' She told him Brenda was with Mr Crawford now, and that Mr Crawford was very poorly, and her lower lip trembled. He turned from her and hauled himself up the staircase, cursing the dead weight of his leg. At what he knew to be Josh Crawford's room he knocked perfunctorily and pushed open the door.

The scene within had the heightened dramatic composition of a painting, a genre scene of a deathbed with attendant mourners. Josh Crawford lay on his back as on a high white catafalque, his arms resting by his sides over the covers, the jacket of his pyjamas thrown open to reveal his huge, heaving chest all furred over with steel-grey hair. An oxygen mask was strapped to his face, and his breaths came in long, laborious rattlings, as if he were hauling on a chain inside him, link by painful link. Phoebe sat on a chair by the bed, leaning forward and holding one of her grandfather's hands in both of hers. Brenda Ruttledge stood close behind her, stylised in her white outfit and her jaunty little hat, the painter's very model of a nurse. On the other side of the bed Rose Crawford stood with one arm folded and a hand lifted to her chin, another stylised figure, representing something certainly unsuitable to her, such as patience, or fidelity, or wifely calm. Hearing him at the door Brenda Ruttledge turned, and with a jerk of his head he signalled to her to come out into the corridor. She did so, and closed the door softly behind her. She was about to speak but he cut her off with a chopping gesture of his hand and demanded:

'Was it you who brought the child?' She frowned, and there came into her face a sliver of guilty fear. 'Come on,' he said harshly, 'tell me.'

'What child?'

'What child, what child! Christine, her name was. Did they make you bring her over here with you?'

She stared at him, shaking her head.

'I don't know what—'

The door opened and Phoebe leaned out, ignoring Quirke.

'Quick,' she said to Brenda, 'you're needed.'

She stepped back inside the room and Brenda hurried after her. Before the door was shut, however, Rose Crawford slipped out in her place.

'Come on,' she said to Quirke in a deadened voice, 'I need a cigarette.'

He followed her downstairs, to the drawing room. He expected to find the maid still loitering there, but she was gone. Rose walked to the fireplace and took two cigarettes from a lacquered box on the mantelpiece and lit both of them and handed one to Quirke.

'Lipstick,' she said. 'Sorry.'

He went and stood at the window. Outside, scant snow was falling in soft, flabby flakes. From here he could see a flank of the Crystal Gallery, a cliff of glass rising sheer against the leaden sky.

'I'm sorry,' Quirke said. She looked at him enquiringly. 'It can't be easy for you,' he said, 'waiting for the end.'

He was trying to remember what it was called, that laboured breathing of the dying; there was, he knew, a technical name for it. He had forgotten so many things.

Rose shrugged. 'Yes. Well.' She touched a log in the fire with the tip of her shoe. 'Phoebe has been very good with him,' she said. 'I would not have thought she had it in her. She's in his will, you know.'

'Oh?' He turned from her to the window, a sort of flinching. It was not news to him and yet it rankled to hear her say it; Quirke had made no will for anyone to be in.

'Yes. He's left her a lot of money.'

'And how do you feel about that?'

She threw up her head and laughed without sound. 'Oh, I feel fine,' she said. 'Don't worry, I get the bulk of the dough, if that's what you mean—and God knows there's plenty of it. But she'll be a rich girl, will Phoebe.'

'I'm sorry to hear it.'

'Why—don't you want her to be an heiress?'

'I want her to have an ordinary life.'

She gave him a sardonic, sideways glance. He looked out at the snow again; half of the flakes seemed to be falling upwards. 'Is there such a thing as an ordinary life?' she asked.

'There could be, for her.'

'If?'

'If you don't try to hold on to her.'

She laughed again, a soundless protest. '"Hold on to her"! Why, Mr Quirke, the things you do say!'

He studied the burning tip of his cigarette. 'She told me,' he said, 'that you asked her to stay here, in Boston.'

'And you don't think she should?'

He walked to the fireplace and flicked the remains of the cigarette into the flames. She took a step forward and suddenly they were standing close together, face to face. There was a tiny flaw in the iris of her left eye, he saw, a splinter of white piercing the lustrous black.

'Look, Mrs Crawford—'

'Rose.'

He drew a breath. 'I came here, to Boston, because Sarah asked me to come. She asked me to look after Phoebe.'

She tilted her head to the side and squinted up at him from under her eyelashes. 'Ah,' she said, 'Sarah, of course—Sarah who hates me.' He blinked. He had never thought to wonder what Sarah might feel about this woman, hardly older than she was, who had married her father and who was therefore, absurdly, her stepmother. She moved even closer to him, gazing directly, big-eyed now, into his face. 'Mr Quirke,' Rose said, in her soft drawl, 'you may disapprove of me, and frankly I don't care that you do, but at least you'll grant I'm not a hypocrite.'

Behind her the log that she had touched with her foot made its delayed, ashy collapse. She was studying him as if she were committing his face to memory. They heard her name called urgently, but for fully half a dozen seconds she made no move to answer the summons. Then, as she turned, he caught the smell of her perfumed skin, the faint, thrilling rankness of it.

It was evening when Josh Crawford died. The house went silent. The ambulance departed, unneeded, followed by the two sombre men, each in his own automobile. Quirke had not learned the identity of this pair; perhaps they were Rose's lawyers, there to authenticate her husband's demise; he would not put it past her. Dinner was served but there was no one to eat it: Rose and Phoebe closeted themselves in Rose's room, and Quirke found Brenda Ruttledge and brought her again to the swimming-pool. She sat in one of the cane chairs, staring into the water. Something seemed poised above them in the swaying air, among the echoes, a large, liquid vagueness. Quirke offered her a cigarette and this time she took it. He saw the inexpert way she held it tilted between stiff fingers, the way she swigged the smoke and blew it out again in puffs, unswallowed. Someone else smoked like that—was it Phoebe? When she moved her feet the rubber soles of her nurse's white shoes squeaked on the tiles. Quirke asked her:

'Who arranged it?'

She pouted, pushing out her lower lip, and for a moment was a stubborn child. Then she shrugged. 'Matron.'

'At the hospital—at the Holy Family?'

'She knew Mr Griffin had fixed up the job for me here, looking after Mr Crawford. She said there was a favour I could do in return. She said I'd be paid. I thought, What harm, to take care of the poor little thing?' She looked at the cigarette she was holding in her fingers and frowned. 'What am I doing?' she murmured to herself. 'I don't even smoke.'

'Did she tell you whose the child was—I mean, who the parents were, who the father was?'

She bent and placed the half-smoked cigarette on the tiles between her feet and trod it carefully under the sole of her shoe, then picked up the flattened stub and hid it away carefully in a pocket of her uniform, and Quirke briefly thought of red-haired Maisie whose child was probably born by now, and perhaps taken away from her, too, for all he knew.

'She said I didn't need to know any of that, that it

would be better if I didn't know. I thought the father must be someone . . . you know, someone big, someone important.'

'Such as?'

She wrapped her arms around herself and rocked herself forward and back in the chair. 'I'm telling you,' she said, 'I don't know!'

'But you have a suspicion.'

Now she unwrapped her arms and banged her fists on her knees and glared at him. 'What do you want me to say?' she cried. 'I don't know who the father was. *I don't know!*'

He sat back in the chair, expelling a long breath, and a ripple of creaks and crackles ran through the woven canes. He said:

'When did Mr Griffin arrange the job for you?'

She looked away. 'Early last summer.'

'Six months ago? More? And you didn't tell me.'

Again she glared at him. 'Well, you didn't ask, did you?'

He shook his head. 'All these secrets, Brenda. I'd never have thought it of you.'

She had stopped listening to him. She looked into the water, its surreptitious slap and sway. 'I did my best for him,' she said. For a second he did not know who it was she meant. She lifted her eyes from the surface of the pool and looked at him almost pleadingly. 'Do you think Mr Crawford was a bad man?'

Quirke turned up his empty palms and showed them to her.

'He was a man, Brenda,' he said. 'That's all. And now he's gone.'

6

SISTER ANSELM was surprised, not by the thing itself but by the suddenness of it, the finality. Yet when the summons had come for her to go immediately—immediately!—to Mother Superior's office she had known what to expect. She stood before the wide expanse of Sister Stephanus's desk and felt like a novice again. All kinds of unexpected, stray things went through her head, scraps of prayers, lines from old medical texts, snatches of songs she had not heard in forty years. And memories, too, of Sumner Street, the games they played, the skipping ropes and spinning tops, the chalk-marks on the pavements. Her father singing and then shouting. Her mother with her freckled arms plunged to the elbows in a tub of suds, her lower lip jutting out as she blew away from her face the strands of hair that had come loose from the bun she always wore. After her father had knocked her down the stairs she came back from the hospital with her leg in an iron brace and the kids on the block were first in awe of her but soon they were calling her names, Peg-leg, of course, or Peggy's Leg after the candy stick, or Hopalong Farrell. The convent had been an escape, a sanctuary; she had told herself, with bitter amusement, that everyone was crippled there and she would not be noticed among them. She had no vocation for the religious life, but the nuns would educate her, and an education was what she had set her heart on, since there would be nothing else for her. They sent her to college, and to medical school. They were proud of her. One of them got an uncle who worked at the *Globe* to put in a paragraph about her—*South Boston Girl's Medical First*. Yes, the Order had been good to her. So what right had she to complain now?

'I'm sorry,' Sister Stephanus said. She was doing that thing she did, her checklist, touching with her fingertips the lamp, the blotter, the telephone. She would not look up. 'I got the call this morning from Mother House. They want you to leave right away.'

Sister Anselm nodded. 'Vancouver,' she said tonelessly.

'St James's needs a doctor.'

'You need a doctor here.'

Sister Stephanus chose to misunderstand. 'Yes,' she said, 'they're sending someone. She's quite young. Just qualified, I believe.'

'Well, that's grand.'

The room was cold; Stephanus was mean about things like that, the heating in the place, hot water for baths, the novices' linen. Sister Anselm shifted her weight from her aching hip. Stephanus had invited her to sit but she preferred to stand. Like that brave patriot—who was it? Someone in an opera?—refusing the blindfold when he faced the firing squad. Oh, yes, lame Peggy Farrell, the last of the heroes.

'I'm sorry,' Sister Stephanus said again. 'There really is

nothing I can do. You know as well as I, you haven't been happy here for some time now.'

'That's right: I haven't been happy with the way things are going here, if that's what you mean.'

Sister Stephanus made a fist and struck the knuckle of her index finger sharply on the leather desk-top.

'These matters are not for us to judge! We have our vows. Obedience, Sister. Obedience to the Lord's will.'

Sister Anselm gave a low, dry laugh. 'And you're confident you know what the Lord's will is, are you?'

Sister Stephanus sighed angrily. She looked drawn, and when she bunched up her lips like that it made the grey bristles on her upper lip stand out. She was getting old, old and ugly, Sister Anselm thought, she who was once known as the loveliest girl in South Boston, Monica Lacey the shyster lawyer's daughter whose family had beggared themselves to send her to Bryn Mawr, no less, from where she came back a lady and promptly broke her father's heart by declaring she had heard God's call and wanted to be a nun. 'Our bride of Christ, by Christ!' Louis Lacey cried bitterly and washed his hands of her. Now she looked up.

'You wear your conscience on your sleeve, Sister,' she said. 'Others of us must live in the real world, and manage as best we can. It's not easy. Now, I have work to do, and you'll need to be packing your things.'

The silence drew out between them. Sister Anselm looked up at the window beside her and the winter sky beyond. What life did they get, in the end, either of them?

'Ah, Monica Lacey,' she said softly, 'that it should have come to this.'

7

THE MORNING OF Josh Crawford's funeral dawned white and cold, and more snow was forecast. The burial had been delayed to await the arrival from Ireland of Sarah and Mal Griffin and the Judge. At the graveside Sarah in her black veil looked to Quirke more like a widow than a daughter. The Judge was rheum-eyed and vague. Mal in his dark suit and dark silk tie and gleaming white shirt had the air of an officiating presence, not the undertaker himself, perhaps, but the undertaker's man, there to represent the professional side of death and its rituals, and Quirke pondered again the irony that such a funereal figure should in his true profession be an usher at the gates of life.

It was a day of solemn celebration for the Boston Irish. The Mayor was there, of course, and the Governor, and the Archbishop officiated at High Mass and later at the cemetery said the prayers over the coffin. The Cardinal had been expected, but at the last minute had sent his regrets only, confirming the rumour that he and Josh Crawford had got into a fight over the awarding of a state haulage contract the previous year. Old men, as some wag at the funeral remarked in a stage whisper, do not forget.

The Archbishop, tall and silver-haired and handsome, every inch the Hollywood image of a prelate, intoned the service of the dead in a sonorous singsong, and when he finished a single snowflake appeared out of nowhere and hovered over the mouth of the grave, like the manifestation of a blessing from above being reluctantly bestowed. When the prayers were done there came the little ceremony of the scattering of the clay, which never failed to catch Quirke's morbid fancy. A miniature silver shovel was produced and Sarah was the first to take it. The earth fell on the coffin with a hollow rattle. When the shovel was offered to the Judge he shook his head and turned away.

The Archbishop put a hand on the old man's sleeve and spoke to him, inclining his film star's fine, silvered head. 'Garret, it's good to see you, even on such a sad occasion.'

'We did our old friend proud today, I think, William.'

'Yes, indeed. A very great man, and a loyal son of the Church.'

Sarah and Quirke walked together towards the cars. She was thinner than when he had last seen her, and there was a vehemence in her look that he did not recognise. She asked him if he had talked to Phoebe, and when he looked blank she clicked her tongue at him angrily. 'Did you tell her what I told you?' she said. 'For God's sake, Quirke, you can't have forgotten!'

'No,' he said, 'no, I didn't forget.'

'Well?'

What could he say? Behind her veil Sarah's lips tightened to a bitter chevron, and she quickened her pace and walked on, leaving him struggling on his stick in her wake.

At the house the family lingered in the entrance hall in an uncertain cluster, awaiting the rest of the mourners. Phoebe's face was blotched from weeping and the Judge looked about him as if he did not know where he was. Sarah and Mal held apart from each other. Sarah took off her hat and stood fingering the veil; she would not look at Quirke.

Rose Crawford put a hand on his arm and drew him aside. 'You don't seem the most popular family member today,' she murmured. The cars were arriving in the drive. She sighed. 'Will you keep me company, Quirke? It's going to be a long day.'

But at once she was separated from him as, first, the Archbishop made his stately entrance and she went forward to greet him. Then the others came in behind him, the clerics and the politicians and the businessmen and their wives, ashen-faced, blue-lipped, muttering to each other of the cold and looking about with covert eagerness, wanting drink and food and warm fires. The red-haired priest from St Mary's was there, and Costigan, in his shiny suit and horn-rimmed spectacles, and there were others whom Quirke recognised from the party for the Judge that night at Mal and Sarah's house. He watched them gathering, and followed them into the drawing room, where the funeral meats were set out, and as he listened to the hubbub of their mingled and clashing voices, a sense

almost of physical revulsion welled up in him. These were
the people who had killed Christine Falls and her child,
who had sent the torturers after Dolly Moran, who had
ordered that he be dragged down those slimed steps and
kicked and beaten to within an inch of his life. Oh, not all
of them; no doubt there were those among them who were
innocent, innocent of these particular crimes, at least. And
he, how innocent was he? What right did he have to stand
upon a height and look down on them, he who had not
even found the courage to tell his daughter the truth of
who her parents were?

He went to where Mal was standing by one of the tall
windows, his hands in the pockets of his buttoned-up suit
jacket, looking out at the garden and the gathering snow.
'You should take a drink, Mal,' he said. 'It helps.'

Mal turned his head and gave him that look he had,
frog-eyed and blank, then went back to contemplating the
garden. 'I don't recall it helping you much,' he said.

The wind blew a billow of snow against the window; it
made a wet, soft sound. Quirke said:

'I know about the child.'

Mal's features registered the faintest frown but he did
not turn. He pushed his hands deeper into his jacket
pockets and jingled something there, keys, or coins, or
the dog-tags of the dead. 'Oh?' he said. 'What child is
that?'

'The child that Christine Falls was carrying. The one
that wasn't stillborn. Christine was her name, too.'

Mal sighed. For a long moment he was silent, and then
said:

'Funny, I don't remember snow, when we were here, all

those years ago.' He turned his glance and looked into Quirke's face in search of something. 'Do you, Quirke? Do you remember snow?'

'Yes, there was snow,' Quirke said. 'A whole winter of it.'

'I suppose there would have been.' Mal, facing the window again, was nodding slowly, as if at word of some far-off wonder. He lifted a finger and tapped it on the bridge of his glasses. 'I had forgotten that.' The light from the garden was dead white against his face. He cracked his knuckles pensively.

'She was yours, wasn't she?' Quirke said. 'Your child.'

Now Mal dropped his eyes and smiled. 'Oh, Quirke,' he said, as if almost with fondness, 'you know nothing. I've told you that before.'

Quirke said:

'I know that the child is dead.'

There was another silence. Mal was frowning again, and glancing here and there distractedly, from the garden to the folds of the roped-back drapes to the floor at his feet, as if there were a thing he had lost that might be found anywhere, in any of these places.

'I'm sorry to hear that,' he said absently. Then of a sudden he turned fully towards Quirke and laid a hand on his shoulder. Quirke looked at the hand; when last had either of them touched the other? 'All this business,' Mal said, 'why can't you let it go, Quirke?'

'It won't let me go.'

Mal considered this for a moment, pursing his lips judiciously. He let his hand fall from Quirke's shoulder. 'It's not like you, Quirke,' he said, 'this stubbornness to see a thing through.'

'No,' Quirke said, 'I suppose it's not.'

And then all at once he saw it, the entire thing, and how wrong he had been all along, wrong about Mal, and so much else.

Mal had turned his head and was watching him again, and when Quirke met his eye he saw what Quirke had suddenly seen, and he nodded once, faintly.

Quirke wandered through the house. In Josh Crawford's library the fire of pine logs was burning as usual and the light from the window gleamed on the upper cheek of the globe of the world. He went to the table where the drinks were and poured himself half a tumblerful of scotch. Behind him Rose Crawford said, 'Goodness, Mr Quirke, you do look grim.' He turned quickly. She was stretched in an armchair under a tall, potted palm. Her tight black dress was rucked at the hips and she had kicked off one of her shoes. She had a cigarette in one hand and an empty martini glass in the other, tilted at an angle. She was, he could see, a little tipsy. 'Do you think,' she said, proffering the glass, 'you could fix me another one of these painkillers?'

He went to her and took the glass and returned to the table. 'How are you?' he said.

'How am I?' She considered. 'Sad. I miss him already.' He brought her the drink and handed it to her. She fished out the olive with her fingers and munched it ruminatively. 'He was funny, you know,' she said, 'in his awful way. I mean humorous. He made me laugh.' She spat the olive stone delicately into her fist. 'Even in these last days, when he was so ill, we were still laughing. Means a lot to a girl, the occasional chuckle.' She squinted up at him. 'I guess you wouldn't have appreciated his jokes, Mr Quirke.' She put out her fist and he opened his palm and she dropped the olive stone into it. 'Thanks.' She frowned. 'Sit down, will you? I hate to be loomed over.'

He went and sat on the sofa that was set back from the fireplace. The snow outside was falling fast now, he fancied he could hear the huge, busy whisper of it as it swamped the air and settled on the already blanketed lawn and on the invisible terraces and stone steps and gravelled walkways. He thought of the sea out there beyond the garden, the waves a dark, muddy mauve, swallowing the endless fallings of frail flakes. Rose, too, was looking towards the windows and the slanted, moving whiteness beyond.

'Coincidence,' she said. 'I just realised, he died on our wedding anniversary. Trust him.' She laughed. 'He probably planned it. He had powers, you know. It's true, you think I'm making it up—he could read my mind. Maybe he's reading it now'—she looked at Quirke with a lazy, sly smile—'though I hope not.' She heaved a shivery sigh, weary and regretful. 'He was a mean old buzzard, I suppose, but he was my mean old buzzard.' Her cigarette had gone out, and he rose and brought his lighter and held it for her, leaning on his stick. 'Look at you,' she said. 'They did beat up on you, didn't they?'

'Yes,' he said, 'they did.' He returned to the sofa; he noticed that his glass was empty.

'But you must be happy, now,' she said, 'with Sarah

here?' When she spoke the name she put into her voice a huskily mocking tremor. She grinned at him. 'Why don't you tell me about her: her, and Mal, and Delia?'

He made an impatient gesture. 'That's all old history,' he said.

'Oh, but the old stuff is always the best. Secrets are like wine, Josh used to say—they get a richer flavour, a finer bouquet, with every year that passes. I'm trying to picture the four of you here'—she waggled the stem of her glass to indicate all that she meant by *here*—'happy and gay. Parties, tennis on the lawn, all that. The two beautiful sisters, the two dashing medical men. How Josh must have hated you.'

'Did he tell you that?' he asked with interest. 'That he hated me?'

'I don't know that we ever got that far in our discussions of you, Mr Quirke.'

She was making fun of him again. She sipped her drink and watched him with faint merriment over the rim of her glass.

'Will you,' he asked, 'go on payrolling this business with the babies that he was operating?'

She lifted her eyebrows and opened wide her eyes. 'Babies?' she said, then turned her head aside and shrugged. 'Oh, that. He made me promise I would. It would be his ticket out of Purgatory, he said. Purgatory! Honestly! He really believed all that, you know, Heaven, Hell, redemption, angels dancing on the head of a pin— the whole caboodle. He would get furious when I laughed. But how could I not? Laugh, I mean.' She looked down. 'Poor Josh.' She began to cry, making no sound. She caught a tear on a fingertip and held it out for him to inspect. 'Look,' she said, 'neat Tanqueray, with just the faintest hint of dry vermouth.' She lifted her head and a palm frond brushed her cheek and she swatted it away. 'Goddamned things,' she said, 'I'm going to have every one of them yanked up and burned.' She let her shoulders droop. She sniffed. 'A gentleman,' she said, in a parody of a bobby-soxer's twitter, 'would offer his handkerchief.'

He heaved himself up again and limped across to her and handed her the folded square of linen. She blew her nose loudly. He realised that he wanted to touch her, to caress her hair, to run a finger along the clean, cool line of her jaw. 'What will you do?' he said.

She wadded up the handkerchief and gave it back to him with a wryly apologetic grimace. 'Oh, who knows?' she said. 'Maybe I'll sell this dump and move to rotten old Europe. Can't you see me, in furs, with a lapdog, the most sought-after widow in Monte Carlo? Would you make a play for me, Quirke? Accompany me to the roulette tables, travel with me on my yacht to the isles of Greece?' She laughed softly down her nose. 'No. Hardly your style. You'd rather sit in the Dublin rain nursing your unrequited love for'—she let her voice sink tremulously again—'*Saarah*!'

A log shifted in the fire and a rush of sparks flew up, crackling.

'Rose,' he said, surprised at the sound of her name in his mouth, 'I want you to stop supporting this thing with the children. I want you to cut off the funds.'

She tilted her head and looked at him, smiling a pursed, lopsided smile. 'Well, if you do,' she said softly, 'you'll have to be nice to me.' She held out her glass. 'You can start by getting me another drinkie, big boy.'

Later, when the snow had stopped and a wettish sun was struggling to shine, he found himself in the Crystal Gallery, not knowing quite how he had got there. He had drunk too much scotch, and he was feeling dazed and unsteady. His leg seemed larger and heavier than before, and the knee had swollen inside its bandages and itched tormentingly. He sat down on the wrought-iron bench where he had sat with Josh Crawford that first night after he and Phoebe had arrived, which seemed so long ago, now. The snow had brought down upon the house a huge, muffled silence. It buzzed in his ears along with the other buzz that was the effect of the alcohol; he closed his eyes but the darkness made him feel queasy and he had to open them again. And then suddenly Sarah was there, as if she had somehow materialised out of the silence and the snow-light. She was standing a little way from him, twisting something in her fingers and looking out towards the distant, dark line of the sea. He struggled to his feet, and at the sound he made she gave a little start, as if she had not seen him, or had forgotten he was there.

'Are you all right?' she said.

He waved a hand. 'Yes, yes. Tired. My leg hurts.'

She was not listening. She was looking towards the horizon again. 'I'd forgotten,' she said, 'how beautiful it could be, here. I often think we should have stayed.'

He was trying to see what it was she was twisting in her hands. 'We?' he said.

'Mal and I. Things might have been different.' She saw him looking at what she was holding, and showed it to him. 'Phoebe's scarf,' she said. 'There was talk of her and her grandfather going for a walk, if Rose can get someone to clear the paths.' Quirke, sweating now from the alcohol in his blood and the ache in his knee, tottered to the bench and collapsed on it again, his stick clattering against the iron of the seat. 'I saw you talking,' Sarah said, 'you and Mal. He has no secrets from me, you know. He thinks he has, but he hasn't.' She walked forward a little, away from him. The palms and the tall ferns rose against her in a green, dense wall. She spoke to him over her shoulder. 'We were happy here, weren't we, in those days? Mal, you, me . . .'

Quirke put the heels of both hands to his bandaged knee and pressed, and felt a gratifying throb that was part pain and part a vindictive pleasure. 'And then,' he said, 'then there was Delia.'

'Yes. Then there was Delia.'

He pressed his knee again, gasping a little and grimacing.

'What are you doing?' Sarah said, looking at him.

'My penance.'

He sat back, panting, on the bench. There were times when he was sure he could feel the pin in his knee, the hot steel sunk rigid in the bone.

'Delia would sleep with you, that was it, wasn't it?' Sarah said in a new, a hardened voice, hard and sharp as the skewer in his leg. 'She would sleep with you, and I wouldn't. It was as simple as that. And then Mal saw his chance, with me.' She laughed, and the laugh had the same hardness as her voice. She was still turned partly away from him, and was craning her neck, as if in search of something on the horizon, or beyond. 'Time is the opposite of space, have you noticed?' she said. 'In space, everything gets more blurred the further away you get. With time it's different, everything becomes clear.' She paused. 'What were you talking about, to Mal?' She gave up looking for whatever it was she had been seeking and turned to gaze at him. Her new thinness had sharpened the lines of her face, making her seem at once more beautiful and more troubled. 'Tell me,' she said. 'Tell me what you were talking about.'

He shook his head. 'Ask him,' he said.

'He won't tell me.'

'Then neither will I.' He put a hand to the place beside him, inviting her to sit. She hesitated, and then came to him, looking at her feet in the way that she did, as if distrustful of the ground, or her ability to negotiate her way over it. She sat. 'I want Phoebe to come back with me, to Ireland,' he said. 'Will you help me to persuade her?'

She gazed before her, leaning a little forward, as if she were nursing an ache deep inside her gut. 'Yes,' she said. 'On one condition.'

'What?' He knew, of course.

'That you tell her.'

A mist was unrolling along the horizon and the foghorns had started up.

'All right,' he said grimly, almost angrily. 'All right. I'll do it now, this minute.'

*

He found her in the high, echoing entrance hall. She was sitting on a chair beside an elephant's-foot umbrella stand, pulling on a pair of black gumboots. She was already wearing a big, padded coat with a hood. She said she was going for a walk, that she was trying to persuade Granddad to go with her, and asked Quirke if he would like to come, too. He knew that he would remember forever, or for however long his forever would be, the look of her sitting awkwardly there with one foot raised and her face turned up to him, smiling. He spoke without preamble, watching her smile as it dismantled itself in slow, distinct stages, first leaving her eyes, then the planes beside her eyes, and last of all her lips. She said she did not understand. He told her again, speaking more slowly, more distinctly. 'I'm sorry,' he said, when he had finished. She set down the gumboot and lowered her stockinged foot to the floor, her movements careful and tentative, as if the air around her had turned brittle and she was afraid of shattering it. Then she shook her head and made a curious, feathery sound that he realised was a sort of laugh. He wished that she would stand up, for then he might be able to find a way of touching her, of taking her in his arms, even, and embracing her, but he knew it was not going to be possible, knew that it would not be possible even if she were to stand. She let her hands fall limply by the sides of the chair and looked about her, frowning, at this new world that she did not know and in which she had suddenly found herself a stranger; in which she had suddenly lost herself.

8

By noon the funeral guests had begun to leave, led by
the Archbishop and his attendant clerics. Costigan and the
others who had come from Ireland, his fellow Knights,
had lingered on in hope of a conference with Rose Crawford, but Rose had gone to her room to rest, taking her
martini glass with her. A subdued sense of crisis made its
way like a gas into the house. In the drawing room Quirke
came upon Costigan and the priest from St Mary's on the
sofa deep in conversation and Mal standing by the fire,
one hand in a jacket pocket and an elbow on the mantelpiece, as if he were posing for his portrait. Seeing Quirke
in the doorway the two fell silent instantly, and Costigan
did his snarling smile and asked Quirke how were his
injuries, and was he recovering from his fall. Mal looked
at him calmly and said nothing. Quirke made no answer
to Costigan's enquiries and walked out of the room. His
head was pounding. He went upstairs slowly to his bedroom. And it was there that Brenda Ruttledge found him,
sitting slumped on the side of the bed in his shirtsleeves,
smoking a cigarette and gazing at the photographs on the
walnut chest of drawers of Delia Quirke née Crawford and
her daughter Phoebe.

He had seen Brenda on so few occasions not wearing her nurse's uniform that for a moment he hardly knew who she was. She had knocked softly and he had turned to the door in a mixture of relief and dread, thinking it must be Phoebe who had relented and come to talk to him. Brenda entered quickly and shut the door behind her and stood with her back to it looking everywhere but at him. She wore a plain grey dress and low-heeled shoes, and had put on no makeup. He asked her what was the matter but she shook her head, still with eyes on the floor, not knowing where to begin. He stood up, stifling a gasp—his knee was very bad today, despite all the alcohol he had so far consumed—and walked around the bed and stood before her.

'I think,' she said, 'I think I know who they gave the baby to.' It was as if she were talking to herself. He touched her elbow and walked with her to the bed and they sat down side by side. 'I saw them here, at the Christmas party. They had a baby with them. I didn't take much notice. Then I saw them again, at the orphanage. She had no child with her that time, and she looked—oh, she looked terrible.' She stared at her hands as if they belonged to someone else. A foghorn boomed, and she turned to the window in vague fright. Outside were fields of snow under a lowering sky of faint, soiled pink. She was thinking distractedly of home, of the year of the big snow when she was seven or eight, and her brothers had made a toboggan and let her ride with them, whooping, down the side of the long meadow. She should never have come here, to this place, should never have let herself be among these people, who were too much for her, too clever and well-off and wicked. Quirke was asking her something. 'The Staffords,' she said, almost impatiently. He did not know who it was she meant. 'Andy Stafford, Mr Crawford's driver—him and his wife. That's who they gave the baby to, I'm sure of it.'

Quirke saw again the back of the young man's sleek, small head and his glossy dark eye in the driving mirror. He reached forward and turned the two photographs to face the wall again.

It took a long time for a taxi to come from Boston. There were more snow flurries and the driver, a miniature Mexican whose forehead was just about level with the steering-wheel, kept up a low, querulous moaning as he negotiated the winding roads out of Scituate under an ever-darkening sky. Quirke and Brenda Ruttledge sat facing away from each other in the back seat. An odd constraint, a kind of embarrassment, almost, had settled between them, and they did not speak. Brenda wore a black coat with a hood that gave her, incongruously, the look of a nun. South Boston was deserted. Skirls of snow swept over the pavements, and in the roadway the tracks of cars were lined with brownish slush. In Fulton Street the frame houses seemed crouched against the cold and the blown snow. Quirke had got the address, not without difficulty, from Deirdre, Rose Crawford's mousey maid.

A narrow-faced woman in a brown apron came to the door of the house and looked them up and down distrustingly, this ill-matched couple, taking in Quirke's walking-stick and Brenda's habit-like greatcoat. Quirke

said they had come from Mr Crawford's house. 'He died,
didn't he?' the woman said. Her face at the side of her
nose bore a recent, angry grey-and-purple bruise. She told
them the Staffords lived upstairs but that Andy Stafford
was not there. 'Far as I know he's out at Scituate,' she said,
sounding suspicious. She did not like any of this, these
two coming to her door, and asking after Andy, and
looking like they knew something bad about him. Quirke
asked if Mrs Stafford was at home and she shrugged and
made a dismissive grimace, baring an eye-tooth. 'I guess.
She never goes out, hardly.'

Despite the snow on the ground she followed them
around the side of the house and stood under the shelter
of the eaves with her arms folded and watched them climb
the wooden steps. Quirke knocked with his knuckle on the
glass of the french door. No answering sound came from
within. 'Probably open,' the woman called up. Quirke tried
the handle; it turned without resistance. They stepped, he
and Brenda, into the narrow hallway.

They found Claire Stafford sitting on a spindle-backed
chair at a table in the kitchenette. She wore a pink housecoat, and was barefoot. She was sitting sideways, motionless, with one hand in her lap and the other resting on the
plastic table-top. Her pale hair looked damp and hung
lankly in strings on either side of her stark white face. Her
eyes were rimmed with pink, and there was no colour in
her lips.

'Mrs Stafford?' Brenda said softly. Still Claire gave no
response. 'Mrs Stafford, my name is Ruttledge, I'm—I was
Mr Crawford's nurse. Mr Crawford, Andy's—Andy's boss.
He died—Mr Crawford died—did you know that?'

Claire stirred, as if at some faint, far-off sound, and blinked, and turned her head at last and looked at them. She showed no surprise or curiosity. Quirke came and stood opposite her at the table, his hand on the back of a chair for support. 'Do you mind if I sit down, Mrs Stafford?' he asked.

She moved her head a fraction from side to side. He pulled out the chair from the table and sat, and motioned Brenda Ruttledge to come forward, and she, too, sat.

'We want to talk to you,' Brenda said, 'about the baby—about what happened. Will you tell us?'

A look of something, of faint protest and denial, had come into Claire's almost colourless eyes. She frowned. 'He didn't mean to,' she said. 'I know he didn't. It was an accident.'

Quirke and Brenda Ruttledge looked at each other.

'How did it happen, Mrs Stafford?' Quirke said. 'Will you tell us how the accident happened?'

Brenda reached out and put her hand over Claire's hand where it lay on the table. Claire looked at her and at their two hands. When she spoke it was Brenda alone that she addressed. 'He was trying to make her stop crying. He hated it when she cried. He shook her. That's all—he just shook her.' Her frown now was a frown of bewilderment and vague wonder. 'Her head was heavy,' she said, 'and so warm—hot, nearly.' She turned up the palm of the hand in her lap and cupped in it the recollection of the child's head. 'So heavy.'

'What did you do then?' Brenda said. 'What did Andy do?'

'He telephoned, to St Mary's. He was a long time away,

I don't know . . . Father Harkins arrived. I told him about the accident. Then Andy came back.'

'And Father Harkins,' Quirke asked, 'did he call the police?'

She drew her eyes away from Brenda's face and looked at him. 'Oh, no,' she said simply. She turned to Brenda again, appealing to another woman, to her good sense. 'Why would he do that? It was an accident.'

'Where is she, Mrs Stafford?' Quirke said. 'Where's the baby?'

'Father Harkins took her. I didn't want to see her any more.' Again she appealed to Brenda. 'Was that bad of me?'

'No,' Brenda said soothingly, 'no, of course not.'

Claire looked again into her cupped palm. 'I could still feel her head in my hand. I can still feel it.'

The silence in the room grew heavy. Quirke had a sense of something coming into the house, wafting in, soft and soundless like the snow outside. He was suddenly tired, with a tiredness he had never known before. He felt as if he had come to the end of a road on which he had been travelling for so long his trudging on it had begun to seem a state of rest; a rest, however, that afforded him no respite but made his bones ache and his heart labour and his mind go dull. Somewhere along that difficult way he seemed to have got lost.

9

ANDY KNEW WHAT the girl was after when he came into the garage and found her sitting in the back seat of the Buick, just sitting there, in a big coat, staring in front of her, pale and sort of shocked-looking. She said nothing, and neither did he, only buttoned up his jacket and got in behind the wheel and started up the engine. He just drove, without thinking, which was what she seemed to want—*Take me anywhere*, she had said that first time, after they had left the big guy in the village. The snow was coming down now; it was not bad, but it meant the roads were empty. They went up along the coast again. He asked her if she had any of them English cigarettes with her today but she did not even answer, only shook her head at him in the mirror. She had that look—scared and sort of paralysed but frantic under- neath—that girls got when they could think of only the one thing. It was a look that told him it would be her first time.

He knew where to go, and stopped on the headland. There was no one around, and there would be no one. The wind was so strong up there it rocked the big car on its springs, and the snow straight away started piling up under the wipers and around the rims of the windows. At first he had a little trouble with the girl. She pretended not to know what was going on, or what he wanted—which was what she wanted, too, if only she would admit it—and although he had hoped he would not have to, in the end he brought out the blade that he kept clipped to a couple of magnets he had fixed under the dash. She started to cry when she saw the knife but he told her to quit it. It was funny, but it really got him going when he ordered her to take off those weird rubber boots she was wearing, and because there was so little space between the seats she had to twist up her leg and he got his first glimpse of her garter belt and the white inner side of her leg right up to the seams of those lace pants she was wearing.

It was good. She tried to fight him and he liked that. He made sure to keep her lying on her overcoat because he did not want stuff getting on the upholstery—or not lying, really, but sort of wedged in a half sitting position, so he had to do some fancy contortions before he could get himself inside her finally. She made a funny little squeaking sound in his ear and he was so fond of her in that moment that he eased off a bit, and leaned up, and looked out through the snowy window and saw away out at the harbour mouth the sea boiling up somehow, he guessed the tide was turning or something, and a big head of blue-black water with a flying white fringe along the top of it was surging in between the two prongs of the harbour, and although he had only started he could not hold himself back, and he arched himself between her shaking legs and plunged into her and felt the shudder begin deep in the root of his groin, and he bit into her neck at the side and made her scream.

Afterward, there was the problem of what to do with her. He could not bring her back to the house. He had no intention of returning to Moss Manor, ever again; with the old man dead, he knew his time there was at an end. That bitch who had suddenly become a rich widow would waste no time in selling—he had seen the way she used to look around the place, twisting up her mouth in disgust, when she thought no one was watching—and move to somewhere more to her la-di-da taste. He had his plans made, and now this thing with the girl had made his decision for him: it was time, and there was no time to lose. He had talked to a guy he knew, a dealer in antique cars, who had moved to New Mexico and settled in Roswell to look for little green men, who had agreed to work on the Buick and make it anonymous and find a buyer for it. But time, yes, time was the thing. He could start by getting rid of the girl. She was lying curled up on the back seat when he drove into North Scituate. The snow was coming down heavy now, and the streets were deserted—not that they were ever exactly crowded, in this one-horse dump—and he stopped at the corner where he had picked up Quirke the other day, and went round and opened the door for her and told her to get out. It was cold, but she had her coat and those boots, and he figured she would be all right—he even made sure she had a handful of dimes for the telephone. She got herself out, moving like one of the living dead, her face all smeared, somehow, and her eyes blurred-looking as if her sight had gone bad. As he drove away he took his last look at her in the rear-view mirror, standing in the snow on the street corner.

He soon came to realise he was in trouble, maybe the worst trouble he had ever been in—it was the knife, he should not have brought out the knife—but he did not care. He was exultant. He had made his mark, had shown what he was capable of. His lap felt wet still but the sweat on his back and on the insides of his arms had cooled and was like oil, like—what was the word?—like balm. He wished that Cora Bennett could have seen him in the Buick with the girl out there on the headland, he wished Cora could have been there, and forced to watch. Cora, Claire, the big Irishman, Rose Crawford, Joe Lanigan and his sidekick who looked like Lou Costello—he imagined them all standing around the car, looking in at the windows at him, shouting at him to stop and him just laughing at them.

Cora Bennett had laughed at him that night when her blood got all over him and he rolled away from her and felt it on his thighs, the hot stickiness of it. 'Why, hell,' she had said, laughing, 'it's only blood!' There had been blood with the girl, too, but not much. If Cora had been there he would have smeared it on her face, and laughed, and said, *Why, Cora, it's only blood!* When she had seen how mad he was she had said she was sorry, though she was still sort of grinning. When she came back from the bathroom she sat down on the side of the bed where he was lying and rubbed her hand along his back and said again she was sorry, that it was not at him she had been laughing, but only that she was relieved because she had been kind of worrying, seeing she was two weeks late and she was never late, and that was why she had begun to wonder if what Claire had told her might not be the case, might just be one of crazy Claire's crazy fantasies. He had sat up on the bed then, all his nerves alert, and asked her what she meant, and what it was that Claire had told her. 'Why, that you shoot blanks, Tex,' she said, with that grin again, and put up her hand and mussed his hair. 'Hence no little Andys or little Claires, or little Christines, either, of your own.'

He could hardly believe she was saying what she was saying. At first he did not understand—Claire had told her it was him and not her who could not make a kid? But when she had come home from the doctor's that day after she got the results of the tests that they had both taken she had said to him that the doctor had told her it was she who was the dud, that there was something wrong with her insides and that she could never have a baby, no matter how hard she tried. Cora, who was beginning to look like she was sorry she had started to tell him all this, said, well, Claire had told her it was the other way round, one day when he was at work and she had gone up to see if Claire maybe needed a cup of coffee or something. Claire was real upset, Cora said, crying and talking about the kid and the accident, and then she had told Cora about what the doctor had really said and how she had lied about it to Andy. As Cora was speaking now, Andy's leg had begun to shake the way it did when he was worried or mad. Why, he wanted to know, why would Claire say it was her if it was really him who could not, could not . . . ? 'Oh, honey,' Cora had said soothingly, not grinning now but all serious, seeing clearly the damage she had done, 'maybe it's just what she told you, a little lie, you know, so you wouldn't feel bad?' That was when he had smacked Cora. He knew he should not have done it, but she should not have said what she said, either. He had smacked her pretty hard, across the face, and his knuckles caught her across the bridge of her nose. There was more blood then, but she just sat there on the bed, leaning away from him with a hand to her face and the blood running down out of her nose and her eyes cold and sharp as needles. That was the end, of course, for them. Cora would probably have kept it on, once she got over being sore at him for smacking her, but the truth was he was tired of her, of that slack belly of hers and her flat-fronted boobs and her ass that was already starting to get puckers in it. Now the laugh was on her.

By the time he had left the girl and got back to the house he had decided to take Claire with him. The decision surprised him, but it pleased him, too. It must be that he loved her, despite everything, despite even the things she had told Cora Bennett about him. He parked the car a couple of houses down, not because he did not want the neighbours noticing the fancy car—they had seen him in the Buick before this—but he wanted to get into the house without Cora Bennett coming out and pestering him. He slipped across the yard and went up the outside stairs three at a time, thankful for the snow that muffled the sound of his boot heels on the wood.

Claire in her housecoat was slumped on the couch in front of the television on which some dumb quiz show was playing—who gives a fuck what the capital of North

Dakota is?—and he paused in passing by her and gave her shoulders a shake and told her to get up and start packing. She did not move, of course, and he had to come back and put his fist in front of her nose and shout at her. He was in the bedroom, throwing shirts into the old carpet bag that had once belonged to his daddy, when he felt her behind him—he had developed a sixth sense, and could feel her presence without looking, as if she was a ghost already—and turned to find her leaning in the doorway in that tired-out, drooping way that she did, the housecoat pulled shut and her arms folded so tight it was like this was the only way she had of holding herself together.

'There were people here today,' she said.

'Oh, yeah? What people?' He had not realised he had so many shirts and coats and pairs of jeans—where did it come from, all this stuff?

'They were asking about the baby,' Claire said.

He went still suddenly, and turned slowly to look at her. 'What?' he said softly. He was holding in his hand a belt with a buckle shaped like a steer's head with horns.

She told him, in that wispy voice she had developed lately, that sounded as if it was wearing out and would soon be just a sort of sighing, a sort of breathing, with no words. It was the Irish guy and the nurse. They had asked her about little Christine, and the accident, and what had happened. As she spoke she paused now and then to pick at stray bits of lint on the housecoat. She might have been talking about the weather. Once she stopped altogether and he had to give her a push to get her started up again. Christ, a clockwork ghost, that was what she was turning into! He would have gone at her with the belt except that she looked so strange, sort of not here, but lost somewhere inside herself.

He paced the room, gnawing on a knuckle. They would have to go tonight—they would have to go now. As if she sensed what he was thinking, Claire took note for the first time of the bag on the bed, the gaping drawers and the closet doors standing open. 'Are you leaving me?' she said, sounding as if it would not much matter to her if he was.

'No,' he said, stopping in front of her with his hands on his hips and speaking slow so she would understand him, 'I'm not leaving you, baby. You're coming with me. We're going west. Will Dakes is out there, he's in Roswell, he'll help us, help me find a job, maybe.' He moved closer to her and touched her face. 'We can start a new life,' he said softly. 'You could get another kid, another little Christine. You'd like that, wouldn't you?' He was surprised how little, really, he minded her saying that to Cora about the doctor's test, or telling the Irish guy about the accident—surprised, in fact, at how little he cared about any of that. The Irish guy, Rose Crawford, that nun and the priest, they were the past, now. But he knew they would be coming for him, and soon, and that the two of them had to get away. Claire's cheek was cold under his hand, as if there was no blood at all under the skin. Claire; his Claire. He had never felt so tenderly toward her as he did at that moment, there in the doorway, with the snow coming down outside and the light failing and the walnut tree in the window holding up its bare arms, and everything ending for them here.

*

He was driving too fast. The roads were slick under the soft new snow. Every time a cop car passed by heading into the city he expected it to swing around on two wheels and come bumping over the central divide after them with its blue light flashing and its siren going. The girl would be back at the house by now and would have told them her story, and he knew, of course, what a story it would be. He did not care. In two days they would be in New Mexico, and Will Dakes would file off the engine number and whatever else needed to be done, and the car would be sold and he and Claire would take the money and travel on, to Texas, maybe, or maybe they would go northward, to Colorado, Utah, Wyoming. The wide world was before them. Out there, under those skies, Claire would forget the kid and be her old self again, and they would begin to live, like they had never lived before. He saw through the swirls of snow the red light flashing ahead, at the crossing. It reminded him of the girl, of Phoebe, and he smiled to himself, feeling good, remembering her sprawled under him on the back seat of the car, and he put his foot down. Yes, life was just starting, his real life, out where he belonged, in those wide-open spaces, on those plains, in that sweet air. The barrier was coming down, but they would make it. They would flash under it and on the other side there would be a new place, a new world, and they would be new people in it. He glanced at Claire beside him. She was feeling the same excitement, the same wild expectancy, he could see it in her face, in the way she was leaning forward with her neck thrust out and her eyes wide, and then they were on the tracks, and suddenly— what was she doing?—she reached out a hand sideways and snatched the wheel and wrenched it out of his grip, and the big car screeched and spun on the snow and the shiny steel rails and stopped, and the engine stopped, and everything stopped, except the train that was rushing toward them, its single eye glaring, and which at the last moment seemed to raise itself up as if it would take to the black air, shrieking and flaming, and fly, and fly.

10

PHOEBE HAD DISLIKED this room from the first time she saw it. She knew Rose had meant well, putting her here, but it was more like a child's nursery than a bedroom for a grown-up. She was tired—she was exhausted—but she could not sleep. They had thought she would want them to stay with her, to sit by the bed holding her hand and looking down at her with their sorrowing, pitying eyes, and in the end she had pretended to be asleep so they would all go away and let her be by herself. Since Quirke had spoken to her in the hall she had wanted only to be alone, so she could think, and sort things out in her head. That was why she had gone to the garage to sit in the Buick, as she used to do when she was a child, hiding herself away in Daddy's car.

Daddy.

She had hardly noticed Andy Stafford when he came into the garage. He was just the driver, why should she notice him? She thought he had probably come to polish the car, or check the oil, or inflate the tyres, or whatever it was that drivers did when they were not driving. She had not been afraid when he got behind the wheel and drove her away, or even when he turned the car off the road and went along the track to the edge of the dunes where the wind was blowing and she could hardly see anything through the snow. She should have spoken, should have said something, should have ordered him to turn back; he might have done as he was told, since that was what she presumed he had been trained to do. But she had said nothing, and then they had stopped and he was climbing into the back seat after her, and there was the knife ... When he left her in the village she had not telephoned the house. There were many reasons why she would not, but the main one was simply that she would not have known what to say. There were no words she could think of to account for what had happened. So she had set off walking, down the main street and out of the village and along the road, despite the cold and the snow and the soreness between her legs. At the house it was Rose who had come to the door, pushing Deirdre the maid aside and taking her by the arm and leading her upstairs. Rose had needed only the simplest words—car, driver, dunes, knife—and at once she understood. She had made her drink a mouthful of brandy, and had told the maid to run a bath, and only when Phoebe was in the bath had she gone off to summon Sarah, and Mal, and Quirke, who was not there, who was never there.

Then there had been the fussing, the tiptoed comings and goings, the cups of tea and bowls of soup, the whispered consultations in the doorway, the bumbling white-haired doctor with his bag and his minty breath, the police detective clearing his throat and twiddling the brim of his brown hat, embarrassed by the things he was having to ask her. There was that strange exchange with her mother—with Sarah: it had sounded as if they were talking not about her but about someone else whom they had both known in another life. Which, she reflected, was true. Before, she had been certain of who she was; now she was no one. 'You're still my Phoebe,' Sarah had said, trying not to cry, but Phoebe had answered nothing to that, having nothing to say. Mal was his usual totem pole. Yet of the two of them, these two who until a few hours ago had been her father and her mother, it was Mal whom she most loved, if love, any longer, was the word.

The worst of it now was the bite mark on her neck, where Andy Stafford had sunk his teeth in her. That was the real violation. She could not explain, she did not understand it, but it was so.

She would not speak of Andy Stafford. He was the unspeakable, not because of the knife, or what he had done to her, or not solely for these reasons, but because there were no words that would, for her, accommodate him. When the police telephoned Rose to tell her Andy and his wife were dead, killed when the Buick stalled on a level crossing, Phoebe was the only one who was not shocked, or even surprised. There was a neatness to their dying, a tidiness, as at the end of a fairy tale she might have been told as a child, first to frighten her and then, with all resolved and the wicked trolls slain, so that she might be satisfied and go to sleep. Toward Andy himself she felt nothing, neither anger nor revulsion. He had been a steel edge at her throat and a hard body pounding down on hers, that was all.

Quirke, arrived at last, came and stood at the foot of the bed, leaning awkwardly on his stick. He asked her to come back with him, to Ireland. She refused. 'I'm staying here for a while,' she said. 'And then I'll see.' He looked as if he would plead with her, but she made her face hard, lying there against the pillows, and he lowered his head like a wounded ox. 'Tell me,' she said, 'there's one thing I want to know—who named me?'

He raised his eyes, frowning. 'What do you mean?'

'Who gave me the name Phoebe?'

He looked down again. 'They called you after Sarah's grandmother, Josh's mother.'

She was silent for a long moment, turning it over in her head, then 'I see,' she said, and without looking at her again Quirke turned and limped out of the room.

Sarah and Mal sat together on a little gilt sofa on the wide landing at the top of the great oak staircase. The last of the day's stealthy light was drifting down from the big curved windows above them. Like Quirke, Sarah felt that she had been struggling all day through mire and ice, over frozen wastes, along treacherous roads, and now had come to some kind of a stopping-place at last. The skin on her hands and on her arms was grey and grainy and seemed to be cringing, somehow, like her mind. The look of the broad expanse of carpet on the landing, like a nubbled, pale pink ice floe, made her feel slightly ill; the carpet, like so much else in the house, had been installed at Rose's command, Rose, who no doubt knew everything, too, that there was to know.

She said:

'Well—what do we do now?'

'We live,' Mal answered, 'as best we can. Phoebe will need our help.'

He seemed so calm, so resigned. *What goes on in his mind?* she wondered. It struck her, not for the first time, how little, really, she knew of this man with whom she had already spent a large part of her life. 'You should have told me,' she said.

He stirred, but did not turn to look at her. 'Told you what?' he murmured.

'About Christine Falls. About the child. Everything.'

He expelled a long, weary breath; it was like listening to a part of his self leaking out of him. 'About Christine Falls,' he said, echoing her. 'How did you find out? Did Quirke tell you?'

'No. What does it matter how I found out? You should have told me. You owed it to me. I would have listened. I would have tried to understand.'

'I had my duty.'

'My God,' she said, with a violent, shaking laugh, 'what a hypocrite you are.'

'I had my duty,' he said again, stubbornly, 'to all of us. I had to keep it together, under control. There was no one else. Everything would have been destroyed.'

She looked at the carpet and again her insides quailed. She closed her eyes, and out of that darkness said:

'You still have time.'

Now he looked at her. 'Time?'

'To redeem yourself.'

He made a strange, soft sound in his throat which it took her a moment to identify—he was laughing. 'Ah, my dear Sarah,' he said—how seldom he spoke her name!— 'it's too late for that, I think.'

A clock struck in the house, and then another, and yet another—so many! As if time here were a multiple thing, different at all levels, in every room.

'I told Quirke about Phoebe,' she said. 'I told him the whole thing.'

'Oh, yes?' He did his faint laugh again. 'That must have been an interesting conversation.'

'I should have told him years ago. I should have told him about Phoebe, and you should have told me about Christine Falls.'

He crossed his legs and fussily hitched up the knee of his trousers. 'You wouldn't have needed to tell him about Phoebe,' he said. 'He knew already.'

What was it she was hearing—could it be the tiny echoes of the clock chimes, still beating faintly in the air? She held her breath, afraid of what might come out of her mouth. At last she said:

'What do you mean?'

He was looking at the ceiling high above, studying it, as if there might be something up there, some sign, some hieroglyph. 'Who do you think got my father to phone me here in Boston the night that Delia died?' he asked, as if he were not addressing her but interrogating that something which only he could see in the shadows under the ceiling. 'Who was in such torment that he couldn't bear the thought of having the child around, to remind him of his tragic loss, and was prepared to give her to us instead?'

'No,' she said, shaking her head, 'no, it's not true.'

But she knew it was, of course. Oh, Quirke. She had known it all along, she realised now, had known it and denied it to herself. She felt no anger, no resentment, only sadness.

She would not tell Phoebe: Phoebe must not know that her father had willingly given her away.

A minute passed. She said:

'I think I'm sick.'

He went still, she could feel it, like something in him stopping, some animal version of him, stopping with all its senses on alert. 'Why do you think that?'

'There's something wrong with my head. This dizziness, it's getting worse.'

He reached sideways and took her hand, cold and limp, in his. 'I need you,' he said calmly, without emphasis. 'I can't do it, any of it, without you.'

'Then put an end to this thing,' she said, with sudden fierceness, 'this thing of Christine Falls and her child.' She turned the hand he was holding and gripped his fingers. 'Will you?' Now it was his hand that went limp. He shook his head once, the barest movement. She heard the foghorns, their forlorn calling. She released his hand and stood up. His *duty*, he had said—his duty to lie, to pretend, to protect. His duty, that had blighted their lives. 'You knew about Quirke and Phoebe,' she said. 'And you knew about Christine Falls. You knew—you all knew—and you didn't tell me. All these years, all these lies. How could you, Mal?'

He gazed up at her from where he sat; all he looked was tired. He said:

'Perhaps for the same reason you didn't tell Quirke, from the start, that Phoebe was his daughter, when you thought he didn't know.' He smiled wanly. 'We all have our own kinds of sin.'

11

QUIRKE KNEW it was time to go. There was nothing here for him any longer, if there ever had been anything, except confusion, mistakes, damage. In the bedroom he turned Delia's and Phoebe's photographs once more to face the room; he did not fear his dead wife any more; she had been exorcised, somehow. He began to pack his bag. The daylight was at an end, and beyond the windows the vague snow-shapes were merging into shadow. He felt unwell. The central heating made the air in the house dense and oppressive, and it seemed to him he had been suffering from a headache, more or less, since the night he had arrived. He did not know what to think, about Phoebe, Mal, Sarah, about Andy Stafford—about any of them. He was tired of trying to know what he should think. His anger at everything had subsided to a background hum. He was conscious, too, of a faint, simmering sense of desperation; it was like the feeling that would threaten to overwhelm him at the start of certain days in childhood when there was nothing in prospect, nothing of interest, nothing to do. Is that how his life would be from now on— a sort of living afterlife, a wandering in a Limbo among other souls who, like him, were neither saved nor lost?

When Rose Crawford came into the room he knew at once what would happen. She was wearing a black blouse and black slacks. 'I think mourning becomes me,' she said, 'don't you?' He went back to his packing. She stood in the middle of the floor with her hands in the pockets of her slacks, watching him. He had a shirt in his hands; she took it from him and laid it out on the bed and began expertly to fold it. 'I used to work in a dry cleaner's,' she said, and glanced at him over her shoulder. 'That surprises you, I bet.'

Now it was he who stood watching her. He lit a cigarette. 'Two things I want from you,' he said.

She laid the folded shirt in his suitcase and took up another and began to fold it too. 'Oh, yes?' she said. 'And what things would they be?'

'I want you to promise me to stop the funds for this business with the babies. And I want you to let Phoebe come home with me.'

She shook her head briefly, concentrating on the shirt. 'Phoebe is going to stay here,' she said.

'No.' He was quite calm, he spoke softly. 'Let her go.'

She put the second shirt on top of the first in the suitcase and came and took the cigarette from his fingers and drew on it and gave it back to him. 'Oops,' she said, 'sorry—lipstick again.' She measured him with a smiling look, her head tilted to one side. 'It's too late, Quirke. You've lost her.'

'You know she's my daughter.'

She nodded, still smiling. 'Of course. Josh, after all, was in on your little exchange, and Josh and I had no secrets from each other. It was one of the nicer things about us.'

It was as if something had swooped down on him suddenly from above: he saw its darkness against his eyes and seemed to feel the beating of its wings about his head. He had taken her by the shoulders and was shaking her furiously. The cigarette flew from his fingers. '*You selfish, evil bitch!*' he said, between clenched teeth, that winged thing still flapping and screeching around him.

She stepped back, deftly disengaging herself from his grasp, and went and picked up the burning cigarette from the carpet and carried it across the room and dropped it into the empty fireplace.

'You should be careful, Quirke,' she said, 'you could set the house on fire.' She kneaded her shoulder. 'What a grip you have—really, you don't know your own strength.'

He saw that she was trying not to laugh. He launched himself forward on his resistant leg, crossing the space between them as if it were not a walk he was doing but a sort of upright falling. He did not know what he might do when he reached her, whether he would slap her, or knock her to the floor. What he did was take her in his arms. She was of a surprising lightness, and he could plainly feel the bones beneath her flesh. When he kissed her he crushed his mouth on hers and tasted blood, whose, hers or his, he was not sure.

The night, glossy and densely dark, pressed itself against the windows on opposite sides of the room. Rose said, 'You could both stay, you know, you and Phoebe. Let the rest of them go back to Mother Ireland. We might make it work, the three of us. You're like me, Quirke, admit it.

You're more like me than you're like your precious Sarah. A cold heart and a hot soul, that's you and me.' He began to speak but she touched a fingertip quickly to his lips. 'No, no, don't say anything. Silly of me to ask.' She twisted away from him and sat on the side of the bed with her back turned. She smiled wryly at him over her shoulder. 'Don't you love me even a little? You could lie, you know. I wouldn't mind. You're good at lying.'

He said nothing, only rolled on to his back, the pain in his knee flaring, and gazed up at the ceiling. Rose nodded, and searched in the pockets of his jacket for his cigarettes, and lit one, and leaned over him and put it into his lips. 'Poor Quirke,' she said softly. 'You're in such trouble, aren't you? I wish I could help.' She went and stood in front of the mirror, frowning, and combing her fingers through her hair. Behind her he sat up on the bed, she saw him in the glass, a great, pale bear. He reached for the ashtray on the bedside table. 'It's probably not a help,' she said, 'but there's one thing I can tell you. You're wrong about Mal and that girl, the girl with the baby—I can't remember her name.' He looked up and met her eyes in the mirror. She shook her head at him almost pityingly. 'Believe me, Quirke, you got it all wrong.'

'Yes,' he said, nodding. 'I know I did.'

He was at St Mary's early. He asked to speak to Sister Stephanus. The nun with the buck-teeth, wringing her hands, insisted there was no one who could see him at that hour, or, her look implied, at any other hour, for that matter. He asked for Sister Anselm. Sister Anselm, the nun said, was gone away; she was in another convent now, in Canada. Quirke did not believe her. He sat down on a chair in the lobby and put his hat on his lap and said he would wait until there was someone who would talk to him. The young nun went away, and presently Father Harkins appeared, his jaw-line rawly aflame from the morning razor and his right eye twitching. He came forward with his smile. Quirke pushed himself to his feet on his stick. He ignored the hand the priest was offering him. He said he wanted to see the child's grave.

Harkins goggled at him. 'The grave?'

'Yes. I know she's buried here. I want to see whose name is on the gravestone.'

The priest began to bluster but Quirke would have none of it. He hefted the heavy black stick menacingly in his hand.

'I could call the police, you know,' Harkins said.

'Oh, sure,' Quirke said with a dry laugh, 'sure you could.'

The priest was growing increasingly agitated. 'Listen,' he said, lowering his voice to a whisper, 'Mr Griffin is there—he's there now, visiting, before he leaves.'

'I don't care,' Quirke said, 'if the Pope is there. I want to see that gravestone.'

The priest insisted on his coat and his galoshes. The young nun brought them. She glanced at Quirke and could not suppress a glint of renewed interest and even admiration—evidently she was unused to seeing Father Harkins made to do what he was told.

The morning was raw, with low, rolling clouds and a wet wind driving flecks of sleet before it. Quirke and the priest went around by the side of the building, through a kitchen garden patched with snow and down a gravelled pathway to a low wooden gate, where the priest stopped, and turned. 'Mr Quirke,' he said, 'please, take my advice. Go from here. Go home to Ireland. Forget all this. If you walk through this gate, you'll regret it.'

Quirke said nothing, only lifted his stick and pointed it at the gate, and the priest with a sigh undid the latch and stood back.

The cemetery was smaller than he had expected, just a bit of field, really, sloped at one corner, with a view of the city's towers to the east, huddled in a winter mist. There were no headstones, only small wooden crosses, leaning at all angles. The size of the graves was a shock, each one no more than a couple of feet long. Quirke walked down a straggling pathway towards where a figure in overcoat and hat was crouched on one knee. All Quirke could see of the man was his bowed back, and while he was still some way off he stopped and spoke. It was Mal's look, hunched and tense; but it was not Mal.

Even when Quirke spoke the figure did not turn, and Quirke walked forward. He could hear his uneven footsteps crunching the gravel, interspersed with the small thud of his stick on the stony path. A gust of wind threatened to take his hat and he had to put up a hand quickly to keep it from flying. He drew level with the kneeling man, who looked up at him now.

'Well, Quirke?' the Judge said, slipping a set of rosary beads into his pocket, not before he had kissed the crucifix, and took up the handkerchief he had been kneeling on and rose with an effort. 'Are you satisfied now?'

They walked three times around the perimeter of the little graveyard, the bitter cold wind blowing in their faces, the old man's cheeks turning blotchy and blue and Quirke's knee keeping up a steady growl of pain. To Quirke it seemed that he had been trudging here like this all his life, that this was what all his life had been, a slow march around the realm of the dead.

'I'm going to get her out of this place,' the Judge said, 'little Christine. I'm going to get her into a proper cemetery. I might even bring her home to Ireland, and bury her beside her mother.'

'Would you not have some trouble explaining her to the Customs people,' Quirke said, 'or could you fix that, too?'

The old man gave a sort of grin, showing his teeth. 'Her mother was a grand girl, full of fun,' he said. 'That was what I noticed about her first, when I saw her at Malachy's house, the way she could laugh at things.'

'I suppose,' Quirke said, 'you're going to tell me you couldn't help yourself.'

Again that sideways grin, lion-fierce. 'Hold off on the bitterness, Quirke. You're not the injured party here. If I have apologies to make it's not to you I have to make them. Yes, I've sinned, and God will punish me for it—has already punished me, taking Chrissie from me, and then the child, too.' He paused. 'What were you being punished for, would you say, Quirke, when you lost Delia?'

Quirke would not look at him. 'I envy your view of the world, Garret,' he said. 'Sin and punishment—it must be fine to have everything so simple.'

The Judge disdained to answer that. He was squinting off in the direction of the misty towers. 'What they say is true,' he said, 'history repeats itself. You losing Delia, and Phoebe being sent out here, and then me with Chrissie, and Chrissie dying. As if it was all destined.'

'I was married to Delia. She wasn't a maid in my son's house. She wasn't young enough to be my daughter—to be my granddaughter.'

'Ah, Quirke, you're a young man still, you don't know what it's like to watch your powers failing. You look at the back of your hand, the skin turning to paper, the bones showing through, and it gives you the shivers. Then a girl like Christine comes along and you feel like you're twenty years old again.' He walked on a few paces in silence, musing. 'Your daughter is living, Quirke, while mine is dead, thanks to that murdering little bastard—what's his name? Stafford. Aye: Stafford.'

Quirke could see Harkins lurking by the gate: what was he waiting for? He said:

'I honoured you, Garret—I revered you. For me you were the one good man in a bad world.'

The Judge shrugged. 'Maybe I am,' he said, 'maybe I am of some good. The Lord pours grace into the weakest vessels.'

The passionate tremor that came into the old man's

voice, that tone of the Old Testament prophet, why had he not noticed it before now? Quirke wondered.

'You're mad,' he said, in the tone of one who has made a small, sudden and surprising discovery.

The Judge chuckled. 'And you're a cold-hearted bastard, Quirke. You always were. But at least you were honest about things, with certain notable exceptions. Don't go spoiling your bad reputation now by turning into a hypocrite. Give over this *I revered you* business. You never gave a second thought in your life to anyone but yourself.'

'The orphans,' Quirke said after a moment, 'Costigan, that crowd—was that you, too? Were you running the whole thing, you and Josh?' The old man did not deign to answer. 'And Dolly Moran,' Quirke said, 'what about her?'

The Judge stopped, holding up a hand. 'That was Costigan,' he said. 'He sent those fellows to look for something she had. They weren't supposed to hurt her.'

They walked on.

'And me?' Quirke asked. 'Who sent those fellows after me?'

'Have a heart, Quirke—would I want to see you hurt the way you've been hurt, you, who were a son to me?'

But Quirke was thinking, putting it together. 'Dolly told me about the diary,' he said, 'I told Mal, he told you, you told Costigan, and Costigan sent his thugs to get it from her.' Out in the harbour a tugboat hooted. Quirke thought he could see from here a section of the river, a blue-grey line humped under scudding cloud. 'This Costigan,' he said, 'who is he?'

The Judge could not resist an amused, malicious snort.

'Nobody,' he said. 'What they call over here the paid help—true believers are scarce. There's a lot who are in it for the money, Quirke—Josh's money, as was.'

'And no more.'

'Oh?'

'There'll be no more funds. I made Rose promise.'

'*Rose*, is it? Aye—and I wonder, now, how you went about extracting a promise of that order from that particular lady.' He glanced at Quirke. 'Cat got your tongue, eh? Anyway, *Rose*'s funds or no, we'll manage. God will provide.' He laughed suddenly. 'You know, Quirke, you should be proud—the whole thing started with you. Oh, aye, it's true. Phoebe was the first, it was her who gave Josh Crawford the idea. He telephoned me, in the middle of the bloody night, it was, wanting to know what happened in Ireland these days to children like Phoebe, children who weren't wanted. I told him, I said, *Josh, the country is overflowing with them. Is that so?* said he. *Well, send them over here to us*, he said, *we'll find homes for them soon enough.* In no time we were dispatching them by the dozen—by the hundreds!'

'So many orphans.'

The Judge was swift. 'Phoebe wasn't an orphan, was she?' His face darkened, the blue blotches turning to purple. 'Some people are not meant to have children. Some people haven't the right.'

'And who decides?'

'We do!' the old man cried harshly. 'We decide! Women in the tenements of Dublin and Cork bearing seventeen, eighteen children in as many years. What sort of a life would those youngsters face? Aren't they better off out here, with families who can take care of them, cherish them? Answer me that.'

'So you're the judge and jury,' Quirke said wearily. 'You're God himself.'

'How dare you, you of all people? What right have you to question me? Look to the mote in your own eye, boyo.'

'And Mal? Is he another judge, or just the court clerk?'

'Pah. Mal is a fixer, that's all—he couldn't even be trusted to keep the unfortunate girl alive when she had her baby. No, Quirke, you were the son I wanted.'

A gust of wind swooped down on them, throwing a handful of sleet like slivers of glass into their faces.

'I'm taking Phoebe home with me,' Quirke said. 'I want her away from here. Away from you, too.'

'You think you can start being a father to her now?'

'I can try.'

'Aye,' the old man said, with high sarcasm, 'you can try.'

'I want you to tell me about Dolly Moran.'

'And just what is it you want me to tell you?'

'Did you know,' Quirke said, looking off again towards that line of lead-blue water that was the river, 'that she used to go up to the orphanage every day, for years, and stand outside the playground, looking to see if she could spot her child, her boy, amongst all the others?'

The Judge's look turned vague. 'What sort of a thing was that for her to be doing?' he muttered.

'Tell me,' Quirke said, 'you were on the board of visitors—did you ever really know what Carricklea was like, the things that went on there?'

'You got out, didn't you?' the old man snarled. '*I* got you out.'

'You did—but who was it put me in?' The Judge glowered and said something under his breath, and set off determinedly in the direction of the gate, where Harkins in his coat and his galoshes was still waiting. 'Look around you, Garret,' Quirke called after him. 'Look at your achievement.'

The Judge paused and turned back. 'These are only the dead,' he said. 'You don't see the living. It's God's work we're doing, Quirke. In twenty years', thirty years' time, how many young people will be willing to give their lives to the ministry? We'll be sending back missionaries from here to Ireland—to Europe. God's work. You won't stop it. And by Christ, Quirke, you'd better not try.'

To the end Quirke was sure that Phoebe would come to say goodbye to him. He waited on the gravel outside Moss Manor, scanning the windows of the house for a sign of her, while the taxi driver was stowing his bags. It was a day of bleak sunshine, and a cutting wind was blowing in from the sea. In the end it was not Phoebe who came, but Sarah. Wearing no coat, she appeared in the doorway and after a moment's hesitation walked across the gravel with her arms folded and a cardigan pulled tight around her. She asked him what time his flight was at. She said she hoped the journey would not be too dreadful, in this winter weather that seemed set never to end. He drew close to her, canted on his stick, and made to speak, but she stopped him. 'Don't, Quirke, please,' she said, 'don't say you're sorry. I couldn't bear it.'

'I begged her to come home with me. She refused.'

She shook her head wearily. 'It's too late,' she said. 'You know that.'

'What will you do?'

'Oh, I'll stay, for a little while, at least.' She laughed unsteadily. 'Mal wants me to go into the Mayo Clinic—to have my head examined!' She tried to laugh again but failed. She looked off, frowning, in the direction of the sea. 'Perhaps Phoebe and I can become'—she smiled miserably—'perhaps we can become friends. Besides, someone has to keep her out of Rose's clutches. Rose wants to take her to Europe and make her into a Henry James heroine.' She paused, and looked down; she was never as dear to him as when she looked at her feet like that, scanning the ground frowningly for something that was never there. 'Did you sleep with her,' she asked mildly, 'with Rose?'

He shook his head. 'No.'

'I don't believe you,' she said, without rancour.

She took a deep breath of the icy air and then, glancing over her shoulder towards the house, she brought from under her cardigan a rolled-up paper scroll and pressed it into his hand. 'Here,' she said. 'You'll know what to do with this.' It was a school jotter, with a dog-eared orange cover. He made to pull off the rubber band that was holding it rolled but she put her hand over his and said, 'No—read it on the plane.'

'How did you get it?'

'She sent it to me, the Moran woman, that poor

creature. God knows why—I hadn't seen her since Phoebe was a baby.'

He nodded. 'She remembered you,' he said. 'She asked after you. Said you had been good to her.' He put the jotter, still rolled, into the pocket of his overcoat. 'What do you want me to do with it?' he asked.

'I don't know. Whatever is necessary.'

'You've read it?'

'Enough of it—as much as I could bear.'

'I see. Then you know.'

She nodded. 'Yes, I know.'

He took a breath, feeling the cold clutch of air on his lungs. 'If I do with this what I think I should do with it,' he said, measuring his words, 'you know what the effect will be?'

'No. Do you?'

'I know it will be bad. What about Mal?'

'Oh,' she said, 'Mal will survive. He was the least of it, after all.'

'I thought—' He stopped.

'You thought Mal was the father of that unfortunate young woman's child. Yes, I knew you did. It's why I wanted you to talk to him—I thought he would tell you how things really were. But he wouldn't have, of course. He's very loyal—to a father who never loved him. Isn't it ironic?'

They were silent then. He thought that he should kiss her, but knew it was impossible. 'Goodbye, Sarah,' he said.

'Goodbye, Quirke.' She was looking into his face with a faint, quizzical smile. 'You *were* loved, you know,' she said. 'Or that's the point, I suppose—you didn't.'

Epilogue

A FRESH WIND was blowing in lively gusts, bringing to the city streets the news of far fields and trees and water. It was spring. As Quirke walked along he lifted his blackthorn stick now and then and took an experimental step without its aid. Pain, but not much; a sharp, hot twinge, the metal pin's reminder.

He was shown into Inspector Hackett's office, where the sunlight made its way but feebly through the grimed window. Most of the space in the narrow room was taken up by a large, ugly wooden desk. Yellowed files sat in stacks on the floor round about, and there was a rack of dusty newspapers, and books with torn, illegible spines— what kind of books, Quirke wondered, would Hackett be likely to read?—and the top of the desk was a raft with a jumble of things swimming on it, documents that obviously had not been moved in months, two mugs, one containing pencils and the other the dregs of the Inspector's morning tea, a shapeless piece of metal, which the Inspector said was a souvenir of the wartime German bombing of North Strand, and, lying curled where he had dropped it, Dolly Moran's diary. The Inspector, in shirtsleeves and wearing his hat, sat leaning far back in his chair with his feet on a corner of the desk and his hands folded across his belly which was fastened tightly into a bulging blue waistcoat.

Hackett gestured at the jotter on the desk.

'She wasn't exactly James Joyce, was she, poor Dolly?' he said, and sucked his teeth.

'But will you be able to use it?' Quirke said.

'Oh, sure, I'll do what I can,' the Inspector said. 'But these are powerful people we're dealing with here, Mr Quirke—you realise that, I presume. This fellow Costigan alone, he has a lot of clout in this town, the same fellow.'

'But we have clout too,' Quirke said, nodding towards the jotter.

Hackett gave his belly a happy little squeeze. 'God, Mr Quirke, but you're a fierce vindictive man!' he said. 'Your own family, as good as. Tell me'—he lowered his voice to a confidential tone—'why are you doing it?'

Quirke considered. 'I don't know, Inspector,' he said at length. 'Maybe because I've never really *done* anything before in my life.'

Hackett nodded, then sniffed. 'There'll be a lot of dust,' he said, 'if these particular pillars of society are brought down. A lot of dust, and bricks, and rubble. A body would want to be standing well out of the way.'

'But you'll do it, all the same.'

Hackett took his feet from the desk and leaned forward and scrabbled among the litter of papers and found a packet of cigarettes and offered it to Quirke and they lit up.

'I'll try, Mr Quirke,' the Inspector said. 'I'll try.'

Acknowledgements

Thanks to: Jennifer Barth, Peter Beilby, Mary Callery, Joan Egan, Alan Gilsenan, Louise Gough, Roy Heayberd, Robyn Kershaw, Andrew Kidd, Linda Klejus, Sandra Levy, Laura Magahy, Ian Meldon, Hazel Orme, Jo Pitkin, Maria Rejt, Beatrice von Rezzori, Barry Ruane, John Sterling.

If you enjoyed *Christine Falls* you'll love

THE SILVER SWAN

the second Quirke Dublin mystery from Benjamin Black

Time has moved on for Quirke, the world-weary pathologist first encountered in *Christine Falls*. It is the middle of the 1950s, that low, dishonourable decade; a woman he loved has died, a man whom he once admired is dying, while the daughter he for so long denied is still finding it hard to accept him as her father. When an old acquaintance approaches him about his wife's apparent suicide, Quirke recognises trouble but, as always, trouble is something he cannot resist.

'Dublin's clammy atmosphere and its oppressive social and religious mores are a convincing backdrop to a moving drama conveyed by a master writer'   *The Times*

'Drug addiction, morbid sexual obsession, blackmail and murder, as well as prose as crisp as a winter's morning by the Liffey ... Quirke is human enough to swell the hardest of hearts'   *GQ*

'The death of Michael Dibdin left a huge hole in crime fiction. Black and Quirke are filling that gap with this wholly gripping account of the shady, priest-ridden and blithely corrupt society of mid-twentieth-century Dublin'   *Daily Mail*

'A romp of a read, a compelling fix'   *Scotsman*

The first chapter follows here ...

1

Quirke did not recognise the name. It seemed familiar but he could not put a face to it. Occasionally it happened that way: someone would float up without warning out of his past, his drinking past, someone he had forgotten, asking for a loan or offering to let him in on a sure thing or just wanting to make contact, out of loneliness, or only to know that he was still alive and that the drink had not done for him. Mostly he put them off, mumbling about pressure of work and the like. This one should have been easy, since it was just a name and a telephone number left with the hospital receptionist, and he could have conveniently lost the piece of paper or simply thrown it away. Something caught his attention, however. He had an impression of urgency, of unease, which he could not account for and which troubled him.

Billy Hunt.

What was it the name sparked in him? Was it a lost memory or, more worryingly, a premonition?

He put the scrap of paper on a corner of his desk and tried to ignore it. At the dead centre of summer the day was hot and muggy, and in the streets the barely breathable air was laden with a thin pall of mauve smoke, and he was glad of the cool and quiet of his windowless basement office in the Pathology Department. He hung his suit jacket on the back of his chair and pulled off his tie without undoing the knot and opened two buttons of his shirt and sat down at the cluttered metal desk. He liked the familiar smell here, a combination of old cigarette smoke, tea leaves, paper, formaldehyde, and something else, musky, fleshly, that was his particular contribution.

He lit a cigarette and his eye drifted again to the paper with Billy Hunt's message on it. Just the name and the number that the operator had scribbled down in pencil, and the words 'Please call'. The sense of urgent imploring was stronger than ever. *Please call.*

For no reason he could think of he found himself remembering the moment in McGonagle's pub half a year ago when, dizzily drunk amid the din of Christmas revelling, he had caught sight of his own face, flushed and bulbous and bleary, reflected in the bottom of his empty whiskey glass and had realised with unaccountable certitude that he had just taken his last drink. Since then he had been sober. He was as amazed by this as was anyone who knew him. He felt that it was not he who had made the decision, but that somehow it had been made for him. Despite all his training and his years in the dissecting room he had a secret conviction that the body has a consciousness of its own, and knows itself and its needs as well as or better than the mind imagines it does. The decree delivered to him that night by his gut and his swollen liver and the ventricles of his heart was absolute and incontestable. For nearly two years he had been falling steadily into the abyss of drink, falling almost as far as he had in the time, two decades before, after his wife had died, and now the fall was broken.

Squinting at the scrap of paper on the corner of the desk, he lifted the telephone receiver and dialled. The bell jangled afar down the line.

Afterwards, out of curiosity, he had upended another whiskey glass, this time one he had not emptied, to find if it was really possible to see himself in the bottom of it, but no reflection had appeared there.

The sound of Billy Hunt's voice was no help; he did not recognise it any more readily than he had the name. The accent was at once flat and singsong, with broad vowels and dulled consonants. A countryman. There was a slight flutter in the tone, a slight wobble, as if the speaker might be about to burst into laughter, or into something else. Some words he slurred, hurrying over them. Maybe he was tipsy?

'Ah, you don't remember me,' he said. 'Do you?'

'Of course I do,' Quirke lied.

'Billy Hunt. You used to say it sounded like rhyming slang. We were in college together. I was in first year when you were in your last. I didn't really expect you to remember me. We went with different crowds. I was mad into the sports—hurling, football, all that—while you were with the arty lot, with your nose stuck in a book or over at the Abbey or the Gate every night of the week. I dropped out of the medicine—didn't have the stomach for it.'

Quirke let a beat of silence pass, then asked: 'What are you doing now?'

Billy Hunt gave a heavy, unsteady sigh. 'Never mind that,' he said, sounding more weary than impatient. 'It's *your* job that's the point here.'

At last a face began to assemble itself in Quirke's labouring memory. Big broad forehead, definitively broken nose, a thatch of wiry red hair, freckles. Grocer's son from somewhere down south, Wicklow, Wexford, Waterford, one of the W counties. Easy-going but prone to scrap when provoked, hence the smashed septum. Billy Hunt. Yes.

'My job?' Quirke said. 'How's that?'

There was another pause.

'It's the wife,' Billy Hunt said. Quirke heard a sharply indrawn breath whistling in those crushed nasal cavities. 'She's after doing away with herself.'

They met in Bewley's Café in Grafton Street. It was lunchtime and the place was busy. The rich, fat smell of coffee beans roasting in the big vat just inside the door made Quirke's stomach briefly heave. Odd, the things he found nauseating now; he had expected giving up drink would dull his senses and reconcile him to the world and its savours, but the opposite had been the case, so that at times he seemed to be a walking tangle of nerve-ends assailed from every side by outrageous smells, tastes, touches. The interior of the café was dark to his eyes after the glare outside. A girl going out passed him by; she wore a white dress and carried a broad-brimmed straw hat; he caught the warm waft of her perfumed skin that trailed behind her. He imagined himself turning on his heel and following after her and taking her by the elbow and walking with her out into the heat of the summer day. He did not relish the prospect of Billy Hunt and his dead wife.

He spotted him straight away, sitting in one of the side booths, unnaturally erect on the red plush banquette, with a cup of milky coffee untouched before him on the grey marble table. He did not see Quirke at first, and Quirke hung back a moment, studying him, the drained pale face with the freckles standing out on it, the glazed, desolate stare, the big turnip-shaped hand fiddling with the sugar spoon. He had changed remarkably little in the more than two decades since Quirke had known him. Not that he could say he had known him, really. In Quirke's not very clear recollections of him Billy was a sort of overgrown schoolboy, by turns cheery or truculent and sometimes both at once, loping out to the sports grounds in wide-legged knicks and a striped football jersey, with a football or a bundle of hurley sticks under his arm, his knobbly, pale-pink knees bare and his boyish cheeks aflame and blood-spotted from the still unaccustomed morning shave. Loud, of course, roaring raucous jokes at his fellow sportsmen and throwing a surly glance from under colourless lashes in the direction of Quirke and *the arty lot*. Now he was thickened by the years, with a bald patch on the crown of his head, like a tonsure, and a fat red neck overflowing the collar of his baggy tweed jacket.

He had that smell, hot and raw and salty, that Quirke recognised at once, the smell of the recently bereaved. He sat there at the table, propping himself upright, a bulging sack of grief and misery and pent-up rage, and said to Quirke helplessly:

'I don't know why she did it.'

Quirke nodded. 'Did she leave anything?' Billy peered at him, uncomprehending. 'A letter, I mean. A note.'

'No, no, nothing like that.' He gave a crooked, almost sheepish, smile. 'I wish she had.'

That morning a party of Gardai had gone out in a launch and lifted poor Deirdre Hunt's naked body off the rocks on the landward shore of Dalkey Island.

'They called me in to identify her,' Billy said, that strange, pained smile that was not a smile still on his lips, his eyes seeming to gaze again in wild dismay at what they had seen on the hospital slab, Quirke grimly thought, and would probably never stop seeing, for as long as he lived. 'They brought her to St Vincent's. She looked completely different. I think I wouldn't have known her except for the hair. She was very proud of it, her hair.' He shrugged apologetically, twitching one shoulder.

Quirke was recalling a very fat woman who had thrown herself into the Liffey, from whose chest cavity, when he had cut it open and was clipping away at the rib-cage, there had clambered forth, with the torpor of the truly well-fed, a nest of translucent, many-legged, shrimp-like creatures.

A waitress in her black-and-white uniform and maid's mob-cap came to take Quirke's order. The aroma of fried and boiled lunches assailed him. He asked for tea. Billy Hunt had drifted away into himself and was delving absently with his spoon among the cubes in the sugar bowl, making them rattle.

'It's hard,' Quirke said, when the waitress had gone. 'Identifying the body, I mean. That's always hard.'

Billy looked down, and his lower lip began to tremble and he clamped it babyishly between his teeth.

'Have you children, Billy?' Quirke asked.

Billy, still looking down, shook his head. 'No,' he muttered, 'no children. Deirdre wasn't keen.'

'And what do you do? I mean, what do you work at?'

'Commercial traveller. Pharmaceuticals. The job takes me away a lot, around the country, abroad, too, the odd occasion, to Switzerland, when there's to be a meeting at head office. I suppose that was part of the trouble, me being away so much—that, and her not wanting kids.' Here it comes, Quirke thought, *the trouble*. But Billy only said, 'I suppose she was lonely. She never complained, though.' He looked up at Quirke suddenly and as if challengingly. 'She never complained—never!'

He went on talking about her then, what she was like, what she did. The haunted look in his face grew more intense, and his eyes darted this way and that with an odd, hindered urgency, as if he wanted them to light on something that kept on not being there. The waitress brought Quirke's tea. He drank it black, scalding his tongue. He produced his cigarette case. 'So tell me,' he said, 'what was it you wanted to see me about?'

Once more Billy lowered those pale lashes and gazed at the sugar bowl. A mottled tide of colour swelled upwards from his collar and slowly suffused his face to the hairline and beyond; he was, Quirke realised, blushing. He nodded mutely, sucking in a deep breath.

'I wanted to ask you a favour.'

Quirke waited. The room was steadily filling with the lunchtime crowd and the noise had risen to a medleyed roar. Waitresses skimmed among the tables bearing brown trays piled with plates of food—sausage and mash, fish and chips, steaming mugs of tea and glasses of orange crush. Quirke offered the cigarette case open on his palm, and Billy took a cigarette, seeming hardly to notice what he was doing. Quirke's lighter clicked and flared. Billy hunched forward holding the cigarette between his lips with fingers that shook. Then he leaned back on the banquette as if exhausted.

'I'm reading about you all the time in the papers,' he said. 'About cases you're involved in.' Quirke shifted uneasily on his chair. 'That thing with the girl that died and the woman that was murdered—what were their names?'

'Which ones?' Quirke asked, expressionless.

'The woman in Stoney Batter. Last year, or the year before, was it? Dolly somebody.' He frowned, trying to remember. 'What happened to that story? It was all over the papers and then it was gone, not another word.'

'The papers don't take long to lose interest,' Quirke said.

A thought struck Billy. 'Jesus,' he said softly, staring away, 'I suppose they'll put a story in about Deirdre, too.'

'I could have a word with the coroner,' Quirke said, making it sound doubtful.

But it was not stories in the newspapers that was on

Billy's mind. He leaned forward again, suddenly intent, and reached out a hand urgently as if he might grasp Quirke by the wrist or the lapel. 'I don't want her cut up,' he said, in a hoarse undertone.

'Cut up?'

'An autopsy, a post-mortem, whatever you call it—I don't want that done.'

Quirke waited a moment and then said: 'It's a formality, Billy. The law requires it.'

Billy was shaking his head with his eyes shut and his mouth set in a pained grimace. 'I don't want it done. I don't want her sliced up like some sort of a, like a—like some sort of carcass.' He put a hand over his eyes. The cigarette, forgotten, was burning itself out in the fingers of his other hand. 'I can't bear to think of it. Seeing her this morning was bad enough'—he took his hand away and gazed before him in what seemed a stupor of amazement—'but the thought of her on a table, under the lights, with the knife . . . If you'd known her, the way she was, before, how—how alive she was.' He cast about again as if in search of something on which to concentrate, a bullet of commonplace reality on which he might bite. 'I can't bear it, Quirke,' he said hoarsely, his voice hardly more than a whisper. 'I swear to God, I can't bear it.'

Quirke sipped his by now tepid tea, the tannin acrid against his scalded tongue. He did not know what he should say. He rarely came in direct contact with the relatives of the dead, but occasionally they sought him out, as Billy had, to request a favour. Some only wanted him to save them a keepsake, a wedding ring, or a lock of hair; there was a Republican widow once who had asked him to retrieve a fragment of a Civil War bullet that her late husband had carried next to his heart for thirty years. Others had more serious and far shadier requests—that the bruises on a dead infant's body be plausibly accounted for, that the sudden demise of an aged, sick parent be explained away, or just that a suicide might be covered up. But no one had ever asked what Billy was asking.

'All right, Billy,' he said. 'I'll see what I can do.'

Now Billy's hand did touch his, the barest touch, with the tips of fingers through which a strong, fizzing current seemed to race. 'You won't let me down, Quirke,' he said, a statement rather than an entreaty, his voice quavering. 'For old times' sake. For'—he made a low sound that was half sob half laugh—'for Deirdre's sake.'

Quirke stood up. He fished a half-crown from his pocket and laid it on the table beside his saucer. Billy was looking about again, distractedly, as a man would while patting his pockets in search of something he had misplaced. He had taken out a Zippo lighter and was distractedly flicking the lid open and shut. On the bald spot and through the strands of his scant pale hair could be seen glistening beads of sweat. 'That's not her name, by the way,' he said. Quirke did not understand. 'I mean, it is her name, only she called herself something else. Laura—Laura Swan. It was sort of her professional name. She ran a beauty parlour, the Silver Swan. That's where she got the name—Laura Swan.'

Quirke waited, but Billy had nothing more to say, and he turned and walked away.

*

In the afternoon, on Quirke's instructions, they brought the body from St Vincent's to the city-centre Hospital of the Holy Family, where Quirke was waiting to receive it. A recent round of imposed economies at the Holy Family, hotly contested but in vain, had left Quirke with one assistant only where before there had been two. His had been the task of choosing between young Wilkins the horse-Protestant and the Jew Sinclair. He had plumped for Sinclair, without any clear reason, for the two young men were equally matched in skill or, in some areas, lack of it. But he liked Sinclair, liked his independence and sly humour and the faint surliness of his manner; when Quirke had asked him once where his people hailed from Sinclair had looked him in the eye without expression and said blankly, 'Cork.' He had offered not a word of thanks to Quirke for choosing him, and Quirke admired that, too.

He wondered how far he should take Sinclair into his confidence in the matter of Deirdre Hunt and her husband's plea that her corpse should be left intact. Sinclair, however, was not a man to make trouble. When Quirke said he would do the post-mortem alone—a visual examination would suffice—and that Sinclair might as well take himself off to the canteen for a cup of tea and a cigarette, the young man hesitated for no more than a second, and removed his green gown and rubber boots and sauntered out of the morgue with his hands in his pockets, whistling softly. Quirke turned back and lifted the plastic sheet.

Deirdre Hunt or Laura Swan, or whatever name she went under, must have been, he judged, a good-looking young woman, perhaps even a beautiful one. She was—had been—quite a lot younger than Billy Hunt. Her body, which had not been in the water long enough for serious deterioration to have taken place, was short and shapely; a strong body, strongly muscled, but delicate in its curves and the sheer planes at flank and calf. Her face was not as fine-boned as it might have been—her maiden name, Quirke noted, had been Ward, suggesting tinker blood—but her forehead was clear and high, and the swathe of copper-coloured hair falling back from it must have been magnificent when she was alive. He had a picture in his mind of her sprawled on the wet rocks, a long swatch of that hair coiled round her neck like a thick frond of gleaming seaweed. What, he wondered, had driven this handsome, healthy young woman to fling herself on a summer midnight off Sandycove harbour into the black waters of Dublin Bay, with no witness to the deed save the glittering stars and the louring bulk of the Martello tower above her? Her clothes, so Billy Hunt had said, had been placed in a neat pile on the pier beside the wall; that was the only trace she had left of her going—that, and her motor-car, which Quirke was certain was another thing she would have been proud of, and which yet she had abandoned, neatly parked under a lilac tree on Sandycove Avenue. Her car and her hair: twin sources of vanity. But what was it that had pulled that vanity down?

Then he spotted the tiny puncture mark on the chalk-white inner side of her left arm.

extracts reading groups
competitions books new
discounts extracts
competitions
books new
events books
extracts
new titles reading groups
interviews
events extracts
discounts
new books events
events new
discounts extracts discounts
www.panmacmillan.com
extracts events reading groups
competitions books extracts new
reading groups
events reading groups
extracts
discounts
events
books
books